KEEPING
SECRETS

Also by Suzanne Morris

GALVESTON

KEEPING SECRETS

A Novel by

Suzanne Morris

DOUBLEDAY & COMPANY, INC.
GARDEN CITY, NEW YORK
1979

Library of Congress Cataloging in Publication Data
Morris, Suzanne.
    Keeping secrets.
        I. Title.
PZ4.M8786Ke [PS3563.087448] 813'.5'4
ISBN: 0-385-11535-0
Library of Congress Catalog Card Number: 78-22233

FOR
Rega McCarty

ACKNOWLEDGMENTS

The background information necessary for writing this novel could not have been gathered without the help of many people. For assistance in finding important documented material, I am particularly indebted to:

Conrad True, Administrator, and Alice Johnson, Librarian, San Antonio Conservation Society;

Ann Maria Watson, Assistant Librarian, Daughters of the Republic of Texas Library, San Antonio;

Marie Berry, Head Librarian, History and Reference Department, San Antonio Public Library;

David S. Bingham, former Director/Curator, Fort Sam Houston Military Museum, San Antonio;

Virginia Wong, Supervisor, and staff of the Interlibrary Loan Department; Helen G. Jones, and all other staff members of the Bibliographic Information Center, Houston Public Library.

Also of great help were Mary V. Burkholder of San Antonio, author of The King William Area—A History and Guide to the Houses, and David N. Johnson of San Antonio, who allowed me the use of his thesis, "Exiles and Intrigue."

I am grateful to the following people for their generosity in sharing personal and family recollections:

Margaret Cousins; Martin Giesecke; Eileen Pike; Mrs. Ferdinand P. Herff, and Mr. and Mrs. William A. Watson, San Antonio;

Vie McKinney and Bryan York, Lufkin;

Espy Baumbach and my parents, Mr. and Mrs. Frank M. Page, Houston.

Edward H. Frank, Assistant Vice President, Bank of the Southwest, Houston, was especially kind in sharing with me his vast knowledge and experience in banking.

I want to express my thanks for the continued friendship and valuable assistance in proofing and typing to *Karen Giesen*, Houston, and *Nancy Rhudy*, League City, Texas.

Suzanne Morris

Contents

Ye who read are still among the living:
But I who write
Shall have long since gone my way
Into the region of shadows.
For indeed strange things shall happen,
And secret things be known,
And many centuries shall pass away,
Ere these memorials be seen of men.
And, when seen,
There will be some to disbelieve, and some to doubt,
And yet a few who will find much to ponder upon
In the characters here graven with a stylus of iron.
The year had been a year of terror,
And of feelings more intense than terror
For which there is no name upon the earth. . . .

Lines from *Shadow—A Parable*
Edgar Allan Poe

PART ONE

Electra Cabot

ELECTRA

FEBRUARY 28, 1917

1

All that matters now is what becomes of Emory.

Though both of us will soon be leaving San Antonio, at least I still have ways of protecting myself. Emory may soon fear for his life, however, because he is a gambler and for that kind of man there is always lying somewhere ahead the risk that will prove too high.

I've known him twice, which is in itself unusual because we've both taken great care to cover our tracks. The first time was twenty years ago in Childers, Texas. Emory was sixteen when he left there. Like his father, he was tall and lean with black hair, and dark eyes already keen and full of contempt. He had, too, that habit of cocking one eyebrow at the end of a question, which caused the people of Childers to reason they'd best look upon him with wariness. He was also a Cabot, and no one in town had ever held that family in high regard.

I was fourteen then, with blond hair still in braids, bony knees, scarcely a hint of bosom, and drab, hand-me-down clothes to wear: the picture of the kid nobody wanted. When Emory began paying me attention that year he left, I was sure it was because no one else liked listening to him brag about how he was going to get out of that town and make a lot of money. Like all the other young girls, including two of the cousins I lived with, I was warned of keeping company with him. Childers was a Bible-worshiping, God-fearing town of farmers and it was clear to all the grown-ups that Emory Cabot, with his big ideas, was headed for no good.

They failed to realize that I had dreams similar to his. The only difference was that he knew how to go about making them come true. Even if I couldn't share in his plans, I was fascinated by listening to them.

I scarcely ever saw him except on school days, when he walked me home. On Saturdays he had a job sweeping out the hardware store, and I usually awoke with a full day of chores to do. One Saturday I finished early, though, and was sent for a walk into town to pick up the liver. The butcher gave it away because he couldn't sell it and my Aunt Eartha, always eager to save a penny, took all that he had on Saturdays so she could fry it in a batter then simmer it down under a mound of onions, to kill the strong flavor. That was our dinner nearly every Sunday.

I always despised the errand of picking up the liver because I was disgraced by taking a handout, but on that particular Saturday I made up my mind to take some extra time for myself and walk by the mercantile window. I'd heard the traveling salesman from the East Coast had been by on Friday and brought a new load of dress material and trimmings. The mercantile just happened to be next door to the hardware store where Emory worked.

There were the most attractive colors of new satin ribbons displayed that day. One bolt each of bright yellow, blue, red, purple, and green were arranged like a fan. I walked back and forth in front of the window enjoying the sight, knowing full well none of those ribbons would ever adorn my hair. In fact I didn't dare walk in and ask to hold them in my hands. Mrs. Turner, the owner's wife, had once caught me looking at some dress material and yanked at my hands, criticized their general untidiness and warned, "Get yourself out of here, Leslie Weems, or I'll tell your aunt, I swear I will."

Emory came out next door, broom in hand, as I studied the ribbons. I hadn't been thinking of him at all and when I realized he was standing behind me with his arms folded over the broom handle, smiling at my foolishness, I bristled and said, "They're just stupid ribbons. Don't know why I'm wasting my time."

"Sure they are," he said, and went back to his sweeping.

I felt he'd shamed me, and I still had to face the condescending look of the butcher, so I thrust out my chin and stalked off.

Emory was out of school for the following week—this was not unusual because if he took a notion to go fishing or camping in the woods, he'd do it and the rest of the world could go hang. Even then he lived mostly by his own rules. I was angry with him for being absent and keeping me from showing I didn't want to talk to him anymore (though by Monday I really did).

Then he pulled the unexpected. The following Saturday he came to our front gate while I was shelling peas on the porch. He whistled, and motioned for me to come with him. I checked to be sure no one was around, then walked very slowly to the gate and asked disinterestedly what he wanted.

"Wanna go for a walk?"

"I'm busy."

"We won't be gone long."

So we walked across a field and down a cow path toward a maze of low shrubs. All at once I stopped and demanded, "Just what do you want with me?"

He dug down into his pocket and drew out a small brown package, which he handed over. "I gotta get back to work now," he said, and walked off.

I had long since forgotten the ribbons as one forgets unreachable treasures, so I was awe-struck to find a yard each of the five colors, coiled around inside the package. Emory was already out of sight. I stood there for a long while, holding the ribbons and smiling.

Back home the gift presented problems.

Anything as flashy as those satin ribbons might be considered sinful by Aunt Eartha and Uncle Jack, who'd raised me since I was orphaned at two. Besides, there were eleven children to feed and clothe in that household, two of the girls older than me. If I appeared with the ribbons in hand, assuming they were deemed wholesome possessions, there would be an excuse made of some kind (I knew from past experience), and my treasures would be confiscated.

I hid the ribbons in the pocket of the coat assigned to me for the coming winter, passed down successively from Bertha and Sue, and missing two buttons. It seemed the safest place in the house. That night I lay awake for a long time, thinking of Emory. There was little telling how he'd gotten the ribbons. All the money he earned went toward the common fund at his home. So what if Emory stole them from some woman's basket as she left the store? I didn't care, and if I ever found out, the information would follow me to my grave. No one had ever cared enough to steal for me, I reasoned, my admiration for Emory zooming higher than ever. Till that night the word "love" seemed a silly one, applied to first one then another of Bertha's many suitors. But now all at once I knew what it meant. I was in love with Emory Cabot.

For the next two days I thought of nothing and no one except him, and counted the hours till class was dismissed on Monday afternoon so I could walk home with him, even while fighting off a sudden and severe case of shyness. At the first opportunity I explained why I had to hide the ribbons. "But I'll save them and one day I'll have dresses to match them all, and I'll be a long way from this town," I added. One thing Emory had already taught me was how to brag.

"Yep," he agreed then remarked, "I'll be going myself before long."

My spirits plummeted. I hadn't really visualized his leaving, though I never doubted his ability to do all the things he claimed he would accomplish. I tried to keep my voice even because I'd overheard Sue and Bertha say that boys hate pushy girls. "Oh, when?"

"Soon as school's out, probably, or maybe before."

"Wish I could go some place and do something," I said, and kicked a rock out of the path.

All too soon the day came when he announced during our walk, "I'll be on my way by sunup tomorrow." We were almost home by then and I couldn't bear the thought of never seeing him again. "It's my turn to milk the cow in the morning. Could you stop around back of the barn? It's a shortcut from there to the main road."

Next morning I stole four beaten biscuits while Aunt Eartha's back was turned, and a jar of pear preserves from the shelf. Taking the preserves was risky—she kept a close count of the jars down in the cellar to be sure the hired hands didn't make away with any—but then if Emory had stolen for me, surely I could chance the consequences of doing the same for him. Had I been two years older I know I would have begged him to take me along, but as it was I would have no more considered doing that than prancing around in the satin ribbons.

I wrapped the biscuits and preserves in a cloth and handed them to him when he came up. He was whistling nonchalantly as though leaving town were something a person did every day. The morning sun was just cresting the ridge ahead and his lean frame was silhouetted against the hills, erect and determined. His face was hidden in shadows, so if he had any misgivings about the unmapped future of his life, he wasn't about to show me.

I was nervous and groped for a parting phrase. "Where are you going, first?"

"A place where I can make some money . . . and this time I'll keep it."

"Then?"

"I'm going to find my mother," he remarked without a pause.

"But she up and left you years ago. Why—"

"That's just what I'm going to ask her," he said.

I wished him good luck; even for Emory, finding someone who might be anywhere in the world seemed a pretty tall order. He turned and headed for the fence along the open road, a quarter of a mile away, and I stood watching him till I could barely make him out. Then I grabbed my skirt hem with one hand and ran after him, hitting the fence with a thud. All at once I realized he'd find someone else one day and forget all about me, and had there been no fence between us my legs might have kept on going. Yet the fence epitomized all of life's limitations on me. I cupped my hands around my mouth and called out, "You will come back, someday, won't you?"

"Not likely," he said from the distance, but already he was out of sight.

Back at the house Uncle Jack was already calling me. "Leslie, you better get back to milking. You sure can figure out more ways to waste time . . ."

All that summer I thought of Emory every day, and often looked up from what I was doing outside to see if he might appear. I'd hear someone whistle like him, and my heart would leap momentarily until I discovered it was not him. As the days went past my longing for his return began to crystallize into bitterness at the cold fact that, whereas Emory Cabot had the ability to do something about his situation, I had little power over my destiny. I'd probably wind up spending my life in Childers or some other equally uninteresting town. Scrubbing the floors, I'd often find myself so lodged in thought it would take Aunt Eartha swinging by with a basketful of laundry to jar me out. "You've rubbed that spot sixteen times, girl, reckon you better move over an inch or two before you go through the floor. I declare, the Lord sent me a burden when you came. . . ."

Once or twice a week, after everyone was asleep, I'd sneak into the box of woolen clothes and reach down into the coat pocket to feel the ribbons. It helped a little, knowing I owned these strands of finery, because it would temporarily dispel my bitterness and renew the belief that there was a world out there with something better in it for me.

As far as I knew there was no wide-range effort by his family to find Emory. As the second eldest son, he was second in command since their father died. His position in the family led to many squabbles because Emory didn't like answering to anyone, and he spent most of his time alone. I would have known this even if he hadn't told me because the Cabots, who didn't attend church or go to town meetings, were always enticing food for gossiping tongues. No one seemed to know them very well; nor did I, except for Emory.

I used to feel quite special when I reasoned that I alone kept alive the memory of the only smart young man in town. While others at first spoke unkindly of him, and accused him of having taken things they were missing, they shortly forgot him as I knew they would. As soon as something new excited their curiosity, they put aside their jealously of the fact he was likely out there somewhere, paving the streets with gold.

I came home from school one evening at dusk, having stayed in town to run an errand for Aunt Eartha. I arrived to find Sue dressed up with two of my satin ribbons entwined in her hair. Some cow-eyed boy was coming to call that evening and, by chance, she had scavanged through the coats to find a lace-trimmed handkerchief she was missing.

I stood by gritting my teeth as she preened in front of the bureau mirror in a way Aunt Eartha would have regarded as sinful had she been around.

"Just look what I found in my old coat," she said snidely.

"Give me those ribbons," I demanded.

"Surely they aren't yours, Leslie . . . my word, where would you have gotten these? I'm sure I bought them some time ago with the money I made working part-time at the cafe. That's just what I told Mama."

"You sorry—I'll scratch your eyes out."

"Now now, little cousin, Mama would be so upset to hear about that."

After shedding many tears of frustration that night, I made up my mind to get out of that wretched town as soon as I could. Less than two years later, in 1898, my chance came and I took it. Nearly twenty years would pass before I would fully recognize the consequences of that mistake.

2

Even as my train pulled into San Antonio on an afternoon in mid-March of 1914, I had little idea of what awaited me. The past three weeks had been among the most puzzling of my life, and had begun with the information that my release had been arranged by a gentleman who wished to remain unidentified.

The agency he'd employed instructed me to leave Denver on the evening of March 10. Enclosed with their letter was my ticket plus two hundred dollars, which I was advised to use for clothing and any other items I might need. At the end of the line in San Antonio, I was to go to the Menger Hotel where a suite had been reserved in my name. There I would be met for the first time by the man seeking me for a "highly specialized position."

With the certainty I had nothing to lose, I agreed to go. I had some money tucked away in Colorado, and if the prospect awaiting me was not to my liking, I would not have to endure it forever. At the sound of the conductor's voice calling "San-an-ton-ee-o," my pulse quickened. I pulled out a hand mirror and straightened my hair a bit, then placed the big gray Gainsborough hat with pink plumes on my head, pulling it far down on the right so that my face remained in shadows. I touched up my pale cheeks with a faint dab of rouge and buttoned my coat. The gray travel suit with pink piping was one of three frocks I'd purchased with the money from the agency, since I'd always been one to buy fashionable, tasteful clothes whenever the opportunity presented itself.

I knew little about San Antonio beyond the fact there was a river running through it, and the site of a battle fought long ago called the Alamo. I'd featured it to be somewhat backward, with horses and cows still wandering freely around muddy roads, few buildings of any consequence, and plenty of smoke-filled saloons. The scene before me as my taxi pulled away from the depot was startlingly different. There were as many automobiles rumbling down paved streets as there were horse-drawn vehicles, and the taxi driver reaffirmed, "The horse and buggy days are about over."

There were blocks and blocks of tall, prominent brick buildings, inviting shop windows galore, and many more people up and down the walks, better dressed, than I'd surmised. There was more of everything, modern and up-to-date as Denver.

"I had no idea this town was so large. How many people live here?" I asked.

"Around a hundred thousand."

I looked out the window once more. Soon, as we detoured time and again to bypass street-paving work under way and other various road obstructions, I realized how strangely the city was laid out. Down one short block we'd go, then turn at such an abrupt angle I was sure we were headed back in the direction from where we'd come. In another block or two the road would fork—dangerously close to the steps of a building looming up in front of us, it seemed to me—and the taxi driver would veer to the right or left, then continue a few yards before crossing a bridge. I could not make heads or tails of the river's course because I soon lost track of the number of bridges we crossed and where. The area looked like an endless maze of sudden crooks and jags, many of them leading nowhere. Finally, my neck aching from looking back and forth so often, I said, "Aren't there any plain ordinary square blocks in this place?"

"A few," the driver replied with a laugh. "People have a saying that San Antonio was laid out by a drunk Mexican, but the truth is, one reason for all the turns is that it's planned around several odd-shaped plazas. We haven't passed any yet, but the

Menger is on Alamo Plaza, for one, so you'll see what I mean
. . . and I guess the way the river runs is partly to blame."

"Where is the river from here? It seems to go in a circle, for
all the bridges."

"Not exactly, but it does a lot of winding. In fact, not far
from here it takes a couple of horseshoe swags. The reason
we've crossed so many bridges right in town, though, is because
it makes a sharp turn to the left, goes the length of a couple
of blocks, turns to the right again and goes back to where
it started." He glanced back at my bewildered face. "It's like
three sides of a box," he added, then shrugged helplessly.
"Lady, you'd better get a map."

I laughed a little nervously and said, "A person could get lost
here and never find the way out."

The Menger suite was large and airy, handsomely furnished,
with great windows showering the bed and sitting rooms with
afternoon sunlight. Upon entering, my spirits rose, and I
walked through the rooms, looking out the windows upon the
garden below, as though wandering through a world of se-
cluded fantasy. A bowl of fruit and some little cakes had been
provided on a table, and also a bottle of good brandy. I
searched for a card with the sender's name, but found none.

After a few minutes my wary nature surfaced, and I began to
assess the business immediately before me. Just fifteen minutes
from now a man I didn't know would come through the door
of the sitting room. So far he had directed all the moves. Shall
I take off my hat and coat, and let him discover me lounging
casually on a sofa, a book in my hand, perhaps?

Decidedly not.

I didn't like being looked over. I unlocked the sitting-room
door, and walked into the adjoining bedroom, leaving the door
slightly ajar. Still feeling at a disadvantage, I switched on the
lamps in the sitting room and returned to the bedroom, pulling
down the shades and closing the draperies. Then I sat on the
edge of the bed and waited.

At a quarter past three my whole body jerked to the sound

of a light rapping on the door. I walked as far as the passage door and called out, "Come in, I'll be with you in a moment."

When he came into view I could tell this was a marvelous figure of a man, beginning with his full black beard. From there down he was more and more pleasing, with broad shoulders tapering to a well-tended mid-section, narrow hips, and long muscular legs, which, as his body shifted around, revealed the well-developed, hard thighs of a horseman. He took off his coat, which he threw absently against a chair as he removed his black wide-brimmed hat. Even then I didn't recognize him.

His back to me, he was pouring himself a glass of brandy when I chose the moment to come through and close the door behind me. All at once I wished he wouldn't turn around. Maybe I wasn't at all what he had in mind. Maybe . . .

"It's been a long time, Leslie," he said, then turned around and smiled. He might have smacked me on the cheek for my surprise.

"Emory Cabot?"

He threw back his head in laughter, then walked right over and swung me around in his arms. I can never recall being so astonished to see anyone in my life. All I could say, over and over, was, "I can't believe it!"

"Let's have some brandy," he said, and we sat down to talk.

He didn't want to discuss his object in getting me to San Antonio just yet, and since he'd started from Childers and trailed me all the way to the little town between Denver and Durango, there didn't seem to be much I could tell him about myself. I insisted upon knowing step by step everything he'd done since leaving our hometown and he didn't mind sharing a good part of it with me for he was not a modest man. He'd gone from place to place as a hired hand in the beginning, then finally made it to the Oklahoma oil fields. He won a lot of card games and saved a lot of money, then bought a very small interest in a well that happened to be one of the biggest strikes in the fields.

"Does good luck always follow you around?" I asked.

"It has so far, but I didn't want to push it too much then, so

I backed off and started investing in land. Went into New Mexico and, later, all the way down into South Texas."

I shook my head in admiration. "Most card players I've known didn't have that kind of sense. Sooner or later they lost it all. You set out to accomplish something and kept your mind on it until you got where you wanted to go. I always knew you would. Now, how does it feel to be a self-made success?"

He paused thoughtfully. "I haven't finished, yet."

The coming of evening threw long irregular shadows across the floor, and the lamplight playing on Emory's face gave him an ever more secretive look even as he continued telling me about himself with apparent candor. He kept our goblets full of brandy and took me through tale after tale of adventure and risk, yet I found myself losing concentration because I was transfixed by his gaze and had to look away now and then as though fending off a wizard's spell. Deep-set and piercing, his eyes were like those of a wild animal, bolder and even more full of suspicion than I'd realized as a youngster. That Emory at thirty-four would have matured into such a dazzling man was a prospect I had never considered. I'd always wondered where he had gone and what he had done, and remembered him as the boy with the smooth face, lean frame, and a sack thrown over his back.

Finally I emptied my glass and leaned back. Emory the man was simply too good to be true. This evening could not be happening to me. . . . Then a question came to mind with a thud. "Are you married?"

"No. I live alone, except for Nathan Hope. He works for me."

"Speaking of work, you've spent a good deal of effort, not to mention an awful lot of money, getting me here. What sort of job did you have in mind?"

He cocked an eyebrow at me and began pacing the floor. "There are a few things you ought to know before I tell you that. First of all, I have never forgotten you, not in all the years. I never forget anyone who is good to me; I've never been one to forgive a person who gives me a bad turn, and I always get even."

Then he paused and looked at me, his expression softer. "I'll tell you something else. I made up my mind when I put that agency to work that if they found you married with a passel of kids, I'd never interfere with your life. As it was . . ."

"Emory, you did me a great favor and don't think I fail to be grateful. But surely when you learned the truth you could have come to me instead of going to all this bother of bringing me here. Why didn't you?"

"I just—" he began, then paused and looked away. "I have too many business obligations to make a trip right now."

"It's all right, Emory. I can understand your not wanting to see me in that place."

He turned to me again, and smiled gently. "I guess that was obvious, wasn't it. Still it was more than that. "I felt that here you could face me with some . . . dignity."

I was too moved by that remark to make a reply. Finally I realized I still had no answer to the question at hand. "Just what is that 'highly specialized position' you mentioned?"

"I want you to be my wife."

I was thoroughly dumb-struck. "But I . . . can't. Surely a man like you could take his choice of any young woman—" I stammered.

"I don't want just any young woman. I want you," he said, then smiled. "Besides, it would take one hell of a female to put up with me."

I sat back, feeling dizzy. "I wish I'd known this before I came down here. As I said, I can't possibly marry you."

"Why not?"

"The reasons should be obvious. . . . I'm not the same Leslie Weems you left in Childers."

He laughed. "I'm well aware of that. When did you change your name? That damned well kept me from finding you."

"Long ago," I told him, but his question provoked another from me. "Just how *did* the agency go about finding me?"

"It was no easy job. Your Uncle Jack was the only Weems

left in Childers, and apparently he was even less friendly than he used to be."

"What did he say?"

"Not much. He opened the door about halfway and when the detectives mentioned your name, he told them you had run off as a youngster and had never been any good. Then he slammed the door. The agency started in a circle around Childers and went from there until they found a record of an Electra Weems. They wrote me to see whether I thought that might be you, and I told them I didn't know but they might as well have a go at it. From then on it wasn't so difficult to trail you."

"Was there anyone left in Childers from your family?"

He shook his head. "I assured them I wanted nothing to do with any of the son-of-a-bitching Cabots if they did run across one. I wouldn't give my boot heel—"

He was so full of hatred that I winced and lowered my eyes.

"I didn't mean to get started on that . . . " he apologized. "God knows your childhood was no more pleasant than mine. It's no wonder you changed your name to Electra—I like that, by the way. I'm lucky you didn't change your last name, too."

He sat down on the opposite end of the sofa and considered me. "Other than that you are very much the same," he said softly. "Your hair is still blond . . . maybe just a little lighter than I remembered . . . your figure has certainly blossomed. You seem to have put on flesh in all the right places," he observed, then moved so near our shoulders touched. "Let me look," he said, and turned my face toward his. "Your eyes are the same when you look at me. I'd almost forgotten how that used to make me feel . . . like I could whip the world."

He ran his finger around my chin then kissed my neck, igniting me. "You tricked me," I said with a gulp.

"You're absolutely right," he answered, then pulled me against him and kissed me hard, and it was good, so good to kiss him back and feel his hand move up and loosen the bow around the neck of my blouse, then, one by one, to fiddle the buttons loose. He picked me up and carried me to the bedroom, which I had darkened earlier for my own protection, and we shed each other's garments easily, naturally as though we had done this many times before. He was dealing the cards now, and could have had it any way he liked, but he took it slowly and gently, caressing my neck, stroking my hair, fondling my breasts, moving his hard thighs between my legs and still going slowly, slowly, giving me time to find my own joy with him first, over and over again, before I felt the final deep thrust, the quick rush, flowing warm inside, which left his body spent and limp above mine. We held on to each other for a long time afterward. It seemed almost as though the years had not come between, and I was doing the thing I had so ardently wished to do the day I watched him walk away . . . to hold him.

Much later in the evening, when finally he rose, he said, "I'll keep no key to these rooms. Think it over for as long as you like, and when you've decided, give me a call at my office downtown. I'll leave my card on the dresser."

At the door he added, "My man Hope has been told a woman—a widow named Mrs. Dexter—is visiting the city. She's an old friend of mine. Should she call while I'm out, he is to find me immediately."

This was my first acquaintance with Emory's style: no bouquets, no bended knees or anxious eyes awaiting the reply; yet I had to smile at his thoroughness. When he was gone I fell asleep and didn't awake until very late the following morning.

3

One week later we were married in a tiny chapel hidden within the confines of a monstrous cathedral. My decision had not been without reservations, which I openly discussed with Emory beforehand. First, there was to be no mention of what he knew of my past. Ever. Neither was he to question me about the parts he did not know.

Secondly, there was the matter of children. I felt a man so well established would expect offspring from a marriage, so when I explained I was barren I watched his expression carefully for signs of disappointment. To my surprise he said quickly, "I got a bellyful of squawling brats growing up. I have no desire for any of my own."

"And you're certain you won't ever change your mind, come to resent me?"

"You can count on it."

Once we had that businesslike conversation behind us, I felt more confident. Somehow this tying up of loose ends helped me to accept the fact that for the first time in twenty years I was truly letting my heart rule my actions. Emory had awakened something in me that I had thought long since dead. Perhaps I'd loved him through the years as he claimed he'd loved me. Yet if so that feeling for him certainly lay dormant until he appeared in my life again. From the morning I awoke in the hotel suite, I missed him terribly.

I tried cold reasoning. I tried mentally listing all the risks that lay at the altar for me. I tried not thinking about him. I tried to convince myself that I would get over him; after all, what were a few hours compared with all the time I'd managed to survive without him? But through it all I kept going back to the day so long ago when he'd walked away from me in Childers, and how it hurt, and somehow that quickly closed the chasm which had widened between us with the years, and I knew that I would be a fool to let the only man I ever cared about walk away again.

On the day before the wedding Emory drove me through a pouring rain to see a house he wanted to buy for us, located a few blocks from downtown. He preferred convenience to his office over living farther out in the newer suburbs. On the way he explained that the neighborhood was fairly old but exclusive —merchants and professional people lived there—and so full of German families and traditions that some called it "Sauerkraut Bend."

I was excited at the prospect of inspecting the house, though the blinding rain ruined my chance of seeing the neighborhood. As it turned out the realtor's car flooded out and therefore he failed to meet us with a key. All I could learn was that the house stood on a large lot backing up to the river, at the corner of Beauregard and Washington streets.

One look at the tall structure convinced me I was going to like it, so I asked Emory, "How soon can we move in?"

A little hesitantly, he said, "I'm pretty sure they'll take my offer, but there's just one thing. I want Nathan to move in with us. He can remodel so that his quarters seem almost completely apart from ours."

"But why? I'd rather have total privacy—"

"I travel some, and I don't like the idea of leaving you alone while I'm away."

"But you don't mind leaving me with another man?"

"Nathan's different. You can trust him implicitly. He'll do anything you ask. I've already made that clear to him."

"I see . . . well, I suppose we can give it a try."

"It's important to me," he said, then changed the subject.

Emory drove a Cole Six automobile, with wide comfortable seats and armrests that must have made it a special luxury for a man of his build. When I remarked on this as we rode to the wedding, he replied, "I get enough horseback riding in Mexico. When I'm in town I want to ride around in something that keeps the rain off and doesn't rub blisters."

"Mexico?" I repeated, beset with visions of a barbaric country crawling with bloodthirsty bandits. "Surely you don't go down there often . . . do you?"

"Only three or four times a year at this point. But I'll explain more about that later."

I slumped in my seat. Following a few moments of silence, Emory asked, "Something wrong?"

"You might have mentioned earlier your travels included Mexico."

"I'm sorry, Electra. There hasn't been a lot of time to give you all the details of my life, and remember, I didn't flinch when you spoke your mind about conditions important to you."

"Yes, but I gave you some forewarning."

"You can still back out. We haven't reached the church yet."

I watched him for a while then, as he faced the street ahead, frowning and puffing on a big cigar. How little I knew about the molding of the character and personality of the man sitting next to me. In a way Emory was like an old picture puzzle you find in a forgotten place one rainy day, and though some pieces have been lost, enough remains for you to complete most of the picture, and fill in the empty, oddly shaped contours with your imagination. The missing pieces may turn up someday, but are of no concern at the moment. . . .

Nathan was the sole witness to our brief ceremony, and proved the biggest surprise thus far. From the time Emory mentioned his name, I had pictured him as someone about the same age, big and burly, maybe a bit crude and boisterous—a good companion for a single man who led an impetuous, adventurous life, matching Emory drink for drink on lonely nights, and keeping secrets when called upon.

He proved instead a slight young man—four or five inches shorter than Emory—with closely cropped auburn hair and light brown eyes, big and round, behind spectacles. He peered down the aisle as we entered, then uttered something to the minister. I didn't intend to stare at him, yet he was so different from my expectations I scarcely heard the brief explanation of the vows being given us, busy glancing toward Nathan as often as I dared. His narrow forehead was pale, his face smooth (was he no more than a boy, I wondered?), and later, as he handed over the gold wedding band during the ceremony, I noticed that his small hands, with meticulous nails, were shaking. In fact he fumbled and nearly dropped the ring, bringing a flash of contempt to Emory's eyes.

When the service was over, Nathan mopped his brow and drew a long sigh. "It's stuffy in here. Why don't we go on outside," I suggested, and would have further invited Nathan to dine with us.

Emory cut in, however, and told Nathan, "Get back to the office and make sure that shipment is priced out right. We don't want any mix-ups now that we have it going again."

Nathan looked at me, then at Emory, and said, "Of course."

On the way out I told Emory, "You could have been less abrupt. I think he wanted to wish us well, or at least introduce himself to me."

"He doesn't have time for that. I've got work for him to do."

The curt exchange was my first glimpse at the strained relationship between Emory and Nathan, and I was both taken aback and filled with misgivings. I wouldn't have guessed the two men were at odds with each other before—if so, why would Emory keep Nathan on, and why would he stay?—yet that day they seemed like two animals of different species, mistrusting each other, at the least. . . .

Outside in the car, Emory's mood had switched again with lightning speed. He took my hand, looked across at me, and smiled. "Well, Mrs. Cabot, how about some dinner?"

"Oh, I do like the sound of that name . . . please feel free to call me that any time . . . and Emory, I'm going to try very hard to make you happy."

"You already have," he said triumphantly, then winked. "By the way, I'm glad you decided to accept the position after all." Then he reached under the seat and brought out a small box, which held a stunning emerald dinner ring. He watched my awestruck expression, then said, "Look inside." And there, engraved in fancy scroll, was the date of my arrival in San Antonio.

Across a candle-lit dinner table, Emory enlightened me on some of his business affairs. The vintage champagne served to the dreamy music of a stringed orchestra enhanced my romantic mood, but not, apparently, Emory's. Yet I was fast coming to know him as one who accomplished a project, only to vault headlong into another. I didn't really mind. In fact I loved listening to him speak on subjects that interested him so intensely, his eyes aglow when he mentioned high profits and shrewd deals. Once during a pause I tried to get him on the subject of Nathan.

He shrugged. "Why should Nathan surprise you? He knows record keeping; he can put up with details that I detest. What makes you think we don't get along?"

"Well, it's obvious you've won his loyalty, anyhow."

"Loyalty?" He raised an eyebrow, then laughed shortly. "I never quite thought of it that way. Now I want to tell you something about Mexico—"

Another question had been nagging at me, so I interrupted, "Emory, did you ever find your mother?"

He paused and eyed me thoughtfully. "Why did you ask that?"

"I don't know . . . something left over from the past, I guess."

"I found her, all right."

I leaned forward, eyes wide. "Where? How is she?"

"Dead."

"Oh . . . that's too bad . . . I mean, I guess—"

"It doesn't matter now . . ." he continued more slowly, "seems she made quite a habit of going about the country breaking up families. I discovered four husbands after my own father. Finally she—oh, well, it's all in the past as you say. My big brother was right about one thing—he always told me she wasn't worth looking for. I used to want to kill him for saying that. It was the beginning of many an argument between us, I can assure you."

Before I had a chance to ask more questions, Emory said, "I've had some good luck in land deals over the past few years. I picked up some property in New Mexico because an acquaintance of mine swore there was water under it. I took a chance on him, and when it turned out he was right—the land was irrigable—the price went off like a bullet. I sold a lot of it before it peaked, and put my money down in South Texas before the big land boom really got going there.

"Late in 1908 I went down into Mexico, and bought some ranching acreage not too far from Vera Cruz. The land just happened to adjoin that of one of the richest families in Mexico—Fernando D. Barrista. You'll probably meet him before long because he comes through here occasionally."

He told me then that he later borrowed money to buy mining properties in lower Sonora and Chihuahua and began Cabot Consolidated Copper, hiring one of the best American mining engineers down there to run things. But then in 1910, about the time he was ready to invest some more money in deepening the shafts, the biggest revolution in thirty years threw the whole country into chaos. "My mines closed down while I still had to meet the loan payments. I came close to pulling out, but Barrista convinced me to try and hang on because he felt things would get better under the new regime."

"Did they?"

He laughed bitterly. "Hardly. The leader of the new regime was double-crossed and murdered by his star general—a son-of-a-bitch named Victoriano Huerta—before there was time to get the country together again, and from then on it has been divided into warring factions."

"Is General Huerta still in charge?"

"Officially he is, but our government won't recognize him because of his underhandedness. And our recognition is all that counts because we've got more money invested down there than any other country."

"Are your mines still closed?"

"They're operating for the moment. Pancho Villa is strong in that territory, and I'm paying him to keep an armed guard on my properties. But I'm producing only enough to meet payments on the original money I borrowed, so I'm having to empty some other pockets to keep going."

"It sounds pretty hopeless," I said, then, noticing his downcast expression, I added, "But surely the fighting can't go on forever."

His eyes brightened. "Someday, when Mexico is a fit place to live again, we'll have a hacienda down there with a fine casa, stables and gardens, long drives—anything you want."

I laughed. "I haven't even had a good look at our house in San Antonio."

He shrugged. "It'll do for now."

On the way out of the restaurant I insisted we take a walk before going to the hotel. "Just as far as that bridge up there," I prodded him. "I haven't had a look at the river."

"It'll be there tomorrow."

"But I want to see it under the stars; please, won't you indulge your bride?"

When we stood in the center of the bridge together, leaning against the rail, I thought if ever there was a moment I would wish to keep, surely it was now. The river below shimmered like a piece of silver cloth rolled out at our feet. The moon hung above as though placed there to make a path of footlights on the water.

"It's almost magical, isn't it," I said, drawing closer to Emory. Yet his perception of the river was obviously different.

He was silent for a few moments, then said, "Hurry up, the wind's chilly off the water this time of year."

4

In the next few weeks, during which we lived in the second-floor suite at the Menger while Nathan readied the house, Emory was more wholly mine than he was ever to be again. The days were long and lazy, drizzled with frequent rains, and while Emory worked at his office on Commerce Street a few blocks away, I spent my time reading in a comfortable chair. The deep branches of a great old magnolia in the garden below unfolded but an arm's length from the window nearby, and often I would look away from the text in front of me to watch the rain plip-plop on ivory blossoms big as dinner plates, and soon be lulled into sleep.

Although matters in Mexico didn't seem to be improving from the newspaper accounts I read, and April brought a confrontation between President Wilson and Huerta when the hard-nosed general mistakenly arrested some of our Marines stationed in Mexican waters at Tampico, Emory did not seem too worried and remarked, "I knew they'd come to blows before long. . . . Wilson will either force that bastard into a formal apology, or die trying."

"Who will take over then?"

"That's a good question. The strongest leader down there right now is Venustiano Carranza, a former governor. His forces control the whole north, with the help of Pancho Villa. But that may not last. Carranza calls himself the 'First Chief,' and I don't think he'll stop till he gets to the top. He needs

Villa now, because nobody can muster troops like that old guerrilla fighter, but he'll ditch him in the end.

"At least, that's my opinion," he added, then changed the subject. He was more concerned at that time with interpreting the confusing new income-tax laws, and was constantly calling Nathan off the house-remodeling job to discuss them. In fact I was astonished the young man could manage so well to fill a myriad of needs for Emory, while making remarkable progress with hammer and nail. By mid-April the rains had subsided, and almost every afternoon I walked to the corner of Washington and Beauregard to see what he'd accomplished. In drawing a map for me, Nathan explained, "Roughly speaking, the neighborhood is rectangular. One long side is bound by the river. The other abuts South Alamo, three blocks away.

"You enter through one end, turning off Garden onto King William Street. The first house has a tall square tower—you can see it from a long way off. Walk past that, then past the triangular park with Spanish oaks around it, then go one full block to Beauregard. Turn right. It's one more block to the Washington intersection.

"Don't worry about getting lost. King William is the main thoroughfare, going from one end to the other, and it's only about four blocks long. The neighborhood dead-ends into Pioneer Flour Mills there—some people still call it the Guenther Mill—but you can see the big plant all the way from Garden, anyway."

Nathan's outline indicated the area was rather small—which was true, but misleading because it left me unprepared for its spaciousness. My first impression upon making the diagonal turn down King William was that I had closed an invisible gate behind me, and left the hustle-bustle of downtown a few blocks distant for a spot of absolute isolation.

On the day Emory drove me to the house, he had short-cut down a cross street so that I had completely missed the view now ahead of me. The wide King William thoroughfare led into a community of scaled-down castles. Each of the two- and three-storied structures with wide galleries and fancy ironwork was like the palace of a small kingdom unto its own. Sprouting up between were just enough smaller cottages to make the grand Victorian mansions all the more majestic and distinctive, and to make the unusual array of towers—some round and pointed, some square and flat, some multisided—more awesome to the eye. Along the way were well-pruned shrubs and abundant shade trees, with wide trunks and thick branches, just taking on their spring foliage.

Looking up and around, I felt at once like a tourist and a trespasser. Many times I lowered my gaze, certain that eyes were looking out upon me from hooded windows and belvederes. I knew my imagination was playing tricks. These people were not out to judge me . . . not yet, anyway . . . and I saw many reassuring scenes. A group of boys were setting up a tennis net at the end of one street; two ladies talked together across a fence adjoining their properties; a young man was busy polishing the trim of a magnificent black automobile at the rear of one house; a small girl rode a wheel, her hat ribbon flying behind and her spaniel loping alongside, his sights fixed upon her ice cream.

Yet there was a quiet splendor about it all, an air of dignity that I supposed must have been the reason for its continued prominence as newer suburbs sprang up around the outskirts of the city. Walking through was an experience akin to turning the pages in a picture book.

I wondered if Emory's choice was a way of thumbing his nose at society, more so than a means of staying close to his work downtown. We were counterfeits here, without the customary lineage. Would I ever chat with a neighbor across the fence, or have someone over for tea?

Our house, I found, was neither as imposing as the larger structures nor huddled out of intimidation as the small ones seemed to be. In fact there was nothing particularly interesting about the two stories of sandy brick and white wood trim, except the main entry was in the corner, with a walkway jutting diagonally across the lawn. Nathan had built a side entrance for his own quarters that, to my mind, was lodged too close to the odd front entrance to look right. Emory swore this was the only way it would work, however, and since the house was by far the nicest I'd ever have hoped to live in, I did not complain. While I still had not grown used to the idea of having an extra man living with us, I did have to admit the way the house was planned, Nathan's quarters—from inside and out—would seem entirely separate from ours.

The house had a deep-pitched shingled roof, and several chimneys which appeared from the outside to have shot up haphazardly as wildflowers in a field. Nathan was busy repairing one of these the first time I stood alone in the dooryard.

Seeing me, he spread his arms wide and said, a little hesitantly, "I hope you like it."

I peered around. "We have our share of good shade trees, haven't we, and that looks like a good pecan. With all this rain, we ought to have a good crop in the fall. I'm going around in the back," I told him, unaware that what I would see was to enrich my whole outlook on the house.

The back yard stretched only about fifteen feet deep—half that of the front—before breaking in a steep incline down to the river's edge. The trees in back were so thick they defied grass to grow along the ground, and in its place grew gnarly, determined vines. My first thought was to have Nathan cut down some of the trees, and provide enough sunlight to encourage grass to grow, but that was before I sat down at the base of one old tree, took off my hat, and gazed idly upon the river for a while.

Undisturbed, that was the word.

Graceful magnolias, cypress trees with knobby trunks, weeping willows stretching their slender boughs out past the banks, tall, moss-hung oaks with straight trunks reaching high as monuments—all made shadows down the wide corridor of water swaying lazily between. Rays of sunlight poked through, glinting off the surface.

Sitting there, forgetful of time passing, was for me a gradual reawakening to a kind of wild, natural beauty which I had forgotten since childhood. I began to hear sounds around me: rustling leaves, snapping twigs. Oddly I never caught sight of any birds that afternoon, yet I heard their brief, high-pitched songs and callings, and now and again their big beating wings, muffled by the roof of tall branches.

I must have been there nearly an hour, when the more ordinary sound of Nathan's voice interrupted the serenity which had possessed me. "I have to get back to the office soon. I thought you might like to go into the house before I leave. Cabot said you'd be picking the wallpaper, and I'll be ready to hang it soon."

"Yes . . . I like the new soft-colored hues. I want lots of light around me, and plants in hanging pots in all the windows, since we don't have much of a porch. And no heavy draperies. I want to be able to look out the back and see what's before me now. In Colorado my . . . apartment . . . was small and confining.

"By the way, what's beyond those trees across the river?"

"The old San Antonio Arsenal is nearby that metal bridge down the way . . . but it isn't used anymore, except as an ordnance depot. Most activity's been moved to Fort Sam Houston up on the north side of town."

"Hm . . . you'd never know anything was out there except wilderness. I hope it's always this calm and peaceful. I'm really glad Emory found this house for us."

He sat down and mopped his brow. "I think I'll enjoy it too, especially the breeze off the water." He took off his eyeglasses and wiped them, then replaced them on his face.

"Emory doesn't seem too taken with the river."

"Oh? Well, he doesn't get excited over simple things."

"Regardless, I'm going to make the most of it. I had no idea the prospect of living near the water would please me so much." He was silent, so I added, "Maybe that sounds like foolish talk to you—did you grow up here?"

"No. I was raised in a sawmill town up in East Texas timber country. . . . I always figured I'd stay there, and grow up to become a sawyer."

That raised the question of how he came to know and work for Emory, but before I could ask he was rising, claiming he had to hurry.

"I'm sorry . . . I guess the river makes me kind of dreamy," I told him.

We spent our first night in the house on April 30, although I expected Nathan's projection of the middle of May would have been accurate. Emory had to leave for Mexico on the morning of May 1, and, in one of his sudden blazes of urgency, insisted we must be moved in before he left. Nathan was already dividing his time between working on the house and figuring Emory's complicated corporate franchise tax—due a month after income tax, by April 30—but the fact that he was forced to close up the books and work for four straight nights until the early morning hours to finish the house seemed of no concern to Emory. Puzzled, I asked Nathan if he wasn't obligated to meet the tax deadline.

"Of course," he answered calmly, while brushing varnish on a baseboard.

"When will you work on it?"

"While the rest of the world is sleeping."

I shook my head and walked past him with an armload of chintz curtains.

Most of the furnishings did not arrive in time, and the pantry was bare except for coffee and some cinnamon rolls Nathan brought from the bakery. However, I was no less eager than Emory to get moved, and was thankful when we had shut the door at last and sat down to rest our tired bones.

It must have been nearly three o'clock before we finally closed our eyes, and even then I slept fitfully. As long as Emory was awake I could fend off unwelcome thoughts of his leaving, but as soon as he fell asleep I was hounded by the fear he wouldn't return. It was a nightmarish feeling I was destined to face time and again in the months to come, and perhaps if I'd known this I would not have wasted my time making up arguments in my head to keep him from going. Yet I did, and finally around five in the morning I fell asleep only to be wakened by a muffled, distant sound of notes that I thought may have been part of a dream. Emory, his arms still around me, was sleeping soundly. How could he, I wondered? If I were the one going to Mexico, my stomach would be in tight knots for days in advance.

It took me a while to nudge him awake and when he finally yawned and nuzzled his face in my neck, I was near to tears. I swallowed hard and said, "I guess you have no choice but to go . . . but I want you to know you have made me very happy."

He opened one eye and said, "Good Lord, woman, I wasn't planning on coming back in a coffin." Then he noticed my pained expression and added, "I've been getting out of scrapes since I can remember. Don't worry about me. If there's one thing I can do it is take care of myself."

I lay back on the pillows while he bathed and dressed. I already missed him. In a few short weeks I'd grown happily accustomed to his attentiveness, and the consistency of waking up in the morning next to him. As hard as I tried convincing myself it wouldn't be so bad if he were not to be in danger, the truth glared back at me. Wherever Emory was, I wanted to be.

He was puffing on a cigar as he buttoned his shirt. "Let me go with you. I can be ready in half an hour," I pleaded.

"That's no place for a female," he said.

"Seems to me it isn't fit for anybody, down there."

He sat on the edge of the bed. "Listen, I think there are going to be some changes for the better soon. Now that Huerta's agreed to mediate through the Latin American powers for a peace settlement with us, we have our foot in the door."

"What about Carranza and his party? Won't they still be making trouble?"

"Once Huerta's out of the picture, Carranza will enter the mediations, if he's smart. Then maybe they can put their heads together and come up with someone acceptable to all parties in Mexico."

"From what you've told me, Mexicans don't put their heads together without knocking them."

He smiled. "Some do. Look, I've had a letter from my friend Barrista. When I get to his ranch—a perfectly safe place, believe me—we're going to talk over some things that may work to my advantage."

I failed to see how that could affect the danger down there in other places he'd be traveling, and I also sensed he was trying to placate me with this line of talk. "All you see in the papers nowadays are reports of lootings and hangings, and unspeakable torture," I told him. "It's a mystery to me why you can't just sell out and buy some more property in the civilized world." I hadn't meant to sound so pushy or vindictive, but it was too late.

He stared at me coldly. "You might as well understand that I will decide when and where to invest our money. I'm not accustomed to having anyone question my wisdom, and I'll thank you to remember that."

There was a long and awkward gap of silence between us while he finished packing and fastened the buckles on his suitcase. I didn't know how to span it—in a way I felt as if he'd cheated me by not telling me beforehand I was in for this kind of life; on the other hand, I knew it was my turn to be on the giving end, and if I didn't show him now that I stood behind him, he'd probably dismiss me as window dressing. He straightened his tie and pulled on his coat. I had to be the one to speak.

"Don't give up on me, Emory. I'm sorry for what I said, but you have to give me time to get used to your darting off without me, especially when I fear for your life. You are the only person in the world I've ever truly loved, and if anything happened to you, I . . ."

He closed his hands around my cheeks and kissed me gently. "I don't take to the idea of leaving you, either, and I'll miss you like hell, but I'm a man walking a tightwire in a circus right now, so bear with me.

"One reason I pushed Nathan into finishing this house so early was so you'd have plenty to keep you busy while I'm gone. That way the time will go faster for you."

"Will I hear from you?"

"If possible. One day the cables are strung, next day they're cut. They're no more dependable than the railroads down there. But I'll be back as soon as I can, you can be sure of that."

"It won't be soon enough."

Later in the day, after he was on the train for Galveston where he'd board a ship for Vera Cruz, I thought of his remark about investing. He had called it "our money." It was good to know he already thought of me as part of him.

That night I had my first chance to talk with Nathan. I offered him coffee after dinner but he surprised me by requesting instead a glass of whiskey. He then proceeded to consume considerably more than I would have expected, though he sipped his drinks slowly, and seemed able to hold his liquor.

He told me a lot about Mill Springs, where he spent his childhood. He became more communicative (as the alcohol took effect), and indicated in many ways without saying so that he had been happy there for the most part.

His father had died when Nathan was ten years old, and he had been very attached to his mother. When I suggested she must have had a hard time supporting the two of them he replied, "She sewed for ladies, worked morning and night, and I helped out a little by doing odd jobs." Then he added, bitterly, "My daddy never made my mother a decent living, and he was gone all the time, peddling notions. So I guess we got by just about as well without him. She always begged him to get on at the mill, where he'd get steady pay, but he wanted no part of it."

"Why not?"

"I guess he figured common labor was beneath him. He was better educated than my mother . . . and I think in a way he was downright afraid to work at the mill, though he never said so."

"Afraid?"

"It's a dangerous place to work. Lost fingers and burned arms and legs are as common as fever," he said, then squared his shoulders before remarking, "I wouldn't have been afraid. After Daddy died I promised my mother I'd grow up and become a sawyer—that's one of the highest paying jobs at the mill, next to filer. I'd have started at seventeen as a water boy, and worked up. I would have given all the money to her."

"That speaks well for you as a son . . . but what happened to change your mind?"

He measured his reply carefully. "When I was thirteen Mother married again—a man named Sam Arnesty who'd come to town and taken over as foreman of the mill."

"How nice," I said.

"I thought so too, at first. But then he turned out to be rotten all the way through."

"I see . . . did she leave him?"

"No. She took sick, and died when I was fifteen. Then I—" he began, but quickly paused. "I left home." Apparently the whiskey had not completely loosened him up, for he again became tense and reserved.

"Is that when you went to work for Emory?"

"No. I"—he hesitated, looking up at me and then again at his glass—"met Cabot two years later, in 1904."

I encouraged him to talk about his years with Emory, but he told me little more, and I could not help believing he regretted the association. Not surprising, I supposed. Surely there were easier people to work for.

As I finally retired that night, I heard the serene melody of taps coming from the arsenal grounds, and realized the brisk notes which had awakened me that morning were not the product of a dream but those of reveille.

I thought for a while about Nathan. His quarters downstairs were converted from what had formerly been a second parlor, so he could enter either through the new door he'd built outside, or from the foyer. Since I'd gotten to know him a little better, I did feel comforted by the thought that he was close by. He'd been so open at first during our conversation—so at ease and natural—you would have thought he had known me far longer than Emory. Then he was secretive and nervous at certain intervals, and I sensed the things he chose to keep to himself were far more important to him than those he talked about. But I had only to look to my own situation to see that, really Nathan acted tonight no differently than I would have. There was no reason why his behavior should concern me.

5

Keeping busy through the month of May was not only a good way of passing the time, but the only means of holding on to my sanity. As conditions worsened daily in Mexico—innocent people losing all their possessions if not indeed their lives, while the warring factions continued to bludgeon each other first in one town then another—I knew what it must be like to have a loved one off in a faraway battle. As a noncombatant Emory's life was worth no more than if he had joined the ranks —possibly less, because Mexicans had a growing resentment against American citizens as the United States continued to meddle in their affairs. In Mexico City their food supplies were cut to a minimum, and their post office confiscated, while we held forth at the port of Vera Cruz with our troops and ships and weapons, serving as handy scapegoats for their lack of needed supplies in the interior.

On top of it all, there were any number of small uprisings led by rebel chiefs whose names disappeared from the news as quickly as their troops deserted them. All of it made me dizzy and caused many a nightmare as the month wore on and we received no word from Emory. Once I screamed out so loud in my sleep that Nathan heard me from his rooms and charged up the stairs. His frantic knocking at the door and calling of my name awoke me. I was amazed my screams were loud enough to be heard as far away as his quarters.

If not for the pleasant coincidence of meeting Geoffrey Woodstone, I sometimes doubt I would have been able to endure the strain of worry over Emory during his trip to Mexico that first spring of our marriage, not to mention the more and more frequent periods he was away as time went on. Woody proved a key which unlocked the door to many new worlds for me.

I had seen him often as he came out of his house a block from ours, on the corner of Beauregard and King William. Every day at three o'clock sharp he took a walk. His small terrier, Scoop, circled his steps and sometimes preceded him, but always stayed near.

An English gentleman, Woody stood nearly seven feet tall and seemed hardly bigger in circumference than one of the gas lampposts along the street. He always wore a formal suit and bowler, regardless of the weather, and kept a cane hooked on his sleeve which I never saw him use for support.

His home was one of the small wooden cottages perched cozily among the majestic residences, and his front garden was a colorful and well-planned array of tulips, daffodils, and other blooming foliage which I admired each time I passed by. Prettiest of all was a thick queen's-wreath just beginning to sport its bright pink blooms, which grew up the picket fence at the side of the house, spilling over and running down like a waterfall across the sidewalk as though it had every bit as much right to be there as the people passing by who were obliged to step around its cocksure runners.

That afternoon several boys, fresh from a swim in the river, came scurrying down the walk near the queen's-wreath vine. Involved in their frolic, they reached the corner without paying attention and smacked right into Woody, knocking his cane off his arm and bringing forth furious growls and barks from Scoop. They hurried past without apology.

I was nearby, and went to Woody's aid. Only then did I see the face under the hat brim and noticed he was well advanced in years. "Children are getting more mannerless all the time . . . thank you, miss," he remarked, collecting himself. "And look, they've stomped all over the queen's-wreath vine. In my day that alone would have been worth a good strapping."

Then he paused and, apparently just then aware he had an

interested listener, smiled and said, "Good day, madam. You're very kind to stop for an old man."

"It's too bad about your vine," I told him, eying the scattered remnants.

"Oh, never mind. The stouthearted vine will be crawling across the walk when those boys are long gone and forgotten. I was just on my way for a stroll. Care to join me?"

It was the beginning of a treasured friendship, one which would have meanings for me that unfolded only with the passage of time. I believe Woody—the name he insisted I call him from that day, though it seemed much too informal to suit him—was at least partly responsible for my breaking the barrier into neighborhood society, because everyone knew and respected him.

Those of the more elite families in the neighborhood admired him for his superior education and well seasoned eye for quality in the arts, and his appreciation of fine music. The hard-working, prosperous merchants liked Woody for his genuine kindness and lack of snobbery. Early in our acquaintance I confessed I felt a little unwelcome in the area. "Why ever should you?" he demanded.

"I don't know . . . I haven't had the advantages of these people. I'm largely self-educated."

"Then you are to be congratulated. Education is an ongoing process, to my mind, and once people stop educating themselves, they wither and die. Don't let any of your neighbors put you off, now. Many of them I taught when they were chaps in the German-English School, and they were just as full of tomfoolery and wickedness as anyone else . . . not a one of them a bit brighter than you."

Soon we were taking frequent walks together, and often would wind up in his small parlor. The room was tastefully decorated with oriental porcelains dating as far back as the seventeenth century, an outstanding collection of cut glass, several wood sculptures, and many original paintings. Using his pipe as a pointer, he showed me these during my first visit, and from time to time would speak on their histories.

He also owned a handsome Victrola, on which could be

heard the piano concerts of Paderewski, the powerful voice of Caruso, or some other musical artist whom he'd identify, discussing the works performed at length while we shared English tea and bread and butter, sometimes with marmalade. Eager to learn, ashamed of what I did not know, I hung to his every word as he spoke on subjects which had never before been introduced to me.

He and his wife, Elizabeth (he always referred to her by her full name, drawing out each syllable with equal distinction), had migrated here some fifty years earlier to take teaching positions in the States. They had soon come to San Antonio, where private schools were begun by the culture-oriented German families, and no expense or effort was spared to bring about high standards of education and discipline. He once remarked, "Of course we arrived long before the advent of the public-school system, and the attendant plunge in principles." That was the closest he ever came to sounding oversuperior, and as I came to know him I realized he was genuinely regretful at seeing anything of merit undermined.

Elizabeth had passed away in 1900, when they were both in their mid-sixties, and he had lived alone in their home since that time, surrounded by the things they loved. Once when I asked if he ever traveled back to England he said, "There isn't much use in it anymore. Elizabeth and I went to the World's Fair in Paris the summer before she died, and went over into England for a fortnight while there; now I really haven't any desire for going without her."

The only living family he ever mentioned were still in England. He had a daughter, "who is one of those suffragettes in the Pankhurst gang who go about smashing things up and burning churches, and protesting before public buildings . . . oh, it is contemptible the things they do, and the very reason they cannot get anyone to take their cause seriously." He also had one grandson, of whom he was obviously fond and proud. There were several photographs of the nice-looking young man around the rooms of the house, and, when I met Woody, he was studying at Oxford University. "Johnny's going to come over here for at least a summer when he finishes his studies," he told me more than once, his eyes lit up with anticipation.

Undeniably, I took advantage of the fact he was an old man, hungry for someone to talk to and therefore eager to accept my friendship. Yet it was not simply that: I was truly fascinated by him and enjoyed the hours we spent together. Woody seldom got out past the boundaries of the neighborhood, except to visit a special art exhibit or attend some other cultural event, and he detested riding in automobiles, so I couldn't repay him by offering Nathan's services as driver now and then.

His digestive tract, which he termed, "brittle and frail with age," kept him on a fairly restricted diet, so I could hardly present him with a fresh fruit cobbler to show my gratitude.

I was searching for some way to reciprocate his kindness to me when I discovered he liked fresh fruit and vegetables, as I did, but was not up to a walk all the way to Haymarket Plaza anymore. So, after that I brought him fresh produce from my frequent trips to the open-air market—first strawberries, which were just coming into season, and later cantaloupes, which were especially good that year.

I was just returning from his home one day following such an errand when I saw Nathan in the yard, waving a telegram. "It's from Cabot—he's in Galveston and will be home early tomorrow," he called.

Forgetting all semblance of propriety, I picked up my skirt hem and ran all the way home.

6

Even then there were subtle changes in Emory.

He returned in better physical condition than I'd expected—no weight loss, as explained by his having stayed for the most part at Barrista's hacienda, where the food stock was ample in spite of the privations in other places—yet he was, if not tired, a little more temperamental, more impetuous, and short with Nathan. In my presence he was making a more obvious effort at control. I sat in the bedroom while he bathed, talking to him through the open bathroom door.

Without him more than a month—surely the slowest period I could ever recall—all I wanted was to hold and love him, and live for a while that idyllic life we had so enjoyed at the Menger. Yet my dream was soon shattered. We were to have a house guest within a week. Barrista had been invited to participate in the Mexican peace talks—what we had come to refer to as the ABC Conference, so named for the Latin American mediators of Argentina, Brazil, and Chile. He would be stopping through on his way to Ontario, where the meeting was under way.

"He was invited by one of the Latin American countries as a special authority on agrarian reform, one of Mexico's biggest problem areas. Barrista is not just anybody, you know. He's one of the country's foremost historiographers, well known in academic circles all over the continent," Emory said.

"No, you didn't mention it to me," I said, wondering immediately why he would be staying at our house, when he surely must have friends far up on the San Antonio social ladder.

My train of thought must have shown in my face, for Emory added, "The Barrista family has never had close personal ties here, because they have never needed them. Fernando takes the liberty of choosing his friends according to how much he enjoys their companionship. He doesn't regard himself as a diplomat when he travels up here."

"I think we can make him comfortable . . . how long will he be staying?"

"Just a couple of days. He has to be in Ontario by the middle of the month."

"Pardon my changing the subject, but having worried over you for all this time, I do wonder just what is going on down there."

"Huerta's about ready to give up—he's nearly bankrupt. Villa is gaining strength all the time; he has about twenty-five thousand men behind him now. And it's beginning to look like I was right about Carranza and Villa—they're quarreling."

I shook my head. "It seems endless."

"I know it, but one purpose of this conference is to find a neutral—someone without ties to any faction—to serve as Provisional President until free elections can be held."

"But will Carranza and Villa go along with that?"

"Villa has indicated he will; Carranza can either co-operate or go hang. If he can't get foreign recognition, he can't hold on to Mexico, and if he doesn't play according to ABC rules, he won't get recognized."

I thought about that for a while, then suddenly something dawned on me and I looked up. "Are you hoping to get Barrista in as Provisional President?"

"Exactly."

Just then he walked into the bedroom, his shirt off, beard trimmed, looking like a pirate who'd won a sword fight and sent the loser down the plank. "I've been thinking about shaving my beard. Facial hair is going out of style, and it's going to be hot this summer. What do you think?"

"I think if you do, you will find yourself short one wife."

I was unbuttoning my blouse with one hand and pulling the pins from my hair with the other. He stood back and watched me, one eyebrow raised. "How quickly you move," he remarked.

"How long you have made me wait," I reminded him.

Barrista proved to be everything Emory claimed and more. By the time he arrived I knew quite a bit about his background —he was educated both here and in Europe, and had married a native of Greece. He was devoted to his country and wouldn't live anywhere else. Now fifty years old, he was a widower with one daughter. His family, including four brothers, stretched to all corners of Mexico, and many of his kinsmen had counted among public office holders and high military officials over the years. "At the same time, they've all managed to keep their noses clean," Emory pointed out.

Because of his enormous land holdings Barrista moved easily within the circles of wealthy Mexicans, but he was also the common man's friend. He helped educate the workers on his plantations and ranch, sponsoring more than his share of foreign exchange students over here, and he also maintained private hospital facilities for his laborers.

"He's a whole lot like Francisco Madero, the leader of 1910, but he's also practical and shrewd—that's what I like about him. He's fed up with war and revolution, and thinks maybe through this conference he can take hold of the government reins peacefully."

Through Emory's description, I had begun to visualize the tall, distinguished man with his flawless command of the English language and all the markings of the citizen of the world; yet he had one characteristic that Emory didn't put into words: there was an immense power in his presence.

As soon as he walked into our house, everything around him seemed to fade in contrast. I got through the hand-kissing introduction as gracefully as possible, though I was almost afraid to speak at the risk of stepping on my tongue. I thought as we walked into the parlor, now I know what it is like to meet a statesman. He had stern, Indian jaws and questing eyes beneath strong dark brows so unruly that here and there the hairs shot up into bristly rings. Barrista looked as if he had once possessed a violent nature, which had mellowed with age and experience into forceful diplomacy. The longer we talked that evening, the more I was convinced this was true.

After dinner, Nathan, servantlike, silently lit cigars for him and for Emory, and at my urgings Barrista began to speak of matters in Mexico. For the first time I began to get a clear picture of why solutions to the problems were so difficult to find.

He spoke at length of the horrible inequities in distribution of property and wealth, begun in the days of Spanish colonialism and compounded down through the ages by first one self-interested government then another. "Even the short and isolated periods of reform have done little to help the common people in Mexico. They have no land, and because they are largely illiterate, would not know how to cultivate it if they did.

"As a result, they will follow any revolutionary leader until another offers them a little something better. Madero disappointed them in 1910 because he lacked the strength and wisdom to hold the government together while he put his reform ideas into action. So, the people are disheartened once again."

"If you were chosen as Provisional President, what would you do?" I asked him.

"At first I could do little more than educate the people about my ideas of reform. But if my official recognition as head of the government were to follow, I would begin to carve up the huge land holdings and set limitations on the number of acres per family in one state—including my own properties and those of my brothers.

"Immediately, I would increase land taxes, and use the revenues for building free schools, and housing and hospitals on part of the land taken from the big estates. Some land would be held aside for five to ten years, while the literacy level is upgraded."

He then explained in detail his ideas of compulsory education for Mexican young people, and broad-scoped foreign-exchange programs both for teachers and medical students.

"For those who chose not to enter the professions, there would be industrial and technical schools," he added, with a nod toward Emory. "Your husband suggested the need for this sort of program."

Emory's face was suffused with pride as he remarked, "They'd be in a devil of a fix with every Mexican walking around with a diploma ten years from now, while no one was able to wire a building for electricity or put in a plumbing system."

It occurred to me for the first time that Emory and Barrista had conducted discussions in Mexico about subjects more far-reaching than I'd known.

Barrista was continuing, "In ten years, the land set aside would be available for sale to the masses able to pass a literacy test and prove they could maintain and cultivate it."

Aside from agrarian reform measures, the Mexican notable had definite ideas regarding compulsory military service with fair pay and benefits, and, finally, a sure-fire way to avoid any future dictatorships in his country. "I would work with the legislature on a new constitution stating there would be one presidential term of eight years, with no re-election rights for the incumbent. Nor could any member of his cabinet, staff, or family run until one full eight-year term followed."

As he ended with a long draw on his cigar, I could see why Barrista commanded so much respect.

In the next few weeks, conditions worsened in Mexico as peace talks continued far away at the Clifton Hotel in Niagara Falls. In the meantime, the rift between Pancho Villa and Carranza stretched at last to the breaking point.

No place in the daily news did I see Barrista's name mentioned, though I looked for it carefully. Near the end of the month the mediators, about to throw up their hands at trying to deal with the obdurate Mexican leaders, finally managed to persuade Carranza and Huerta to agree to send agents to a separate treaty table in Washington. Men from each side could have a copy of the peace plan drawn up in Ontario, and look over it together.

Barrista sent a letter to Emory informing him of this, adding that the Ontario conference would adjourn until a Washington treaty meeting could be held. He would be coming to San Antonio to stay until such time as he had to return to Ontario, or could go home to Mexico. He asked Emory to reserve a suite at the St. Anthony's for him and his daughter Aegina, who would be joining him there.

"It'll be nice to meet her," I said.

"Aegina won't get here for another week or so. I doubt we'll see her," he said.

I thought no more of it at the time.

Barrista returned looking tired and somewhat dispirited, and more out of kindness to him than for any other motive, I opened up the dinner-table conversation by asking if his daughter Aegina had arrived in San Antonio. Barrista glanced quickly at Emory, then at me, shifting nervously as he answered, "Why, no, not yet. I expect her within the week." Something in his manner made me uncomfortable, but I couldn't tell what. The moment passed.

When he turned to the subject uppermost in our minds, his voice was far less animated than when he had visited us before, and Emory listened to the unfolding of muddled events with a frown of concern, puffing on his cigar.

"Time after time my name was mentioned as a possibility for the provisional government, and each time overlooked. I did not realize how blinded the ambassadors could be. I have been in the forest, yet I can better see the outlines of the trees than they can."

"They're all stupid," Emory said abruptly. "I never thought it would work, and I told you so."

Barrista leaned back and drummed his fingers on the table. "It is going to get worse down there. I need to get back to look after my own affairs. Yet I'm afraid I would be a fool to be absent if the meeting takes up again."

He lacked the decisiveness he'd shown before, and throughout that evening I was able to see where Emory's traits fell into place to allow for his shortcomings. It occurred to me that if Barrista were king, Emory would be the power behind the throne, the "trusted advisor" you often read of as being in accompaniment with heads of state. Then I remembered something Emory said just before he left for Mexico in May about talking over things with Barrista that might prove advantageous. That, put together with Emory's dinner-table remarks and Barrista's answers, evoked a frightening prospect.

I interrupted their conversation. "You men have discussed the possibility of staging a new revolution in Mexico, haven't you?"

They both looked at me thoughtfully. "Hopefully one far less costly in human lives than ever before," Barrista added.

7

I lay awake for many hours that night, still in awe of what had been said. It began to dawn on me how deeply involved Emory was. Every time I felt I'd come to grips with one aspect possibly facing us, another would come to mind. Emory would surely be away a lot. All right, I suppose I could learn to endure that, if it did not go on forever. He would be facing dangers thus far unfamiliar. Well, he had already proven he could look after himself, and certainly knew the territory well enough after all the traipsing north and south between his copper mines and his ranch. Some Mexican might try to pick him off, though, just because he is American. But then, surely he'd be somewhat protected by his friendship with Barrista. Or would he? How safe would Barrista be, after the revolution was under way?

The worries were endless, like sparks from a forest fire being carried by the wind to ignite other dry timber, farther and farther away. . . .

Emory lay rigidly beside me. He wasn't sleeping either. Finally I said, "I suppose there's a small chance Barrista could yet be named—"

"He isn't willing to give up on that, yet."

"How nice that would be," I said with a gulp. "No more blood spilling . . . oh Lord, I'm afraid."

He pulled me closer to him. For all the questions bursting in my mind, I was unable to frame one of them aloud. It was comforting, at least, that he was there, warm against me. "Don't worry; nothing can be done, at least for now," he said.

"I never thought you'd be involved in anything like this."

"Neither did I." He kissed my hair; his voice was placating. "Please, don't worry—I wouldn't go down and enlist in the troops or anything. Hell, I'm too young to die and too vain to risk losing an arm or a leg . . . or something worse."

I couldn't help smiling. Sometimes his sense of humor came just in time. "Well if that means you won't be taking a direct part, I feel better already," I told him, but could not resist the temptation of reminding him he still could pull out, sell his interests, and put his investments in San Antonio alone.

"I have a good bit more than you realize down there," he said, "and while it's a big risk, if it works it could bring in the biggest dividend of all. So it's worth it."

"I've a good mind to go up to Ontario and tell those numb-skull mediators what's what," I told him.

"You sound like a suffragette."

"It's obvious they're all too busy parading around like peacocks to see the facts."

"You've probably hit the nail squarely on the head. And you're probably just sassy enough to push your way right into the exalted chambers up there, but once they got a look at you, they wouldn't be able to concentrate on Mexico anymore.

"Which reminds me, right now I'm a little tired of the subject myself. Doesn't this damned nightgown of yours have a bottom?"

In July Barrista returned to Mexico, and, anxious for his daughter's safety, left her in San Antonio to enroll for teaching courses at a small Catholic college in the fall. I felt a little sorry for her, alone in a foreign country, and offered to have her stay with us from time to time. However, Emory was against the idea and assured me she was well-educated, world-traveled, and had many friends among the students here with whom she would be in contact. "Nathan might like to meet her, though. They're probably near the same age."

"He has already met her, once or twice in Mexico, and believe me there were no sparks between them. Aegina wouldn't be interested in staying with us."

I dismissed her from my mind.

Whether because word had gotten around that the Cabot home was the guest residence of a Mexican notable, or because of my continued friendship with Woody, I began receiving occasional invitations to tea receptions, for various women's clubs, and one Thursday afternoon was invited to a coffee klatch. I had seen them in progress on my way to the market from time to time, at one or another of the larger and more impressive houses. I suppose the heat drove the ladies out on the big porches, and they'd be sitting around a table with formal tea cloth and silver service, dainty china cups, and a variety of cakes and pastries. Probably eight or ten in number, they seemed an impregnable force as I walked in solitude down the shady lanes, their chitchat halted momentarily as I passed by and gave and received a polite nod. They never invited me to join them at those times, and as soon as I was a few steps down the block, I would hear the drone of neighborhood gossip start up again, always half believing they were talking about me.

On that hot Thursday afternoon in July, a young woman named Lyla Stuttgart, who'd surprised me by introducing herself a few days earlier, came by at two o'clock and invited me to go with her to one of the more stately mansions on King William.

"Are you sure it's all right? They aren't expecting me."

"I can bring anyone I please," she said breezily. "We aren't all that formal around here." I could have taken exception to that remark, but didn't.

Lyla was twenty-four years old and married, with three children. She had grown up in a house on King William, and moved but three doors down when she married Arnold. Their home—a wedding gift from her parents—was one of those raised cottages which looked deceivingly small from the front, yet spread far to the rear of the lot and included three levels: two above, with one a few steps below ground for the kitchen. On the day we met she was sitting in a little breezeway under the tall front porch, with her feet propped up, swinging a palmetto fan. When she first called out to me, I thought I was hearing things. Then I saw her, partially hidden from view by the porch stairs. Our introduction didn't seem very promising —she didn't bother to walk over to the fence—but I stopped to chat.

"On your way somewhere?" she asked.

"Haymarket Plaza. Care to come along?"

"Heavens, no. I once had my purse snatched there. You'd better be careful. Why don't you send someone to do your shopping, or have it delivered? Butler's up on River Avenue is good. My housekeeper swears by his meats."

"I don't have a housekeeper."

"My goodness, how do you manage without one?"

"Oh, I like doing things for myself, and the house doesn't get all that messy."

Just then, as though by signal, two of Lyla's children came charging out of the kitchen door nearby, quarreling over a toy and bringing our conversation to an end.

Lyla had auburn hair, freckles across her upturned nose, and green eyes that lit up when the subject of high fashion arose. On coffee-klatch day, she was formally dressed in white tunic, hat, and gloves, and carried a smart-looking parasol with an ivory handle.

"I go to these things to get away from the children," she remarked as I put on my hat. "Even with their own nurse and a housekeeper, they're under my feet all the time. How many do you have?"

"Children? None."

"My dear, how did you manage that?"

I ignored her question and presented myself. "Do I look proper for a coffee klatch?"

"Hm . . . well . . . except that hat is awfully large, isn't it?"

"I prefer large hats."

"You do have the carriage for them—wish I had! Last week I bought three of the new smaller ones with single plumes in the back—they're just in from Paris. Arnold nearly died of heart failure, poor dear, but I told him he could send the bill to Papa. That always shuts him up, and quick."

Lyla's voice was light as a butterfly most of the time. She continued to speak on whatever subject came to mind all the way to the awesome-looking house with the mansard roof two blocks away, and quietened down only once we entered the stifling parlor—why, I wondered, did they not have coffee on the porch that day? She was quickly introducing me to a dozen or so ladies, several of whose German surnames I could not quite grasp. The conversation centered mostly on homes and children, with incidental comments now and then—some young girl's canoe ride down the river lately, and the daring new tango steps; the alarming frequency of automobile accidents out on the South Loop near the asylum, and many veiled remarks and raised eyebrows about the females involved in them.

One lady leaned near and, raising an oriental fan to shield our faces, whispered, "Until a few years ago I taught school down that way, close to Santa Rosa and Matamoros. I soon learned to spot a night lady from a mile away." She nodded, sat back, and fluttered her fan.

My eyes widened. "Oh, and how's that?"

She leaned forward again. "Ah, you'd have to see a few to tell, but they usually go around in pairs or groups, and wear the most striking ensembles. Now and again I see them shopping downtown—" she began, but the hostess interrupted with a call to refreshments. She snapped away and flipped her fan closed, as a schoolgirl would do when caught with a naughty book. I just managed to keep from smiling.

Thankfully, a cold punch was provided as well as coffee. I filled a cup, and arranged some fancy sandwiches and cookies on a plate, then found a chair near a window and sat back contentedly to enjoy the chitchat. Lyla had long since gotten involved in gossipy whispers with one lady, and no one seemed to notice me very much, so it was easy to observe at a distance. There was something nice about the ease with which these women kept company—their world one I had never known, full of gentility and carefree days, the stability of having lived in a certain place over a long period of time, of using china and silver passed down from one generation to another, and of knowing many people close by with common interests. . . .

I was sitting there in something close to a reverie, when I gradually became aware of an exchange between two women not far away. They were speaking about the new popularity of the tango over here. The dance had been favored in Europe for a long while, but up to now had been held back in this country because so many considered it vulgar.

"Of course they're always ahead of us abroad," said one. "Correctly done, I find it a stunning sight, don't you? Just last Friday I was leaving a meeting at the Menger when their afternoon tea dancing began. I stopped to watch the most handsome couple, executing the tango. When she turned to face my direction I realized it was Aegina Barrista. I met her and her father once at a party at the International Club. She's such a striking young woman, you know."

"And who was she with?" the other asked.

"I didn't really get a good look at him, but he was dark, full-bearded—an attractive match for her. . . ." The remark was like a cold breath on my neck, and I clutched my half-empty plate harder.

The breeze across the river was cool that early evening. I sat at the edge of the bank and looked down the sharp curve, sounds of the ladies talking echoing over and over in my mind, vaporous images of Emory and Aegina touching, bending against each other, closely, closely, the satin ribbons of her shoes winding around her legs, meeting the edge of the slit skirt as she moved, back and forth, back and forth, her whispers in his ear and her soft giggles, his beard brushing her cheek. . . .

Now it all came together. Emory's refusal to invite her to our home, his comment that there had been no sparks between Aegina and Nathan, the awkward moment when I'd mentioned her name while Barrista sat at our table.

Yet it couldn't be. Emory didn't know the tango. We had watched a captivating demonstration once during an evening at the St. Anthony's, but he hadn't said he knew the dance and hadn't offered to perform it with me. . . .

At the Menger? Impossible. Short blocks from here. I could walk there this minute and see for myself . . . no, last Friday. This is Thursday. Tomorrow, then?

What did she look like?

Like Emory, of course—they made an attractive match.

But at the Menger, where we'd been so happy together.

Nonsense.

I pulled up an encroaching vine, felt the little suction cups pop under my hand as I loosened it, inch by inch, from the earth. The vines climbed all over, up the trees, along the ground, up the fence nearby. Who did they think they were?

Why, Emory, why?

Nathan stopped by and looked at the vines clutched in my hands. "You can hardly kill them," he observed.

"What?" I glanced up.

"At home when I was a kid, we had a big tree right in the center of the front yard. The vines grew up the trunk and all through the branches. Dead of winter, the tree would be bare, but the vines would be thriving still . . . it looked so odd."

"Nathan, does Emory know the tango?"

He looked perplexed. "I have no idea."

"I think he's doing it, with Aegina Barrista. Would you go to the Menger next Friday, and see?"

"Electra, I can't just—"

Then a thought flashed like a beacon. "Of course, you must know where Emory was last Friday afternoon. Think, where?"

He paused. "Why, at the office of course—"

"You're positive?"

"Let me think." (An interminable pause as he studied the ground.) "He did leave early, though, to go by the bank on some busi—Electra, listen, I'm sure you are wrong about this."

"Oh, Nathan, could you just check next Friday?"

"Me? But why?"

"You could so easily explain your looking for him if he were there and he saw you—a pressing business matter. And then I'd know the truth and have some time to . . . gather . . . to . . ."

"Don't cry, Electra."

"Please, help me."

"Would that be helping? I mean, I just couldn't risk it, really."

I looked at him squarely then. Beads of perspiration covered his forehead. His eyes were wide, intense.

"You're a coward!"

"No, you don't understand . . ." He was drawing away and backing toward the house, arms held out, entreatingly. "I can't, you see . . ."

Presently I recovered and turned to look up at the house. He was inside, watching me from the window. Poor frightened fellow, strange shadow of a man. I threw a rock into the water and watched the ripples spread.

8

Nathan and I shared dinner alone that evening.

Every sound of knife grating across meat, spoon stirring in a glass, fork scraping plate was deafening. We soon gave up and faced each other.

"I'm sorry," I began. "You see, I've tried so hard to please Emory but . . . today a lady at the coffee said—"

He looked away.

I ran my tongue across my mouth. "If there is something going on behind my back, you could tell me and I swear to you I would not let Emory know where the information—"

"I know of nothing," he said, staring at a fixed point across the room.

I sighed. "All right. I don't suppose you could imagine what it's like to—"

His hard glance shot through my words. "But I could . . . I could imagine more than you think."

"Well then, just tell me, was there ever anything between Emory and Aegina Barrista? My suspicions are based on more than what I overheard today."

"Why don't you ask him?"

"I can't."

"Why not?"

"I just can't, that's all," I said. I could not tell him the true reason was that, since I had forbade Emory to mention my past, I had no right to trespass on his unless I was certain he had failed to leave part of it behind.

As I hesitated, Nathan studied me, then queried earnestly, "You're afraid to ask him, aren't you?"

"Of course not . . . I just . . . don't want to bring on a confrontation that would make me look foolish, that's all. If you'd rather not say, it's all right."

"Well, if it will ease your mind I'll tell you what I know, but you must give me your word you will never tell Cabot what I said."

"I already have."

He relaxed somewhat and leaned back. "They courted when Cabot first came to know Barrista, but he stepped in as things became serious."

"Why?"

"Several reasons, from what I gathered. . . . Aegina was only twenty-one years old, and her father felt Cabot was too old for her. Also, I think he wanted Aegina to marry a Mexican *caballero*—one of his choice, probably.

"But mainly Barrista didn't want his daughter marrying out of the Catholic faith."

"I see. How long ago did all this happen?"

"About a year before you came here, it was over and done."

I swallowed hard, realizing for the first time I may have been second choice, our marriage one of rebound for Emory. "Knowing Emory as you do, would you be willing to wager a guess about the two of them now?"

He considered. "I suppose he could be seeing her. She was—is—a beautiful young woman, with dark eyes and hair. He was taken with her, all right. They used to throw big parties at the ranch in Mexico when Cabot was there, and he and Aegina would dance all night—" He stopped abruptly and blinked. "I never saw them do the tango."

I nodded, and he continued, "Next day they'd be off to the bull fights together. They both enjoyed the bloodthirsty sport. She had a wild streak in her, just like him."

"I see."

"But she couldn't stand next to you, Electra, not by any stretch of the imagination. Finally a man—even one like Cabot —likes to settle down to a fine lady, and live respectably," he said, then leaned forward and added, "Listen, you probably don't realize what a different man he was before you came. He has straightened up a lot, by comparison." He rose from his chair. "That's all I know."

"Thank you. And don't worry, Nathan. This will work itself out." I watched him leave the kitchen, his steps quick and jerky, and wondered again at his fear of Emory. He was at times like a figure of spun glass, resting precariously on the open palm of an unpredictable hand.

I retired early and lay in bed thinking. It was just possible that even if nothing were now between Emory and Aegina, the fact that there once was might make for discomfort between Emory and her father. Perhaps it was a subject that had once brought them almost to blows, and now that so much depended upon the friendship of the two men, they took extra care to avoid conversation about Aegina. That would explain a great deal. The man seen with her at the Menger may have only resembled Emory. . . .

A couple of hours later Emory came in and I pretended to be asleep. I heard his hat plop on the bureau, his pants being shimmied off, and smelled the strong odor of his cigar. He didn't bother me, although he lay for a long time awake.

Finally I could stand it no longer, and framed the question that would be the quickest, easiest stab at the truth: "Emory, is there someone else?"

He didn't answer. I decided, with relief, he was asleep. The question had sounded disgustingly superficial. At daybreak I awoke to the feel of his fingers stroking my hair, and turned to him.

I believe from that time on Nathan took it upon himself to try and make up for any way he felt Emory was letting me down. He was always offering to drive me to one place or another, though it was easy to see he was reluctant to get behind the wheel of Emory's automobile because he drove as though there were a traffic officer breathing down his neck all the time.

Should I make the slightest suggestion or just hint at something needing to be done, he was at work on it immediately, even when there was obviously no hurry necessary. One morning I told him I'd noticed a charming little summerhouse in one of the yards on King William.

"I could build you one even finer than that," he offered at once.

"Oh, I don't know whether Emory would like—"

"He wouldn't mind, as long as it was for you. I'll work on some plans tonight, and when I get them to suit you, I'll go down to Steves Lumber and buy the wood. Maybe we could situate it in front of the Spanish oak in the side yard, between those two big magnolias. That way you'd have plenty of shade on it."

"Yes, and I could plant roses around it. Let's paint it white, to match the trim on the house," I said, infected by his enthusiasm.

As a matter of fact, while the summer of 1914 wore on, I was eager for something new to occupy my mind and demand my energies. I found myself constantly expecting Emory's announcement that he was bound again for Mexico, and would brace myself for the worst each time he broached a new subject in conversation. He spoke little at first about his plans with Barrista, and as he was often preoccupied I didn't urge him to discuss them (I wished more than once that something might happen to make the Mexican troubles dissolve).

Only the daily newspapers kept the situation near. In mid-July Huerta finally gave up under Wilson's pressure and left the country, friendless, and reportedly "subtle and bitter" in his denunciation of the United States. Reading the Huerta story—assuming then it was an epilogue—I could not help but wonder why Fernando Barrista wanted the weight of Mexican troubles on his shoulders. And Emory—how much wealth or personal gratification could possibly be worth the strain and pressure of involving himself in matters he needn't even bother with? His insatiable thirst for winning went back, of course, to the indignities he suffered in his bringing-up.

Sadly, as much as I loved and understood him, my presence in his life could not completely fill his sense of need. In a way I was even a part of what drove him: as his wife, I could always be referred to as the "reason" he had to make good. How badly it would reflect on him if I did not have a big home and lots of expensive clothes to wear . . . and, several years hence, what a failure for him if I did not have even a second home, a staff of servants for each, and a substantial amount of the year spent traveling to one place then another. That I wanted none of this did not matter to him in the least. And I couldn't tell him why I had every reason to remain modest about wealth. . . .

Emory was spending fewer and fewer evenings at home, and I was certain he was putting up Nathan to lie for him about the reasons. The young man never looked me in the eye when he told me another, then another excuse about why Emory would be arriving home late.

Yet this concern was pushed aside by something far more ominous.

9

One morning as I was picking over fruits and vegetables at Haymarket Plaza, enjoying the sunshine and the pleasant sounds of chatter and general hustle-bustle of the market, I suddenly had the feeling someone was watching me from behind. I turned around, expecting to see a familiar face approaching. By now I knew enough of the vendors and patrons to exchange a greeting now and then or discuss a good find among the produce. Yet there was no one I recognized, though I shaded my eyes and looked both ways.

Imagination, I decided.

I began comparing the color and texture of fresh peaches, and was soon lost again in the business at hand. I selected several, and moved along to the next table. My basket was growing heavy by now so I stopped to reverse it with my handbag in the other hand, and in doing this I looked about, an uneasy feeling taking hold of me though I couldn't say exactly why. Then I thought of Lyla's warning about purse-snatchers and clutched my handbag tighter. I decided to call it a morning and head for home.

It is odd to recall how I fought off misgivings during the long walk. Several times I was tempted to board a trolley or hire a taxi. Yet I kept telling myself I was behaving foolishly, walking a little faster all the time, never daring to look back to see if anyone were following yet listening for the sound of footsteps. . . .

By the time I arrived at our door I was winded. I hurried inside, locked it, then went to a window and looked out. Nothing. Silly. Still, my nerves were unsettled so I sat down with a glass of cold fruit juice and tried to concentrate on a magazine. After an hour went by I was convinced my anxieties were groundless. Then I heard a knock at the front door.

"Who is it?" I asked. There was no view of the porch from our windows. Breathless, I repeated, "Who is it?"

"Oh, just an old friend. Hey, open up!"

I knew then, even before I opened the door, who I was about to face. I was only thankful neither Emory nor Nathan were around as I let him in.

Mark's husky frame had gone to fat; his face, once having had a boyish pudginess about it that made him seem younger, was by now graded with wrinkles, his chin lax. His color was unhealthy, and his brown eyes were puffy underneath. It was as though his looks, never attractive, had over the years become a badge of his character.

"Well, well," he said with an insolent smile. "Looks like you done all right for yourself, Mrs. Cabot." He walked through the foyer and poked his head into one room then another, as I stood rigid against the doorjamb. I already knew what he wanted. The thing was to deal with him as quickly as possible and get rid of him. I directed him to the sitting room and offered him a chair, then sat across from him and asked how long he had been out.

"Not as long as you, but long enough to do some looking around and take a little stock." He propped a foot upon the table nearby and looked at me steadily, still smiling ever so little.

"How did you find me?"

"Oh, we had some real helpful friends down the line. It wasn't so hard. When I heard you'd come to San Antonio I came down and started hanging around one place then another. I knew it was only a matter of time till you'd turn up somewhere."

"Were you at Haymarket Plaza this morning?"

He grinned. "You still got good instincts. But I was real curious as to where you might be living by now so I didn't want to reveal myself too quick."

"How did you find out my name?"

"You got real accommodating neighbors. I must say I was surprised, Mrs. Emory Cabot," he said, drawing the name out. His eyes circled the room again. "From the looks of things, you sure knew which coattail to hang on to this time. Maybe I ought to stay around awhile . . . when does your new husband get home? I might just—"

"He'd kill you if he found you here," I interrupted.

"Now, now. I don't want you to think I came all this way just to cause trouble, now that you're wealthy and all. That might be fun but it wouldn't do no good. You just give me what I've got coming and I'll get out of your way. I never was one to hold grudges . . . not like some people."

"Listen, it's not that simple," I said quickly. "I can't get my hands on that kind of money. At least, not all at once."

His expression hardened and the corners of his mouth turned down. "Come on, sister. Who are you trying to kid? You're Mrs. Rich-lady Cabot now, ain't you? Just ask for it. Tell him it's a little family obligation you got to take care of. I'm sure he'll understand that," he said, and grinned again.

I just stared at him, my stomach churning. Soon he walked over and brushed a hand against my cheek. "Course, maybe you'd just like to come away with me . . . it shouldn't be too hard for us to come up with a solution to your problem if we worked together on it. After all, there was a time, you know . . ." His face was close now; I could smell his sickening breath. I pushed him away and stood up.

"Look, I've got a little money of my own in Colorado, about five thousand. I'll have to write a letter to get it. Leave me an address and I'll send it to you. Then as soon as I can get more, I'll forward it."

"Hold on a minute. I'm not near as trusting as I used to be. I want it all now."

"I just can't get it. Our money is not in cold cash. And even if it were—look, if you'll just give me time I'll figure out a way to get it all to you. But it won't do you any good to badger me."

He seemed to consider that for a few moments, then walked over and took my face in his hand. "No remorse? No apologies for double-crossing me?"

"Oh, I'm sorrier than you will ever know. But I didn't have good sense then. If I had, I wouldn't have taken up with you in the first place. Now leave an address and get out."

He squeezed my face a little tighter. "Don't start giving orders, Mrs. Rich-lady. It may take me a little while, but I can prove a lot, and I got nothing to lose. If you don't want the truth to come out, we're going to have to keep in close contact. Supposing you rent a post-office box where I can send you a little note now and then, to remind you of your obligation in case you have another lapse of memory. Otherwise, I might have to come back and visit you again."

"Yes . . . all right."

"I'll be waiting in the lobby of the post office at ten o'clock in the morning, and we'll exchange addresses just like old friends who meet up again after a long spell. And if I don't get the first five within the month, I'll be knocking on your door again. Got it?" He pressed his mouth against mine and I lurched free and flung the back of my hand across his face. He stood there rubbing it for a minute, then started to laugh in that maniacal way I remembered so well, his voice starting low then pitching higher and higher. . . .

When he was gone I rested on the door. My heart was beating wildly and my hands were icy. How long would the first five thousand abate him, and where would I go for the rest?

There was no opening for me now. Emory considered my past a closed case and even if some part of it cropped up again he might be understanding. But I was sure he knew nothing about my involvement with Mark, and if he found out it would be the one thing that would turn his love for me to hate. Neither would I surreptitiously take Emory's money to pay what Mark was demanding.

There was also the good possibility that once I'd paid off

Mark he would turn greedy and blackmail me for more. I had never even thought of that until now. If that were to happen . . .

The print of his hand was still like a flame against my face. I wished more than ever I had believed in Emory and his feelings for me twenty years ago faithfully enough to have stayed in Childers all these years, awaiting the day he'd come back for me.

10

Within two weeks I had obtained my savings from Colorado and forwarded it to a New Orleans address Mark gave me. I soon received a letter that he'd gotten the money, but, as I expected, the letter contained an underlying threat about the future installments.

The savings, begun long ago, had originally been intended to go toward paying Mark off. But in the meantime Emory had proposed marriage. I saw his proposal as my one chance for the good life I wanted so badly, and so I fooled myself into thinking Mark would never find me. So much time had passed, and now not one new name, but two . . . surely that was ample protection.

At least the five thousand had been sufficient to appease him so far. I felt almost safe again as weeks passed without word from Mark. And as Emory's affairs in Mexico continued to mount, I managed to shove the question of where I might next look for money to the back of my mind, although it resided there like a haunting specter.

The provisional presidency of Mexico was denied Barrista and handed to someone else, with the stipulation that regular elections would be held in the fall. Emory scoffed and said, "Carranza is still the strongest man down there and it looks now like he'll get recognition by our government, if he just hangs on long enough.

"When that happens you can say good-bye to free elections and look for more bloody strife than ever before because

Pancho Villa will never stop fighting Carranza, and the rest of the country will be divided into as many rebel bands as there are bandidos able to gather a few troops."

By early August, Emory's predictions were proving true, and I was discussing this with Woody one morning over the fence as he tended his flowers. "It seems trouble is breaking out everywhere," he said, mopping his brow. "And I must say the incident that has brought Europe to the brink of war is a lot less reasonable than the problems causing trouble in Mexico. Over there the monarchs have nothing to do but sit around thinking of new territories to take over, more jewels for their crowns, and they only need a little nudging to fight. Ah . . . now it's begun, I'm afraid the whole of Europe will fall in line like dominoes."

"Maybe you should see about getting Johnny to come here to school for a while. I heard that one of the neighbor girls is coming home from school in Switzerland. Her family came home a month early from their ranch in the hill country to pack up and go to Europe for her."

"Oh, Johnny would never come. He'd stay and fight, if it came to that." Then the old man wiped his brow and folded his hands over the handle of the garden hoe. "I only pray it doesn't."

He looked somehow a little older as he stood there, tall and weathered as a tree which has withstood many a season of hard frosts, to face one more spring of rejuvenation. "I'm going to an art exhibit at Carnegie Library this afternoon—a mixture of local and international artists' work—why don't you come along?"

"I'd like that."

"Then we'll have tea. I've just received a new tin of tea biscuits from a niece in Glasgow . . . she thinks of me once in a while."

It occurred to me as I walked away how alone Woody was, with only his terrier Scoop for company and a woman from the Irish Flats who came by to tidy up the house twice a week. I ought to invite him for dinner one evening, I thought, but then I couldn't quite see him seated across the table from Emory.

Nathan was just finishing the summerhouse, on which he had spent many an evening sawing lumber and driving nails. Less ornate and lacy than the one I'd seen nearby, it was hexagonal, with open sides and six latticework columns under a peaked roof. The crowning touch was an onion-shaped finial for the rooftop.

Raised off the ground by three steps, the summerhouse was breezily inviting, and large enough to hold a small table and eight wicker stools, which I had bought and arranged for delivery before the final coat of paint had been applied.

Nathan was undeniably proud of his work, and I was delighted. It added so much to the looks of the yard, I thought, yet when I mentioned this to Emory he was noncommittal. He'd had a few drinks too many that evening, and wasn't inclined toward pleasantries anyway. I shouldn't have persisted, but I did. "When Katherine Brooks saw it, she offered to pay him twenty-five dollars just for the labor to build her one similar to it."

"Who the hell is she?"

"A neighbor over on Turner Street."

"Oh, one of your coffee-time chums?" he asked with a sneer.

"Not a chum exactly. . . ."

"Well Nathan doesn't have time to go around building summerhouses for people."

"Forgive me, your most highest, I didn't realize it would put you off so badly."

"Hell, I bought the lumber, the nails, and the paint."

"I'll be only so glad to reimburse—"

He laughed. "With what, my dear?"

I could have turned the whiskey bottle over on his head for that remark. Thankfully, the sound of Nathan coming through the back door made me pause, and I kept my temper. Once I'd heard Nathan's door close and lock, I continued, more softly,

"I don't mean to start an argument over this . . . I just believe it wouldn't be too difficult for you to show a little more kindness to Nathan now and then. You're lucky to have him in your employ. With his variety of talents, I'm surprised he stays with you . . . I mean, bookkeeping is such tedium."

"Don't worry. Nathan isn't going anywhere."

"How can you be so sure?"

He paused. "Because I own his son-of-a-bitching soul."

"My God, what a thing to say," I told him, bringing a hand to my chest.

"I've got to go out."

"Seems you do an awful lot of that lately."

"It beats staying home."

I stood there a few moments after he walked out, scarcely believing how easily we'd gotten into a quarrel. Then I ran out the back door and caught his arm just as he reached the garage. "Emory, why are you angry with me?"

"Who said I was?"

I shook my head. "Could we talk for just a few minutes?"

"What's so important? I have an appointment."

"With whom, about what?"

"None of your business. Anything else?"

"I suppose not. Shall I wait up?"

"Don't bother. I'll be late."

I lay awake far into the night, thinking how simple the message Emory was relaying to me, yet still unwilling to accept it. We'd been married less than a year and for most of that time I had been so sure I was making him as happy as any woman could. Certainly he found me a responsive bed partner—the ingredient most basic in a good marriage from a man's point of view—and I had made every effort to be more than was normally expected in a wife. I studied the Mexican news like a dedicated student pores over his textbooks, not only because I was directly concerned with Emory's welfare, but also because I wanted to be able to talk with him intelligently about the subject of most importance to him. I took special care in the way I conducted myself, in the way I selected my clothes, so that he'd be proud of me. I kept our home clean and presentable, and never complained of having a boarder though at times I felt Nathan's presence put an extra strain on our relationship, especially during Emory's nasty moods. Nor did I pry into their association with each other, even while it was a source of great puzzlement to me. Owning Nathan's soul . . . what could he have possibly meant by that remark?

It seemed to me I did everything within my power to please him. Yet it wasn't enough, obviously. While I was lying on my side of our bed, he was undoubtedly lying beside Aegina Barrista. It was so simple, yet so impossible to fathom. Maybe he'd lived the life of a bachelor so long, he was uncomfortable with the responsibility of a wife, and those less constricting ties along the way now begged to be picked up again. . . .

I tossed and turned, wondered and speculated, until finally it occurred to me I was letting the whole thing get out of hand . . . jumping to conclusions. That was a comforting prospect, and upon it I finally dozed off, too numb to have come close to shedding a tear.

The following morning I awoke to the jovial sound of Emory singing in the bathtub. "Good morning, my dear," he said as I walked in, his cigar hanging precariously in the corner of his open mouth. I stared at him sleepily for a few moments. Finally he said, "You're supposed to demand to know where I was all night."

"You said that was none of my business."

"Oh . . . so I did. Well, I'll tell you anyway. I tied one on with a business friend in the Menger Bar. That place hasn't rocked like it did last night since Teddy Roosevelt hit town with his Rough Riders."

I turned and reached for a cake of soap, so he couldn't see the look of relief on my face. I could usually tell when Emory was being honest. Then I pulled the cigar from his mouth and threw it into an ash can.

"What are you doing?"

"Move over. I feel like a bath, too."

He watched quietly as I let the gown fall slowly around my feet; then, leaning forward to toss it aside, I looked him in the eye.

"Get in here. Damned if you aren't like a bad habit," he said with a devilish grin.

Before leaving for his office that morning, he apologized for his remarks about the summerhouse and said, "That was liquor talking. You can have anything we can afford, and someday I hope to be able to give you much more."

I felt ashamed of myself for entertaining the suspicions of the previous night. "Let's have dinner out tonight, just the two of us," I suggested.

He hesitated then said, "I . . . uh . . . can't tonight. I have another appointment."

I nodded with a casualness I didn't feel.

11

In early October, Emory went to Mexico for a planning session with Barrista. Thankfully, this was a short trip—he was away only a couple of weeks—and I was kept busy much of that time gathering and shelling pecans from the tree in our dooryard.

We received several party invitations, which I held aside for his return. Emory took a jaded view of most social functions, and knew few people in the neighborhood, so I was reluctant to commit us on my own. Besides, it would have been fine with me could we have gone away somewhere together for the coming holiday season. I didn't mind having Nathan live in our house all that much, and was many times grateful for his presence, but I never felt we had complete privacy. The house was old, the limestone walls thick. You could not hear what was being said in the next room unless the doors were open. Yet I often found myself guarding my conversation when Nathan was at home, as though he were crouching somewhere, listening. . . .

Emory looked among the engraved cards hurriedly, and said, "Let's not go to any of them. Parties don't matter to me." But then he picked them up again and said, "No, maybe we ought to attend a few, especially this one at the Casino Club."

"You changed your mind awfully fast."

"I have to feel out some people about money to finance the revolution. If I've got to socialize, at least I can do it with a purpose."

He was eager to tell me of the plans drawn up in Mexico,

and even before changing from his traveling clothes he filled a whiskey glass and sat down. As he talked it was easy to see Barrista had the long-range ideas for the good of the country; Emory provided the short-term means for putting them into operation. Barrista had named his manifesto Plan de Pacifica Reforma—plan of peaceful reform. I asked Emory how and when the operation would begin, my pulse pumping a little faster as I uttered the words.

"Early next year I'm going down quietly and take a little tour, covering five or six Mexican states and paying a visit to each of the Barrista brothers and a few trusted friends. I'll be gone a few months, probably."

My heart fell as I thought of the dangers, with railroads operating only here and there, and half of them blown up by revolutionaries.

When I voiced this to Emory he said, "I'll be on horseback mostly," which did not make me feel any better.

"Why can't Barrista do that?" I asked.

"If a man like Barrista were seen riding horseback from one end of the country to the other, it would look a mite suspicious. I can do it easily, and besides, I want to meet the people we're enlisting and get a feel for them." He paused. "I have my doubts about his brother Carlos, especially. He's a little too ambitious and competitive to suit me. . . . Maybe I'm just measuring him by my own experience—Barrista seems to think he can be trusted—but family ties don't mean a hell of a lot to me."

"What then?" I asked quickly.

"We're going to try and create a national spirit by circulating Barrista's plan around the country, and make sure it is told to those who can't read."

"Won't that give him away?"

"No," he said, with a smile of satisfaction. "Barrista is going to be known as Apostol de Reforma—Apostle of Reform—only no one will know who the Apostle is until the end. At first we'll be dealing only with education as to his proposals. Later —probably around the end of 1916 because it will take time to get people to talking and understand what is going on—will come the call to arms, and hopefully a very short decisive battle coming from three corners toward the capital."

The statement gave me goose bumps head to toe. Emory made it all seem so possible, that if everything were carried through as carefully as it was obviously mapped out, it could not fail. He was looking at me. "What's wrong?"

"It just occurred to me I'm in the presence of a man certain to change the course of history."

"Yes, or perish in the effort."

During an autumn cool spell near the end of October, I gave my first coffee for the neighbors. It was long overdue because I'd attended several in other homes, and although I agreed with Emory they were largely time-wasters, I still maintained an unquenchable interest in the sense of permanence and belonging they gave me. I was never called upon to give monologues about my past—the ladies seemed all too busy speaking of their own long-standing families in San Antonio—and I enjoyed sitting back and listening. Besides, Lyla had given two since the day she had called on me for the first time, and had hinted lately it really was my turn to have a day-at-home.

Though the morning was leisurely spent for the most part—I was practically ready by noon—my mind was not nearly so at ease. Around a week prior, I had received another letter from Mark. I hoped the first installment would quiet him for at least several months longer. Yet he was apparently living high down in New Orleans. The letter said, "You know how it is. Money gets away from a person quicker than cornmeal spills out of a slit in the sack, don't it?"

I had already burned the letter over the kitchen stove just as I had the first one . . . somehow this ritual gave me an odd sense of comfort. Yet the problem of Mark could not be dispensed with so easily. Half an hour before the coffee was to begin, just as I was beginning to place refreshments on the table, the doorbell rang.

My whole body jerked, and I nearly dropped a platter of

finger sandwiches on the floor. Then I walked to the door as though there were irons on my feet, hands still shaking, thinking, oh no, not now, Mark, not now. . . .

It was Lyla. She breezed in wearing her newest afternoon frock, kissed my cheek gaily, and headed straight for the table. "Oh love, you've forgotten the coffee spoons," she said after a brief inspection. "Where do you keep them?" She was removing her gloves. "You can fit them over on this end with a little rearranging." Finally she paused and looked at me. I was still standing at the door of the parlor. "Electra, you look positively ill. Don't worry. You have plenty of time to fix things and even if you didn't, no one would notice. These coffees have been going on for such a long time.

"Isn't it lucky I came early?"

The talk that day began with the usual gossip. Someone complained of a maid scorching the kimono sleeve of her new evening gown, and this served as Lyla's cue for a few minutes' descriptive chatter about her new creation by the famous designer "Jenny"—its tunic coming just ten inches above the skirt hem. Then she sat down and lit into, ". . . the new velvet hats—have you seen them?—exquisite!" For the first time I began to notice the other ladies seemed little interested in what Lyla had to say. They'd probably known for a long time what I was just beginning to learn: Lyla was extremely self-centered and unable to see beyond her own nose.

Aware suddenly that, as hostess, I was obligated to switch the center of attention elsewhere, I was about to open my mouth to speak when someone addressed Vera Frederick, just returned from Europe to pick up her daughter in school there. I had not met Vera before, and she struck me as being a good bit more intelligent than Lyla.

"The conditions over there were abominable," she was saying. "We had a taxi confiscated right out from under us in Paris—"

"Whatever for?" someone asked.

"They need them for war vehicles. We had an awful time cashing those embassy checks—the lines of people were endless. Our steamer was stopped four times on the way home, and when we got here Mathilde was missing a valise and I was minus a trunk. All the same, we were grateful to set foot on the dock in New York. It's like the whole world has gone mad over there—crowds of people everywhere, animals running all over, turning over garbage bins . . . the streets are unsafe. . . ."

One lady said timidly, "My goodness, and to think how I've griped about rising prices over here because of the Great War. I guess we're lucky it hasn't touched us any worse."

Then someone else said, "It's a puzzle to me who's winning."

"Everybody's winning, or says they are," Vera replied.

"And the Germans dropping bombs from those Zeppelins all over the place. You'd think they'd have more regard for human life than to do what they did in Antwerp," said Treva Morse. A moment of awkward silence followed.

"If you were fighting for survival and the British had effectively cut off your food supply, you'd do well to have a port like Antwerp at your disposal. You can't fight a war with clean hands," said Vera.

"The Germans will win," said Melva Scheiner. "They are persistent and determined. No one will get them, you wait."

I was beginning to think there was a miniature war threatening in my own parlor. Worse still, all the tensions of the day had combined to give me a throbbing headache. I needed to get this coffee over with so that I could be alone to get a grip on myself.

Quickly I spoke up, "Ladies, shall we have coffee now? And Lyla, suppose you do the pouring . . . you are so good at that kind of thing."

Her look of consternation was small price to pay for keeping my unsteady hands from everyone's attention.

After the ladies were gone I pulled a shawl around my shoulders and went out to sit above the river, hoping its peaceful reflection would help to quiet my nerves. It seemed I was losing control of everything at once. While Mark had not shown up in San Antonio—thank heaven the incident of this morning had proven a false alarm—his letter made it obvious I was to have little peace. Though I had replied that I was working on something and would soon have another payment for him, I knew there was nowhere for me to turn.

I had seriously considered seeking a job. I had a ready-made excuse for Emory in case he protested. He was out of town so much, and I just didn't have enough to keep me busy. Yet I had no training. . . .

One morning shortly after that as I pored over the classifieds at breakfast, Emory asked, "What are you looking for?"

I kept my eyes on the print before me. "Oh, nothing in particular."

I was aware he continued to watch me and in a little while I looked up at him. His expression was concerned. "Lately you're getting circles under your eyes," he said. "Aren't you sleeping well?"

I started to tell him of course I was, then thought of a better reply. "I have to know you're home safe before I can rest and sometimes half the night passes before—"

"Have you thought of what you'll wear to that Casino Club party on the eighteenth?" he asked, changing the subject.

"Actually . . . no."

"Well it may be an important event, so get all gussied up. Buy something new."

"All right," I told him, and he brushed my cheek with a kiss and walked out.

After that I looked in the mirror and realized he was right about my harried appearance. If he was having a second look at Aegina Barrista, maybe I had no one but myself to blame for letting my problems take hold of me. I had to do better. I had to be more of a wife and helpmate to Emory, quit hiding in the shelter of the pillars at social gatherings—my usual custom, since I felt so ill at ease—and make myself noticed both as a woman and a good conversationalist.

First I had to concentrate on improving my looks. I parted my hair in the center and pulled it back into big braids winding down from the crown of my head. Lyla Stuttgart bragged of her Limoges hair fashions from Europe, but I had plenty of my own hair to work with, thick and wheat-colored, especially if I applied lemon juice rinsings regularly. I hadn't gone to that trouble lately.

I bought the most expensive dress of my life for the Casino Club party. It had a daringly low-cut white silk bodice that tapered to the waist and draped becomingly around my hips before dividing into three snug, beaded tiers. For just a nod at propriety, the dress was topped by a sheer overblouse that silhouetted the curves of my breasts in front and fastened down the back, beads winking here and there on the butterfly sleeves.

I purchased my first pair of long white kid gloves to match and white shoes and stockings. The sales clerk at Blum's was obviously envious when she saw me in it, and Emory, on the night of the party, looked pleased and proud but said, "With a cloak and a train, you could ride on a float in the Battle of Flowers parade."

"Is that a compliment?"

"Of course. I've always had good taste in women"—he winked—"and how do I look? Like a prosperous gentleman, on his way up in the world?"

Actually he looked so well in his new midnight-blue suit and waistcoat that I couldn't wait to get him home from the party, but stung by his flippant remark I said, "You'd look swell as a riverboat gambler." (This was true in a way; and he certainly was a high roller.)

Sobered somewhat by the match of wits he said, "You know damn well you'll have every man's eyes coming out of their sockets tonight."

"That was the idea, my dear. Shall we go?"

"Just one thing . . . what do you think of this?" he asked, slipping a large ring over the index finger of his right hand. It was an oval-shaped black onyx cradled in a high gold-tub mounting—a beautiful piece, and the only one of its kind I'd ever seen.

I was praising him for his taste in gems when he interrupted, "And this is for you—an early Christmas present," and opened a box which held an exquisite necklace, earrings, and bracelet ensemble made of Mexican opals. He'd had all the stones for months, he explained, and ordered them mounted in San Antonio by a jeweler renowned for his gold filigree designs.

I was filled at once with delight, and quickly exchanged the jewelry I was wearing for the stunning opals. They were perfect for my dress, almost as though they'd been ordered especially to accompany it. I was so touched by Emory's generosity that I thought of nothing else at first. But then as I turned from the mirror and reached for my handbag a sordid question presented itself to my mind.

"What's the trouble, don't you like them?" Emory was saying.

"Why, of course. I love them," I said glancing at him.

"Well that's reassuring. You looked just now like you thought they belonged in the trash."

"No, I was thinking of something entirely different," I said nervously. "Hurry up. We don't want to be late."

Midway down the stairs we saw Nathan just closing his door to our right. His mouth opened in surprise, then drew closed. He mumbled something about a gay evening as I wished him good night. Outside Emory said, "You even had Nathan all agape and he is not exactly what you would call a man who runs with women."

I don't know that Emory already had designs on Adolph Tetzel as the banker who would be likely to finance the Barrista revolution, but it was well known that the Casino Club was still made up largely of upper-class German people who mixed with members of the military and, sometimes a bit reluctantly, with other German merchants who came up the hard way. Surely a party there would likely serve as the setting for financial overtures—reason enough to whet Emory's interest in attending.

Lyla and her husband, Arnold, had invited us for this occasion. Her grandfather was one of the founding members long ago, when it was "strictly for the German culturally elite." She had told me all I knew of the club's strata, adding, "Arnold could never have gotten in without Papa's help."

Just where Tetzel and his wife, Sophie, fit into this complicated echelon I wasn't sure. He owned the big International
Bank of the Southwest downtown, but as I soon learned, he
had migrated with his family from Germany in the 1840s, and
took great pride in the fact he'd been in San Antonio when the
railroad came in 1877, and had worked hard to build his fortune in the city. Almost from the beginning of the ball that
evening, Emory made it his business to stay involved in conversation with him and, while I was aware of the fact he was feeling him out as to his views on Mexico, I was kept busy myself
with no end of attentive gentlemen who cut across the dance
floor during the fox trots, hesitations, and waltzes with remarkable grace. The balding, sallow-faced Arnold was often at my
elbow while Lyla gossiped with a group of women, and I kept
wishing to rid myself of him because our only common interest
was the boring subject of street widening on Commerce.

Around ten o'clock Emory was at my elbow, guiding me over
to meet the Tetzels. "Is he *the* one?" I asked, and Emory nodded confidently. Tetzel was tall and slender with wavy, gray-
streaked light-brown hair, and a German accent as strong as
Woody's British dialect. He was not overfriendly to me, but
polite. Sophie's hair was grayer than her husband's; she was
chunky and awfully plain. She was also distant. As we engaged
in stilted conversation, I kept wondering how Emory managed
to get Tetzel to warm up to the point of talking business.

As we drove home Emory explained, "Oh, I've met Tetzel
before and we have some mutual acquaintances. We didn't get
down to brass tacks tonight—oh, speaking of brass, did you see
all the military around there? I was afraid one of those majors
or whatever they were would overhear something, so I really had
to keep it guarded. Now that the troops are coming back from
Vera Cruz, I wish the Army would figure out some place other
than Fort Sam to send them. I don't like them under my
nose."

"So what did Tetzel say?"

"He agreed the right man might be able to make it in Mexico, regardless of all the fiascoes since 1910."

"How about money?"

"I mentioned it would be costly, but he said now with the new reserve laws in effect, banks have more money to work with than before."

"Hm . . . doesn't sound like very much."

"I know it. However, he invited me to lunch week after next."

"I see . . . well, maybe I could curry Sophie's friendship. She might not behave so stiffly next time I see her."

He was pensive for a few minutes. "They're a little funny on the surface, but maybe it's to be expected. I've heard a story that just after the Tetzel family came over here and started farming up near Fredericksburg, there was an Indian raid. Half the family were wiped out. Their house and barn were burned, the animals stolen—they lost everything. But Tetzel is a fighter. He stayed and built it all back long before he moved here and went into banking. That calls for a strong consti-tution, and it's one reason I think he might be the right man to help us."

"Sophie said they lived on King William up until a few years ago. I guess I could have another day-at-home and invite her, for old times' sake."

"Don't worry about it yet, not till I'm sure Tetzel wants to give."

He's shutting me out, I thought. "By the way, they didn't do the tango tonight. I was hoping they would, weren't you?"

"Hm? I—" he began, but then we both heard a loud pop and he said, "Oh, damn, we've got a flat tire. I should have had Nathan drive us." He pulled off the road and reached for the tools, forgetting my question. For the next thirty minutes he worked on the tire, intermittently cursing, and returning once to throw his coat into the car. I couldn't resist a chuckle at his wanting of any mechanical ability, especially as I thought of Nathan, at home and probably in bed by now, peacefully sleep-ing.

My cunningly phrased question went unanswered.

13

Early in January of 1915, Emory made a pact with Adolph Tetzel.

As Emory explained it to me, Tetzel would lend money directly to him, as needed, to finance the revolution to put Barrista in power. Tetzel fought for stock options in Cabot Consolidated Copper in exchange, but Emory, still stubborn about giving away any of his holdings, managed to persuade him to settle for a percentage of the profits, payable as soon as the first amount was deposited into Emory's newly opened account.

At the time the revolution was successfully carried through, repayment of the loan would begin in installments over a five-year period. The period was negotiable, however, depending upon the sum total loaned. Quarterly interest on the unpaid balance would be due ninety days after the first amount was drawn.

"How long will he continue to receive a percentage of the profits?" I asked.

"As long as it takes me to repay the principal."

"But if the mines are only turning enough profit to repay your original loan on them now, won't that put you into a bind?"

"I intend to sell some of my stock in other interests, if need be. Tetzel offered to pay off the original notes, but I declined."

"I hadn't expected anything quite so complicated . . . or maybe a better word is 'obligated.' "

"You're certainly right about that," he said with a wistful look. "It is by far the greatest risk I've ever taken. But I am sitting on one of the richest mining districts in Mexico. As soon as we get this blasted revolution over with and I can begin producing to the optimum and picking up more properties, repaying Tetzel will be the least of my worries."

I gave him a reassuring smile and thought with frustration, my debt probably amounted to a pittance compared with the figures he was talking about, yet as a woman, my means of repaying it were frighteningly limited.

Before the end of the month it was time for Emory's trip to Mexico. He would carry no more than would fit into saddle-bags. Nathan had painstakingly typed and proofed eight copies of Barrista's lengthy Plan de Pacifica Reforma—one for Barrista, one for each of his four brothers, and three for trusted friends of the family. I was charged with sewing special pockets into the vests of two of Emory's suits. As I did so I thought of Emory charging in his rumpled clothes through the mountains and valleys on a horse, camping out at night, eating God-knows-what and smelling worse than a Mexican bandit, while his Cole Six sat quietly in its place in the garage, gathering dust.

Conditions south of the border had never been worse, with outbursts of fighting first here, then there, as Villa declared open war on Carranza. The two great leaders were reduced to a couple of fighting cocks. The American Red Cross sent a large group of volunteers down in a valiant attempt to aid the war-torn Mexico City while one self-assumed leader after another declared himself President.

The great proclamations of the ABC Conference up in Ontario now seemed pathetically inadequate, if not downright laughable, and I wondered how I ever could have been naïve enough to think their attempts at peacemaking inside Mexico would amount to anything. Down there the term 'Provisional President' might as well have been an entrée on a bandido's lunch menu. It was hard to tell who was official anymore, even for the United States, and members of the diplomatic corps were leaving regularly, doubtless with their hands thrown up in despair if not in response to the undeniably clear orders issued from the other end of a pistol. I knew now that Emory had shown remarkable wisdom in his views on the situation all along —what would have become of the peaceable Barrista, sent down under the auspices of the ABC, to lead the country? Would he by now be drawn and quartered, a sacrificial lamb instead of a leader with a growing list of disciples?

Even so, as the day of Emory's departure neared, I wished more and more that matters could have developed any other way than behooving him to fulfill the dangerous job ahead of him. I imagined a bandit behind every bush, the nose of a gun poking through the leaves at Emory as he rode around like Paul Revere. By the time his last night at home arrived and all the work of preparation was done, I was in a fit of nerves.

To make matters worse, rain was pouring down as though from storm clouds slit with razors. I walked testily to the window as Emory flipped through an old issue of the *Mexican Mining Journal*. I wanted to tell him I never thought marriage to anyone could be this hair-raising, that I might not wait around for his return, that he was greedy as hell for going through with this nonsense, and an absolute scoundrel for presuming to leave me without him for an untold number of months.

Then I looked around at his face, the picture of outward calm, and all I could say was, "Is there any way you can get word to us once in a while?"

He closed the *Journal* and looked at me. "I'll try. I might at least get a message through when I stop at the mines. I can wire you, or tell Jones, the engineer, to write you of my safety. Maybe I can send word through Barrista. But remember, no one knows what I'm doing down there—no one here or there—and keep in mind that my safety may well depend upon that."

"Don't speak to me as if I were a gossiping old woman. Don't you think I know that?"

He sighed. "Come here, Electra."

"No, you come, if you want me."

He rose and walked to the window. Lightning fractured the skies and thunder rattled the window glass. He put an arm around my shoulder and nuzzled my neck. "Emory—" I began.

"Sh. Listen . . . when we were kids and I walked away from Childers, what do you think kept me going for the first few long weeks? It was the thought of you, pasted against that fence, wishing me luck. I wouldn't have made it to the next town if not for that." I shut my eyes tight. "You were the first person to ever believe in me—I never forgot that—and if you can't believe in me now I just won't make it. I know I won't."

For a few moments I couldn't speak for fear that the confession of all my deceit would come pouring out. Finally I turned around and looked up at him. "I'll be here, Emory."

He took my face in his hands. "I warned you in the beginning I wasn't a man just any woman could put up with."

I managed a smile. "That statement was hardly considerable enough to cover what you're putting me through now."

He threw back his head and laughed, then swept me off my feet and carried me toward the stairs. "Time's wasting. It will be months before I feel anything under me softer than a saddle."

Up the stairs I held him as tightly as if some force were threatening to take him from me forever.

Three weeks after Emory left I received a letter from Barrista. I held my breath as I opened it, but relaxed as I read the first line: "Your husband passed through here—"

The letter said little else, nor had I expected it would due to the risk that it might have fallen into the wrong hands before it reached me. I read it twice, then refolded it.

He had not mentioned his daughter Aegina. I assumed she was still attending school in San Antonio, and since nothing had ever been proven of my earlier fears that she was seeing Emory, the youthful heiress appeared less of a threat just then. I was glad I escaped the confrontation with Emory which I had dreaded yet felt compelled to bring about at one time. Even now I wasn't sure she might not one day get in my way, but compared with the other threat hanging over me, she seemed a small aggravation.

Earlier in the week I had picked up a letter from Mark. He was allowing me two weeks to make a payment, and if none was received, I could then look for him at my door. I checked the date of the letter. Ten days to go. If not for this letter, so explicit in its demand, I might have been more wary of the sound of my doorbell that afternoon. I stopped just short of opening the door.

"Who's there?"

Before answering, the man cleared his throat. "My name is Richard Boscomb. I wish to speak to Mrs. Cabot on a matter of business."

The voice was well modulated, deep, and refined—certainly not that of Mark. I felt suddenly a bit foolish. The man obviously thought he was speaking to a servant. I hesitated, and finally said, "I am Mrs. Cabot. What do you wish to speak to me about?"

"I've some literature in my case which I think might interest you, if you would allow me to come in for a short while. I won't take much of your time," he said, still evenly.

I opened the door a few inches. Mr. Boscomb was a slight man, neatly dressed, with a small mustache. He wore a black bowler, which he did not remove, even after I showed him into the parlor. I was convinced by then he was a salesman of some sort.

He went directly to a table and opened his leather case. I pulled up a chair nearby. Now that he was inside, there was an air of pompousness about him. Certainly a salesman would have been more . . .

"To put it simply, madam, I am in the business of selling information, among other services," he began without facing me. He drew some papers from his case and laid them on the table, then looked directly into my eyes at last. "A mutual friend in New Orleans has recommended that I pay you a call."

I leaned forward then. The blood was rising to my temples. "You must be mistaken. I have no friends in New Orleans."

He observed me for a moment, then a small smile played on his lips. "Shall we say, then, a mutual acquaintance?"

"What do you want?" I demanded.

He picked up a slim folder and handed it to me. "Have you ever seen one of these?"

I flipped through the pages of names, addresses, and telephone numbers, then handed it back. "No," I answered truthfully.

"Quite. It happens to be peculiar in this area," he said, then paused before continuing. "My firm is interested in establishing a network of such indexes over this and other surrounding states; ultimately, we hope, on a national basis. We are already under way in a number of strategic points along the eastern seaboard.

"We believe that as the war in Europe continues, as well as the Mexican border troubles, there will be an ever-growing market for contacts such as you see in this volume, to be distributed with the utmost discretion, of course."

My lips felt like parchment paper. I ran my tongue over them. "What has this to do with me?"

"To put it briefly, your . . . associate in New Orleans . . . felt you could be of invaluable help in compiling information that we need, that is, contacts who might wish to participate, over a broad area which we are most eager to encompass."

I started to interrupt, but he added, "I can of course guarantee you substantial remuneration."

I narrowed my eyes. "Where did you come from?"

He smiled pleasantly. "My work takes me to all corners of the world."

"Well you can tell our mutual acquaintance that I am not interested. Good day."

"But I was given to understand you are in something of . . . shall we say . . . an embarrassing financial situation just now. Temporary, of course, I'm sure."

I rose and handed him his folder, so angry I dared not speak again.

"You might be well advised to hold on to it, madam. There

may come a day when you will alter your opinion. Think about it."

"I don't think you'll be hearing from me. Now, get out."

He drew up his shoulders and picked up his case. At the door he turned and said coldly, "I assure you, madam, I personally will not trouble you further. Here is my card. Feel free to telephone or write to me any time. I receive messages through my office."

I stood on the porch and watched until he was out of sight around the block, then looked both ways. Seeing no one except a group of children riding their wheels across the street, I closed the door. Then I went upstairs and slipped the two items into the rear of a drawer in my lingerie chest.

The following morning I took the Mexican-opal ensemble to a pawnshop on the outskirts of town. I was in such a state of despair that I rode all the way with my eyes fixed on the window glass, seeing nothing but a blur of shapes and colors pass by, ignoring the friendly attempts at conversation by the driver.

Since receiving the opals from Emory in December, I had tried several times to bring myself to sell them. I had even investigated a number of shops far from where we lived as possible places where I might exchange the jewelry for cash, without the risk of someone recognizing me. Yet each time I found I simply could not do it, and wound up writing a letter to Mark instead, trying to put him off, while racking my brain for another solution.

The visit from Richard Boscomb had sharpened my fear of Mark to a keener edge than before because now it was evident he had friends who could all too easily tighten the noose around my neck even while he remained miles away. How many others like Mr. Boscomb had been alerted to my situation? Had he confided in anyone here before he left for New Orleans?

"Lady, that's four bits," said the taxi driver.

"What? Oh, of course, thank you."

While in the shop I realized that if the pawnbroker—a small, scrubby little man with garlic strong on his breath—purchased and in turn sold the ensemble, there might come a day when Emory would see another woman wearing it, or at least a piece or two from it.

"Just the stones, take them out," I told him, my throat constricted.

He peered at me above his eyeglasses, and for a moment I feared he would change his mind and send me away without taking any of it, but then he said, "There's a lot of gold here. I'll have to reduce my offer quite a bit—"

"It's all right. Go ahead," I told him quickly.

From there I went straight to the post office to forward the money, then walked back home. I clutched the box that held the empty gold filigree settings and tried to console myself that at least I had these. Maybe one day I could somehow get money to have them reset with some opals that Emory would mistake for the originals. Yet I knew that hope was futile. For now, I would have to say nothing for as long as possible, and when the day came that Emory demanded to know why I had not worn the ensemble, I would think of something to tell him.

Once in the house again I went straight to our room, lay across the bed, and wept. After a while I heard a rapping on the door.

"Is anything wrong?" Nathan asked.

"No, nothing."

"Did you hear something from Cabot?"

"Yes," I answered. Why wouldn't he go away?

"Is he all right?"

"Yes."

He paused for what seemed to me quite a long time before I finally heard his footsteps on the stairs.

14

Emory arrived home at the end of the first week in April—less than three months since he left. Having expected the tour to keep him away half the year, I was delighted to have him back so soon, amazed at his reports that the trip had gone so smoothly, the response a solid vote of favor and support—even including Carlos Barrista. Indoctrination of the people by word of mouth would soon begin.

He was exultant as he reported, "To get around fast in Mexico, all you need is a good horse, a little luck, and a tough ass," but by the middle of the month an unpleasant surprise caused a quick change in his mood.

General Huerta, who had double-crossed Madero and overthrown the Mexican Government established by him, only to be forced into exile himself the previous year, suddenly appeared in New York. Emory flew into a tirade, which I could not understand at the time.

"I agree he has some nerve, but surely he can't cause much of a fuss," I told him. "One thing all of Mexico agrees on is their hatred of him."

My remarks fell on deaf ears. Emory paced back and forth in the sitting room, puffing abrupt and volatile clouds of smoke from the end of his cigar. Presently he put on his hat and said he was going out.

It wasn't long before I was able to see at least part of the reason for his anger. Huerta soon began issuing frequent press releases, claiming that he had been wrongly accused of killing

Madero, but that he knew who was responsible, and was keeping it secret. What a despicable character he was.

Then on the first of May the fuse was lit. Huerta, we learned, was fomenting a new Mexican rebellion while installed in safe quarters in New York, meeting with "friends" in the style of a corporate official in a board room. He was suspected of being aided by one of the belligerent nations in Europe.

If Emory took the news badly, it was no worse than the way President Wilson viewed it. He immediately issued a statement to the effect that anyone caught planning a rebellion in the United States would be prosecuted severely. Only when this statement was published did I begin to see the full nature of Emory's wrath.

Government officials were going to be redoubling their efforts to nip revolutionaries in the bud, and one obvious place they were going to comb pretty closely was San Antonio. From then on we would be living under a new burden of danger, heavier than that before. It was a fairly certain guess we wouldn't be seeing any more of Barrista for a long time because he didn't dare step across the border. Possibly I would never see him again, if plans for the revolution failed.

Yet that was only a part of the mounting complications around us. The sinking of the steamer *Lusitania* had all of us, for the first time, more directly involved in the European war than anyone over here cared to be.

Actually there was less said about it around our neighborhood than I would have expected, considering the fact that what began as a predominantly German settlement years ago was by this time so interspersed with people of other origins—English, Italian, French, and Irish among them as well as people like us, with lineage they'd rather not discuss. Maybe it seemed safer to concentrate on the fact we were all Americans, first, and that was why the subject was largely ignored during across-the-fence chitchat sessions and coffees.

I suspect inside the privacy of homes a different story was being told. It certainly was in ours, and I know I was at least partially responsible for the conflict which arose between Emory and me one night because, in the back of my mind, I was always looking out for Woody. The situation was not helped by the fact that Emory had been drinking for a while when we began to talk. I'd learned only that day that a small newspaper in the German language called *The German Frie Presse* was printed by a man over on King William. Astonished I had never heard of it before, I asked Emory if he knew about it.

"Sure, so what?"

"I just thought it was interesting. I'll bet that poor fellow feels uncomfortable right now . . . since the *Lusitania* was sunk."

He shrugged.

Irritated by his drinking as well as his attitude, I stupidly forged on: "I hope we don't get pulled into that war because of it. Do you think we might?"

"How should I know?" he replied belligerently.

"After all the dust was kicked up down in Mexico because old Huerta wouldn't salute the U.S. flag, I can't see Wilson letting Germany get by with killing a bunch of innocent Americans."

"They were warned beforehand to stay out of those waters."

"Well they have a nerve, declaring all waters around the British Isles, including the English Channel, a war zone."

"That'll teach the British to cut off their raw materials and food supply."

"The British search and seize contraband, all right, but they don't kill."

"If they're starving the Germans to death, isn't that killing?"

"The *Lusitania* was a neutral ship, though. The Germans should have checked before they opened fire."

"The ship carried a cargo of explosives. You expect them to just merrily let them pass through with it?"

"It also carried innocent civilians, and flew a neutral United States flag."

"The German sub couldn't see the flag because the stupid British patrol boats got in the way. And there were no markings on the freeboard, either, to show it was neutral. Besides,

Britain switches flags whenever it suits her purpose on those ships."

"But they don't kill innocent people. German subs have torpedoed twenty-nine ships since they declared the war zone."

"Well then why didn't the Americans heed the warning sent and stay off the ship in the first place?"

"I guess they couldn't believe anything that preposterous would happen."

"Probably the Germans couldn't either."

"Well if they were aimed for the *Lusitania*, do you think if they had seen the flag and an insignia on the freeboard, they would have held their fire?"

"That is a question they don't have to answer. The point is, they didn't see it," he answered, and walked out.

Afterward I was dismayed with myself for letting an argument take shape over the incident, especially when I recognized Emory's points were as valid as mine. I was thankful when the whole affair was laid to rest. I pitied President Wilson, trying to get out of the mess gracefully, appealing to Germany for an explanation he could accept and thus buy continued neutrality. Between the Great War and problems cropping up now and again in Mexico, he must have felt as if he were riding the rapids in a canoe, paddling from first one side then the other to stay in the middle and avoid the rocks.

By late June we had begun to see the early results of our own efforts south of the border. Copies of the Plan de Pacifica Reforma had now been circulating for two months, and according to Barrista the term "Apostol de Reforma" was being heard from many voices. Since the whole country was in a state of chaos, I thought this reaction a very positive sign.

On the other hand a chilling episode occurred, which was to be repeated more than once in different areas, and reported in the papers. A group of six Mexicans were found near the city of San Luis Potosi—Madero's stronghold, and the namesake of his manifesto of 1910—with the Plan de Pacifica Reforma in their possession. They were immediately shot by a police firing squad in a public square.

Emory shook his head regretfully and said, "Now we have our first martyrs . . . I guess that makes the revolution official. . . ."

15

Emory was so happy when American agents arrested Huerta in El Paso, you might have thought him personally responsible. He bought two bottles of imported French wine—becoming expensively scarce—and sent Nathan out of town to deliver some papers. There was no possibility he could return before one or two in the morning.

I, too, was in a state of elation because, since the last payment to Mark I had not heard from him, nor had any of his friends come around. His silence had puzzled me at first because the payment was considerably smaller than the first had been, but as time went by my mind became privy to all sorts of plausible reasons. The most likely was that he had come to some form of destruction. I was almost ashamed of myself for entertaining the thought, but then I was also desperate to be rid of him and perhaps I would never have to know what really happened to him. . . .

I was eager to take full advantage of a whole evening of privacy with Emory, who was in an expansive mood. I cooked a big dinner and lit candles on the table, then changed into a new robe before we sat down to eat.

"I don't mind telling you I was edgy about that old bastard. He had his friend Orozco gathering troops just across the border, getting ready for the big assault, when they picked him up," Emory said.

"Regardless, he couldn't have been much of a threat at this point, could he?"

"I don't know. There was a rumor he had some friends over in Germany backing him with money, and apparently a lot of it."

"Oh . . . well, at least he's out of your hair now. I've always had the feeling you held something personal against Huerta."

"You're right. When he was in power he forced me to loan him money—he did the same thing to Barrista and everybody else with money down there. I don't like people who tell me what to do with my money, and since the day I left Childers I've tried to avoid them."

I raised my wine goblet. "Huerta's capture calls for a toast to success for the Plan de Pacifica Reforma," I said, trying to keep the mood light.

"And all the new mines I just bought," he added, and raised his glass.

I gulped. "You mean, you bought more?"

"This spring, I found some good properties available for next to nothing, so I picked them up. Now my operations will stretch farther south and east. Of course, if Barrista doesn't come into power, I might lose title to all I've got, so there's another reason why Huerta would have been in my way now more than ever."

"Emory, where is all this money coming from? Has Tetzel begun financing your real estate ventures, too?"

"To some extent. . . ."

"I have a feeling there is something about this I haven't been told."

He paused for a moment, as though to measure my reaction. "Virtually everything my mines produce is being sold to Germany."

"Germany? You mean, for—"

"As the war goes on, they have a growing need for copper to make munitions. Tetzel has connections high up in the German Government. He has arranged for shipment through Norway to avoid the damned British blockade. It's part of our bargain, and the price is more than generous."

"You didn't mention that in the beginning."

"It didn't come about until a little later."

I sat back for a few minutes, trying to take it all in.

"There's nothing wrong with it," he said. "Look at all the munitions sold to the British from over here. And we are supposed to be neutral, aren't we?"

"Sure . . . I just didn't realize you were involved."

"Well I am, like it or not."

"With things in such a mess, why press your luck further?"

"I told you, because the price is down and the market for copper is up. If I have properties spread over a wide area, I can produce in at least some of them all the time. Others are doing it. I'm not the only mine owner in Mexico operating with one arm tied behind his back."

"Are the others selling to Germany?"

"I don't know. It's of no concern to me."

"Is that why Tetzel was really interested in helping the rise of Barrista originally—just using the two of you as a means of making a deal on the purchase of copper?"

"Of course not. We both know Barrista is going to be friendly with foreign investors; Carranza certainly isn't, and whatever other fools might get into power—well, it's anybody's guess how they'll feel about the country's natural resources. So Tetzel's just a smart investor, that's all."

"Does Barrista know about all this?"

"He knows enough."

I gazed down at my plate. Suddenly the food looked less appetizing. "I'm confused about the Germans, I must say. If Tetzel's working with them, why would they send down Huerta—or pay his way—back into Mexico?"

"I didn't say Tetzel was doing anything but selling copper to them. He had nothing to do with Huerta's return, I can assure you. Don't forget, he's going to make a pot load of interest off the money he loans us, and his bank needs capital to grow on."

I couldn't say anything.

He asked, "Why do you look like someone just slapped you on the cheek?"

"Well . . . it's only that . . ."

"You think it's dirty money."

"I didn't say that."

"But you thought it," he said.

I looked down. "I . . . uh . . . you mistake my feelings."

He leaned back then and said, "Feel free to elaborate, my dear."

Weakly, I began, "If the war ends tomorrow, what becomes of you and Tetzel and your market?"

"There's always a market for copper. Don't worry about that."

"But what if it continues, and the United States enters?"

"That depends upon which side we go in on. If we take the Allies, I can't do what I'm doing lawfully anymore. If we go to the other side, I probably can. Only, if the United States enters the war, I'll have a ready market right here at home."

"And what about Tetzel, then?"

"What about him? He's only serving as an agent over here. If we get into the war, he will cease to do it, that's all. He isn't getting rich off it, and he'd have little to gain by going on with it. Wouldn't you think?"

"I suppose you're right." I shook my head. "It's very complicated. I wish you—"

"Wish I wasn't involved with the Germans; go ahead; say it."

"All right. I guess that's it."

"Why?"

"It's—it seems dangerous, and you're already involved in enough danger just getting Barrista to the top."

"Why don't you be honest? You have already taken sides, with England. It's that damned Woodstone down the street who has you hoodwinked into it."

"He has not. Woody's been over here longer than either of us have been alive. You're just angry about my remarks on the *Lusitania* incident. It was plain the day we talked about it that you were irritated with me."

"Just take my advice and be careful what you tell that old man."

"Woody? I can't believe you're serious. Anyhow, we don't discuss the war very much, only insofar as his grandson is concerned."

"I know. You spend your time discussing the arts, and music and 'what not.' Becoming very hoity-toity, aren't you? Little Miss High Society."

Common sense would have dictated that I shift the subject then. Emory was now full enough of whiskey and wine he wasn't even making sense anymore. Yet, drawn right into the fight he was bruising for, I said, "I believe you're jealous of the time I spend with him. It isn't as though you're always attentive to me, that's certain."

"Well if you don't like the way I am, maybe you'd prefer 'attending' your British friend. I understand he's worth a lot of money. Maybe he'll remember you in his will. . . . At least you'd have a better chance at securing your future with him, than with me."

I threw down my napkin. "This conversation is absurd. I'm going to bed."

"I was thinking along those lines myself."

"I didn't mean that."

"I did."

I awoke very early the next morning—before the sound of reveille from the arsenal—and sat in the kitchen drinking coffee. Too exhausted to think straight by the time I finally closed my eyes the night before, I tried that morning to look objectively at what was happening to Emory and me, at all the unexpected curves and twists our marriage had taken, and decide whether I should go on with it.

We had argued more and more as the months passed, and it seemed to me that I would no sooner feel the presence of a strong bond between us than he sliced it in two. I knew he was under enormous pressures and I wanted so much to help relieve them, even while I was facing some pressures of my own.

I knew that morning I shouldn't have allowed the argument to get going, but I didn't see it coming in time to head it off. Besides, I was trying to see if Emory had guessed something I didn't want him to know. I truly believed he hated himself for letting others manipulate him, and I was sorry for that, but I wasn't willing to take the brunt of his anger. Maybe I was less than a good wife. Maybe I should have let my mind overrule my heart and refused his offer of marriage in the first place . . . perhaps that would have been more fair to both of us.

I sat and thought awhile longer, trying to analyze our difficulties objectively. Yet I could not get past the way he behaved toward me. His abuse hurt too much and had come so unexpectedly. Had he come to me honestly and told me of his growing predicament, I would have offered him comfort. Instead he baited me, got me mad by twisting my words into false meanings, then on top of it all, forced me right into the bedroom, where I'd always counted on his sensitivity to my needs and desires. I wasn't able to fight off his advances, though I tried hard, and in the end I was being pushed down roughly and plunged into, with no rights whatsoever.

Emory walked in sleepily and poured a cup of coffee, then sat down at the table. I rose and walked to the icebox. I didn't want to look at him.

"It was pretty cold up there last night," he said, finally. "Has the climate warmed up any down here this morning?"

"Not much."

"Could you come over and sit with me?"

"Nathan will be awake soon. I have to get breakfast."

"Damn it, you're not married to him. You're married to me."

"You made that all too clear last night."

"Look, I'm sorry for that. I can't remember all of it, but I know I was a real jackass."

"I've been thinking this morning that maybe you made an error in marrying me. I don't seem to be able to make you a very good wife after all."

"Don't talk like that. You mean more to me than anything. Look, just forget everything I said . . . or did . . . I'll make it up to you. I know what. We'll go to the Roof Garden for dinner tonight. Get all dressed up. Did I ask you to have the waist in my blue suit taken in? Never mind, it'll probably do. How about it?"

"No thanks. I think I'll just stay at home and try and get some rest tonight."

"All right," he said, and rose. I thought he was leaving for work when he walked from the room, but he returned in a few minutes and tossed a big envelope on the table. "I intended handing you this last night, before things got all balled up between us. Then from what you said I decided maybe you wouldn't want them," he said as he drew some papers out. "I don't know . . . maybe I was right after all."

I found myself looking at several stock certificates for Cabot Consolidated Copper, each made out to me. I didn't know what to say.

"That represents fifty percent of all I own down there," he said. "It isn't worth the paper it is written on now, but I hope someday it will be worth a hell of a lot."

"Oh, Emory—" I began, but he'd walked out.

I felt very low as I stood there holding the crisp parchment papers, and as the prospect of paying Mark crept into my mind, I was thankful to God that Emory had given me something that for the time being was unredeemable.

16

Emory stayed in San Antonio all through the summer of 1915, relying upon his mining engineer, Ralph Jones to keep him apprised of conditions in Mexico. For this I was thankful: regardless of reassuring news now and then that chaotic conditions were going to improve, they never did. Carranza's forces grew stronger, but Villa's forces followed suit, and the bandit Emilio Zapata and his mad warriors were running rampant over Mexico City.

Like some other mining concerns, Cabot Consolidated Copper was hanging on as best it could, getting supplies in when transportation was available; putting laborers to work when they were to be found; keeping looting and vandalism to a minimum. When enough time had passed so that I could put our quarrel into perspective, I marveled at Emory's ability to behave with relative calm most of the time since he had so much at stake, and overlooked his occasional black moods as Nathan seemed to. In fact when I counted the many times at home that Emory lashed out at Nathan, as opposed to the one serious conflict between us, I took a lesson from it. Surely next time he picked on me I'd deal with it more deftly, I told myself. . . .

In August we received an invitation from the Tetzels to attend their thirtieth wedding anniversary celebration at their home in Laurel Heights.

"I'd have thought they would have been married closer to forty years, judging by their ages," I remarked to Emory.

"Tetzel's original 'intended' bride was killed in the Indian raid I told you about. Sophie migrated several years after that," he said, then switched the subject. "Another Pan-American Peace Conference is in the planning. Barrista wrote that he thinks they might ask him to sit in. He couldn't say so, naturally, but he hopes to have his name brought up as Provisional President." ·

"Maybe he will."

"I doubt it. He's determined to get in without a fight, but he can't be allowed to fool himself that there's much possibility. I wrote him to say he ought to stay out of it. Things are going steadily now, and there is no use in taking chances."

I looked at him squarely. "Why don't you admit you'd really like a good old-fashioned fight, and you are itching to lead the troops?"

I expected an equally kidding reply, but was met with silence.

"It would be nice to see Barrista again, though, and he'd probably come through San Antonio—certainly it would seem routine, and would give you a chance to meet with him. He might—uh—like to see Aegina. She is still here, isn't she?"

"As far as I know."

"I never have met her—"

"Be sure to set aside the date of that party. And we ought to give the Tetzels a present. Will you pick up something suitable?"

The Tetzel house—or mansion—surrounded by galleries laced with gingerbread trim, and topped with pointed towers— stood upon a small hill. Its landscaping was built up with four stone tiers and spiced with colorful gardens flanking the curved path up to the front and bordering the circular porches.

We arrived during a lull between the rain showers which had gone on intermittently all day long, and the white house and well-planned garden scheme cut a startling contrast against the bleak gray sky, like a picture trimmed from a magazine and mounted on a scrapbook page. In spite of the bad weather, the street was lined up and down with automobiles, so Emory suggested Nathan let us out under a portico on the north side of the house.

I had felt no particular excitement about the party until I saw the windows lit up and people arriving in evening wear. Emory was persuaded to wear a top hat, which he despised—only a hat with a wide brim suited him, and he quickly dispensed with it as soon as we crossed the threshold. I wore a rose-colored taffeta gown with organdy and lace overlays, and matching pumps with Cuban heels. The ensemble was fashionable, yet conservative. Although there were times, such as the party at the Casino Hall the previous December, when I made a point of being a little *outré*, I still usually concentrated on fading into the background at parties, talking little and trying to remain as obscure as possible. If I did not talk very much, there was less margin for a mistake that might give away something I did not want known, and now with all of Emory's secrets strung on to my own, I had to be doubly careful.

I was in for a surprise when Tetzel led us into what he proudly termed "the grand hall." It was a near replica of the Menger Hotel lobby, on a smaller scale.

Surrounded by an open second-floor gallery which was supported by tall columns, the square floor of black and white inlaid marble was ample for dancing space, and Tetzel directed my gaze above to a skylight made of stained glass he'd purchased in Europe during a trip abroad. "Why, it's remarkable," I said in all sincerity.

"Yes, it is," he agreed.

Tetzel was still brusque, yet a little more friendly that night than times before, and as he left I considered the fact both he and his wife still spoke in broken English. I wondered if they retained the German language at home in privacy, as did many of the families where we lived.

Emory had already disappeared, so I found a little table near a pillar behind a huge vase of flowers, and sat down. He would just have to look for me, since he was thoughtless enough to leave me alone in the first place. Several minutes passed before a voice behind me said, "You are much too pretty to be hidden away, madam."

It was Arnold Stuttgart, and close by, looking elegant in her newest Jenny creation with a tight skirt and tiered lace over-skirt—the frock a good three inches shorter than mine—was Lyla. She wore a headband with a jewel in front and one long feather extending straight up above her forehead. Even if Lyla's head was full of shallow observations, she had to be credited with a perceptive eye for fashion. She was truly a trend-setter in San Antonio, and it seemed to me that was at least one trait to her credit.

"I hadn't expected to see you here," I told them.

"Arnold believes in cozying up to his bankers," said Lyla. My eyes met Arnold's. She'd apparently gotten a head start at the cocktail table. I think she'd embarrassed him, because he said quickly, "Adolph and Sophie are nice people, you know, and he has seen me through some lean times in the printing business. How about some champagne?"

While Arnold was away Lyla sat down. "I thought you were going to spend the whole month at your father's cottage in the hills," I said.

"We were, but Arnold insisted we get back for this con-founded party. I was happy with my feet in the creek and a fishing pole in my hand, but you know how it is when duty calls."

"I can't feature you with your feet in the creek, Lyla."

"Actually, it wouldn't matter where I was as long as it is away from here. I mean, it gets so hot in the summer. The kids get cranky and drive the nursemaid crazy, who in turn drives me insane. . . ."

Emory soon returned—he'd been sidetracked by some business associate or another—and once the party got under way it was a great deal more fun than I'd anticipated. The orchestra was one of the best I'd heard, and someone said they played from time to time at the Top O' the Town at the St. Anthony's. We went through waltzes and polkas, fox trots, and several variations of the tango. Up to then, I still hadn't tried it, though I had seen the dance demonstrated several more times since the day I suspected Emory and Aegina were tea dancing at the Menger.

I was into a second goblet of champagne when a man named Terence Brown approached and Asked Emory's permission for my hand. "Oh, but you see, I've never—" I stammered, for suddenly I was afraid of this man I didn't know.

"It's quite easy, just follow me," he insisted, and after a few moments his open, friendly manner put me at ease. So many people were dancing, the orchestra repeated several melodies with the tango rhythm. I stayed out there with Terence, enjoying it more and more as I gained confidence in my ability to perform the dance, following him with new twists and steps and twirls, really forgetting myself and allowing his compliments to persuade me to relax and experiment with the endless variety of little dips and sways. All of these certainly fell within the realm of propriety, and even more so in my case because there was no slit in my evening gown to allow completely free movement.

Suddenly I twirled around to see Emory on the floor with a woman I did not know, and it was obvious he was quite familiar with the dance. My partner noticed my sudden stiffening and asked, "Something wrong, Mrs. Cabot?"

"Oh no, it's just—maybe I'm a little tired. Let's sit down."

All the way back to the table I speculated. So what, if he knows the tango?

Everybody else knows it nowadays.

Why didn't he invite me to the floor?

Maybe Terence beat him to it.

No, he didn't come by till the second time . . . or was it the third?

But then, it's only a dance after all. Silly.

No, the tango is more than just a dance. . . .

"Are you sure you are all right?" my partner asked.

"Certainly. Fine."

"I didn't mean to exhaust you. My wife and I dance quite often, you see, and I'm accustomed to going on for hours and hours. We have a player piano at home, and—"

"No, really. You were marvelous out there. Thank you."

"I'll freshen your drink."

Before he returned, Emory came back and sat down. "I didn't know you could tango," I said.

"I noticed you cut a pretty good figure on the floor yourself."

"I've learned by watching other people."

"That's how I learned. It's easy."

"Did you go dancing a lot before I came here?"

"As a matter of fact I did. Everybody dances in this city, and when things were sane in Mexico City the parties made this one look like a small neighborhood get-together."

I was about to ask him if he danced with Aegina very much, but it probably would have been a fairly obvious question, so I was just as glad that Terence Brown came back and asked to sit with us for a while.

"I'm a poor bachelor tonight. My wife's visiting her parents up in Newport. I left her off there when we got back from Europe."

I was interested in how he found conditions abroad, and he said, "Remarkably the same in many places. In Vienna the theater and opera go on as though nothing could interfere with them, and in Paris it's as crowded as ever. Lots of reservists are over there on leave right now, so the sidewalk scene is a little drab, with all those uniforms. And of course you notice a great difference when you visit the Louvre—so many of the art works and paintings have been removed for safety.

"Train service all over Europe is sporadic, and in many places there are no dining cars anymore because the armies have confiscated them for carrying troops. But all in all, it was easier to cope than I expected."

"From what I understand, it's the same in Mexico," I said, glancing at Emory. "That is, wherever the fighting is not going on, it isn't so bad—"

"Ah, Mexico . . . I haven't been there in years. I wouldn't dare go down right now, would you?"

When I mentioned Emory had business interests down there, more in an attempt at drawing him into the conversation than anything else, the man could not hide his surprise. "What in?" he asked.

"A few real estate holdings here and there," said Emory.

"Well, I must say that calls for raw courage. I'd have run when old Diaz got booted out in 1910. He was one of a kind when it came to courting foreign investors, wasn't he?"

Emory smiled wryly and drew on his cigar. "I certainly hope not."

There were no more tangos played that evening, though soon the Tetzels led into a special anniversary waltz that was followed by several more lilting tunes. Emory moved me smoothly and confidently through the one-two-three rhythms, making for a merry finale to the party close to midnight. I'd forgotten the bad weather, which had worsened through the party. Rain was coming down like a barrage of splinters, and was causing quite a bottleneck of people at the main door, trying to get their gear together before braving the storm. The poor girl who was taking care of coats and hats was having an awful time in all the confusion. My heart went out to her as people grew impatient. She was a plucky little thing with long straight red hair flowing down around her white uniform cap, straight bangs in front, and a kind of elfin face with wide brown eyes and a few freckles across her nose. She couldn't find Emory's despised top hat, and, while he could not have cared less what happened to it, I was in charge of returning it to the rental store.

"I know I can find it if you will just go back in and wait a few moments," she said nervously. "I'll bring it to you when the crowd clears out."

Tetzel appeared. "Something wrong?"

"My confounded hat got lost in the shuffle, I guess," said Emory.

"Well, Camille, what have you done with—"

"I knew you looked familiar," Emory interrupted, looking at the girl.

"Allow me to introduce Mr. and Mrs. Cabot," Tetzel offered with surprising graciousness. "This is Camille Devera. She began as my secretary at the bank recently, and extended herself to help us tonight. Camille, my dear, I think some of the things got taken to the room behind the kitchen for lack of other space. Why don't you check, and I'll tend to matters here."

I wasn't sure whether his civility in the awkward situation was supposed to impress us, or he wanted to assure Camille she stood a rank above the hired servants. His gaze fell upon her as she walked away, then he turned to handing out hats and gloves himself as we chatted with people around us. When Camille returned, Emory's hat in her hand, Tetzel took it from her and remarked, "You see, Miss Devera can always be counted upon to come through in a situation." She avoided his eyes and went back to work.

Nathan was waiting outside with a big umbrella. When we were inside the car Emory told him about seeing Camille.

"I'm not surprised," he said, over his shoulder. "She pops up everywhere."

"Camille delivers papers to our office for Tetzel now and then, and she is sweet on Nathan," Emory told me with a side glance.

"She's just a squirt, a bratty kid. She drives me crazy," said Nathan.

"Well I think it's a good thing for a young girl to learn a trade," I said. "With prices soaring all the time, it doesn't hurt either to have a job now and then on the side, like helping out at parties. I wish I'd known how to do something at her age."

For the rest of the ride home we all stared at the nearly invisible road ahead. The rain was gushing harder and harder—our share of the severe flood which had hit Galveston earlier, testing its famous seawall.

Later, as we got into bed, I asked Emory if he noticed how Tetzel looked at Camille.

"No, how?"

"Oh, a little too . . . interested . . . I think."

"Aw, she's just a kid."

"I know, still . . ."

"You can't put a man behind bars for his thoughts."

"I've known plenty who ought to have been put in jail for their deeds."

"Why should you worry about that girl? I'm sure she can look after herself, and I'd be amazed if Tetzel had any but an aboveboard interest in her."

"I hope you're right. Women on their own don't have much of an advantage when it comes to—"

"The hell they don't," he said suddenly and rose from the bed. I thought he'd misinterpreted the remark somehow. I searched for something to say while he stood at the window, watching the rain. I had never felt the heat of his anger rise so quickly or unexpectedly.

"Usually it's hard for a woman to find a decent man unless he happens to come along before she leaves home," I began nervously, but he interrupted with a sharp turn. His whole face was in darkness, but I will never forget the frozen glare in his eyes.

"My mother didn't exactly fit into your picture of down-trodden females, did she?"

"Oh, I'd forgotten . . . I wasn't thinking about her," I said meekly.

"I know you weren't, but I think about her, and what she did to me. It is on my mind a lot, as a matter of fact."

"I . . . I didn't know you were so bitter."

"There is a lot you don't know about me. When you decide to pick up your banner for all womankind, I'll thank you to remember there is another side of the coin."

"Oh Emory, I'm all too aware of that. Just look what you did for me. Listen, I'm sorry for what I said about Camille. It was probably just my imagination anyway," I said gently, but he was not thinking of Camille. He was lost in a poignant memory of his mother. He paused before continuing softly.

"She didn't love my daddy. I was the only one in the family she ever pretended to care about . . . but she left me behind like all the rest. I was just a little runt then, you know. . . . I waited for days and days, certain she'd come back for me, but she never did. My brother said I was crazy, that she never loved me either, and I hated him for that. He was twice my size, but it took three of them to pull me off him. My daddy just stood by and did nothing."

He took in a long breath. "After that I vowed I'd have nothing more to do with any of them, and that I'd go off one day and find her, and prove to them all she did love me, that she'd go away with me and stay with me . . . forever. . . ."

As his voice drifted off, I measured my words carefully. "It's too bad you weren't able to find her before she died. You might have been right. She may have had reasons for her ways that you never knew."

"Yes, it is very unfortunate her untimely death kept me from finding out."

"I'm so sorry for you . . . I had no idea. . . ."

For a time he said nothing. Finally he shrugged and remarked, "Let's forget it. There's no use in talking about it. It was all over . . . long ago."

I pitied him as he stood there, looking so alone. "Come back to bed," I asked him finally, and when he did his body was shaky and moist. We held each other fast as two young children, afraid of the dark.

By morning he seemed himself again, though he was a little withdrawn at breakfast. Yet afterward he and Nathan went off together, talking shop, so I supposed he'd shoved it to the back of his mind again—there was little else he could do.

I couldn't quite shake off the doldrums myself, however. I decided to pay a call to Woody. Maybe he could cheer me up. The sky was dull gray, threatening more rain, and thunder rumbled like cannon in the distance as I walked down the windy street. I was expecting Woody to be in the parlor having tea, but found him instead out in his dooryard, cutting back the queen's-wreath.

"The storm last night destroyed the blooms and, anyway, it's time to cut it back," he said. "It will grow just that much faster until the frost nips it. Get back Scoop, don't want to get in the way of this hoe, old boy . . . and how are you this morning, Mrs. Cabot?" Then he stopped to look at me. "Not quite up to par, eh?"

I leaned against the fence. "Maybe it's just the weather. I thought I'd come by and get you to cheer me up."

"I think I can do that, as a matter of fact. I've had a letter from Johnny. He has assured me he is enrolled in school for the fall semester."

"That's a relief. Maybe by the semester's end, the war will be over."

"I certainly hope so. And not only for Johnny's sake, although he is my main concern. I've been around long enough to know that no one really wins a war. A few miles of real estate change hands and they term it a 'victory.' It hardly begins to do justice to such a powerful word."

"And people over here are foolish to talk about taking sides, don't you think?"

"Like the President says, it is our place to be rock-ribbed Americans, first."

I smiled at his strong British accent, which he habitually exaggerated at times like these. His words made me feel better about at least one thing bothering me—Emory's business with the Germans. I couldn't wait to tell him Woody's opinion.

"Of course if the Germans and Austrians continue with their submarine warfare and the British continue with their confiscation of neutral ships, we'll find ourselves right in the middle of it."

"What if we threw in our lot with the Centrals?"

"I rather imagine we'd side with the Allies, but I've been in this country long enough to side with any common, ordinary people who want only to live and hold on to what they've got, regardless of whose flag rises above them." He paused. "By the way, I'm not acquainted with anyone else who takes the matter of the war in Europe so seriously—or at least, so it appears. Why do you?"

"Oh, I just try to impress you with my knowledge of world affairs, Woody," I said, and smiled.

"When I was a teacher, you would have been just the kind of student I would have encouraged and taken pride in. I'd forgotten that feeling I used to get every few years, when I'd find a youngster, not only bright but also eager to learn . . . the lump in my throat as I watched him—or her—graduate. Ah, it has been such a long time, yes, I had quite forgotten. . . ."

"You compliment me more than you will ever know," I told him.

17

By early October of 1915 the sheer stubbornness of First Chief Carranza paid off, and he won his hard-fought battle for recognition. To clench the deal, a few days ahead he made magnanimous guarantees for amnesty to his political enemies, freedom of religion, and protection of foreigners and their properties, none of which Emory trusted him to honor. And apparently few people in Mexico believed in him either because he no sooner issued his statement than new revolutions began breaking out, one of the largest headed by Pancho Villa.

Emory immediately threw his clothes into a suitcase, headed for Mexico, afraid Barrista might want to back out. "But he says things are settling down now, the Plan is getting well known," I argued. "Maybe by the time the next election rolls around—"

"Once Carranza gets a grip on Mexico, he isn't about to let an election stand in his way."

I just shook my head. I couldn't blame Barrista for his willingness to compromise at this point. As Emory buckled his suitcase I marveled as I had many times over how hard it was to separate Emory's idealistic side from his selfish one. I could not ever pin him down on how much he did for himself alone as opposed to how much it meant to him to see Barrista save Mexico. There was one thing that became more and more evident, however, and I told him:

"You're the iron in Barrista's soul."

It proved to be a most prophetic statement over the next year.

Emory had more than one reason for going to Mexico at that time. Ralph Jones was in need of money and a number of supplies that only Emory could get to him. He needed to have a look at the properties working and confer with Ralph on preparing to get others started. Now that the transportation situation had eased up in some places, he wanted to get machinery moved in where possible. He also had to get some idea of money needed for repairs to damage and replacement for looting suffered in some of the mines over the past few months. When he told me of this, I was reminded of what a small concept I had of the turmoil he was enduring daily, how many loose ends were dangling in his financial empire. Surely he was pouring more money down into those mines than their natural wealth could yield up for a long time to come. Of course I could only speculate on this because he confided so little in me. I received information like a yard dog receives table scraps.

With Emory gone for what he expected to be at least a month, time soon hung about like moss on an ancient tree. I decided to buy two season tickets to the San Antonio Philharmonic concerts—I'd put it off earlier because I thought Emory would be in town—and coaxed Woody into going to the evening performances. To his protests that he did not see well at night, I countered, "Nathan will drive us to Beethoven Hall, and you certainly don't have to be able to see to appreciate the music."

A few days after Emory left, I went down to pick up the tickets, and made a side trip by the post office on my way home. So many months had gone past without further threats from Mark that I was becoming convinced I'd heard the last from him. Yet I didn't know for certain so I had no choice but to continue my little side trips, and I was always nervous about being seen. While the postal station was blocks from Emory's office, I always found myself hurrying along, looking both ways in case Nathan might be afield running an errand, or Emory himself might pop up. I had a couple of excuses made up for going there should I be found out—I was picking up a package for Woody, or buying some postage stamps. Thankfully I never had to use my made-to-order escape tactics, because as far as I know I was never discovered.

On this particular afternoon I mounted the steps with my usual caution and circled the postal lobby with my eyes before checking the box. It was empty. I strolled away, thinking maybe Mark had really found himself a "rich lady" who could at least temporarily keep him busy. Yet, surely there were sections of New Orleans that could be dangerous, even for a man like Mark.

One late November day, Woody came to my door around noontime and invited me for a stroll. This departure from his regimented three o'clock walk with Scoop was so unusual that I took off my apron and followed him without question.

Soon he said, hoarsely, "I have a letter from Johnny. He has decided to enlist after all."

"Oh, no . . ."

"They're having quite a bit of trouble over there you know, with Lord Derby's efforts at getting up enough force, although he has raised thousands and thousands of volunteers. Asquith's conscription bill is being fought tooth and nail in the House of Commons . . . it's a very bad situation."

"Well, I'm sure—"

"It's a matter of pride in Britain, you know," he interrupted, raising his shoulders and setting his jaw. "Johnny wouldn't be called a shirker, no sir, not he, even if it means sacrificing his studies for a while. I only wish it would be over soon."

I didn't know what to say. I walked along, looking at the ground. In a few moments he continued, "It's such a horrible thing, all those young lads . . . doesn't matter whose side they're on . . . so many down in the trenches in the cold and the rain, with no food, bullets whizzing by and shrapnel showering—"

"Woody, maybe you oughtn't to speculate on—"

"Have you read Stephen Crane's *The Red Badge of Courage?*"

"No."

"When the novel was first published I used my own money to get enough copies so that my students could read it. It is about war, about the fact the common soldier can't even tell which way he is going and whether he is making progress . . . he is lost in an abyss of destruction and death all round . . . and none of it makes sense to him, you see?"

Then he stopped and turned toward me. "It is a novel of the War Between the States, but it is more than that—a universal story of war and its criminal waste. . . . Mrs. Cabot, do you ever go to church?"

"No."

"Neither do I, anymore, but I still pray. Will you pray, too, for Johnny?"

18

Emory returned in mid-December with the good news that Barrista was willing to go on, but unfortunately the trip had taken a strike at his health. A few days before Christmas he became ill—he was in such excruciating pain in his limbs, especially his legs, and running such high temperatures that we were afraid he'd contracted dengue fever while in Mexico. That and typhus were on the spread down there and growing worse. Nursing him, I found myself wondering over and over why anyone in his right mind would want to have anything to do with Mexico. I wished the whole matter of Barrista's rise to power could be discovered to be a very bad, delirious dream from which I would soon awaken, and Emory could be involved only in land in the San Antonio area, just as I'd believed at first. Now, with the worry of Mark apparently behind me, I would be well settled with Emory into the life I'd so looked forward to when we were married almost two years ago. . . .

The doctor diagnosed Emory to be suffering from a case of mild influenza, brought on, he surmised, by exhaustion. The prospect of a week of his recuperation in bed was one which I did not particularly relish, because he was already bored and restless. On the way out, the doctor told me privately, "I've recommended a week, but I'll figure in about three days he'll bust out of there like an angry bull."

Within forty-eight hours I was marveling at how well the doctor was able to calculate Emory's behavior, and wondering if doctors in general had the special gift of knowing just what to expect of a patient. I squared my shoulders and prepared for the worst. Although I tried to avoid upsetting him, there were many conversations between us that began innocently enough, yet wound up with him turning away or looking sullen, or growing so irritated that I'd leave the room for fear of setting him off in a rage. One such began with my remarks about Colorado having passed statewide prohibition.

"I read in the newspaper they had 'bargain days' shortly before the law took effect, and there were between two and three million dollars spent on liquor during the sale. Can't you just imagine the same thing happening in Texas? With all the saloons in San Antonio alone probably twice that much money would change hands the first day," I said, laughing. I stopped and looked at Emory, who didn't seem so amused.

I was about to shift the subject—I'd become fairly apt at that—when he said thoughtfully, "Do you ever feel that everything is changing, and nothing will ever be the same again? It's like being caught in quicksand without a rope or a tree in sight, or anything else to catch hold of, and feeling yourself going under. . . ."

"What does that have to do with—surely we won't get prohibition here."

"Why not? Nearly half the country has it now, and anyway, if not that it's something else. Wilson is campaigning for a national defense plan, and he'll wind up paying for most of it by jacking up income tax. It used to be free country, you know, but more and more the bastards we vote into office are telling us how to run our lives. Can't you feel it coming, faster and faster?"

"You look tired. Maybe I ought to leave so you can take a nap."

"Take a nap," he repeated snidely. "It'll all go away then, like a bad stomach ache. They can all go to hell, do you hear?"

"You don't have to get nasty. It's nearly dinnertime. I'll go down and fix you a tray."

"Don't bother. I'm not hungry. I want to be alone."

I needed a breath of fresh air, and could have used a dose of the river's quieting effect on my nerves. Yet the breeze off the water had a bite to it this time of year. I put on a coat and sat on the front-porch steps, arms wrapped around my knees. Soon two mockingbirds arrived simultaneously at a parcel of food halfway down the walk. They moved away and circled around, then lit into it again, bouncing the tidbit into the air and engaging in a good sparring session that sent a few feathers aflight before both birds realized the prize had been lost in the conquest for it. After a while they flew off in separate directions.

I sat there until it began to grow dark, and I saw the lights of Emory's Cole Six nose down the street and turn into the drive. Nathan had equipped it with new tires that day. I heard the motor stop and the door open and close, and thought again how right Emory had been to insist Nathan live with us. He took great care of everything that was Emory's—including his automobile. He kept it in perfect running condition all the time and spent hours waxing it and polishing the trim. In fact I had kidded him once that when he wasn't busy shining his own shoes—a task which consumed much of his spare time —he was shining Emory's car.

He'd seen me as he passed, and walked around to wish me good evening and ask about Emory. "A little testy," I said. "The doctor was here today. Uncanny how well he predicts Emory's moods. Wish I had the same talent."

"You're not alone," he said, and sat down. "Where I grew up there was a doctor like that. The mill kept him on to take care of injuries and look after the families of the employees. He did everything from dispensing medicine to delivering babies. Doc Barnes knew everybody, and everybody liked him.

"I knew him before my mother married Sam, because he came down to the depot once in a while for a shoeshine. After they got married and she took sick, I'd go down to Doc's office and pick up her medicine. I think he felt bad there wasn't much he could do for her."

"I guess he stayed pretty busy, with so many injuries at the mill."

"Yes, he did at that. . . . I remember going by his office one day, just as they were bringing in a head-end dogger who'd gotten his leg sliced by a saw blade. He was out cold, whiter than that summerhouse over there. I thought he was dead. But when Doc Barnes hit his leg with iodine, he shot up like he was resurrected from the grave."

"My heavens, he doesn't sound like a very gentle man."

"Oh, he was, nothing wrong with Doc. He was kind to my mother, and honest about the fact he couldn't help her any. He didn't have much besides epsom salts, castor oil, quinine, and calomel. What happened wasn't his fault. . . ."

Just then Emory bellowed my name from his sickbed.

"Well, speaking of illness, I think I hear my patient calling," I said. I'd left the front door slightly ajar, and walked in to find Emory, already halfway down the stairs, demanding to know where his dinner was.

I sometimes wonder whether the melancholy moods Emory suffered during his illness when he wasn't vacillating toward the other extreme, cursing and yelling, were not harbingers of things to come. Soon after he was up and around again, we were in for another blow.

One day in mid-January of 1916, a train chugged peacefully along a track fifty miles outside of Chihuahua City. Its main cargo included mining supplies for ASARCO mines, and a large sum of money sent by one mining concern to the suffering natives in the Chihuahua mining country. Also aboard were a group of mining men.

Along the route, the train was halted by a group of Villista forces, who emptied it of its American passengers—eighteen or so men—stripped them of their clothing, lined them up like feed sacks against the railroad cars, and opened fire on them. One man managed to escape from the impromptu execution, and fled across the sharp cactus and stones of the god-forsaken desert terrain back to Chihuahua City, where he arrived badly injured and bleeding profusely. By a stroke of kind fate, he was met by a group of friendly Mexicans who cared for him.

His report of what had happened was soon to blacken the headlines of the American press, and cause outrage in Washington. I had been told that Villa in defeat could be as bloodthirsty and cruel as he was magnanimous and friendly in victory.

But for the sporadic wire service between San Antonio and Mexico, we would have known before we read the newspapers that Ralph Jones was not among those killed. Yet because Emory believed he might be, we spent two very long days agonizing over the matter. Conditions in Chihuahua territory had been so dangerous that a good many of the mining men had been out of there for some weeks, and now, under the assurance by Carranza that they could safely return, many of them were going back to work.

Although I thought the miners were a bit dense for failing to listen to the cautions later added by Carranza agents that Villistas were in the immediate area and they ought to stay out for the time being, I was as frightened as Emory that Ralph might be on that coach. He was known to have been near there picking up supplies, and could easily have taken that train. After two days of conflicting reports as to the number of men killed and their names, and a frustrating attempt at getting information from closer to the site, which had Emory pacing the floor in his nightshirt and sending thunderous clouds of cigar smoke into the air, while Nathan was dispatched to send telegrams to every possible address where Ralph might be, were he safe, we received the wire confirming he was in El Paso. All of us breathed a sigh of relief. Unfortunately, the relief was not to last.

Several nights later we got word Ralph had been killed in a knife fight in El Paso. I couldn't believe it was all happening as I packed a suitcase for Emory before daybreak. Still pale from his illness, he hurriedly dressed for the trip to the border town. Nathan, roused from his sleep, dressed and went out to warm up the automobile while I fried bacon and eggs and made coffee. I was too shocked to react. Only hours earlier, Emory had gotten a wire from Ralph's parents, who lived in Michigan, thanking him for the wire he'd sent them several days previous, with the message, "I trust you have been notified of your son's safety." The exchange between them had astonished me, and brought to mind that side of Emory he kept in check most of the time . . . that compassion for others which emerged so unexpectedly now and then. I would have looked for Emory to be angry at the loss of a valued employee, but not to have a thought for the feelings of the man's loved ones.

By midmorning Emory was well on his way and Nathan was at the office. I sat down with the paper and a cup of coffee, looking for an account of the strange and tragic event. I read something of an American man being killed in a bar in El Paso, at the hand of a Mexican, but there were no names mentioned and by that time a new and more formidable news story had largely displaced items of interest to a relative few. General Pershing, in charge of Fort Bliss, had declared martial law in El Paso because of widespread street fighting brought on by the massacre of the train passengers.

Adolph Tetzel had heard the news of Ralph's death, and stopped by after dinner. It was unusual for him to pay an impromptu call, and I wondered at first how he'd found out about Ralph, before I realized that, of course, Nathan might have told him during the day. He handed me a note with a name and address included on it, and asked it be given to Emory. "I'm leaving town early in the morning. Please see that Cabot gets this name. I think the man might be able to take over operations for him down there. Tell Cabot to contact the man immediately. I'll return in two weeks," he said brusquely, then added almost apologetically, "It was a very sad thing about Jones, eh?"

His early appearance with Ralph's replacement seemed almost cold-blooded, but then that was business, I supposed, and anyway, Tetzel had been very understanding about the reduced production of the past few months, and had extended notes on money borrowed as well as lending more to Emory, until things could get straightened out. It escaped me how anyone could be helped very much by depending upon Mexican copper, especially when in the market for quantities huge enough to make munitions to fight a war, but then I really never was very clear on how much production went on—perhaps more than anyone could have imagined—and I'd heard that lately a Frenchman had paid two and a half million dollars to buy the big El Oro mine in Mexico. I guessed prospects down there must be fairly good for anyone able to hold out a little longer. I shook my head, frustrated by my own ignorance of the situation.

Emory was kept away almost as long as Tetzel. After identifying Ralph's body, he felt it his duty to accompany it by rail all the way to Michigan, remain long enough for the funeral, then travel back home. When he arrived at mid-day in a taxi, he looked tired and drawn again, and more depressed than I had ever seen him. I gave him Tetzel's note, which he folded and put into his pocket without reading. "I talked to Ralph's buddies in El Paso," he said. "It seems one of his best friends was on that train Villa massacred and since then Ralph had spent most of his time drowning his sorrow in whiskey. He got into a fight with a Mexican one night; the Mexican pulled a knife, and that was the end for him. Damn it, he ought to have known better."

"Did they get the Mexican?"

"No, he disappeared, a very easy thing to do down there."

"Why don't you try and get some rest."

"I can't. I've got to get right down to the office. I can't seem to get anything done anymore."

I watched him walk toward the garage, a beleaguered-looking figure with shoulders a bit more angular than they used to be, his black suit rumpled from the trip, and hanging more loosely on him than it used to. I thought with a shudder, is the world changing, Emory, or just your luck?

Although Emory did not go into Mexico during the first few months of 1916, he carried on a constant exchange of letters with Barrista, who seemed often to be looking for ways out of the movement the men had begun together. Each time Carranza made some positive attempt at restoring order in the country, or announced some new phase of his reconstruction plans, Barrista would write about it.

His white stationery was like an ebbing flag in Emory's hand, as he read the messages again and again, then fired back with six new reasons why they should go on with the Plan de Pacifica Reforma. I sometimes felt sorry for Barrista. He was so tired of the bloodshed of his countrymen, so weary of the separation from his daughter—he could not bring Aegina back until he was assured of her safety—that he was willing to compromise if Carranza could do the job even half as well as he himself could have done. He often reminded Emory that Carranza was stubborn but reasonable, and he was sure that the man would not be so arrogant as to turn the foreign investor out.

One day in February as Emory angrily wadded up a letter from Barrista, he grumbled, "Well, at least his daughter's got some fight in her."

"Is that so?" I said, bristling. "And what does she do that's so important to the revolution?"

"She writes literature, for one thing. Her essays tell young people about the educational opportunities promised."

"And her writings are circulated across the border?"

"Yes."

"I'd like to meet her sometime."

"She wouldn't interest you."

"She interests you, no doubt."

He smiled and put a hand under my chin. "Something tells me you are a little jealous." I looked away. "Why do you hide things so? You didn't always do that. You're getting very matronly, Electra."

I caught his hand, and held it against my neck. "How would you know, as much as you stay gone?"

He pulled his hand away. "I'm busy. You know how much I'm involved in. If you wanted a husband who worked from seven till six and came home for lunch, you ought to have thought twice before you took up with me."

"Emory, let's go away together for a little while. Maybe to

Corpus Christi for a few days. Wouldn't it be nice to get away, just the two of us?"

"Yes, yes, we will when I have some time. Right now I'm too busy. And I'll be late tonight. I have a meeting."

"With Aegina?"

"No, damn it, with somebody else," he said, and strutted up the stairs.

Oh God, I hate this, I thought; who does he think he is fooling?

Later as I lay in bed I thought once again of leaving Emory. I was quite objective about it all for a few minutes, until I thought of the afternoon he tapped on my door at the Menger and gave me the chance for something better than I'd ever had before. Surely if he'd wanted only a replacement for Aegina as his bride, he wouldn't have reached back twenty years to find her.

After that I just lay there and let tears stream down my face. I didn't beat the pillow in frustration, or even cry hard. I just let the sadness come warm and soft across my cheeks, and thought how much easier it would have been had we both come into this marriage with nothing behind us.

19

Many times I found myself in agreement with Emory about his views that we were all being duped, led along by the nose, and being robbed of our freedom little by little. German U-boat warfare continued right into 1916, though it was dealt with through reams of paper memoranda between our government and theirs that often dwelled more on legal terms than on human rights. The German Government was unwilling to accept an agreement for settlement, terming the *Lusitania* incident of so many months ago "illegal," so we batted back through the embassies a substitute word: "unintentional." I don't suppose one word or another made much difference to the families of all the people who lost their lives when the steamer was torpedoed.

At the same time, the British arrogantly continued to confiscate the cargo of our merchant ships and had begun the further assault of our mails: opening and inspecting them as they saw fit. One mention of this sent Woody into outrage. To be sure, Wilson was caught squarely in the middle . . . at this point, both sides seemed to be doing their utmost to alienate our friendship and force us down a neutral course in Europe.

To make matters worse, he still could not extricate us from troubles to the south. Border raids continued to erupt like infected sores in Mexico, while Carranza pranced around the peaceful part of the country bragging about his reforms in progress. Yet it struck me as ironic that as Wilson himself toured the United States speaking on the importance of na-

tional preparedness, the need for a League of Nations that
would ensure freedom of the seas for world powers and sovereignty of small nations (costing a few more tax dollars), the
President seemed to forget these high ideals momentarily when
Pancho Villa raided Columbus, New Mexico. He immediately
requested permission of Congress to send a battery of our
troops down into the Mexican interior to pursue the trouble-
some "outlaw." This would be, Wilson promised, a "punitive"
expedition, which must have been a handy word to substitute
for the much-hated term "intervention." When Carranza demanded to know how far we proposed to come into his country
with our guns and troops, and how long we intended to stay,
and whether he'd have reciprocal rights to cross our border if
need be, I couldn't help noticing that the First Chief added he
was bound to protect the "sovereignty" of Mexico, using Wilson's own words to slap him in the face.

When in the spring of the year we learned Pershing would
take nineteen thousand troops south of the border, Emory
remarked, "Hell, that's nearly the whole army. We'd be in a
hell of a fix if we got into the war in Europe."

Nathan, seated at the dinner table, turned pale. "Oh, you
don't think—"

Then Emory leaned back and eyed him, puffing on his cigar.
"They might have to increase the forces, pass a conscription
bill in Congress, just to be on the safe side."

"But they'd federalize the state militia instead of that, didn't
they say so?" Nathan asked anxiously.

"Yes, but in all-out war, there wouldn't be enough. Young
. . . single men . . . would go first," he added, drawing out the
words cruelly.

Nathan started to raise his fork, then put it down and took
his napkin from his lap. "I'm not very hungry. I think I'll go to
my room."

When he was gone I told Emory, "It's too bad Nathan isn't
smaller. Then you could capture him in a jar and stick pins in
him."

"What goes on between Nathan and me is none of your

business," he said, then left the table and went out the back door.

I felt sorry for Nathan, and felt I ought to apologize for Emory's vicious behavior. While a lot of young men were talking earnestly about joining to go down with Pershing's forces, Nathan clearly wanted no part of it, at least at this early point, and I saw no reason he should be shamed for his feelings. It wasn't as though we were being threatened with a massive attack on our country.

I knocked on his door. "Can I come in for a moment?"

"If you want to."

He sat at his rolltop desk piled high with papers, trying, I am sure, to look much busier than he was. Without looking up he said, "It's those new income tax laws, new rules coming out all the time. You can spend all your time filling out forms."

"Nathan, I'm sure Emory didn't mean to sound quite so cruel just then—"

"Oh yes, he did," he quickly answered, then paused. "Of course, when it came down to it Cabot would try to figure out a way to keep me from going into the service because I know too much . . . about his business affairs. I mean, no one could walk in and take my place, and he knows that."

"Well Emory has a lot on his mind lately . . . things are getting so complicated in Mexico. There is still so much fighting down there that Carranza might use it as an excuse to bend the rules and put off regular elections. If that happens, Barrista might be forced into an all-out revolt, with more guns and smoke and blood."

"Good. Then Cabot will have his fight."

"Oh no, you're wrong. Emory just wants to protect his property, and he thinks Mexico can be made into a country as good as ours with Barrista leading it."

He smirked. "If not Barrista, Cabot would have found someone else to help him stir up trouble," he said, and the look on his face told me what I had long suspected: Nathan's loyalty to Emory was based on something other than sincere devotion or even some sort of twisted gratitude because Emory taught him a trade. My husband's despise of him was more than equally returned.

Shaken, I rose from my chair and said, "Emory could get killed down in Mexico. While it may not matter to you, it is a source of great concern to me."

"Oh no, seeing Cabot dead is the last thing I want," he said quickly, then beneath his hostile eyes a smile curled up like a burning piece of paper.

Through the spring I was feeling glum and everyone else seemed to be in the same frame of mind. Even if people insisted on saying the only effects of the war in Europe were the highly suspicious rise in food prices and the welcome boom to that intangible term "our economy" as we sold more goods to the warring countries, we all felt uneasy about the fact it continued to drag on and on and force us closer to a position on one side or the other.

Lyla was no doubt unaware of most of this, but typically was bothered if anyone was moping around, in which case she felt they became boring. She suggested Emory and I throw a big party to celebrate our anniversary. "But we're a month too late," I protested. She insisted that didn't matter, and even Emory seemed in favor of her idea so we set on an April date.

"You must hang Japanese lanterns all the way from the house to the summerhouse, wired with electric lights, and you can set up a punch bowl in there. Little tables and chairs should be put around outside in case the house gets stuffy."

"That's an awful lot of work."

"Yes, but it's the way people entertain around here," she said. "You don't have a third floor like some people, where you can serve a midnight supper, so you have to make the most of what you do have.

"Really, I'll never understand why you don't hire any help. At least one maid certainly—"

"I still like doing things myself."

"That's absurd. No one does that. If you ever had a couple of bawling kids to contend with, it would change your mind."

"Well I don't, and so that's an end to it. I know what—I'll see if I can get that young girl from Adolph Tetzel's bank to come. She helped out at his party."

"Oh, yes—that dizzy redhead—I'm all for doling out the dirty work."

"I have noticed that."

Emory would probably have squawked at the suggestion of inviting Woody to the party, and I didn't believe he would be interested in coming to our evening get-together anyhow, although he had readily accompanied me to the Philharmonic concerts all the way to the end of the season. Just the same, I went by one afternoon to ask him. He was happier than I had seen him in months, and proudly displayed a photo of his grandson Johnny in uniform. Light-haired and bright-eyed, the boy looked very dashing in his military getup. Woody's chest swelled as I mentioned these obvious facts. "It isn't so frightening after all, when you see him this way, is it? Makes you realize he's among a group of able men who are going to do their best to win," I told him, thinking guiltily of Emory's copper bound for Germany.

"Right, it does. He'll come home with a chest full of medals, watch and see. Maybe when all this is over, he'll take a leave and come over here before going back to school."

"Oh, I hope so. It would be so nice to meet him."

"Perhaps he might even enroll and finish school over here, at Harvard or Yale. Ah, how I miss him! I keep this photo beside my bed."

I had guessed correctly—Woody declined the invitation to our party—but everyone else accepted and we ended up with better than thirty people at our house. From the mood of gaiety that prevailed until around two in the morning, I had to admit Lyla's timing was good.

Camille Devera eagerly accepted the job of helping out, and proved even more of an advantage than I'd imagined. Although she kept a close watch on Nathan, who seemed bent on avoiding her, she stood duty in the kitchen and at the serving table, and freshened drinks—she seemed to have a talent for being several places at once. I liked her very much for her spunk and plain-spoken ways. She wasn't frivolous or coy, like some of the young girls around; rather, she was quick-witted and candid, and obviously knew just how to look after herself and what direction she was taking. I asked her how long she'd been on her own.

"Seems forever," she said. "My mother travels all the time with the National Suffrage Movement. My father's been dead for several years."

"Have you lived here all your life?"

"No. My father was stationed at Fort Sam Houston when I was born and for three years after, then we were sent to first one place then another."

"What brought you back here?"

"We lived here another two times before my father's death —he was quite a bit older than my mother—and since it was the only place we'd lived more than once in my lifetime, San Antonio seemed like home. When Mother started traveling so much, I decided to roost here. That was a little over a year ago."

"Does she visit you often?"

"Yes. She's up in Oklahoma helping establish a branch of the Congressional Union right now, but she's coming down to Texas for the state democratic convention in May, hoping to get a pro-suffrage plank into the platform."

"Do you think they'll—we'll—win?"

"It's as sure as prohibition," she said, then smiled. "Pardon me while I take out these cocktails."

I watched her as she walked toward the parlor, looking very energetic in her starched uniform, and realized she had a quality that made me feel good just being around her. If there were a lot of seriously negative events taking place in the world right now, Camille's unusual common sense and self-confidence certainly were a positive sign a few things were going right . . . and her mother's work, in which she was obviously well versed, was without doubt a ray of hope that good things were to come.

I felt very cheerful through the party all evening long, and could not remember when last I had felt so carefree. After it was all over, Camille stayed to help until everything was cleared and put away, while Nathan mysteriously disappeared and Emory went to bed.

I thought little of Nathan's behavior at the time, even though he usually put forth a lot of effort for me. He had spent the greater part of the day working on the Japanese lanterns Lyla had insisted upon, although from all appearances they were wasted because the punch bowl brought in from the summerhouse was still full at the end of the party, and the evening had turned too cool for people to spend time at the little tables clustered around it. I explained all this to Camille as I washed and she dried dishes, and she suggested Nathan was probably worn out, then suddenly sliced her finger on a knife edge. "Oh, fudge! How stupid," she said. In looking after the small wound, we both forgot about discussing the subject further.

Around two in the morning I finally went to bed, exhausted but still too keyed up to fall asleep. I thought I heard a sound —the cracking of a dry limb maybe, from the back yard—so I walked to the window to investigate. Under the light of the full moon, Nathan paced back and forth along the riverbank, his hands pushed deep into his pockets. I started to go back to bed and leave him to himself, but then my curiosity got the best of me. I pulled on a robe and went down.

He was quite engrossed in his own thoughts, and seeing me gave him a start. "Oh, it's you," he said, and turned to face the glistening water.

"Having a time getting to sleep?"

"Yes . . . I . . ." He dropped his gaze to the ground.

"Something troubling you? Can I help?"

He shook his head. "You know, if a fellow doesn't behave in certain ways, everyone thinks he's crazy or, you know . . . not manly."

I knew then it was Camille. Either because of Emory's occasional fun-poking, or her continued interest in him, he was beginning to feel as though there must be something wrong with him for not returning her affections. I asked him if that was it, and he looked wide-eyed and said, "Did you see, tonight?"

"I noticed she kept her eyes on you, and you seemed eager to avoid her."

"Oh, that . . . yes," he replied, then appeared to relax somewhat.

"Well don't worry. You're young yet, still have time to find the love of your life. I have to admit I can't understand how you can pass up someone as cute and sweet as Camille, but when you don't like someone, there's no help for it."

"There was someone . . . a long time ago. Her name was Cynthia. She was very pretty, with brown hair and green eyes, and a nice smile. But no one approved of her."

"Oh, here in San Antonio?"

"No, much further back. I was fifteen at the time, still in Mill Springs. It was the year my mother died."

"I see. Why didn't people approve of her?"

"They called her 'easy,' 'common.' She was just eighteen, and went to work for the mill, as cashier in the commissary.

"I was having a bad time around then, and she'd talk to me. There were deep, thick woods between the big ponds, and we'd go for long walks through them on Sunday afternoons. Sometimes I'd walk the logs in the log pond while she watched. . . . I was fair at that, with a good leveling stick. Once in a while we'd walk across the long railroad trestle; she liked that, flirting with danger. Often we'd just lean against the big iron pump at pond number three, and talk about things.

"It was pitiful because she was so kind, and the men in town always talked about her. I used to listen to them, while shining shoes. What did they know? Still, they said ugly things about her—all speculation about what she'd done before she came to Mill Springs. The more they talked, the more I liked her. I guess it wasn't right, but that was how I felt."

"What did your mother think about it?"

"For a long time she didn't know . . . but then one day, after . . . well, she found out somehow, and got furious with me, told me she knew what was going on and I shouldn't be fooling around with trash like Cynthia. . . . My mother got kind of . . . mixed up . . . near the end. She'd just lash out over the least—"

"I think I know what you mean," I told him gently.

"After that my mother and Sam got into a big argument. Mother wanted him to have Cynthia fired, said it was the least he could do for her. He argued she was the first cashier they'd been able to find who knew how to count change and send it back through the chutes to the right department.

"But Mother won. Lord knows, it was the only thing Sam ever did for her. I guess he felt obliged. I never saw Cynthia again, and Mother died three months later."

I couldn't see Nathan's face, and could only sense how painful the memory was for him. In a moment he looked at me, though, and his eyes were moist. "I was so ashamed," he said. "Can you understand?"

As in many of our talks, I was left to figure out Nathan's message from what he did not say. I was certain that young girl had seduced him into an illicit relationship, undoubtedly his first; and his mother, with the queer, highly developed instinct reserved for people at the brink of death, guessed and reprimanded him for it. Knowing she'd soon be powerless to shape his morals probably intensified her reaction, as well. She may not have realized she was dabbling with the fledgling manhood of her young son. I felt very sorry for Nathan, and determined this was his reason for steering away from women in the following years. He held his mother in such high esteem, what a blow it must have been for him to have disappointed her so near the time she died.

As I returned to the house that night, I thought I finally had the key to many of the crippling legacies locked up inside Nathan, that Emory was guilty of mocking him for his lack of manhood, and therein lay the reason they despised each other. In their early years of working together, it was probably easy enough to bully Nathan into believing he was some sort of freak, lucky to have been taken in by someone who could teach him a trade then provide him employment for it. Emory had once said Nathan was not the sort who "ran with women." As a young, single man who obviously was not wanting for female companionship, Emory could easily have nosed out Nathan's reticence with women and played it to his advantage. He was all too capable of convincing others of what he wanted them to believe, and this would have been especially simple with someone as weak and malleable as Nathan.

I now felt certain the present situation was one in which Emory, under pressures growing daily, was returning to his old ways with Nathan and despising him more and more for lacking the courage to fight back or turn on his heel and leave.

20

By early summer, San Antonio was teeming with boys in khaki uniforms, as Fort Sam continued to serve as the distribution center for forces en route to the border. The soldiers could be seen everywhere, from the shady plazas in the busy part of town to the normally quiet avenues and parks of the neighborhoods such as ours. It was common to see a young man smartly clad in uniform with a pretty young girl on his arm, strolling along the streets or resting in the triangular park between King William and Washington, she reposing against the trunk of a Spanish oak while he stood a proper distance from her, holding his hat as they talked.

Emory was increasingly impetuous as Barrista appeared to side with Carranza, and whether in conference with Tetzel or out late at night for what he always announced were "meetings," he was less and less at home. When at home his moods fluctuated from open hostility to cold withdrawal. Watching him lose his normal cockiness as new worries were added to the old ones was very painful to me, regardless of whether I could be certain of his true reasons for staying out so much. One night I made a strong appeal to him to give it all up.

"I know you will lose a lot down there, but you can make it back," I said. "We could move from here, sell this house and buy something smaller. I wouldn't mind, truly. Think how uncomplicated it would be, Emory, to be rid of this mess. We could be happy again, and within a few years—"

"No!" he all but shouted. "Don't ask that of me. I've worked too hard to give up now."

"But sometimes giving up is the only thing left to do. Then, you can start over again."

"I can't do this again, can't build what I've built again. It's too late, can't you see? Are you ever going to come out of that cocoon and face what is happening?"

"No, I don't understand what you mean. It seems all too clear to me. It is a business venture that didn't work out. Maybe being shut out of it, I can see it more easily than you."

"I wish it were that simple."

"Maybe if you could just get your mind off it—we could go away for a week or so—"

"Damn it, keep your nose out of it."

"You don't have to shout. It seems that's all you do lately, when and if you speak at all."

He took a deep breath, as one does in dealing with a petulant child. "I know. Look, if we give Carranza enough rope he will hang himself, you will see. We've gone too far now to turn back."

"But if Barrista is not enough of a man to stick it through—"

"I will make up what he lacks."

"It seems to me you've been doing that for a long time."

"You don't even know a small percentage of it."

I stroked his shoulder. "I would if you'd tell me. I feel like a person who walked in on episode three of a motion picture. You can tell me, Emory. You can tell me anything."

"No, there is a great deal I hope you will never have to know."

The curious note of finality in his voice stayed with me through the night and part of the next day, and I was so preoccupied with concern for him and for us that my hand was lying on top of a small envelope in my postal box before I realized it was there.

"I done a stretch in jail down here, but I'm out now and flat broke. Hoping you can do something about that in the very near future. Perhaps you need someone to help you out. I could send a man around to collect the dough."

Dizzy with anger and frustration, I stalked across the lobby and out the door, nearly barging into another postal customer. All the way down the steps I tore at the letter, again and again, until at the bottom I regained my composure, looked around, then crammed the pieces into my handbag.

At home I opened my jewel case, which contained only one item of value. I picked up the emerald ring that had been Emory's wedding gift to me and turned it over in my hand. I had never even considered giving this ring up because of its great sentimental value to me. The date of my arrival here was still clearly readable inside. I wore the ring to every social function we attended, and Emory would notice its absence immediately if I left it off. He was very proud of the ring and always pleased when someone complimented its beauty. With the one large emerald stone, surrounded by two tiers of diamonds, it was a handsome ornament which had even drawn a comment of envy from Lyla Stuttgart.

Although it was as dear to me as my wedding band, I had no choice now but to sell it. Should Emory find out, it would draw me into an even bigger lie than the fib I had prepared for the missing opals. This time I would simply have to say the ring had been stolen. Oh God, if the Mexican quagmire seemed endless it was nothing compared to this, I thought, then remembered something Emory had told me long ago of the revolutionary martyr of 1910, Francisco Madero. "Madero was rich like Barrista when he started," he had said, "but by the time he finished he'd lost his fortune, had all his properties confiscated, and even had to hock his wife's jewels. And for all that he wound up with nothing, not even his life."

One afternoon shortly after, Lyla came by as I sat above the river. I had not seen her lately, hadn't even seen Woody except to exchange a word or two over the fence about where Johnny's outfit was going next.

Lyla patted the ground to be sure it was dry, then sat down beside me among the vines.

"How can you sit by the river so much, and do nothing? I simply can't just look at the water—what a bore—I have to be fishing or something."

When I didn't answer she continued, "You keep to yourself too much lately. Why don't you come along to the railroad station with my ladies' club tomorrow and take food for the boys coming through on their way to the border? Chicken-salad sandwiches and lemonade—I have to make up six loaves and eight gallons of the lemonade. You could get me out of half the work."

"I knew there must be some reason you wanted me along."

"Don't be so touchy. What's wrong with you, anyhow?"

"Nothing. Maybe the summer heat taxes my strength."

"Isn't it the truth? As soon as I get this obligation off my neck, I'm taking off for the hills. It'll be nice when this idiotic European war is over so we can plan another summer abroad. I'm getting sick of the hills, but it's the only place to go right now.

"Anyway, why don't you go along? The boys are coming from all over the country, and from what I hear they all have two things in common—they're afraid of Texas rattlesnakes—I've never even seen one!—and they're hungry. They've cleaned out the restaurants and fruit stands already."

"All right. Maybe getting busy will do me good."

Next morning I carried a loaded basket down to Lyla's house, where we'd be picked up by some other lady in an automobile. On the way I glanced at Woody's cottage and wondered what he was up to. I would have stopped, but was already running a little late. Scoop, out in the dooryard, scampered up to the fence. I reached over and patted his head. "It's awfully hot for you to be out this morning, old boy. I'm surprised you're not on the back porch catching the breeze." I glanced up at the windows, then walked on.

There are many things that will stay in my mind about that day.

The train station was hot and dusty, noisy with engines starting up and roaring off, or screeching to a halt. A good many Red Cross volunteers were trooping around among the soldiers, as the city had been named a distribution point for them also.

We served the sandwiches and lemonade, and the iced-down watermelons some other organization had provided, from tables set up lengthwise close to the tracks, and I met many men—some young, and some surprisingly older fellows who'd interrupted important careers in the professions of medicine and law to answer the muster into active duty. I could not help thinking of Nathan. Surely these men were leaving work equally important with his, yet they seemed to do so cheerfully; or maybe they put on smiling faces for the benefit of all the ladies who stood around wiping perspiration from their own foreheads and necks, dipping out punch and wearing looks of cheerful reassurance as they backhanded impudent flies. It occurred to me a stint in active service might be just the needed dose of medicine to stave up Nathan's confidence in his own manhood . . . maybe I ought to suggest it to him . . . but then, something told me not.

I saw a young Mexican woman down the line, sitting with her legs crossed on the pavement. She had a huge box of Mexican candy in front of her, which a group of seven or eight youngsters were distributing to the soldiers. On second glance I noticed she was selling it, rather than giving it away, but then the boys were eager enough to pay for it, and the children would return and prance around, some of them taking in hand thick locks of the woman's waist-long black hair and twining it around her head maypole-fashion. I was about to draw Lyla's attention to her, when I realized Lyla had disappeared. I found her sitting back near the depot on a chair, looking pale, so I went to see if she was all right.

"It's this killing heat, and the smell of that chicken salad," she said. "It's quite overpowering. I'll be glad when it's time to go."

"I don't think it will be long. We're about cleaned out of sandwiches already. I could call a taxi for you, though."

"No, I'll wait." She shifted sideways in the chair, as though in hopes of avoiding the smell of the food. It seemed to me the body odor of returning troops was far worse than the chicken salad, but I didn't mention this to Lyla.

On the way home in the crowded little Electric auto, I thought of one young soldier who'd muttered bitterly under his breath at being called to duty in Mexico, and how red his face became when he realized I'd overheard his private feelings. Didn't we all put up a wonderful, courageous front. Hardly any man would have risked tainting his honor by saying, "Look, it's all right for anyone who wants to go down and play cowboys and Indians with Pancho Villa, but if it's all the same to you, I'd rather not risk my life over it."

It occurred to me then that even Nathan had less to say lately about his fears of being called to duty, though I was sure his feelings had not changed. Perhaps Emory's remarks were not the only ones putting pressure on Nathan. . . .

The lady driving made a point of stopping by Lyla's house first, though she seemed completely recovered by then. I wondered whether her little sickness was indeed a good trick to save her from standing in the heat.

I couldn't wait to get out of the car myself, and as soon as I got inside the house I changed clothes and sat down with a glass of iced tea. I considered moving to the summerhouse, then looked at the clock. Three-fifteen. I was amazed at the hour. We'd passed by Woody's house just a few minutes before, and I had seen Scoop outside, snoozing on the porch. I took another sip of tea and thought, he should have been out for his walk. Well, maybe Woody had other plans today . . . yet. . . .

Silly, worrying over a thing like that.

However, where would Woody be? There were no art exhibits that I knew of, and concert season was long since over. In fact, this time of year there was scarcely anything going on. . . .

At three-thirty I gave up fighting off the feeling of uneasiness that was coming over me. Within two minutes I was inside Woody's gate, holding Scoop in one arm, knocking on the door.

"Come in." It was Woody's voice, low and even, as usual. I

felt relieved as I opened the door, but even as Scoop hopped out of my arms into the darkened room and scurried to his master's feet, I knew.

Woody sat in his wingback chair, still clad in robe and house slippers. On the table next to him was a Western Union envelope, its contents nearby with the impersonal square letters of its message marching across. Woody was very still, with one hand clutching Johnny's picture, and the other covering his forehead. I knelt in front of him, groping for words, and, thinking of none, finally reached hesitantly and closed my hand over his.

"There was no reason to bother about the Somme," he said, almost inaudibly. "After the Marne, there was no reason at all. I was so glad Johnny was attached to Rawlinson's Fourth there. It was a good place to be. They were all young recruits, wet behind the ears, you know. Must have thought they were poised above the splendor of victory. The Germans laid them out across the fields by the thousands."

My teeth were clenched. All I could do was grip his hand as he continued, "Some general, for whom youngsters are only numbers on a sheet of paper, decided there must be a battle; perhaps it would gain us a few feet of ground, he thought, and we won't lose but a small percentage of our troops. A percentage."

"Woody, let me make you some tea."

"Yes, that would be nice, Mrs. Cabot."

"Are you hungry? You should have something in your system, even a piece of fruit or a tea biscuit."

"No, just the tea, strong and hot."

I went about his kitchen, so long familiar to me, as though in a fog. I knew where to reach for the tin of tea and where to find the matches to light the stubborn burner on his little stove. I fixed a dish of food for Scoop, who ate as though he had not been fed for a long time, and put fruit and tea biscuits on a tray for Woody, hoping I could change his mind and get him to eat, and hoping more that all of these rituals would give me words to say that would substitute for my inability to comfort him.

Scoop followed me back and lay down at Woody's feet, his head between his front paws, his eyes wide, ears perked with curiosity. As Woody took the scalding tea he said, "You're very kind, Mrs. Cabot."

"I only wish there was more that I could do. I feel so . . . so helpless, and so sorry."

"I know . . . don't worry. There are no words anyone can say that are of help just now. I'm an old man, you know. I've seen a lot in my lifetime. I've been sitting here awhile, thinking of that. When I lost Elizabeth I thought I would not be able to go on, though I did. I never expected to lose Johnny."

"Why don't you come home with me for a little while? Let me look after you. We have plenty of room and I think Emory is going off to Mexico again in a day or so. When you get your strength up, maybe it will be easier to accept—maybe not—but at least you won't have to do it alone."

"No, I appreciate it but I don't want to go anywhere. It's kind of you to try to think of ways to help me, but I don't think you can."

I sat back with a sigh. "All right. But I'll come by to check on you every day, and any time you want to talk to me, just pick up the telephone. I wish I could make you know how terribly sorry I am. . . ."

"I know that, Mrs. Cabot, I know. . . ."

It was almost five o'clock when I walked home, my steps as heavy as though my feet were bound in chains. I saw Lyla's cousin Gregory Brandon, all spruced up in his straw hat and Palm Beach suit, with a daisy in his pocket. He alighted from a car three houses down from ours where the young Elissa Franck would be awaiting him. It seemed a short time ago that I'd first met Elissa's mother at a coffee klatch, and she'd told me Elissa despaired of ever having a suitor because Beauregard Street was so short and difficult to find. Yet, close by all the while had been Gregory. Lyla had snorted at the match, and said, "Oh God, another Arnold and Lyla story. It's like an abyss in this neighborhood."

The pair of young people were now engaged to be married, and all the ladies of the street were beginning to talk of wedding showers and gifts for the bride-to-be. Gregory's social club, the Merry Knights of King William, would be throwing a party for him soon—launching him in fraternal fashion out on the vast sea of matrimony and continuity, on a wave of good-natured jokes and predictions. . . .

Pausing momentarily to watch him step confidently up to Elissa's door, whistling a tune, I was seeing another image in the back of my mind, of Johnny—his most promising moment captured in a photo—lying among a field of fragmented bodies, waiting to be carted off, thrown in a sack, and tagged for shipment home. I shivered and walked on.

Nathan met me inside the house with news that Emory had taken the afternoon train for El Paso. "Carranza's talking about free elections now, so Cabot's gone down to work out some propaganda strategies with Barrista."

"Well I sure hope they can manage this without killing anybody," I said bitterly and started up the stairs.

21

Emory was gone a couple of weeks, and his failure to write didn't surprise me. I read of another Mexican Peace Conference getting under way—this time the order of business was to figure a way for our troops to get out gracefully without an international incident, while at the same time persuading the angry First Chief to leave a border patrol on his side while we left one on ours, of twenty thousand troops each. Again the Pan-American countries would act as mediators, meeting with Secretary of State Lansing. As I read I thought, they have so many peace conferences, why don't they just set up a permanent one and save the trouble of getting it together every year or so? Then I realized that was probably the reason behind Wilson's desire for a League of Nations. If it could save any more bloodshed, it certainly would be worth the try.

There was little Woody would allow me to do for him. His cleaning lady now came in every day but Sunday, and would for the next few weeks. He seemed fine enough within a few days, though he was less talkative and I found many awkward silences when we had tea together—something that seldom used to happen. He didn't seem inclined to play the Victrola in the background, to bridge the conversation gaps, and I never stayed long with him. I mentioned once that, in a month or so, season tickets for the Philharmonic would be on sale, but he didn't seem particularly interested so I decided to drop the matter until the time arrived, and perhaps if I could persuade

him to begin going again it might do him good. I didn't want
to demean his grief by behaving as though it did not exist, yet
neither did I want to let him slide into a state of depression. It
was very hard walking the fine line between.

One thing Johnny's death had done for me was to bring into
sharp focus a very high regard for human life that had been
seasoning since the day we first learned of a group of poor Mexicans being executed over possession of the Plan de Pacifica
Reforma. It seemed too shabby a consolation to mention to
Woody, but it led me to become involved more in the human
effort afoot to make the soldiers feel as though they were not
just so many numbers. I helped gather reading material, paja-
mas, and cotton socks and towels for the Red Cross, and went
again with Lyla's ladies' club to distribute food to the arriving
soldiers.

Lyla herself had left for the hills and wasn't expected back
until the end of August. It was in fact a little earlier that she
returned. She appeared at my door one morning, eyes red and
puffy, her hair untidy as if she'd slept with it in a knot the
night before and come to visit direct from the bed, stopping
only long enough to put on a dress.

"I'm going to have another baby," she said as I offered her a
chair. She sat forward, one hand gripping the chair arm, the
other draped across her abdomen.

"I gather that doesn't please you."

"Another kid!" she scowled at me. "I've already been
through this three times." She paused, then noticing I didn't
reply—there was hardly anything I could say—continued, "I
won't be able to wear any of the frocks I've ordered for next
season . . . oh, what a lousy thing to happen."

"But there'll be other seasons—"

"That's what Arnold says." She leaned back and stared at
the rotating ceiling fan. "It's all right for him, of course, he's
not the one who loses his figure. While I'm moving about like
a German Zeppelin ready to drop a bomb, he cuts around playing
Romeo, pinching his secretary's bottom—oh, excuse me, I
feel one coming on." She shot up and made for the bathroom,
with one hand over her mouth. In another moment I heard the

door slam and the flush of the water closet. She was so comical, I could hardly keep from laughing out loud. When I knocked on the door and offered help she said softly, "It's all right. I'll be out in a minute. Confound it all!"

When she came back I had some tea poured for her. She sat down and sighed heavily. "I just bought this wonderful motor coat with military braid and double buttons down the front."

"Surely you can wear that."

"No, it'll be too tight—you haven't seen how big I get— then, by the time I can wear it again the war will be over and the military look will be out."

Impatient now, I said, "You worry too much about clothes, Lyla. Just think about having a healthy baby, another one to love."

"Sure, that's easy for you to say. I told Arnold *no more*," she said, then narrowed her eyes. "I told him never to touch me again. I'm not going to spend the rest of my life having kids."

"Lyla, I don't really think that's—"

"I can't stand him anyway; all he wants from me is a good tussle in bed. Let him hire a whore." She paused, then, ignoring my stunned silence, continued, "I've lived in this neighborhood all my life, and it's absolutely stifling. Arnold was picked for me before I was fifteen years old, even before I made my formal debut at the Casino Club. Would my father dream of giving me a say-so? Hah! A woman doesn't have a chance in this world. Those suffragettes are just kidding themselves. . . ."

I sat quietly, figuring she needed to get it all out of her system, although she was becoming less amusing by the moment. I had not known her to be so caustic or vindictive.

Finally she said, "I envy you."

"Me?"

"Married to a rich, good-looking man who stays away enough so you don't get tired of him. You have no idea how lucky you are."

I picked up a spoon and stirred my tea.

She continued, "And no kids. How do you manage that?

Don't tell me you've kicked Emory Cabot out of bed. What's your secret, love?"

I never thought I'd be embarrassed by a conversation, not after all I had listened to in my lifetime, yet I found myself looking down, avoiding her eyes. "It's a private matter. I'd have several children if I could."

She was thoughtful for a moment, then shrugged. "Well, I guess I'd better go before I have another retching spell. Oh, this is appalling. I'd give my inheritance if Arnold would join the Army."

I watched through the window as she went down the walk, back toward home, thinking what a spoiled little tart she was, and what a nerve she had barging in and cluttering my parlor with her vituperative tongue. But I continued to think of her throughout the day, going over the things she said, soon realizing she was a pathetic figure whose options for living her own life were no better than mine. But before that day it had never occurred to me that money and good schools, travel and opulence could be limiting factors.

In the evening Emory returned, and what I had seen of Lyla's frustrations of the morning seemed mild in comparison with his. He was among the first passengers to return on the newly reactivated through train from Laredo, but the way he was blowing off steam I wondered he needed a train at all. He nearly had me dizzy, watching him pace up and down the sitting room. Barrista had virtually backed out altogether.

"He believes he can get a post on Carranza's cabinet as Minister of Education and Agrarian Reform, and advise him on improving the programs Carranza has in mind. Then, in a few years, maybe he'll be in the position to run for President himself."

"But what about the Plan?"

"He wants it killed, doesn't want his name attached to it. If his connection with it becomes known, he'll be thrown in jail as a revolutionary."

I sat quietly for a few minutes, trying to digest the news. Then I said, "What will you do now?"

"Sit around and wait, like all the other miners, to see what Carranza is going to do to us next."

"Does Barrista realize the extent of your investments down there?"

"Not entirely."

"Well, does he expect you to repay all the money borrowed from Tetzel to finance his revolution?"

"No. He has insisted upon helping. He's a man of honor. I hate his guts right now, but I've got to hand him that."

"I'm going to see Tetzel," he said, putting on his hat.

Emory was surprisingly calm when he returned. The German banker had suggested he quit pressuring Barrista and give him time to come around. He also offered to extend the notes, as long as Emory could keep producing the copper.

"Can you?" I asked.

"I think we can dig out enough to meet his demands, but until things are settled in the north long enough to get the repairs done and the new machinery in there, it won't be enough to turn a profit for me. And if Carranza gets too horsey, I could lose it all, then Tetzel might not prove so patient." He paused, then said, "You know, all my life there is one thing I've been careful to avoid—being in the position of depending upon someone else to call the shots. It's a hell of a note to see that is exactly where I've got myself."

"Well you could hardly start a Mexican revolution by yourself."

"Yes. That was the ultimate gamble. It could well prove to be the final one."

The note of despondency in his voice was much more unsettling to me than his earlier angry mood. He had been depressed before, but not to this extent, and try as I might I was powerless to bring him out of the doldrums over the next few weeks. He stayed at home more, coming in early from the office and seldom going out at night, but whereas I would have welcomed this at one time, now I dreaded seeing him come into the door. He went straight for the liquor cabinet, and drank steadily until I finally coaxed him up to bed, or he passed out in a chair.

Sometimes I'd wile away the long evenings by sitting outside with Nathan, who was all for staying out of Emory's way. Sometimes I would drink with Emory, hoping to get him into a conversation that would take his mind off his troubles. Yet there seemed to be nothing we could talk about that did not wind up in an argument. I couldn't be the understanding wife all the time, and the mounting tensions took their toll on me after a while. If I mentioned Woody, he'd get on to the damnable British blacklist recently established, and we'd soon be squabbling about some academic theory on the war in Europe over which neither of us had any power. If not, we'd fight over his constant riding of Nathan. Dinnertime at our house had become a battlefield itself, during which he would pick on Nathan about a paper at the office he couldn't find, accusing him of losing it, or jump on him about his failure to pick up a tax break that would have saved money, or, even more cruelly, would taunt him about his impending military status.

I knew he was churning inside like a wild animal, newly captured and locked in a cage, but I didn't have the key to open the gate and was tired of having his anger vented on me. I was coming to know that when one feels love as passionately as I had for Emory, there is but a thread separating it from hatred.

What happened finally was inevitable, I suppose, and, like everything else going on during that period, formed a link in a chain of events that seemed deceivingly unconnected.

22

One night in September, after his usual consumption of nearly a whole whiskey fifth, he lay in bed pensively and said, "Dear old Fernando has proved a disappointment to everyone. Even his own daughter is furious with him. She told me so, coming back from Laredo."

I sat up and looked at him. "She rode back on the train with you?"

"Yep."

"I see."

"I see," he sneered.

"You didn't mention it before."

"You're so touchy about Aegina, my dear, always afraid she might outdo you in bed."

"That's a lie."

"No it isn't, Electra. You've been giving a lot of thought to that since you first met her father. I've been waiting for you to get up the courage to ask me. I could satisfy your curiosity—"

"No, Emory, let's not discuss—"

"I'll tell you how she is in bed. She's pretty good . . . maybe not as good as you . . . but good."

I sat there like a stone.

"Then again, there's a lot to be said for the bloom of youth, not to mention—"

"Shut up. You're drunk. You've been drunk for weeks."

"I know it. Come down here," he said, and pulled me by the hair.

I yanked it free. "Leave me alone. I don't want anything to do with you when you're like this. Go to sleep."

He pulled me down and got next to my ear. "What's the matter, dear, haven't I paid enough for you?"

"Go to hell."

He smirked, then got up, weaving. I could not believe this was happening. "Where are you going? You can't even walk straight," I said.

He turned on me with a glare. "I'm going to find a woman I can afford."

Next thing he was pulling up his pants and reaching for his shoes, and I was doing just what I would not have expected. I was wondering what the neighbors would think if they saw him out in this condition. I decided to try diplomacy. I reached up and barely touched his elbow, entreating him to stay home.

He pulled his arm forward, then with piercing suddenness, wheeled around and struck my face with the back of his hand, grazing my temple with his big finger ring. The force of it knocked me across the bed, against the pillows. I lay there stunned and wide-eyed, my hand pressed against my bleeding temple.

He turned to dressing, no more bothered than if he had swatted a fly. I couldn't speak until he was ready and at the door, then I said, "I won't be here when you get back. There isn't a man alive who can get by with striking me."

He slammed the door and stomped down the stairs. In a moment I walked to the door, opened it, and looked down across the gallery to the foyer below. He was gone, and I found myself staring into the upturned face of Nathan.

I closed the door again and went back to sit on the bed. I was shaking hard and unable to think. A glance in the mirror told me the cut was small, but I could already feel the rising underneath, and for several minutes I had to keep a cloth on it to stop the blood.

I sat holding it impatiently. I must get dressed, put my things together, buy a train ticket . . . all of these things seemed insurmountable obstacles in front of me then. How could I buy a train ticket with no money? I sat there and shook, and tried to think of how I could get money quickly. Go to Lyla? No, I didn't want her to know. Woody? No, I couldn't. Nathan?

He was knocking at the door. "Are you all right, Electra?"

I tried to steady my voice. "Of course. Emory had to go out, that's all."

He kept standing there. "Go back to bed, Nathan. Everything is fine."

He hesitated awhile longer, then at last I heard him walk softly down the stairs. I realized I couldn't do anything until morning, yet I did not want to be there should Emory come back. My head was beginning to throb. Finally I decided to stay, but not undefended. I took a small lamp off the dresser and put the base underneath the covers. Made of hollowed brass, it was heavy enough to be useful, but light enough to lift. I brought a fresh, cool damp cloth from the bathroom and put it next to my temple before going back to bed. Then I looked across at the mirror again, and the sight of myself, lying like a wounded soldier braced for another enemy attack, made me start to laugh nervously, then to bite my lip and weep.

I fell asleep, finally, and around sunup I was awakened by the ringing of the telephone downstairs. Nathan answered quickly. Had he lain awake? I couldn't make out his words, but as soon as he hung up the phone he bounded up the stairs and knocked on my door. "It's Cabot. He's been in a wreck out on the South Loop, but he's all right. The police phoned. Someone has to go out there and get him."

"Well, call for a taxi, Nathan. Thank God, he's all right."

"Uh—you know the South Loop, out there by the asylum."

"Yes?"

"I—uh—I could call a taxi for you. I'm sure he'd want you to come."

"Nathan, that's absurd. Get going," I demanded through the door.

"Please, Electra, I really—"

Oh, this is too much, I thought. The wound on my temple

was now the size of a small bird's egg. I raised my hand to it, then quickly took it down. The whole situation rivaled the plot of a cliff-hanger at a matinee. I didn't know whether to pity Emory or murder him. "Nathan, was anyone with—I mean, anyone else hurt?"

"The police said his car swerved off into a gully. They didn't say any other autos were involved. Apparently he was lucky—the Cole Six was demolished."

"You've got to go, Nathan. I'm ill this morning."

"All right, but what do you think the police will ask me?"

"How should I know, Nathan? You're wasting time. Go on."

At times Nathan's indecisiveness and cowardice were enough to drive me mad. It was no wonder he got on Emory's nerves. He was fortunate Emory would put up with him.

A couple of hours passed before the taxi carrying both of them arrived in front of our house. I'd kept cold compresses on my face most of that time, and had gone about the regular daily task of cooking breakfast. Later, I would talk to Emory about leaving in a way that I could do so with some dignity. For now I would just have to tell Nathan I'd gotten out of bed and slipped from dizziness, thus the small gash and goose egg on my temple.

I heard them chatting amiably as they came up the walk. Emory looked as though he were none the worse for wear, and the first words I heard him speak concerned ordering a new Overland—he'd been wanting one anyway, and the 1917 models were soon coming out. He was telling Nathan about the Model 85 Touring Sedan with the new hard top and lush gray upholstery when they came through the door. When he saw me, his voice fell silent. Nathan's eyes widened in astonishment.

"I had a little accident myself this morning—" I began, and turned back to the stove.

Through breakfast Emory did the most enviable job of idle chitchatting he had ever managed, while I went along with the game just pleasantly enough to signal him he might as well be prepared for a good raking over the coals. Soon Nathan dabbed at his mouth, threw down his napkin next to the plate of food he'd scarcely touched, and mumbled he needed to get down to the office. My little tale of the "accident" hadn't fooled him any more than Emory.

"See about that Overland, first thing," he told him.

When Nathan was gone, I said, "What did they do with the Cole Six?"

"Towed it away to the junk heap."

"Was anyone hurt?"

"What you mean to ask is, 'Was there anyone with me?' No, I was alone."

"Well that's a blessing anyway."

"Electra . . . did I do that?" he said, nodding at my temple.

"You know damned well you did."

"Actually I can't remember . . . much of anything. Were we fighting?"

I shrugged. "Never mind. It doesn't matter anyway, now."

He looked anxious. "You're not going to leave me, are you?"

"I was turning it over in my mind," I said, and scooped a spoonful of sugar from the bowl.

"Well, I wouldn't blame you. I've been a real bastard lately. But I wish you wouldn't. I love you very much and I need you, now more than ever."

I was moved by that remark, but unwilling to show it. "I'm worn out with serving as your whipping boy, as I am sure everyone else is. I hope that wreck last night shook some sense into you."

"I'll straighten out," he said earnestly, avoiding my eyes. "I guess sometimes you have to go all the way to the bottom before starting up again . . . but promise me you won't leave."

"I'll think about it, but first let's get something settled. I want to know whether or not you're carrying on with Aegina Barrista, and I want the whole truth. You owe me that, at least."

"No. There is nothing between us except business, I swear. Once things were different, but that was a long time ago and it is all over."

"Someone saw her with a man of your description, at a tea dance, not too long after we married."

"Oh, is that what got you started on her? Well it must have been one of her boy friends—she has plenty of them. Hell, I don't have time for tea dancing, never have. And I don't see much of Aegina. Since we got back from Mexico I haven't seen her at all."

"And why was she with you in Mexico—just on a nice little visit with her old man?"

"She had been there for a few days before I went. She tried as hard as I did to change her father's mind about the movement. It was almost time for classes to begin here, and Barrista is always worried about her safety, so he asked that we return on the same train."

"And you expect me to believe nothing happened between the two of you on the way back?"

"I'm telling you the truth. We talked a lot, mostly about conditions in Mexico and about Barrista himself. But she has someone else now, and I wouldn't have come after you if I'd wanted anything more to do with her. I don't see why you've always felt so threatened by her."

"Ah . . . men! All right, but I want to see some changes in your behavior or I swear I'll walk out that door and never come back. You ever talk to me again the way you did last night, and you will see how fast I can get my baggage together. Is that clear?"

"Yes."

"All right. We'll overlook last night," I said, and began to tidy the kitchen. He walked up behind me as I stood at the sink, and kissed the back of my hair. Then he whispered, "All my life, there has never really been another woman for me. You've got to believe that, and stick by me through the hard times."

"It's a pity you weren't around to help me through when I was having them," I said caustically. I wanted to be kind and forgiving, wanted to tell him I supported him more than he knew, but something kept holding me back. Everything came out in spurts of bitterness. He kissed my cheek, and probably could have used his old advantage against me, but instead he mumbled something about being exhausted. I told him he ought to show the first signs of common sense he had in months, and skip the office today so he could rest. Without another word, he went upstairs.

I stood holding a plate and a hand towel, fighting back a disgusting urge to cry for him because, while I'd seen him hurt by other things, I had never been so hard on him, or ever expected to be.

I don't know whether he would have been able to better deal with what he stood to lose in Mexico by virtue of the encounter between us, because he never had the test of time. Within a few days the situation south of the border—like one of our city streets—had taken another abrupt turn.

Throwing caution to the winds, Barrista was on the way to San Antonio, fire on his breath.

23

From what I gathered between Barrista's frequent lapses into frenzied Spanish during dinner at our home the next evening, Carranza was showing all signs of installing himself as a dictator. He was rolling out decrees that spelled assurance of his own election to the presidency the following spring. The title that he had carried for almost three years—First Chief of the de facto government—would not keep him from succeeding himself in effect, but would, on the other hand, give him authority to change the constitution immediately.

"He has called a constitutional assembly for late November, and picked the delegates from among his sympathizers. By spring he will have a new constitution representing his ideas alone. He has written his ticket to absolute power," Barrista said, then emptied his wine goblet in one gulp. "The man is contemptible. He must be stopped."

Emory cocked an eyebrow. "Are you ready now, Señor Barrista?"

"You have my word, amigo. There is no backing out."

He then began to detail his plans beginning the first of the year. He wanted to make the perfunctory gesture of getting his name on the presidential ballot, and was confident he could get the backing of the most powerful rebel chiefs, including Pancho Villa, plus the solid support of mine workers, textile workers, and ranchers. "Once I announce my candidacy, and become a public figure in this new respect, I can associate my name with the Plan de Pacifica Reforma safely. Carranza cannot persecute me or my followers without the risk of being labeled a dictator."

"You still better post an armed guard around your hacienda," Emory told him.

"I intend to."

"And if you run for President, only to find there has been a 'slight discrepancy' in the vote count, causing you to lose, what then?" Emory asked.

Barrista shrugged. "A call to arms."

My pulse quickened. It seemed Emory was locking all the windows.

The expected course of events, on the other hand, was that Barrista would not be allowed candidacy, so the final coups would be pulled a little earlier. The signal would be the single name of Carranza on the ballot. Within one week following the election, Barrista's four brothers, in co-operation with the other Mexican revolutionaries, would have a band of troops numbering close to 150,000 by Barrista's estimation, prepared to form a chain around the radius of the capital and close in. Emory would be in Mexico while it happened, but Barrista himself would co-ordinate the forces. "I know I can get the trust of these men, but they will never put their trust in a gringo," he said, and, remembering all the jesting about Emory's love of a fight, I glanced at his face. His expression was calm and thoughtful.

"All right, let's have a look at the maps you brought," he said.

I had no desire to see territorial maps scarred with red marks, so I went outside and sat on the front steps. Although the early autumn night was chilly, I hardly noticed. Every nerve in my body was charged with excitement because I knew the plans which had proved so elusive before were now destined for reality.

The aspects discussed that night smacked more than ever of

risk and hidden dangers, of the appearance of turncoats and disappearance of the faint of heart, but then I thought, what revolutionary plan did not? What force for change on such a grand scale did not bear heavy burdens of this kind? The only question at hand was whether or not it was worth it, and that had already been answered by Carranza himself.

Under the glow of a full moon I rested my face in my hands. It was like touching a cold cloth to fever. The bruise on my temple already seemed to be getting smaller. Either because he was too busy concentrating on other matters to notice, or he was too diplomatic to make reference to my wound, Barrista had said nothing about it.

The hour was very late when he and Emory folded up the maps. Barrista was to be our house guest overnight, and by the time I got everyone settled down it was nearly two in the morning. Yet I was still too excited to sleep. I waited until Emory had bathed and come to bed.

"It seems a hundred years have gone by in the past couple of days. I'm exhausted," he said.

"I hope you weren't thinking of going right to sleep."

"Did you have something else in mind?"

"Come a little closer and I'll show you."

He sat down near me and smiled. "I've left something to be desired as a husband lately, haven't I?"

"You might say that. I want to catch you while you're sober."

He ignored the last remark and said, "Well, you see my dear, what with little revolutions here and there, dormant copper mines, and other minor incidentals, I do get preoccupied now and then."

"That's all right as long as you're not preoccupied with other women."

"How could I be? It takes all I've got just keeping you satisfied."

"That hasn't seemed of major concern lately," I said, and turned away from him. I wasn't really mad. I just wanted to see whether he'd come after me. The feel of his lambent fingers up my spine and around my breasts brought a small smile of triumph to my face.

Emory's behavior was a great deal more civilized for the next couple of months, and he cut back to his more normal consumption of whiskey, even then so considerable I stopped wondering why he should blow up every time he read something new on the growing movement of the Anti-Saloon League toward national prohibition. Still he was a man relatively at peace, since Barrista finally had taken the helm in Mexico. There was probably never a time prior to that when I was more tempted to relieve my own burden onto his shoulders, because the truth was that I could no longer handle it alone.

Mark's letters since the receipt of the proceeds from the emerald ring had been increasingly frequent and nasty. It seemed to me that the larger the payment I made, the more apt he was to press for more immediately. Perhaps he thought Emory and I came into money sporadically—that was likely, considering the uneven pattern of my ability to forward him money—and that he would take as much as he could get while it lasted.

Several of his letters made reference to the "little business deal" I had turned down with Richard Boscomb, and one said, "If you could let a good chance like that slip by, you must not be having as hard a time gettin' your hands on cash as you said."

There was also the hint that he was laying the groundwork for blackmail, for he began to include such phrases as "You know, it kinda seems like I been through an awful lot to get this money. It don't really seem fair, over what must be about like a handful of change to someone in your class. I kinda think somewhere along the way there ought to be an extra bonus. . . ."

I wrote him a note ignoring the new threats, and saying I could not send him more just now, but would forward the balance due him within a few months. The promise was total fallacy, of course, except for the wishful thought contained in it. I wadded it up and threw it away, then thought again and burned it in the stove. I went upstairs, pulled out Richard Boscomb's material again, and looked it over, then put it back into the drawer.

By that time my nerves were in such a state that a letter from Mark could put me near hysterics, and there were many times when the unexpected appearance of Nathan at home during the day, to pick up an item from his desk or tend to something else, would startle me so I would jump as though I had seen a ghost.

24

Around ten o'clock on a morning in late September, Woody's neighbor Mrs. Hormby rang the doorbell. "Do you know where Mr. Woodstone is?"

"If he isn't at home, I have no idea. Why?"

"I've been hearing Scoop bark since I got up at five this morning—off and on, you know—and finally I went next door to see if anything was wrong. No one answers. Do you suppose he went out of town and left the little dog alone?"

"Of course not." I followed Mrs. Hormby down the street toward Woody's house, more fearful with every step. When we came in view of the house I could see Scoop, first at one window then another, barking, tail wagging. Seeing me, he scratched against the glass.

I circled around to the back door of Woody's house and knocked, while Mrs. Hormby, aware, I think, of what might possibly have happened, stood reluctantly by the front gate.

Woody's bedroom was at the back of the second floor, so the only thing left to do was go through a window and see if he was all right. I found a kitchen window unlocked, and climbed in. At once, Scoop was jumping on me, yelping hysterically. He wouldn't let me pick him up, but ran instead to the foot of the stairs and stood barking. I took a deep breath and followed him up.

I don't know exactly how long Woody had been dead. He'd apparently gone in his sleep, peacefully. There was a book of English poetry, spine up, at his side. On the table near his bed was the picture of smiling Johnny in his uniform. Not having been this close to death before, I would not have believed I could feel so uncertain upon seeing it. I touched his hand and called softly, "Woody?" Then I moved away and raised the back of my hand to my mouth. Scoop kept yelping and scratching at my legs, until finally I came out of my daze and grabbed him up. But he needed a conveyor, that was all, and leaped right from my arms onto the bed, sniffed around Woody, climbed up on his chest, and licked his face, then quietly scrambled down and lay beside him. He glanced up at me as if he sought an explanation.

I stood watching him, unable to move. In a moment he went to the end of the bed to the lump of his master's feet and lay down again, his head resting across them, ears perked, eyes still curious.

I held the stair rail tightly as I walked back down, then remembered Mrs. Hormby and opened the front door. She remained stationed at the gate. "Do you know his doctor?" I called.

Her eyes were as wide as Scoop's. "Is he alive?"

"No."

"I think I have the doctor's name written down. He treated my husband once." She scurried down the walk, no doubt relieved at having a purpose, and I went back in to wait. Scoop neither made another sound nor came down the stairs. I sat for what seemed a long time in my usual place, across from Woody's chair, and thought about all the times we'd sat together with music from the Victrola making interludes between the words we shared. He had regarded me almost as a special child. He never quizzed me on my schooling, or my bringing-up. He didn't know where I had been before he came to know me, and I had never told him, although several times I had come close. It would have made no more difference than the fact the annuals in his garden had to be dug up and replanted each year. In his view, each day one started from the beginning to learn something new. With me he simply started from scratch. He was the only real friend I ever had. By the time the doctor knocked at the door, my eyes were filled with tears.

At Woody's funeral there were people I recognized, though I had never met them; people who lived in the bigger, finer houses of the neighborhood that I had seen alighting from their automobiles or talking to one another in their dooryards. There were people who lived elsewhere in the city, and drove Packards and custom-made automobiles up to the curb of the church. They wore fine clothing and had their names linked to the best clubs and cultural societies. Their pictures often appeared in the paper. They did not speak to me.

There were probably near two hundred people at the service, and more floral remembrances than I had ever seen in one gathering. It all seemed so queer, when he had been so often alone, that all of these people should have known him well enough to attend his funeral. Of all the times his genuineness had struck me, I had never been more aware of it than on that day. His remarks about the people who'd been his students, and his social friends from all the literary and musical and art clubs that registered his and Elizabeth's names, came back to me, sitting in the pew. I felt very much alone and out of place among them, and felt that having lost this lifeline Woody had offered me when we first met, I was no longer a part of anything he claimed. Yet it wasn't his way of life I would miss. It was Woody himself.

"He was an old man; his death was inevitable," said Emory when we spoke of him at dinner, then he shrugged and added, "I tried several times to save you from this."

"What do you mean?"

"I told you not to become involved with him—or tried to give you a subtle hint."

"You 'hinted' that I shouldn't take sides in that god-forsaken war overseas. Well, that had nothing to do with my friendship with Woody. Maybe you can turn your feelings for people on and off, like a faucet, but I can't."

"I'm surprised you haven't learned to by now. . . ."

"I'll tell you what killed Woody. It was that war. It took from him the only person he had, and that killed him. He would have been around long enough to see his grandson again, one day, if the kid had not been massacred."

Emory turned around, furious. "What do you expect me to do about the war? You seem to believe it's my fault."

I wanted to tell him it sure wasn't a British gun that put an end to Johnny's life, but I stopped myself just in time. It wouldn't have helped Woody.

Finally Emory put his hands on my shoulders from behind. "I'm sorry . . . believe it or not, I try so confounded hard to save you from being hurt. It never seems to turn out that way, though," he said, and squeezed my shoulders, then walked off.

He refused when I asked if we could keep Scoop permanently, but agreed to let me care for the dog until I could find him a home. I think he felt far worse about the war in Europe than he would admit, and didn't want a constant reminder around of a casualty he'd been even vicariously responsible for.

I decided to offer Scoop to Camille Devera—I'd seen her lately while I was helping to serve the hungry soldiers at the railroad station. She might enjoy the little dog, being a young single girl without much social life, judging from all the little odd jobs she took on. Yet that could wait. In the meantime, Scoop knew me better than anyone else, and I was more than happy to have him around for company. The will found among Woody's papers in a bank vault was dated more than ten years previous. Everything in the Woodstone estate passed first to Johnny, and in the event he didn't survive Woody (that must have seemed a remote possibility then!), the estate went to Johnny's mother, the militant suffragette. I couldn't see her coming all the way over here to pick up a dog. The way things were overseas, she could not even catch a steamer to arrive in time for the reading of the will.

An inventory would have to be taken to arrive at the worth of the whole estate, and until this could be arranged, the house was to be locked, and left with all its possessions intact. I learned this one morning from two official-looking men whom I saw at Woody's house while passing by.

That afternoon I sat alone, stroking Scoop and thinking of all Woody left behind . . . all the things he treasured so. . . . Suddenly an idea occurred to me which I dismissed almost as quickly, despising myself for entertaining it even for a second.

But then in the night, lying in bed, I thought of it again. I still owed Mark more than ten thousand dollars, and short of asking Emory for it, which I could never do, I simply could not pay it. In the very near future Mark would appear and I would have to go away with him, as he had threatened in the beginning. Then my life would go into reverse and I would start down into the quagmire that had gripped me from the moment I took up with Mark so long ago.

Woody would not have wanted that. He would rather have helped me than to let that happen, surely, if he were as much my friend as he seemed to be. So if I took just one. . . .

No, I couldn't. To steal would be the same as to arrange my own admission back into what I was trying to escape. Yet . . . from whom would I be stealing? Someone who didn't care about Woody, who never even wrote to him as she paraded around England as a militant crusader, destroying property. . . .

Destroying. She had destroyed the property of others—crashing windows, setting fires—without a care as to its value. Yet she would get all that Woody had cared for so tenderly, then left behind, as soon as she could take a short leave from her "work" and come over here to fetch it.

Oh, it was wrong, I knew as I rose and dressed, and no amount of rationalizing would make it right. But maybe I could somehow, someday, make up for this one last plunge into transgression . . . someday . . . when I was rid of Mark, and Emory's problems were over and life was normal. . . .

Right now I wouldn't allow myself to think about it, but do it before I lost courage.

When I returned from Woody's house I felt very unsettled about what I had seen and done, and whether I should have gone still further than I did. All things considered, I knew I should not feel bad about having taken the small vase from the shelf of his breakfront, yet I did. It was so odd—Emory had been right. I made myself a whiskey and water, and sat down in the dark sitting room to try to calm my nerves and get my thoughts together.

After a few sips of the drink I began to relax somewhat, and to think way back over the years, about how easy it had always been to take what was not mine. Curiously, the first time I remembered stealing was the day Emory left Childers, and I took food from my Aunt Eartha's cupboard. I did not think it was wrong to take the food; in fact I was even proud of myself because I was doing it for Emory. I didn't have to tell myself sneaking from my aunt was all right; it came naturally to take what I could get, to make up for the feeling of loneliness and emptiness that comes from being an unwanted kid.

After that, as I grew older, it was still always easy, and there was always a handy reason, regardless of what the property was or who it belonged to. Even the last time. . . .

Tonight was no different from any other at first. I had thought it out, rationalized something that was dreadfully wrong into something right because it suited my need. Then, as though in a kind of hypnotic state, I had gone through with it. No one saw me as I slipped in and out of the house where I had received so much kindness over the past few years from a man who never asked anything in return and even, after death, continued to offer more. . . .

Until tonight I had always managed to slough off aspersions people might cast on my character, never letting them get under my skin. But now, at last, I saw myself from the inside out and felt rotten all the way through. I had to make this up to Woody, and I would, and free myself of Mark into the bargain.

Lyla's cousin Gregory Brandon and his new wife, Elissa, rented Woody's house once the estate was being processed for settlement. All of his beloved antiques and paintings, his old Victrola and stack of classical records, his books, his wingback chair and all other furniture—everything I had seen but not taken—were hauled away in a van to be inventoried, then

stored until after the war when his daughter would supposedly
come to claim them.

I watched from Lyla's upstairs window as the van was loaded
—her house was not far from Woody's. I caught my breath as I
saw the enormous breakfront go trooping down the walk on
the backs of two men. The other porcelain pieces had been removed. The books were still intact.

"I wonder how long it takes to go through and inventory all
those things," I said.

"Oh, that can go on for months," Lyla replied. "When my
grandfather died they were nearly a year appraising all his
things and getting his estate settled. Wouldn't you hate to be
the one to dig through all that old man's bric-a-brac? Must be
tons of it."

"Yes, quite a lot of work I suppose. . . ."

A few days later, while taking Scoop for his afternoon walk, I
noticed Elissa chopping back the queen's-wreath vine, still
blooming in all its glory. The bright-pink petals rustled at the
chop of the hoe, then fell in one last flash of color and lay
softly on the grass and walk.

I chatted with Elissa over the fence while Scoop sniffed
around, trying to detect familiar odors through the fresh paint
job on the house and fence. "I'm getting rid of this thing once
and for all," she said of the vine. "You can't walk down the
sidewalk without getting tangled up in it or walking on the
curb to keep from stepping on it. Besides, the place will look so
much neater without it, don't you think?"

25

The porcelain vase that I took was one of many objects Woody had pointed out to me during the period of our friendship. Though I was certain before I chose it that the vase was one of considerable value in his collection, I realized all too soon that I was mistaken and had chosen instead a piece of lesser value.

As the third antique dealer I visited confirmed two earlier reports that it was worth only around twelve hundred dollars, I silently despaired of my unpracticed eye for rarity in art treasures. I should have known . . . should have remembered this as one Woody had compared with another long ago, and explained why this was less worthy of note because of the later period during which it was made, and the place.

It seemed I had no sooner mailed the proceeds to Mark than I found a scurrilous note about his receipt of the money, which included a warning that made the hair rise on my neck. "I gave you your chance to pay me off through one business deal a long time ago," he said. "There are other deals that ain't so neat and clean as that, and I'm sure you know what I mean. I'm givin' you till the first of the year to pay me at least the rest of what you originally owed me, then we gonna do some talking face to face about another payment plan, one that I can personally oversee."

I knew then I had to act immediately. I would have to attempt to borrow money—something I'd hoped never to do—and the only collateral I could offer was at this point in time questionable at best.

I telephoned Adolph Tetzel and explained that I needed to see him on a strictly confidential matter. He agreed to meet me for lunch the following day, at a place far from Emory's office.

I hardly slept all night. While Adolph's telephone voice was friendly and reassuring, I had a strong sense of foreboding about meeting him face to face. I went over and over my approach to him, like an actor studying lines for a play, and I tried too to look at the proposal from his standpoint, to consider what he might think but not say which would weigh in his decision. By the next morning I was sure I was prepared with every piece of information, every phrase which would convince him to make me a loan, without telling him the object I had in mind.

I was to be thankful for this forethought as the meeting took place and he seated me across from himself at a little corner table, because he proved to view my request with far more suspicion than I would have guessed, and, already nervous, I was soon muttering under my breath like a frightened servant.

I told him I had to meet some obligations that came about before I married Emory, and that I did not wish to burden him with them, that I knew everything about his dealings in Mexico, all about how involved he was, and I felt I couldn't add to his troubles now. I was trying to make Adolph understand that Emory considered my judgment sound enough to confide in me. He did not seem to interpret my meaning correctly, though. He seemed instead to suspect I was dealing behind Emory's back—his stern expression and probing questions about my life before I came here indicated this. While I was in a way betraying Emory, I was doing nothing that would bring him ultimate harm, and I couldn't figure why Adolph should be so wary of me.

He warned me I was dealing in "risky business," and perhaps it was true that I was a bit naïve in my request. This was the first time in my life I ever had property of value to borrow against, and it did not help matters that the value could not yet be redeemed. Still I was desperate. Surely he could see that in my face. Even if he were laughing to himself behind that businesslike, inscrutable mask he wore as the meeting continued, he must have guessed that if I failed to come through with repayment of the money he could always take Emory aside without my knowledge and demand he make good the loan. The way he eagerly handed out money to Emory in amounts many times what I asked, his reluctance to associate himself with me or have any sympathy for my needs seemed quite odd.

In the end he refused to give me an answer. He said mine was a highly irregular request and he wasn't sure he'd be able to honor it. He mentioned something about "banking rules" and "loan committees," but by that time I was hardly listening.

When we parted he said, "I'll let you know something soon," and I felt then more disconsolate than I had felt since the day I sold the Mexican opals Emory had given me, and it seemed the pounding in my temples was like the ticking away of a clock as time ran out.

In the days that followed I tried to remain calm, and to concentrate on the fact that Tetzel had not given me an unequivocal "no." I wrote to Mark that I was working on something which I was confident would bring enough to pay him the rest of what I owed, all in one payment, by sometime in January.

Except for this preoccupation, we had many good days and nights that fall which I always want to remember. Never since the beginning of our marriage nearly three years before had Emory been so attentive, or talked with me so openly. I soon realized more than ever what a strain we had both been under for the previous months as he began to laugh again over simple trifles and I stopped having to worry about his being so touchy should I say something on a sore subject.

Nathan was becoming more and more withdrawn, even though Emory wasn't bothering to taunt him over the growing possibility of national conscription, or in fact, bothering with him much at all. Now that pressures were off, Emory was pleasant to Nathan, at least whenever I was around. I thought I could foresee a happy ending to their story: eventually, conscription would touch Nathan, and when it happened, he would go off to service (I'd help to bolster his courage, myself), and prove to himself once and for all he was a bright, independent young man. While he was away, Emory would see how valuable an employee he had been, and upon his return, their association would change.

We went to many parties over the holidays, beginning with a small Halloween party at the Tetzels' home. Emory's pearl-gray Overland had arrived earlier that day and he insisted upon driving us to the party to show it off. I had never dreamed of riding around in such luxury—the seats were soft as bed pillows when compared to the cars I'd ridden in before, including the Cole Six. The automobile provided more privacy to passengers, too, which I found I liked, and I enjoyed watching Emory show it to guests arriving at the Tetzels. His demonstration included everything from the dome light to the tumble locks, and he proudly pointed out the silk curtains on the rear windows and heavy silk-cord rails on the back of the front seats. It gave me a special, warm feeling, seeing a man who had worked so hard and worried so much during his lifetime take joy over something his work had earned him. The immediate reason for the purchase of a new automobile had worked its way to the back of my mind by then. I really didn't believe he'd cause any further scars on our marriage to equal that night in September.

I'd half dreaded the Tetzel party; yet it turned out to be one I enjoyed most. I had not seen Adolph since our private lunch several weeks earlier and wasn't sure whether or not to approach him about the answer I anxiously awaited. To my surprise, he took me aside at the first convenient moment and assured me he was giving the matter consideration. Perhaps as desperate as I was, anything would have given me hope, but I thought I read a positive sign in his smile.

"Don't worry," he added. "Let's enjoy ourselves, shall we?"

Everyone seemed to share his jovial mood. I met a woman who was having her portrait painted in miniature. The portrayal was being created on a piece of ivory, and would be made into a brooch and given to her mother as a Christmas gift. "When people grow as old as my mother, it is harder and harder to think of gifts they might enjoy," she said. "At least this will be something no one else can give her. I don't know what I'll do when her birthday comes up in February."

Immediately the idea crossed my mind of having one of myself painted for Emory, and framed on a small stand for his dresser. I wrote down the artist's name—Eleanor Onderdonk—and put it away in my handbag. Woody had mentioned knowing the girl's father—a famous Texas artist himself—so I had a feeling Miss Onderdonk might be very talented.

Closing my bag again I realized I had no money to pay for a portrait of myself, but at once I knew that was a foolish thought. Emory would pay the fee, as any husband would do for his wife when he was her sole support. I could see my problems over the previous months had taken a toll on my perspective.

I wonder if, when we are about to lose something dear to us, we instinctively take on a new awareness that will enrich the memory of it later. It seems to be so as I look back on the afternoon following the night of the Tetzel party that fall of 1916. I sat for a long while shelling pecans—my third season to take care of that time-consuming task—and as I worked I gradually began to perceive my surroundings differently, now and then pausing to gaze at the limb of an oak tree, its golden leaves brushing the window against the backdrop of a fine, chilly blue sky.

I was awakened to the nameless squeaks and groans of the old house, so long heard that they were hardly noticed by now, and, outside, the noise of a car trundling down the street, its horn honking above the shouts of a group of children using the pavement as their playground.

It struck me that these were the very things of which the permanence and continuity I had so long envied around me were made. I don't believe there has been another moment in my lifetime when I felt so content or fulfilled.

I wonder whether there ever will be again.

26

There was no reply to my letter to Mark promising payment in full, and in fact I never received another letter from New Orleans. The sudden discontinuance of his letters worried me all the more, so I began sending him reassuring notes every week or so.

Once Emory was on a train bound for Mexico in early January, I did not expect to hear from him again until he returned, probably without any notice, within a month or two. Knowing he would surely be busier than ever, I was prepared to depend upon the newspaper for reports from across the border, and upon the talk of people coming and going that I chanced to see. Yet within the first couple of weeks I had the beginning of many letters, which, though they were brief, proved at least I was on his mind a great deal.

The letters were always covered with so much postage there was room enough only for my name and address (as he explained, the amount of postage down there necessary to mail a letter was increasing faster than anyone could keep up with it, and he was never sure whether or not a letter sent to me would arrive). The messages were often from places I had not heard of before, located all over the interior of Mexico as proved by a check on the map, and were always completely devoid of any word which might betray his work down there. He told me only what I needed to know for piecing together the true conditions, and most of this vital information was between the lines. What surprised me was his thoughtfulness of keeping me apprised. Through most of our marriage, his doing so had seemed largely a matter of his own convenience.

Throughout January he wrote of all the laws and decrees being handed down by Carranza to make it rough on miners, and indeed all foreign investors. Later he alerted me that Barrista's circulars outlining his platform were being mysteriously pulled down around the villages almost as soon as they were posted, and his literature was being confiscated and burned by the *jefe* politicos.

Then came the final letter, which was so delayed in getting to me I had already read more than what it told me in the papers. Carranza's "delegates" had concluded their constitutional assembly, and the new constitution was ready for signatures. Presidential elections were set for March 10. Carranza was not to be opposed.

Emory would be home by the third week of February.

The next three weeks were the longest of my life.

Whereas before I had always looked to Woody or to Nathan to help me pass the long evenings during Emory's absences, now when I needed company the most, I had no one. I could have attended the last of the season's concerts at Beethoven Hall, but without Woody I had no interest in going.

Nathan rarely came in for supper. I presumed he was kept busy long hours at the office, poring over income tax figures. Just as well, I thought. Since Emory's wreck on the South Loop I hadn't felt comfortable with Nathan. Often I'd glance up to see him staring at me. At first I thought he was anxious about the wound on my temple, and perhaps he was. After a while however, I noticed his expression was somewhat transfixed, as though he were concentrating on me, yet placing me somewhere else. I never mentioned this to Emory because I was afraid the words would not come out sounding sensible. There was no telling how Emory would interpret them, and he might be inclined to jump on Nathan, all because of something which might turn out to be quite innocent. I certainly did not want to cause unnecessary trouble between them.

One evening he surprised me by asking if he could use the Overland. "Of course," I told him. "Emory's never minded your driving his car." He nodded and went off. He returned sometime after eleven o'clock, and I heard him pass through the foyer and into his rooms. All evening I had wondered where he was. He'd always had such a fetish about avoiding the wheel of Emory's car unless compelled to drive. Maybe he has found himself a girl friend, I thought.

The following night he requested the car again, and repeated the strange procedure. Then for five more consecutive nights he checked to see if I wished to be taken somewhere, and when I told him I did not, he walked to the garage without further adieu. By then I was convinced he was having a fling, and was too shy to tell me. That's wonderful, I thought, especially as he won't be breathing down my neck anymore. On Saturday I slept later than usual. When I awoke the car was gone. Nathan returned with it sometime in the afternoon, and instead of coming in to wish me good day, he stayed outside and washed, waxed, and buffed it until it gleamed from one end to the other. For the rest of the time Emory was in Mexico, he never drove it again.

I became more and more nervous, not only due to my own predicament but for Emory and what he faced. Mexico was in for a new bloody revolution known of by only a few at this point. Within three weeks the Apostol de Reforma would be a title inextricably connected with Fernando Barrista. His followers, so long and carefully indoctrinated, would be forced to take up arms once again, convinced this would be the last of the revolutions, the quickest and best organized, the one that would bring Mexico into the twentieth century on the coattails of her neighbor above. And the catalyst was my husband. Who would have guessed our hopes and dreams so many years ago in Childers would have brought us together in this?

I had to talk to someone, about anything, or go insane with worry.

Lyla was now two weeks away from expected child delivery. Victim of a difficult pregnancy, she was confined to bed. I rose early one morning and baked a cinnamon-pecan coffee cake—

this was a long and tedious chore, made especially so because my oven wasn't working properly and I had to regulate the temperature myself by putting pans of cold water in alongside the cake. Finally, dripping with perspiration from the oven heat, I bathed, changed clothes, and went to call.

I'd made a point of stopping by occasionally over the past few weeks, but seldom stayed very long. Today I made up my mind to listen to her chatter for as long as I could endure it, as a means of shortening my day.

I found Lyla in anything but her usually flighty mood. She was quiet and introspective, lying motionless among the pillows. She had not exaggerated when she told me she grew very large during pregnancy.

To break the unexpected silence, I went to the window and looked out. "It's begun to rain. Good day for being a shut-in, isn't it."

"I suppose. I've been a shut-in all my life."

"Oh Lyla, you're just down in the dumps today. When the baby comes a couple of weeks from now, you won't remember how long it seemed."

"I dread it, you know."

I sat down near her. "Lyla, what difference does one more child make? The worst is almost over. Back to your beautiful frocks this summer. The nursemaid will look after the child most of the time. You can go back and poke your feet in the pond, and forget the past."

"It's the future that worries me."

"Oh . . . you mean Arnold?"

"I wasn't kidding about what I said. I don't want any more children, and there's only one sure way to avoid them as far as I know."

I looked down. "I wish there was something I could say."

"Forget it. You couldn't guess what it's like to be in my place. I'll tell you one thing. If I had my life to live over again, knowing what I know now, I would play my cards just like you have."

I looked up again, startled. What did she know, I wondered?

"You don't let things control you the way I do. I envy you for that, more than you could imagine."

"Oh well, perhaps—" I stammered. "Perhaps you shouldn't compare—"

She interrupted me with a shrug, and looked out the window. "Arnold says we're going to get into that bloody war."

"I hope he's wrong."

"We can't keep out of it much longer. He thinks that is why Wilson pulled most of our troops out of Mexico. We've been tied up down there, like being stuck to a wad of chewing gum. To hell with Mexico. It's like a Sunday-afternoon cock fight compared to what we're going to get into."

"I guess that depends which side of the border you view it from."

"Those greasers will be fighting from now till the end of time. It's the way they are. Emory must be hauling in the money by the trainload from down there, or he surely wouldn't consider the risk worth it. Arnold pointed that out."

"Look . . . perhaps I ought to go. You don't seem to be in a very good mood today."

She pulled forward. "Don't go, Electra. No one comes around to visit me except you. Let's get the maid to bring some coffee, and we'll cut the cake."

Later as we ate the cake she said, "You will have to forgive my rudeness. I feel the whole world's crumbling around me lately."

"That's understandable."

"The odd part is, I think the world really is coming to pieces. Everything's beginning to change. This morning I was thinking, six years ago when I was carrying little Arnie, I was in bed for the last eight weeks. Mostly what I saw from this window were children going around on wheels and splashing around in the river. Occasionally you'd hear a team of horses shuffle down the street, or the tinkle of a bell—someone signaling it was time for coffee in the afternoon. . . .

"There used to be a street vendor—an old man—who came around in his wagon early in the morning. He'd call out, 'Cu-

cumbers, Cu-cumbers, five cents for roasting ears.' I don't think he comes around anymore. I never hear him.

"All I hear now is the sound of automobile motors; that plus the noise coming from the arsenal, now they've begun using it again, obliterates all the old sounds."

I was surprised at her perception. In a moment she continued, "You know, we had a lot of fun growing up. On holidays all my mother's sisters and their kids would come to town and stay with us. Every year on the Fourth of July we'd go out to San Pedro Park for a big picnic. We took so much food, we had to carry it in big wicker baskets. I had a beautiful white lawn bonnet that I wore . . . sheer as a hummingbird's wing. We laughed and played all day, and were tired when we all got home, just from having fun. . . .

"Christmas was the same. We began baking cookies weeks ahead of time—at least a dozen kinds—and on Christmas Eve we'd unveil the tree and sing 'Silent Night' altogether. Everyone had a little pile of gifts of their own, and everyone a plate of cookies and candy. We all sat down to dinner together, and Papa would rise at the end of the table and say the longest blessing in German you ever heard, while the kids made faces at each other and slapped hands under the table.

"I guess I'm not putting this very well . . . but the point is that we do the same things now, but it's no fun anymore. Somehow nothing turned out exactly the way I thought it would. Have you ever felt that?"

"From time to time," I said.

"I've always liked you, Electra. It used to get on my nerves that you wouldn't spend a little more time picking fashionable clothes but I've learned to accept that in you."

"How generous."

"I'll tell you a secret. I buy a lot of clothes because I like being admired by men. That's what most women like, isn't it? If I know someone is staring from off the side, thinking what a terrific dish I am, it makes facing Arnold a little easier. I realize that sounds strange . . . still, it's true.

"Most of the time you keep your greatest feminine assets

well concealed. I've often wondered whether that's because you've got a husband who makes you so happy, you don't want to be looked at by other men, or else he doesn't like having you looked at."

I sat silently. Lyla had the most weird sort of logic I'd ever heard, and she could come within a hair's breadth of being downright vulgar, for someone of her upbringing.

When I started home—some three hours after I'd arrived at Lyla's door—I thought over many of the things she had said. Mainly, her thoughts about the prospect of our entering the war echoed my own all too well. Though the Centrals had offered a peace settlement through Wilson as mediator, Britain, France, and Russia acted as though they were more insulted than anything else. The German peace proposal had seemed a lot more reasonable to me, with its territorial exchanges and indemnity payments, than did that of the Allies, who wanted to democratize the German Government altogether and divide her navy among the entente nations.

The fact, however, was that Germany was in a good bargaining position now, with her U-boat warfare having proven so effective. On the other hand, while the Allies were losing, they didn't want to settle on the down side. The only real way to keep the war from dragging on endlessly was a tip of the scales in one direction or another, and everybody knew there was not one nation capable of doing that. You could not live in San Antonio without getting a feel for the immense effort being put forth toward national defense all over the nation. It was hard to believe this much money and time were being spent on preparation without something specific in mind.

Evening was falling as I approached our front walk. All the windows in our house were dark, and the shades were drawn. The whole view presented a lonely, forlorn prospect. The rain had ceased, and I was warm enough in my coat and hat. I decided to keep going and have a long walk.

Lyla was right, too, about the way things had changed. Even in the time we had lived at Beauregard and Washington, many families had moved from the neighborhood, to be replaced by new ones. Children who were just tykes when we came now played unchaperoned around the streets. Everyone had an automobile now, and few people retained their horse and buggy anymore. The carriage houses—many of which were large enough to be comfortable homes—had been converted into garages.

Downtown, which I approached rather quickly it seemed, was trying to keep the growing number of jitneys from getting tersections busier—so busy, in fact, that now the city council was trying to keep the growing number of jitneys from getting in the way of the streetcars. But they would fail and they knew it. The time for streetcars was rapidly passing. . . .

All the streets in this section were now lit by electric bulbs instead of gas flames, and it was underneath the bright glow of these lights that I walked around, looking in shop windows and thinking of what Lyla had said of my clothes. She had been on me from the beginning about my big hats, then later about my skirt hems, while I ignored her because I was so certain my clothes were well chosen. Once (apparently in desperation), she said, "If only I could just get you to try. You can go to any of the finer stores in town and take something out on approval. If you decide you don't like it, return it. Yet—how can you be certain unless you've worn it, and gotten people's reaction, eh? So, you just be careful about wearing strong perfume—keep it off the frock—and after you've worn it once, then return it. I do it all the time, for heaven's sake, and the stores never know . . . if they guess, they wouldn't dare say anything for all the bills we run up. Arnold was never a day late on paying one."

I'd looked at her, aghast.

However, there may have been something valid in what Lyla harped on. I'd never forgotten the night Emory referred to me so readily as "matronly." He'd be home now in about a week, and there was a dinner-dance invitation for the seventeenth of February from the Tetzels, which we would no doubt attend during Emory's brief stay in town. This time, I decided, I would send him back to Mexico remembering me in a special way. If he was to be involved in battle plans and secret conferences in hideaways with men he could only hope to be able to trust, let him think of me fleetingly as an added impetus for coming through it safe and sound, not only because I loved him but because other men might find me more alluring than before. . . .

I smiled to myself as I looked at a store display, thinking, no, I'm above all that. Then I noticed a mannequin wearing a black dress with a plunging neckline, the skirt slit up one side, and a headband with a black feather aigrette on either side. On her feet were black satin pumps with ribbons wrapped criss-cross all the way up her calves. I hesitated . . . a few minutes from now the store would be closing. I started to walk off, then considered again and decided—the hell I am.

Feverish with excitement, I rushed inside to order a fitting of the ensemble, so sure of the great sensation I would create when I appeared in it at the Tetzel party.

27

Emory returned on Saturday, February 17, 1917, a date which I will never forget. After arriving in the afternoon he went straight to the office, then called. He seemed preoccupied, and spoke to me as if we'd seen each other fifteen minutes earlier, rather than six long weeks ago.

"What time is that party tonight?" he wanted to know. I told him we could miss it if he was too tired, but he replied, "No, I've got to see Tetzel anyway. Are my clothes ready? Do I have to wear one of those silly hats?"

In fact I still had to pick up his suit after alterations. His weight had dwindled gradually by twenty pounds in the past three years. I also had to pick up my miniature portrait. I was disappointed there would be no time for having it framed, but then I wanted him to carry it to Mexico if he wished, so a frame would only have complicated matters. I was very pleased with Miss Onderdonk's work. She had insisted my hair be left loose and flowing for the portrait, and the result—perhaps the intent—was a kind of ethereal quality. I was eager to hear Emory's reaction, though, knowing him, I expected a cursory glance and a good-natured but vulgar appraisal.

He phoned again at six-thirty, one hour before the party was to begin. "I'll be on my way in five minutes. Fill the tub with hot water, will you?" I told him I would, bristling. He could stand reminding I wasn't his maid. Six weeks away, he could stand reminding a lot of things. . . .

It is almost painful to look back at myself on that night, recalling my confident mood as I stared into the mirror and placed the headband on my head—the final touch to my new "look," which would have made Lyla Stuttgart sit back and take notice, masking her envy with a smile of approval.

When Emory walked through the door at seven o'clock he took one look at me, standing across the floor, and said, "My God."

"It's the newest thing, don't you like it?"

"I've never seen you look more becoming . . . or should I say, tempting? What time is it anyway? Ah, never mind. Wait till I get you home. We won't be staying late." He winked.

A little later, as he buttoned his shirt and reached for his tie, he glanced at me and asked, "How about your opals? Wouldn't they look good against—"

"I—I'm having the catch repaired on the necklace," I interrupted quickly, then added, "Besides, I think maybe this dress is statement enough in itself, don't you?"

"You're probably right," he agreed. I folded my hands, hoping he wouldn't notice the absence of the emerald ring from my finger.

I sat back on the bed and watched him pull on a tapered black waistcoat. Thin as he was now by comparison to three years before, he still did more justice to a suit of clothes than any man I had ever seen before or since we married. In truth, I wanted nothing so much as to walk up behind, put my arms around him, and forget the Tetzel party altogether. Yet, for him the party was business and therefore not to be missed. And I needed to speak to Adolph myself.

He turned around and opened his arms. "How do I look?"

"Handsome as ever."

"Why do you look so glum all of a sudden?"

"Oh, I just wish we didn't have to rush out so fast. You've been away so long. . . ."

"I know. I've missed you, and I have a lot to tell you about, but it can wait till after the party. I feel good. Let's get going . . . I'm anxious to show you off."

Well, that answers one of Lyla's questions anyway, I

thought, and smiled to myself. Emory's good mood was becoming infectious as we left the bedroom, and started arm in arm down the stairs. Nathan had been dispatched to pull the car around to the front, and I could see its headlights moving toward the edge of the walk. But just then a white envelope at the foot of the stairs caught my eye.

Emory picked it up. "Your name's on it," he said, handing it over. "Looks like someone slipped it under the door." He walked out on the porch and looked around as I loosened the glue.

Shaking violently, I reached inside and pulled out a slip of paper, on which there was a short typewritten note: "A lucrative business opportunity at little personal risk is available. Come to the corner of Durango and Flores, three o'clock next Wednesday. An auto will be waiting."

I read the note twice before I grasped its meaning, then stood stock-still, unable to speak.

"What is it?" Emory said, and snapped it from my hand.

I made for the nearest chair and slumped into it. I thought I was going to faint, but I could not take my eyes off his face as he read the words. He started to look toward me, then read the note again, one eyebrow cocked. Then he asked, "What's it all about?"

I looked down, and shook my head.

"Have you ever gotten one of these before?"

I looked up. "Of course not."

He considered for a moment, then asked, "Have you been talking to anyone about my financial affairs—at the coffees or—"

"Certainly not," I said, head down again. Could he have only seen, the meaning was very clear.

I looked at his face. His eyes were full of questions yet he didn't utter one. Finally he flung it aside and said, "Some son-of-a-bitch is pulling a cheap trick, that's all."

"Yes . . . maybe that's it," I said, weakly. My voice sounded hollow and faraway.

"Look, don't worry about it. Let me think on it. Let's go on to the party—we're late now. We'll talk about it when we get home."

I stared at him. "Party?"

He knelt down in front of me and pressed his hands on my shoulders. "Now, you listen to me," he said. "Maybe some maniac has been watching us and knows more than we'd like him to about our business. Maybe he knows I'm out of town a lot and thought he'd have a little fun with you. I don't know. But I can tell you one thing for damned sure. He didn't send you that little greeting to make your day more pleasant, and if he were outside somewhere watching, he'd love to know you're in here white as an Easter lily.

"No one is going to do that to my wife, do you hear? Now, get up."

He must have lifted me to my feet. He helped me on with my coat. I felt like a drifting feather. In a moment we were at the door and I could feel the chilly air hitting my face. The car sat at the curb, lights glowing. I hesitated at the porch steps, and Emory, mistaking my thought, said, "It isn't Nathan. I can assure you of that." He kept his hand on my elbow and guided me to the car.

Inside he asked Nathan, "Did you see anyone around here just now, leaving the house?"

"No. Were you expecting someone?"

"No. Let's go, and hurry up, we're late."

He sat back and clasped my forearm. All the way there he neither looked at me nor spoke to me. He just rubbed my hands, over and over, and kept talking to Nathan about nonsensical things, as people do on the way to a funeral.

"We were about to begin without you," said Sophie as we entered the dining room. I couldn't make out the inflection in her voice, but I heard Emory apologize and say he'd just arrived from out of town. He was close, very close, but sounded very distant. I looked over the crowd of expectant faces—it seemed like hundreds, each one peering right through me, yet there must have been no more than twenty guests. I could not seem to remember the occasion for the highly formal affair. Sophie was hurrying us around the table, explaining introductions could be saved for later. I spotted familiar faces, and tried to return their smiles, unsure what showed in my face. Emory was speaking, covering for me, guiding my elbow. It seemed a long way from one end of that white-clothed table to the other. Tall candles in huge silver candelabra, their flames glancing off mirrors underneath, and gleaming silverware, gilt-edged plates, and beveled crystal goblets graced the festive board. All of it shimmered in front of me. I think I was close to fainting.

Finally a servant seated me near the end, beside Emory. I was grateful to be positioned behind a huge, footed bowl of winter fruit. I managed to get through course after course of obviously sumptuous food that tasted like paste to me, my only comments as people began to notice I hardly touched the food, "I've been feeling a little off today, you see." This explanation served very well because the look in people's eyes told me they speculated Emory and I were in the family way.

Tetzel was at the end just to Emory's left, and though they exchanged guarded comments throughout the dinner, Emory kept giving my knee a reassuring pat under the table so that I knew he wasn't ever disregarding my predicament. In fact he did not leave my side all night. He was unusually attentive, and though half the time I did not grasp what he said, I could not have been more grateful.

I wished to hide behind a pillar and sip champagne once the dancing began, but I was only halfway through the second goblet when Emory noticed Terence Brown, whom we'd met at a Tetzel party before and who had proved to be so divine on the dance floor. He was on his way toward me. Emory murmured, "Oh hell," and, in order to save me from him, rose to his feet and took my hand. "Come on, we're going to dance."

"Can we just go now?"

"No."

It seemed everyone talked louder, laughed more, and behaved with more abandon than I'd noticed since I came to San Antonio. Maybe my shattered perspective was to credit, yet there seemed a tacit arrangement that we would not hold one another responsible for what happened that night. Did they all feel the time for grand parties such as this one was grinding to a desultory halt? No, I thought, it is only me . . . this kind of life will go on and on. . . .

Round and round we waltzed, as more people, not included in the dinner party, arrived for the dance. Emory held me closer than ever and once I looked down in shock to see the white crescents of my breasts above the plunging neckline of the black dress. It was the first time I'd even thought of the dress since I saw the envelope. "Oh heavens, I look indecent," I whispered to Emory.

"Shut up. You do not. You look stunning, right in style."

"What if it was someone here?" I said . . . maybe Mark knew someone here. . . .

"It wasn't, and even if it was I don't give a damn, do you hear? Will you ignore the bastards who pulled that nonsense? They're not fit to wipe your shoes. Now, throw your head back where everyone can see your beautiful face." He clenched my spine tightly, forcing my head up into the glow of lights.

"Can we go now?"

"No."

I looked at him then, and measured at last the strength of the man and the depth of his feelings for me. He had assumed my innocence of any dealings with the sort of people here in San Antonio who work in filthy, underhanded ways. Though he must have wondered tonight more than ever since he brought me here, he had not asked the one question I could not dare answer honestly: what were the things he did not know of me, the parts left out of what the agency he sent after me learned that might come back to haunt us both?

I knew at that moment I had been the petty one, gathering meager shreds of evidence against him and another woman; building up cases against him which did not exist, constantly setting limits upon the amount I was willing to give in our marriage because I did not understand any more than the tokens that lay on the surface of love. Little did I realize, until tonight, I wanted the Emory who had brought me ribbons so many years ago.

It was then, at last, I finally let go of the fantasy I'd clung to, and fell in love with the man Emory had become. Once I had entertained the notion that many years from now, after my debt was paid, and I was rid of Mark for good, I might tell Emory what I fought so desperately to hide over the past few years because it would lessen the guilt I endured alone. But I knew now that day would never come because I loved him far too much to hurt him that deeply. . . .

Afterward I relaxed somewhat as we danced, and enjoyed the feel of him next to me, the smell of him, the look in his eyes, riveted on me, and gradually found myself being carried along by the growing momentum of the party mood.

In a while we sat down again. Every few minutes, more champagne. Once I looked out at the floor to see Adolph Tetzel whirling around with Camille Devera, and soon after he was approaching our table, asking for my hand. An excellent dancer, he moved about the floor with sure-footed grace, and complimented me on my natural ability to hear the rhythms and follow. I told him he could thank his excellent champagne for that, whereas I wouldn't ordinarily have made such a statement. Tetzel threw back his head and laughed. His uncharacteristic reaction brought me to my senses and I said, "Have you an answer yet . . . please?"

"Now, now, my dear, you must trust me in this. I'll have more definite information shortly."

I nodded, looking up at him hopefully. Uncertainty surfaced again as I realized that, like my husband, I had placed myself in Adolph's hands. I brought my face nearer his and said, "By Wednesday, you must," then glanced quickly at the face of Emory, who sat alone at our table, watching us through cigar puffs. Adolph kept smiling and dancing. Had he not heard me?

"Doubtful," was the only word I caught in his parting phrase, but I knew then he had heard.

Back to the table for more champagne, to make the prospect of Wednesday seem farther away. . . .

Near the end of the party, as Emory sat near me with his hand on my knee under the table, the orchestra began to play tango music. Never before had I felt such a rise of expectancy at the uneven beat of the music, nor become so charged by the dark, mysterious tones followed by shrill, exciting chords. Emory, apparently of the same mind, caught my hand and led me to the floor. What happened soon after was a rare space of time that could never be recaptured.

We began to tango with several other couples around us, all in "proper" form, stepping down the floor, knees slightly bent, arms straight out like arrows, moving together but as separate figures, conscious of the four short steps, then the long pauses as the tortuous music wound tighter and tighter.

Like all the rest, Emory and I were the pictures of correct execution, keeping our distance from each other, measuring time, concentrating on graceful control as the steps followed by closes went carefully ahead . . . one, two, three, four, close. . . .

Then all at once I saw a change in his expression, the crafty gambler caught off guard, revealing he was on the verge of wiping the table clean. Our bearing switched: our bodies were closer than skin to bone, moving as one, heads pressed together, thighs locked, two black contours closed, like a finished puzzle. The dance became a ritual of twirling, curving, sensuous motions . . . one, two, three, four, close, together, hold, turn . . . and the music went on and on until at last we were alone on the floor and all the people watched as we continued dancing, mesmerized by each other, nothing else in the world existing, the music flowing around and through us until, finally, we ended in the last prolonged close followed by the sudden deep bend, my head nearly touching the floor, and Emory above, his eyes fixed on mine, triumphant.

The audience cheered and clapped, and whistled as we left the floor together and Emory said, "Now, we will go."

At home the spell remained unbroken. In front of a log fire in the bedroom Emory unwrapped the satin shoe straps from around my legs and lifted my feet from the shoes. Gently. He helped me off with the daring dress and tossed the headband aside. I unbuttoned the waistcoat slowly from around him and encircled his body with my arms. I raised my face to his. He pushed me down on the bed then and held me away for a moment, as though what he had been acting out all evening must be emphasized again, now, with words. I pressed my fingers to his lips and pulled him forward, too eager for the feel of his warm hands on my buttocks, drawing himself in, first slowly, then pumping faster and faster, and, please God, never stopping. . . .

In the morning I awoke before Emory and stood by the window to look out at the cold, bleak February day. The river below meandered along its well-traveled path, silent and calm, remaining the same through all the changes, protected from the world around it by steep banks and insulated even from unwelcome noises by the trees above, which it nurtured into thick, strong webbing.

So much was the same as in the beginning. We had loved again last night with the urgency of the first time. It seemed as though the past three years had never really happened at all . . . in fact, in a sort of grim, twisted way, the note which had thrown me into limbo was much like the note from Emory's agency . . . offering a "highly specialized position. . . ."

I turned and looked toward the bed. He was just awakening. "Come here and lie close to me. I have so much to tell you.

"I'll be here only till about the first of the month, then I've got to get back down to Mexico. I have an awful lot of loose ends to pull together before I go," he said.

"I expected that."

"Yes, but the thing is . . . I probably won't return."

"For how long?"

"Forever."

28

I sat straight up in bed and stared at him. "But why—"

"As soon as it's safe down there, I'll be sending for you. There won't be any reason for either of us to have to come back here, once it's all over. It'll be a brand-new life for us."

"But I don't know whether I—"

"Let me start from the beginning . . . there's so much you don't know," he said, then rose to stoke up the fire. He seemed nervous. "I hate this lousy place, and no doubt you do too, after receiving that note last night.

"Most of the money I made before I bought property down in Mexico was in the saloon business here. I owned interests in two, and owned two others outright, down on Matamoros and South Santa Rosa. In fact I'd put some money down on a couple of brothels . . . they're damned good money-makers."

It seemed that everything inside me was struck motionless by his words. I couldn't even take a breath.

He was looking away now, into the fire. "But then once I found you and brought you here, everything changed." He shook his head. "It's funny, but I didn't think it would matter because I expected you to be . . . harder . . . more like me. But then, talking to you, seeing that same look of admiration in your eyes . . . knowing you had never stopped believing in me, it was as though we were kids again and I had to make good—can you understand?" He paused and stared at me intently. "I wanted to go back and start over . . . to be all those things you thought I could be. For the first time in my life I was ashamed."

I lay back on the pillows. Soon he was beside me again, and I locked him in my arms, his head on my breast. He was at once the child I never had and the boy full of dreams who never grew up, but just left town and kept journeying farther and farther away. . . .

In a moment he continued, "I never lied to you about anything I said . . . but I just couldn't tell you everything. I felt so guilty about what you endured all those years, as if they were my fault, that I ought to have taken you with me in the first place.

"Soon after we married I began getting myself out of that mire. But I was in one hell of a position because I'd used profit from the saloons to develop the land I already owned in Mexico and I had to hold on to them for a while. I got out of the other deals on the brothels, though I lost the money I'd already put down. That's why I couldn't tell you where I was going night after night that first year. I couldn't talk to you because I've have had to lie, and I didn't want to lie to you.

"Then, later I needed big chunks of cash to move down into my mines, so I had to try and sell the saloons . . . even when I was acting like a bastard a few months ago, it was over those damned saloons. With the threat of prohibition all the time I couldn't make nearly the deals I should have. If not for that, I could have made three times what I finally came out with, and wouldn't have had to borrow any extra money from Tetzel.

"As it happened, I was forced to borrow quite a lot from him, to get my hands on some of the richest mining property down there. No one else would touch it the way things were, and Ralph had tested out a whole slew of properties that promised to be worth millions.

"My God, when Barrista tried to back out I thought I'd go mad. Everything depends upon his success."

"Does he know this?"

"No. He doesn't know how deeply I'm in, or how much I've borrowed from Tetzel. He doesn't know my copper is going to

Germany. He thought he could repay me what I'd lost, and help recoup the money we'd already spent on the revolution. He didn't know a fraction of how complicated it was, and I couldn't tell him. I couldn't let him know how I had used him. . . ."

I kept holding him. I didn't know what to say. After a while his body relaxed a little and he said, "If you got my letters, and kept up with the newspapers lately, you know as much about the Mexican situation as anyone else. Barrista's name will not appear on the ballot. There is talk that people have been warned against writing in names, or showing any signs of protesting Carranza's victory.

"The only thing left now is the call to arms. And Carranza is so strong down there, it isn't going to be an easy fight. Everything will depend upon precise timing and swift movement. One week from election day, March the tenth, the uprising will take place. That'll be on the seventeenth. Except for Carlos Barrista, everything is set."

"What about him?"

"Even if Barrista trusts him to follow through, I don't. So I haven't shown him the battle plan for his sector yet. It's still up here in my head. I won't lay it out until the last moment. Until then, only I will know what he is to do. Carlos will control the most important area of the uprising, and the one with the largest amount of troops. We can't chance his being a turncoat. I'm going to see him when I return. He'll have just enough time to get his final organization under way."

"And in the meantime?"

"I figure on leaving here on March first. Before I go, I have to arrange for the safe shipment of currency across the border. It's being printed here in San Antonio. There are a lot of other details I've got to take care of, too. It's going to be a busy week."

"What about Nathan?"

"I'm leaving him here until you are safely across. Then I'm going to let him go."

Again, he spoke of Nathan as though the man were enslaved

to him. I'd fought down the temptation of insisting on the full story before, but I found I couldn't hold back any longer. "Please, tell me how you two came together."

"No . . . I just can't, yet. Maybe someday I will, but not now. It isn't a very pretty story."

"All right," I said. I was in no position to press for information. "If . . . when . . . I come down to Mexico to join you, shall I put up the house for sale?"

"Tetzel will see to that, and deposit the proceeds," he said, then asked, "Is there some question in your mind about going to Mexico? I wouldn't have thought so, especially after last night."

"I want to be wherever you are," I told him honestly. "It's just that I'd never really thought we'd live in Mexico permanently." I didn't tell him that I wasn't sure Mexico would be far enough to run, that even there, Mark might one day show up if I didn't square with him before I left. . . .

"I'm going down to Durango and Flores myself next Wednesday," he said, looking at the note again.

I nearly leaped from the bed. "No, you mustn't do that," I said.

"Why?"

"Because . . . because, you're probably right about its being written by a maniac. He'd take just as much satisfaction out of seeing you go down there as—"

"Not after I blew his ass off."

"Oh, Emory, no, please," I begged him. "Just think. Now, when this whole thing in Mexico is about to take place, Barrista depending on you, you can't risk it. It wouldn't be fair. Oh please, promise you won't go."

He shrugged, but he wouldn't promise me.

I had to convince him. "Emory, what if the revolution fails?" I asked, hoping this would remind him of his own value and make him think twice about next Wednesday.

"I'll be shot, and you won't have to come," he said with a laugh. Then he raised up and searched my eyes. "Say you will come, Electra. Give me your word. I've got to know."

It was the closest I've ever known Emory to approach begging.

This morning I awoke as usual to the sound of reveille, and lay there for a while, thinking how I would miss that sound, and this place, especially my little spot above the river. Would someone else occupy the tranquil place, or would they fell the trees as I once considered, and replace the wild beauty with well-behaved grass and uniform gardens?

Early tomorrow we'll be leaving, and there won't be time to savor all the small things that have come to be such an important part of my life. Through all the clouds of uncertainty before us, one fact remains clear: after tonight, neither of us will ever live in San Antonio again.

As Emory predicted, the past ten days have been full. Within a few hours of our talk the morning after the Tetzel party, Emory decided I might be better off away from here while he is involved in the revolution. "I suppose you'll be safe enough, but something could go wrong, and if Carranza has any agents up here, you might be in danger," he said. "If any United States agents get wind of our activities, they might cause you some trouble. Of course, there's the note, too. . . .

"I'm going to have Nathan pick up train tickets for both of us. There's a connection to Corpus Christi within the same hour as my train leaves for Laredo, on the first. I'll have Nathan book a room for you at the Nueces Hotel there, and I can contact you when it's time, and let you know what to do. No one else needs to know where you are, except Tetzel. He may need to contact you should anything . . . go wrong . . . with the revolution. Of course, I'm confident now. Within a few weeks all this will be behind us, and you'll be on your way to join me."

He looked at me with a question in his eyes. I still had not committed myself. But I told him the trip to Corpus seemed a good idea, and to go ahead. In the following week, however, Nathan informed me my train on the first of March was already full, so he'd bought me a ticket on the mid-day train February 28. Had Emory been at home I would have told him about it, but he was away, busy with final details. Somehow this unexpected development nagged at me. I'd counted on the last final hours with Emory because, regardless of my decision about Mexico, it would be a long while before I'd be with him again. It seemed a little strange that tickets for the Corpus train would be sold out so early, this time of year. I decided to check at the train station myself. The clerk looked puzzled and said, "Must be some mistake. There are plenty of seats available on that car."

So I changed my ticket, and made a long-distance call to the hotel, to switch my night of arrival back to its original date, March 1. I didn't mention it to Nathan. Perhaps the ticket salesman had given him the wrong information.

I was grateful to Emory for his foresight in thinking about the trip because, with or without the threat of Mark, I really didn't want to live out the Barrista revolution in the same house with Nathan. When I told Emory about his use of the Overland for several nights back in January, he shrugged off the young man's odd behavior as meaningless and said, "Nathan's the least of our worries. As long as he works for me, you can trust him implicitly."

Through all the plans we made, the approach of Wednesday was never far from my mind. I kept checking the post office for further letters from Mark, but found none, and this seemed to confirm that my instinct about the note had been correct. Let Emory think what he will; I knew the danger ahead. When on Wednesday morning I checked the box and found it empty, I considered canceling it effective the day we were to leave. But then he'd know I had bolted as soon as the first letter was returned to him, and he would waste no time in hunting me down again. Leaving the postal box open might buy me more time. . . .

Though I left the house just long enough to tend to that errand, and returned home by nine-thirty, I never heard from Adolph Tetzel. I hadn't really expected to. Somehow I guess I never really fooled myself he would come through. All that day I spent half my time listening for the ring of the telephone, and the other half watching the clock. For a while I considered going down to Durango and Flores myself, to tell Mark he had to give me just a little more time, but then that would have been foolish when I considered the danger and the fact that I may have run squarely into Emory.

As the hour of three neared, I went into the parlor and watched the clock like someone awaiting execution. Was Mark, or someone he had sent, looking for me out the window of an auto? When I didn't come, would he drive away and forget about me, or would he come here and threaten me?

Three o'clock.

I wiped my brow. Unable to sit still any longer, I went to the phone and called Emory's office.

"He isn't here," said Nathan.

"Do you know where I can reach him?"

"No. He hasn't been in since early this morning. I could try and find him if you—"

"No, no. It's all right."

A quarter past three. I pulled the shades down.

At five o'clock Nathan came in and found me sitting rigidly on the sofa in the gathering darkness. "Where is Emory?" I asked, hoarsely.

"I still haven't seen him . . . anything wrong?"

"Of course not, why should there be?"

He gazed at me doubtfully, then squared his shoulders and walked past. How silly I'm behaving, I thought then, and rose to prepare dinner. Emory must have been right. The note was the product of a mean, sick mind . . . but not Mark's. Yet, where was Emory?

Finally at six-thirty he arrived. He saw my worried expression and took me in his arms. "You didn't go down?" I asked.

"Yes, I did," he confessed. "No one showed up."

"Oh, Emory," I said, breaking at last into tears.

"It's all right," he said kissing me. "Only a few more days and we'll be out of here. I told you it was a prank."

"Yes . . . yes," I said, and held him tighter.

Last night I finally gave Emory his answer. "You are my life. I will come to you," I told him.

And in time, I will.

PART TWO

Camille Devera

CAMILLE

JUNE 4, 1918

1

When I came back to San Antonio in 1914, all I wanted was a place to call home and a normal life. The most I dared hope for was a good job, a taste of big-city excitement, and a room overlooking the river. The least I expected was a fair job, a Sunday matinee now and then, and quarters at the YWCA until I could afford something better.

Instead I wound up with more jobs than a farmer's wife and little more pay, enough excitement to last me forever, though not exactly the kind I had in mind, and a strong doubt that anything, anywhere, will ever be normal again.

Right away I landed a job at the Telephone Company as an operator-trainee on the Crockett exchange board, and found that living at the Y wasn't going to be so bad. They'd built a new one on Avenue C since I lived here before. My roommate, Cecelia Freeman, was the quiet bookworm type, and the food in the lunchroom was cheap. For the first few months I stuck plugs into a switchboard and put up with a supervisor breathing down my neck, all the while telling myself if I could hold on to that job for six months I could look for something better, without the risk of being labeled a floater.

The job at the phone company was horribly monotonous once I caught on. I got tired of people yelling into the transmitter—oh, the times I wanted to point out that as loud as they talked, they didn't need a telephone—and tired of trying to put calls through to lines that were continuously busy, acting as the mediator between the party trying to make the call and the one tying up the phone. There were many nights when I repeated over and over in my sleep, "Line busy, line busy, would you care to try later?" Cecelia pointed that out one morning. She was soft-spoken and very intellectual, and always seemed to be in our room with a book hiding her head, or in the library. I think that, having come from a sheltered background in Houston, she was a little shocked at my ways altogether—especially my nervous energy. I spent as many hours working out in the gymnasium or swimming in the pool as she spent reading, and at night, all keyed up with no place to go, I'd scrub the floor and dust and rearrange furniture while she relaxed with a magazine or a book of poetry.

On Sundays, my only day off, I rode the trolley to San Pedro Springs or took walks in Brackenridge Park, or just meandered around downtown looking in shop windows, imagining what I would buy when I had enough money saved up. I began the day with services at Travis Park Methodist, because I promised Mother I would, but more often than not I'd be anticipating the classified ads all through the sermon. By the time the church bells were silent I'd be sitting on a bench in the plaza, turning the pages of the newspaper.

Finally one Sunday a job appeared that looked like the answer to all my dreams. They needed a filing clerk at the International Bank of the Southwest who was willing to train and work up to stenographer. The pay started off at two dollars more a month than I made as an operator, and I knew, as my heart beat in double time, that I was going after that job and nothing was going to get in my way. I'd had stenography at business school in Philadelphia, and stayed consistently at the head of my class. I could use a typewriter with equal skill. The following morning I lied to my supervisor that I was ill, and went for an interview, a blossom of self-confidince.

The job had been filled on Friday—too late to cancel the Sunday ad—but something even better awaited me. A full-fledged secretary was leaving. As I was about to be ushered out by a clerk, crestfallen over life's injustices, I overheard the assistant personnel manager talking over the phone about it. I nearly knocked down the puzzled clerk, trying to get back in there and plead my case. Mr. Terrell hardly had a chance to take the receiver from his ear before I was introducing myself.

He looked disapprovingly over his bifocals. "You're much too young, and I'm sure Mr. Tetzel will want another gentleman to assist him. He owns the bank, you know."

"Oh, he does . . ." I said, wilting momentarily. Then I remembered my mother's mettle in the face of impossible odds in the suffrage movement, and drew up my shoulders. "All I want is a chance. I know I can do it. Just look at the qualifications on my application," I told him.

He called for the paper, then rubbed his chin as he eyed it with increasing interest. Finally he said, "Mr. Tetzel has been looking quite a while, and he is getting impatient—understandably, of course. All right, young lady, close the door. I'll need to ask you some questions. . . ."

When I finished that interview—more like an interrogation —I learned I had still another to face, with the department manager. In between I sat on a hard bench just inside the department entry, surely positioned to challenge the ebbing confidence of any job applicant. My skills, which had seemed so important and impressive when I walked in, began to seem less and less so as others, already employed, briskly paced about, talking to one another in precise, businesslike tones. I could hear the clacking of typewriters manned by people with surely double the speed I'd shown on my typing test. Often I was passed by men and women who shot me a condescending glance, as though I were a smelly pair of stockings. I raised my chin, smoothed out my gloves, and gazed ahead with a mask of self-assuredness.

By the time I faced the personnel manager, Mr. Hicks, I told myself the worst was over. Then he began: "I see two typographical errors here on your test."

"I was a little nervous."

"Here in the bank, this kind of error is not tolerated. Everything must be letter perfect. Anything less will endanger your employment." He looked across at me sternly, before continuing, "In fact, banking is a very precise business in every way. A teller out of balance is a teller out of a job. Often our tellers work through the night to get their numbers reconciled."

I started to point out I wasn't applying for a teller's position, but then he said, "You will find policies regarding work procedures are the same throughout the bank. Should you be employed as Mr. Tetzel's secretary, you must expect your supervisor to be the most exacting. . . . After all, the whole reputation of the bank rests on his shoulders."

After fifteen minutes with Mr. Hicks, I was certain he was endeavoring to frighten me away. Unable to do so, he asked me to wait outside while he set up an interview with Mr. Tetzel himself. It was twelve o'clock, and since I'd skipped breakfast as usual, I was famished. Some busy clerk pulled out a tuna-salad sandwich across the room while she worked away at her desk. I sniffed hungrily, and thought, wouldn't it be just my luck to be stuck here till after the lunch period is over. Mr. Tetzel probably goes out for those marathon business lunches. . . .

Just then a kind-looking woman approached with my application in her hand and said, "Mr. Tetzel will see you now. Hurry up, he has a meeting at twelve forty-five."

He certainly looked like a distinguished, well-established banker as he offered me a chair across from his huge mahogany desk. After giving my application a cursory glance, he said, "I see you have lived here before."

"I was born here, and went to high school at Old Main. In between I lived all over—"

"Yes, I see your father was an army sergeant. He was posted here long enough for you to complete your education?"

"Actually, he died at the end of my first year. Mother let me finish before we moved to Philadelphia, where I went to business school."

"Um-hum, and how were your marks in school?"

"All right, except I almost flunked cooking. I overcooked the pot roast for the final exam."

He laughed. "No, I mean in business school—we can and will order a transcript, of course."

He seemed satisfied with my answers. He had a stiff-necked

look about him, but smiled readily enough, and when he did his face looked kind and fatherly. He told me he had been here since he was a youngster, migrating with his family from Germany. "There was simply no means of fighting the class distinctions there, of getting ahead. So my father decided we'd come over here where a man was given a fair chance," he said. Then he reminisced about living in this area when he was my age, and spoke of swimming in the river down by what was then the Guenther Mill at the foot of King William Street. "It is very deep there—we used to say the river had no bottom—and a little closer to the arsenal is a whirlpool. But then, we were young and inclined to be daring. . . .

"Did you ever eat chili at the stands on Alamo Plaza?" he asked, but before I could answer, he added, "That chili was so hot it would start your ears smoking. We'd follow it with a Menger beer—"

Suddenly he seemed to realize he was talking to a young lady. He cleared his throat and took on a businesslike demeanor again.

"What we want here, Miss Devera, is someone who can work up to fill the position of my secretary within a few months time. Claude DuChauncey is leaving sometime after the first of the year. You're a bit young—just shy of twenty-one —and inexperienced—"

"Oh, but I could do it, I just know I could. I'll stay late, come in early, learn everything I can. Just give me a chance to prove myself."

He considered for a moment, studying me, then said, "You might be called upon to do just that." He looked at his watch. "I must go now. Suppose I think about it and call you tomorrow?"

"I get back to my room at the Y at six. I'll be waiting." I stood up and offered my hand. "Thank you very much for considering me, Mr. Tetzel." He nodded and I left. I was less buoyant than I hoped, although I consoled myself I was expecting too much, looking for a firm commitment on such an obviously important job on the same day I applied. They probably had lots of people wanting that position. In fact, they obviously had so many qualified people within their ranks, it seemed odd so much time had been spent filling the job. I speculated on that point all afternoon.

I had figured on taking the whole day off if I got the job, risking the chance of being seen by someone from the Telephone Company, and being reported for lying. But since I was still for all purposes without a new job, I went back to work and told them I was feeling better, and feigned a cough now and then to make it more convincing. Then at three o'clock my supervisor remarked that I looked a little pale, and suggested I go back home until tomorrow. I felt like a rat.

Considering all the lying and cheating I soon became involved in, however, the incident would later seem minuscule by comparison. . . .

The following night Claude DuChauncey called to say Mr. Tetzel wished me to begin after suitable notice to the Telephone Company, so on Monday, September 14, I walked in through the main banking lobby, climbed the impressive marble stairs up to the third-floor office of the president, and glanced with condescendence at all the curious faces along the way.

My first task was in learning the files, just as I had expected. Yet I was surprised to find that dealing with Mr. Tetzel's correspondence—both business and personal—would deny me the chance of learning about the pulse of the bank. Claude, who was preparing to move to California and go into business for himself, seemed more anxious to get me trained in Mr. Tetzel's administrative work than teach me the rudiments of banking. After my first day I had an uneasy feeling I would have been better off with the filing-clerk job, so that I could learn from the ground up. As it was, I would probably soon look foolish to clients who expected me to know something about the business, and other employees would be bound to chatter about my lack of knowledge behind my back.

I meant to say something about this during my second day with the bank, but Mr. Tetzel called me in for dictation and I forgot everything else. He replied to ten business letters and four personal notes, including one about water rights on a property he owned up in Fredericksburg. I was not prepared for this sudden plunge into the pot, and my hands were cold and shaky throughout the whole session. Mr. Tetzel was very concise about what he wanted to say in each case, and spoke loudly enough that he was easy to follow. Each time he paused, I wondered if he could hear my knees quivering. Yet I endeavored to hide my misgivings, and, in the end, satisfied him of my capabilities.

Though I didn't realize it at the time, I later reasoned he'd planned to give me a stiff tryout, and if I failed there would still be plenty of time to find someone else and have her . . . or him . . . trained by the time Claude left. I know he certainly had no ideas about involving me in his secret affairs, and even at this point I can't help but respect that.

Claude had little to say to me outside the subject of work, and even my training consisted mostly of digging out information for myself. I believe the most he ever told me in one conversation was, "All you have to do to please Mr. Tetzel is center his letters on the page, avoid all errors in typing, spelling, grammar, and punctuation, never misfile anything, and be sure he has his daily banking reports on his desk first thing in the morning.

"Oh yes, and always keep his inkwell full. He gets furious if he starts to use his pen and finds it empty."

"Is that all?" I asked nervously.

"He's fairly self-sufficient in keeping his own appointments straight . . . oh, but he's absent-minded about his homburg. He's always leaving it on the shelf above his coat hook."

"Thanks for the pointers."

"The job is easy . . . I'm certain you can handle it," he said snidely.

I was really happy at the bank over the first few weeks. Claude was more and more often slipping out early as I became capable, and there was no denying the fact Mr. Tetzel was pleased with the situation. Once he realized I was a sharp secretary, able to anticipate his needs and carry them out accurately, he became more and more friendly toward me. I sensed he considered me attractive—I'm no Lillie Langtry, but after five years with a male secretary it must have been refreshing to have a young woman attending him. What seemed to impress him the most was my energy. "I told my wife, Sophie, about you, and she asked me if you were a German girl," he said one day.

Who knows how long I would have continued, never guessing the things going on right under my nose, had my mother not come for a visit when she did?

2

Mother had been active in the woman's suffrage movement since my father died in 1909. Before then she worked on various women's committees and in clubs wherever we lived, but she had remained overshadowed by other women more deeply involved. My brothers and I were all astounded as she began to speak before groups, to travel, and serve on important commissions all over the place. What shocked us most was the fact she had grumbled and groaned every time my father's change in military orders caused an uproot. After his death she hardly ever stopped long enough to unpack her suitcases.

Following many long talks with her, however, I finally decided my father's career was the cause of her involvement. Although she never let us know because she wanted her children to have a high opinion of their father, she resented having her life manipulated constantly. Her work in the suffrage movement was a strike back for personal freedom. Her gripes about moving us kids from pillar to post expressed only the surface of her feelings. What really disturbed her was her own sense of violation carried on the print of military decrees.

Once all of her children were educated, and my three older brothers were married and building their own lives, she dedicated herself to the movement for the rights of all women, giving up once again her own personal freedom and forcing me gently from her nest.

My mother is a very serious-minded individual, but she does have a great sense of humor and a certain amount of mischief in her eyes. She also has an amazing talent for stirring up what she calls "constructive activity," and what my brothers and I have long since referred to as "trouble."

She is short and plump, with steel-gray wavy hair and the clearest skin I have ever seen on a woman in her fifties. She always wears a small watch in a filigree case, hanging from a long chain around her neck—a wedding gift from my father—and when she reads she wears a small pair of wire-rimmed spectacles. I thought of her motherly looks when I picked up the telegram awaiting me at the Y, saying she was coming for a visit. I'd written her all about my new job, and couldn't wait to tell her in person that my salary was to be raised another five dollars per month in December.

I hadn't seen her in months. Before the war in Europe began, she had been in London, working with the antimilitant faction of suffragettes. She was among those trying to reason Sylvia Pankhurst out of her hunger strikes and violent protests, and her displays on the steps of Premier Asquith's residence on Downing Street. She was in agreement with the higher-ups in the suffrage movement in this country who believed women who continued to react to rebuffs from any government dramatically and violently hurt the cause for all women, and she was mobile and thus able to represent them in England. Over there she had seen windows crashed in by rocks, churches burned, bombs set off, and all sorts of destructive and terrorist acts by the militants, "putting their cause back by hundreds of years," she wrote.

Now back in the United States since the war began, she had been touring the country, speaking on the changes that had occurred since the first of July in the whole suffrage movement. Formerly unreasonable women were now showing men they could do their fair share of man's work in his absence, and in the process showing in any number of constructive ways that they were equally capable of casting ballots in elections. The thrust of Mother's speeches was that American women were once again proven correct in their nonmilitant, more patient approach to suffrage. Whereas over in England they were only now getting the attention they wanted and deserved from the government, women in the United States had already managed to swing many state legislatures to their side. Yet, there was much left to be done. . . .

Her letter about that speech ran sixteen pages, and I could tell by the more and more indecipherable scrawl as the letter continued that she was thoroughly wound up on her subject. I was proud of her for having the ability to communicate her enthusiasm to others, and I believed in what she was doing, but regardless of her prodding I was not yet ready to take up the flag and follow her. Neither was I reluctant to tell her so.

The last time she left for Europe I had told her I was thinking of moving to San Antonio after I finished my course in business school, and when she seemed surprised I said, "You're never at home anyway, and I don't want to live with any of the boys and their families. San Antonio is the closest thing I've ever had to home. Also, Dad's buried there . . . it just seems like a good idea."

That argument satisfied her, and she wished me well and left in a flurry of kisses and hugs, and with instructions that I was to go to church regularly and behave myself. One thing both of us knew: the years of living in so many different places had taught me self-reliance. She didn't have to worry much about my welfare. Even if I were her only daughter and the youngest of her brood by several years, I could look after myself.

She arrived in early December of 1914, checked in at the Gunter, where her conference was to take place, and left a message at the Y that she'd be in touch the following day, in between a tight schedule of meetings. I told myself I didn't mind that she put her meetings before me. She had important matters to tend to. . . .

Up to then, everything was normal.

She called on Saturday afternoon to say she wanted me to meet some people in her room at the Gunter, and since they all had to attend a banquet that night—would I like to come?—to please stop by as soon as I could. I'd just gotten off work, and told her I'd be over after I changed clothes. I didn't hurry, though. I had counted on a private visit, and was irritated by her inviting guests. That was thoughtless, and unlike her.

Mother looked well, and after going through the usual maternal routine of looking at me aghast, and declaring I was getting too thin, and turning me around to give me a cursory inspection, she introduced me to a small man with black wavy hair and a neat mustache beneath a large nose. His name was Michael Stobalt. Their companion was a tall, stately woman named Frieda Miles. What occurred in that queer little meeting soon had me sitting forward, eyes wide.

Mother had met Frieda at a women's club meeting a couple of days earlier, and they had talked over coffee. The woman, of Czech origin, seemed especially interested when Mother mentioned the name of the bank where I worked. By that evening she'd contacted Mother again and brought along Stobalt. He dominated our meeting in Mother's room.

He began in slightly broken English, "We of the Bohemian National Alliance feel a kinship with the women involved in the suffrage movement both here and in Europe . . . basically our goals are the same—personal and national freedom. Miss Devera, there are many important women of your mother's organization working in ours as well.

"The provinces of Bohemia, Slovakia, and Moravia have been working for independence for some time, and our work becomes especially crucial now that Europe is at war and the German empire threatens to aggrandize in the Austro-Hungarian empire—in the process robbing us of our last hope for an independent republic. Here is our scheme. The BNA, along with several fellow organizations, is working on the side of the Allies in the hope that, should they win the war, they will in turn help us in getting our independence. The best we have to offer the English is in the field of espionage."

"Spies?"

"Over the past few months we've learned of an extremely powerful underground movement by the German espionage service to undermine the Allies in various ways, through this country."

"For example," I said.

He glanced at Frieda, then Mother, before continuing, "Sabotaging shipments of arms from the United States to Britain; stirring up labor strikes; spreading propaganda through the buying of newspapers here in the United States to sway sentiment away from the Allied cause."

"I'm sure the Allies do their share of dirty work, too," I told him. I could see Mother smiling from the corner of my eye. She loved a good debate. "What about the crummy British blockade? Seems to me if the English are cutting off the guns and food on its way to Germany, they'd be pretty desperate to counter somehow. Don't you agree?"

"Let me assure you, miss, we of the BNA branches in the United States consider ourselves first, last, and always American citizens. While we are secretly organizing our forces to help the Allied cause, we will stop short of committing any deed whatsoever that will endanger the position of our country or risk one human life. We are simply in the frightening position of having our families in the fatherland completely at the mercy of German aggrandizement, and only those of us who have had the privilege of freedom are able to help those of us who have not.

"We're like sailors in a ship, throwing life buoys to drowning victims. It is because those of your mother's group work for the cause for equal rights for women that we find ourselves so greatly in sympathy. Freedom has many different faces, but only one meaning in the end."

I recognized his powerful rhetoric, but failed to understand what this had to do with me. "You want me to hand out circulars or something?" I asked.

"No, no. We enlist your help in something far more serious in consequence, demanding absolute secrecy. It is only by virtue of your mother's vocation and your own unique position—as well as what we trust to be your irreproachable morals—that we consider asking your help."

"How?"

"You have recently taken a job in the bank owned by Adolph Heinrich Tetzel?"

"Yes . . ."

"We have information which indicates Tetzel is involved in the underground activity of the German espionage system through the buying of certain newspapers in this area, the purchase of arms for Mexican revolutionaries, the granting of certain loans in Mexico, and the buying and transshipment of copper from Mexican mines. We do not know to what extent he is involved. However, we do know of plans under way for sabotaging munitions factories and blowing up munitions ships in United States harbors destined for Allied countries, and we have strong reason to suspect Tetzel is an active participant."

I sat back. "Well, you're mistaken, that's all. Where did you get those ideas, anyway?"

"We have definite proof regarding several of his associates."

"But none against him."

"Not as yet."

"And you want me to snoop around and look for some? Well, you're asking the wrong person. I won't do it. Besides, I happen to have easy access to his personal papers, and I've never run across anything incriminating in the least."

"Hm . . . I wonder, does he keep a safe in his office?"

I thought for a moment about that implication, then said, "Yes . . . but that doesn't prove anything."

"Have you ever taken a careful look at the interior of that safe? There is likely to be a small inner compartment in the upper left-hand corner, with a special lock."

"No . . . I haven't had any reason to get into that yet, and we've been too busy. I've never really looked, but I'm sure—"

"Do you have the combination to the outer lock?"

"No. I suppose I'll get it when his present secretary leaves."

"Well, then you could check inside for the small compartment."

"Something tells me your activities might be illegal."

"Our organization does nothing more than channel evidence to the proper officials for their perusal, and we are within our rights as long as the United States remains neutral."

I looked at the three faces across from me. It irritated me that they presumed to choose sides on my behalf in a war that meant nothing to me. "You certainly take a risk—how do you know my sympathies might not lie with the Centrals?" I asked.

"My good woman, surely you would not be in favor of either side setting off explosions here in your own country, killing and injuring innocent people.

"Let me hasten to explain that most German people in our country have but one allegiance—to the United States—only a small percentage have loyalties elsewhere. The discovery that Adolph Tetzel may be involved in espionage does not in any way discredit the multitude of naturalized citizens from Germany or the Austro-Hungarian empire.

"Further, we would not have considered imposing upon your personal feelings regarding the war under ordinary circumstances. But in this instance we are facing plots that may well endanger the lives of hundreds of your own innocent countrymen."

"But you only suspect Tetzel—"

"You are correct. Yet, as I explained, we have definite proof regarding several of his close associates, and his name is one of several which are spoken continually in circles of these people. Certainly you would agree it bears some investigation."

I did not like the direction this meeting was taking. He kept dissolving my arguments. I looked across at Mother, whose expression now indicated she was clearly in favor of the BNA's plans for me. Frieda looked as though she were about to add something, then changed her mind. They all stared at me. I felt perspiration rising on my forehead; I despised them for putting me on the spot. Finally I realized there was an all too easy way to get myself out of the predicament. "I'll think about it, and get in touch with you."

Michael Stobalt drew up his shoulders and said, "As you wish. But remember, time is not on our side. I'll be here in the hotel until tomorrow evening, then I must leave town. Please call me as soon as you have made up your mind. If you are interested, we'll arrange a further meeting. If not—"

"I won't call you at all."

From his expression, I think he understood. "All right, but keep in mind, aiding in the freedom of an oppressed people is a rare opportunity, and one which you would never regret. As to citizens of your own country—"*he began, then stopped. He glanced at Mother, then he and Frieda left the room and shut the door behind them. Mother sat looking down, tracing her finger along the piping of the chair arm. I didn't know whether she was ashamed of herself, or of me. I couldn't quite find the words to sum up my exasperation with her for ganging up on me with those people, but I was about to give it a try when she spoke.

Meekly, she said, "You're not going to do it, are you?"

"Of course not. You're expecting me to jeopardize my job for some cause I've never even heard of?"

"I know it's asking a lot, but—"

"How do you know these people are sincere? Surely you couldn't find out much about them in two days."

She shook her head. "I became acquainted with their movement for liberation while working with Emmeline Pankhurst in Europe."

"Oh . . . I see. Is she heading it?"

"No. The Czech Nationalist Leader, Thomas Masaryk, is at the top, and he's a friend of hers."

"Is Stobalt in charge over here?"

"No. A man named Victor Voska heads the movement in this country, but I don't think Stobalt is too far down the line. I really don't know much about their chain of command over here."

"So you're not actually a member."

"No . . . though I did promise my support once I got back over here."

"Did you set me up for all this?"

"No indeed. But when you mentioned Tetzel's name and I passed it on to Frieda Miles—purely by coincidence—she told me of their suspicions about the man and I agreed to let them talk to you. You're in a perfect spot. Stobalt traveled a long way to make his appeal today. I do wish you'd reconsider."

"How do you know they're not a bunch of radicals, like Pankhurst?"

"Emmeline has a clear head, and a lot of wisdom. It's Sylvia, mainly, who is so hard-headed and overdramatic—the head-lines-maker. The people in the BNA are not hotheads like her."

I looked into her eyes for a few moments, then said, "You're still hurt that I didn't follow you into the suffrage movement, aren't you? And that's why—"

"No, that was your decision and I respect it. Believe me, I'm only serving as an intermediary here. Though I must say, knowing it's an important crusade—virtually a life and death situation—I couldn't help feeling proud of you if you'd co-operate. They've assured me they wouldn't expect much from you . . . just a little sleuthing and reporting back what you find."

"You seem to forget you're asking me to pry into the business of a man I like and respect, and who, incidentally, took a chance on my ability. You heard my feelings when Stobalt was here. Mr. Tetzel just wouldn't—"

"I'm not calling Tetzel a blackguard, Camille. But people have loyalties, and they're not always where they ought to be."

"But you don't mind traipsing over my loyalty to Mr. Tetzel."

"Wait a minute. Do you really think the BNA would bother with him if there weren't good reason to believe he's up to something? You heard about the plans for blowing up—"

"But in this case they're wrong."

"How can you be so positive? You really haven't known the man that long, have you?"

I just stared at her. It was like a repeat of our arguments over the suffrage movement so long ago. We just couldn't get through to each other. Finally she said, "Look at it this way. If you prove he isn't guilty of anything, you will have been doing him a service. Now that they're on to him, the BNA will have to find some way—eventually—of investigating him. If not you, then someone else who is in a less accessible position will be chosen. If you're right—and I hope you are, believe me—you have the wherewithal to lay the whole thing to rest."

I spent the balance of the day and part of the night struggling over what Mother said, and in the end decided to trust her judgment. More than anything, it was her final remark which convinced me.

The following morning I met Stobalt again in Mother's room. First I made my position clear. I was willing to help the BNA only as long as it took to exonerate Mr. Tetzel. Then I was finished. Stobalt listened attentively while I spoke, then nodded and briskly began, "Now, what you must do first of all is familiarize yourself with his habits. What time does he go to lunch? What time does he leave his office in the evening? Who are his regular visitors? Telephone calls? See if you can over-hear his conversations, whenever possible. Note how much time he spends alone in his office, with his door closed."

"Shall I look after these little incidentals for a week or so, then dash off a little note to you?"

He shook his head. "One week from tomorrow, you will meet your contact, and work with him from there. If you have nothing to report, he will give you further instructions; if you have, he will advise you accordingly."

Suddenly it all seemed more ominous. "Where will I meet this man? What time? And how will I know him?"

"At one o'clock in the afternoon, on a bench at Alamo Plaza, Menger side. He will approach you. You will know him by this phrase—'There is rain today in Paris.'"

"All right. I'll keep my eyes and ears open next week, but I'll bet you Tetzel comes out looking cleaner than a Golddust twin."

He nodded. He is more certain than he pretends, I thought.

Mother and I had the rest of Sunday together, until her train left at eight o'clock. As soon as Stobalt was out the door, she began bustling about in her usual way, making plans. "We'll visit your father's grave, of course, and I'd like to see your room at the Y and meet your roommate. How about dinner at a really nice restaurant? Honestly, if I see one more roasted chicken half or fruit salad I'll give up conferences for-ever. . . ."

Yet as the day wore on she became more and more subdued,

especially after she stood at the foot of my father's grave. I had been there only once since moving to San Antonio, and, unable to reconcile my memories of him with a small plot of ground marked by a stone with his name, I had not stayed long. Yet Mother lingered, standing perfectly still with arms folded under her bosom, as though her thoughts were somehow communicating themselves to him. Upon his death several years before, she had talked a great deal about what was to be done next. With her stiff-upper-lip attitude she was as much like a soldier as he was. Yet as she stood above his grave that day I realized she must have missed him far more than she ever let on to us kids.

We didn't speak again of the BNA, but as she was about to board the train she said, longingly, "Do take care of yourself, and eat properly . . . and . . . remember to keep your guard up."

"Mother, you sound like I'm about to be thrown to the lions."

She hugged me tight and kissed me, then looked as though she might add something. But the train whistle blew and she scurried down the walk, weighted down yet balanced equally between her proverbial enormous purse, carried by the strap in the one hand, and her bulging portfolio packed in the other. It occurred to me when I stepped away that my remark might have hit a little too close to home.

I made it through most of the next week with growing confidence. I was thoroughly convinced that anyone who spoke so fondly of life in the United States, and particularly anyone who had been able to amass so much in terms of wealth and position in a foreign society, could not possibly be involved in what the BNA people were trying to pin on Tetzel. He had no reason, first of all. He had been here since he was a kid. What could he gain by working with agencies of the government he had fled as a youth? Why risk the loss of everything to help them?

Mr. Tetzel ate lunch in his office, door closed, on Monday

and Tuesday. Both days Claude brought him a sandwich and a cup of coffee. On Wednesday Tetzel went to a regular meeting of San Antonio bankers, which included a luncheon at the St. Anthony's. After he left I wondered if I should have followed him, but by then I was convinced the BNA was all wrong, and counted the days until Sunday so that I could tell them so. On Thursday Tetzel spent much of the day behind closed doors, speaking on the telephone. I could hear little of the conversation because Claude had me working on a file near the front of my office, but whenever I did catch a phrase as he slipped into Tetzel's office or came out, to leave a message or take one, the words seemed to pertain to banking and certainly gave no indication of anything outside the law. Another point was that he had only one phone, which was connected into the bank switchboard. Early it occurred to me that if he were carrying on cloak and dagger activities, surely he would have had a separate phone direct to outside. Arranging for it would have seemed innocuous on the surface—an understandable executive luxury. I made a mental note to tell my contact of my sound rationale.

When I left at six o'clock on Thursday night, Tetzel was still in there. After putting on my coat I stepped up to his door and knocked softly.

"Come in," he answered immediately.

I asked if I could get anything for him before I left.

"Nothing," he said, and smiled. "I was just going to call it a night myself. Can I drive you home?"

"No, thanks. I don't live far from here."

I saw nothing unusual on his desk. There were a lot of papers, but I couldn't make an issue out of glancing down at them, so I could only assume, from his relaxed behavior, that I had not been threatening discovery by coming in when I did.

On the way out I looked up at the windows—his office faced the Navarro Street side of the building. The lights were still on. I was really feeling smug and crafty by then, and spending a lot of time thinking how I'd impress my contact—whoever he was—with my thoroughness in proving there was nothing wrong with Tetzel. I decided to go by a little cafe for some

Mexican food, then double back after I had eaten and look up at the windows, to see if he had left. I pulled my coat collar up around my chin. The winter air was chilly, especially near the river.

An hour later I was back on the spot. I did a double take when I noticed Mr. Tetzel's office lights were still aglow. Too late for the cleaning people to be in there. By seven o'clock they were up on the fourth floor. Half the windows on that floor, Navarro side, were now glowing, proof my timing was correct.

I walked back to the Y, crestfallen. I'd have to mention this to my contact. Yet, what could it mean? He'd been tied up longer than he expected? It was only an hour, for heaven's sake. In a week of absolutely normal routines, what did an hour prove?

I had more nervous energy than usual that evening, and scrubbed floors, then emptied the bookcase along the wall of Cecelia's books, dusted each one, and put them back into place. I repotted a languid ivy and mended a blouse. I was so involved in my own thoughts that I stared at Cecelia dumbly while she repeated twice, "It's almost nine-thirty. Aren't you ever going to bed?"

"I—I just remembered . . . I have to go out for something," I told her, pulling on my coat. I know what nagged at me was Stobalt's certainty. I had a feeling he already knew plenty, before my help was enlisted. And if that were true, I just had to be extra suspicious of anything unusual. Maybe Tetzel did pal around with some unscrupulous characters, not knowing that's the sort they were. Then I would be doing him a favor by clearing his reputation. I walked back to the bank building to check once more. To my relief, all lights were out. I turned to walk back, a smile on my face, when I caught a glimpse of him, crossing a street just a few feet ahead of me. With the streetlights on, there was no mistaking it was him. Should I follow, I wondered? Just fifteen minutes left before curfew at the Y. I didn't have time. He was probably going home anyway, but what if not?

No, I just couldn't risk it. I didn't have any money with me, and could not possibly catch him up, once he'd gotten into his car, without hiring a taxi. This is ridiculous, I thought angrily. Here I am feeling obligated to go chasing after a perfectly decent man, right on the point of spending my own money to rent a taxi I can't afford, all for some organization that means nothing to me. I slipped upstairs and into my room—stubbing my toe on a table because Cecelia had turned the lights off—undressed quickly, and got into bed. Cecelia turned over and said sleepily, "I was worried about you, Camille. It's awfully late for a single girl to be out on the streets. Anything could happen to you."

"Thanks," I told her, and was soon asleep.

By Friday I knew my case wasn't as strong as it had been on Monday, but I was still sure my evidence against Tetzel was minimal. Then around noon I happened to walk in while his safe door was open—Claude was putting something into it—and noticed there was undeniably a separate compartment in the left side. I approached and said, "Oh yes, before you go you'll have to give me that combination. What would happen if you got off to California without telling me? Oh say, how do you get into that little door inside?"

"I don't go into that, and neither will you," he said without turning around. "Mr. Tetzel keeps the key himself."

3

By the end of the week I knew I was bound to get involved
more deeply, because I had learned just enough to cause the
BNA to want more. Sunday was a clear, breezy day with blue
skies and white clouds crossing over like brush strokes. I sat out
on a bench, enjoying the sun's warmth on my face. Within a
couple of minutes I saw a man come from the front door of the
Menger lobby, fold a newspaper under his arm, and cross the
street. Certain to be him, I thought, then was surprised to see
him stroll off toward the post office, passing me by. Just after,
another man approached from behind and sat down on the
bench. His complexion was light and his hands were long and
slender, with prominent veins. His hat brim covered his forehead, so I didn't get a good look at his face or his eyes. Though
he proved to be the man with whom I would have frequent
and intimate meetings, I never did get a good view of his facial
features.

I looked ahead. In a moment he said the code words, in a
clipped dialect. I sighed and said, "All right, mister—what shall
I call you?"

"My code name is Edwin."

"What do you want to know?"

"Everything you have learned this past week."

"Who do you report to?"

"Stobalt."

I still couldn't look at him, but I knew he was smiling at my
thoroughness in checking him out. I reported fully, playing up

the fact that my evidence was very inconclusive, hoping the frailty of what I said would cause him to suggest we part company forever. Instead he nodded slightly, and replied, "Your next step will be to have a look at the general ledgers to see whether any unusually large amounts are being transferred regularly into individual accounts. I'll need a list of the names and addresses of these accounts, along with amounts and dates over the past three months."

"Now see here, maybe Michael Stobalt didn't enlighten you on this, but I don't work with ledgers. I work for Mr. Tetzel directly. I couldn't possibly get my hands on them without arousing suspicion."

"You will display a desire to learn all you can about the running of the bank, in order to be of more help to Tetzel by better understanding your job," he said. I had an uncomfortable feeling Edwin had been reading my thoughts. He continued, "One day, you will ask to be taken to the room where the records are kept, and have a brief lesson from a bookkeeper or whoever is in charge. Then one night, after everyone has gone, you will find a way of getting back into the room to look around."

I was aghast!

"It may take several nights, of course, to get the job done. By the way, have you got to go through the main lobby to get to the other floors?"

"No. There's an employees' entrance, with a separate staircase."

"Is there a night guard?"

"One, but he stays around the main lobby most of the time."

He nodded, and I thought the instructions were over, but I was mistaken.

"Oh, and we will need pictures of Tetzel and all his immediate staff, and as time goes by, anyone who proves to be involved with him in his espionage activity. There's a vest-pocket camera in the package I've brought along here. When I leave, you should pick it up. Instructions are included on how to use it. Of course, if you could find another way to get pictures— maybe you're a Kodak enthusiast—you could easily find excuses to photograph people. They don't have to know your reasons. Usually people love to have their picture taken."

"Anything else?"

"Yes, you must move into a private place. Find an apartment."

"I can't afford an apartment—they're expensive," I protested. At that point I was boiling mad, and talking louder, using my hands. Edwin put a finger to his mouth and folded his arms. I took the hint and said softly, "Do you expect your organization to pay the bills?"

"Unfortunately, we're a poor bunch of amateur spies. We don't have much money. Many of the top people in our outfit are spending from their own private funds. We aren't like our enemies, who have unlimited amounts to spend in this country. I'll try and get some extra cash for you, though, and maybe in a few weeks you could ask for a raise in pay."

"I just got one."

"Prices are going up everywhere. Use that excuse. It's for—"

"I know, a good cause."

"Is there any way you could get access to that little compartment in Tetzel's safe—maybe you could search his suit coat for a key, or his desk—"

"Look, I always considered myself brave, even reckless at times. But do you realize you are endangering my job if I get caught? Do you know what kind of position you are putting me in?"

"Keep in mind that what you are doing might ultimately save not only the jobs, but the lives, of many innocent people. And if you act discreetly, no one will have reason to suspect you're up to anything."

"At least tell me what you expect me to find in his safe, and in those confounded bank ledgers."

"He may have some vouchers or invoices for the sale of arms or metals in his safe. As for the ledgers—just have a look and give me the information. I can instruct you from there."

"Well he certainly wouldn't be stupid enough to carry on that kind of business through the records of the bank."

"We have certain evidence ammunition is being sold to Francisco Villa, as it has been sold to Victoriana Huerta in the past. We want to find out whether any of these sales are channeled through Tetzel's bank, via other parties. Nothing would be shown on the bank's registers except amounts of money. From the list of names you get, we can check out the sources."

I let out a long breath. "I'll do it, but you have to get me more money."

"I'll work on that. Meantime, if you could also be put in charge of carrying outgoing mail—you might find an apartment with the post office between it and the bank, so you could feasibly suggest taking on the job of dropping it off—except that you also have to be in charge of posting it.

"You would slip it out unposted, steam open the envelopes, and take what is important to Sam's Print Shop at the address I have written down inside the package. Ask for Sam and tell him the papers are for Edwin. He'll duplicate them for you on a machine in the back."

"What if he isn't there?"

"Usually he is, and after the print shop closes at six o'clock, you can knock on the back door. Normally he stays pretty late. But don't let anyone else handle the papers.

"After you have that done, reseal the envelopes, stamp and mail them. You must not unseal the envelopes once they've been posted."

"Why not?"

"That's a federal offense."

"Oh . . . I'm not sure I wouldn't rather run that risk than to do all these things you have planned for me. Besides, I doubt I can manage the mail. The International Bank is big. It has a huge mail room, and mullets—runners—take care of the mail."

"I speak only of Tetzel's private mail. You might offer to take what there is at the end of the day, rather than have it wait till the morning. You are in the position to capitalize on your youth and enthusiasm for your new job. That can be your excuse for all the extras you do."

"Up to now all my enthusiasm has been genuine. . . . Where and when do we meet again?"

"I've written down a telephone number where I can be reached between six at night and eight in the morning. Call me when you have something and we'll arrange a meeting."

"*If* I have something."

"Sure. And thanks, Camille."

When he was gone I sat awhile longer, wondering why in the world I let myself get mixed up in this and wishing my mother had not chosen to come to San Antonio when she did. Most of all, I wished Edwin had not said "thanks."

During lunch hours all the following week I looked for an apartment which met the specifications, though the closest I could find, considering my small salary, was hardly more than a room. Located on Houston at River Avenue, the apartment building was at least fifteen years old. It was not between the post office and the bank, but close enough so that I could reasonably offer to drop off the mail on my way home.

The place was not fancy by any standard, and right away I knew I was going to miss the indoor swimming pool and gymnasium at the Y. However, it did have several redeeming features, which the manager was careful to point out. "This unit was painted last summer," he said, taking in the main room, tiny private bath, and kitchenette of which it consisted in one sweep of his hand. "Formerly this whole floor was rented by one family of high means, and for that reason a kitchen was built at the other end, and this little kitchenette was added for the maid. You're lucky. These rooms are on the corner, so that you have a view of Houston and River Avenue both, and two balconies.

"There's a laundry room and storage space in the basement, and you're within a block of a small grocery store with a bakery and a good meat counter, back on River Avenue."

"But you see, I have no furniture."

"That's no problem, miss. I can have some brought down from a vacant apartment up on the fifth floor. Small bed, chair, couple of tables and lamps. One dollar extra a month. How about it?"

I gave notice at the Y and moved in by the end of the following week. My renting a private place seemed to shock Cecelia, but she soon recovered and picked a roommate who shared her tastes in leisure activities. When I loaded the last of my possessions and started out, she looked over the top of her book and said, "You ought to be careful. The streets aren't safe for women nowadays, remember."

"That's the least of my worries," I said.

When I was about halfway down the hall she suddenly hurried toward me with our sickly-looking ivy plant. "Take this as a going-away present," she said. "It never grew very well in our room—probably not enough light. You could put it out on one of your balconies, but don't let it freeze."

I thanked her, and as I had no extra hand in which to carry it, she put it in the crook of my elbow and said, "Well, good luck now," and hurried away. Thanks a lot, I thought. What I needed was a sick ivy plant.

The furniture promised by the manager was waiting inside the rooms, and when I put everything down and sat on the edge of the little iron bed, I suddenly had an overflowing feeling of satisfaction. This was the closest thing to a place of my own I had ever had, where I would be the one to say when I'd come and go, and whether or not to fix a meal or leave a lamp burning late at night. I was possessed of a strong urge to bounce up and down on the bed, but then remembered it did not belong to me, so I got busy scrubbing and putting my things away in the chest provided by the manager and the small closet next to the bath.

I could get a bright-colored spread for the bed and some pictures for the walls, I thought. When I watered the ivy and set it out on the River Avenue balcony in the sunshine, I noticed the grocery store across the street and down the block. Butler Grocer Co. It reminded me I hadn't stopped to eat all day and it was nearly three o'clock. I decided to walk down and buy a few things for the pantry. As I descended the steps in the apartment hall, my spirits went in just the other direction. If one good thing came out of this whole spy mess, it was having my own apartment. True, it had no river view, but it was mine, and I was truly on my own at last. I went humming into the grocery store, past the pickle and cracker barrels near the door; I picked up a loaf of bread, a tin of George Washington Coffee —having no coffeepot, I'd have to make mine in a cup—a pound of butter, a wedge of American cheese, a can of Gebhardt's Chili with rice, a box of chocolates, and some grape juice. I didn't know how to cook so I skipped the meat counter and the produce section. Then I saw someone opening the pickle barrel, and made a quick detour to dip down and get a big juicy one for myself.

The young fellow who tallied my bill and boxed my groceries was tall and muscular with not quite but almost blond closely cropped hair. He had a strong, prominent jaw and a serious expression across his otherwise pleasant face. He put all the things carefully into the box, then looked across at me with eyes that were an almost startling shade of ocean blue. "We have green beans on special today—five cents a pound—and carrots a penny a bunch."

"Thanks, I don't need any."

"Do you need meat? Got some good beef for pot roast."

"I don't cook much."

"Can I carry these to your car, or deliver them?"

"I'm walking, but thanks anyway," I told him and picked up the box.

"If you live nearby, I could walk you home and carry these."

"Is that part of the service?"

"No, but I could get away for a few minutes."

"All right."

Out on the street he introduced himself as Keith Butler. His father had been in business on that corner for twenty years. He had an older brother, Kenneth, who'd become a dentist, and Keith went to college part-time and helped at the store. His father was the butcher, his mother ran the bakery and kept the books, and two other employees, with Keith's help, took care of just about everything else. From his description, they sounded like a wholesome, respectable group. We discovered we'd gone to the same high school, but he was two years ahead of me and we had never met.

"You live with your folks?" he asked when we got to the apartments.

"No, I'm strictly on my own."

From his expression I wasn't sure if he was shocked or impressed. He offered to carry the groceries up, but I told him not to bother and thanked him for his help.

"You'll come by again, won't you?" he asked. "Mother's been baking special breads and pastries for a party we're catering tonight, but usually on Saturdays she makes butter streusel kuchen—the best in town."

"Are you German?"

"No, why?"

"Just wondered. Well, good-bye."

This unexpected meeting of someone so nice, whose life seemed a sort of sturdy fabric of uninterrupted threads, kept my sunny mood intact for the balance of the weekend, until Monday morning arrived and I was forced to realize again that I was faced with insurmountable tasks.

The morning was bitter cold, and rainy. As I walked to work under my umbrella I was passed by automobiles inching slowly along behind glowing headlights. When I reached the corner of Navarro and Houston, Mr. Tetzel pulled over to the curb and offered me a ride. He'd been so nice to me. I still felt guilty about spying on him that night he worked so late, and had purposely put off doing anything further for the BNA because I didn't want to find out anything bad about him. For the short distance to the office that morning, he proved interested in hearing about my new apartment and how I liked it, and said if I needed some extra time to get settled in I could leave a little early.

"Claude will be in the bank's employ until the end of the month. Surely he can stay at least one full day, between now and then," he said, then winked.

I laughed and told him no thanks. It was now a common joke around the bank that Claude was leaving a little earlier every day, but he was sure that Mr. Tetzel was too busy to notice. He let me out right at the entrance and drove on to his parking space, and as I closed the door I felt determined more than ever to get this nasty business of spying out of the way and prove, once and for all, that he was not guilty of taking sides in the European war. Once I had done that, I would certainly have proven by all my willingness to help out in extra ways that I was the sort of secretary any man would be grateful for, and he would wind up prizing me in the end. It was like having a nagging toothache. One painful extraction, and things would be fine again. . . .

The first matter was getting to the general ledgers. While filling Tetzel's inkwell that morning I told Claude, "You've taught me just about everything about this office, but I know little about how the bank works. Don't you think I would benefit by having a look at each department while you're still around? I'd feel like I know at least a little more about what's going on."

He shrugged, and shot me a petulant glance that I suspected he had been saving for a long time. "There's really no reason to start getting into people's hair for a while—"

Just then Mr. Tetzel came through the door and cut him short. "On the contrary, if Camille is that interested I see no need to waste time. She's already caught on to the work in here. But since you're too busy to familiarize her with our procedures, I'm sure we can find someone who can spare the time. Get Giddeon Sparks down here. She knows more about how this bank is run than anyone else."

After he walked out, Claude slammed a file drawer shut and picked up the phone, without looking at me.

I'd seen Giddeon—whom everyone called Giddy—around the bank before, though we had never met. She was a widow, and had been with the bank since her husband died ten years before. She always wore dark skirts and white ruffly blouses on her stocky frame. She had a chubby face, kinky hair, and wore a pair of spectacles on the edge of her pug nose. Giddy looked like somebody's grandmother, though she'd never had any children. She had the vocabulary of a sailor and an infectious laugh. She was merry and fun. I adored her right off.

Before we left on a tour of the bank, Mr. Tetzel told me she was the assistant auditor, and a "most valued employee." On the way down the hall I asked how a person worked up to such an important position.

"Aside from knowing how to keep a general ledger and understanding bookkeeping, you've got to have excellent penmanship," she said.

"That leaves me out. Say, what sort of information goes into the general ledger, anyhow?"

"All deposits, withdrawals, transfers, loans—virtually everything, including a financial standing of the bank itself. It is the key to the whole operation, and has to be balanced to the penny each night."

"Sounds like a tall order."

"That's why the auditor has an assistant. I've always done most of the work, while my boss sits around in meetings. Lately I've had a bookkeeper helping me. But even when the boss retires a few years from now, I won't have a prayer for taking his title or salary. Personnel will move a man in to fill the job and hold me back, because I wear a skirt instead of trousers."

"But that isn't fair. Mr. Tetzel doesn't seem—"

"I know, honey, but that's how it is. The personnel department is like a fortress. It takes a good deal of conniving to get past them to Mr. Tetzel's ear. He's a big advocate of line-of-authority. Around a bank, women are treated second-class, or haven't you noticed? No, I guess not. You're in a unique position."

"I get unspoken messages from Claude, though. I think he's insulted at being replaced by someone as young as me, aside from my being a female. I just ignore him."

"You've got plenty of fight. That's good. I never give up either. I keep hoping someday my capabilities will be appreciated. . . ."

We began on the main banking floor with the four tellers' cages, and I soon found Giddy had access to every corner of the bank because of her job function. She tapped twice, then paused and tapped once again on the door of the head teller's cage. In a moment I heard a lock turn, and the door opened.

The teller explained that once he'd opened his money in the morning, he locked his door and stayed in there until he closed his pouch and left. "I understand you have to balance every night," I told him.

"I once spent Christmas in this cage."

When we left Giddy said, "From here a mullet picks up the checks and deposits, and sends them upstairs in a basket. Transit is up on the fifth floor. Mullets also send checks to the clearing house, and take bad checks to the merchants who issued them. They hand deliver statements to some of the customers who work in the downtown area.

"Now, on the day a check is written it goes to the credit department for posting. A pair of bookkeepers work together on this. We have a double entry system. They're also in charge of checking signatures, dates, and stop-payment orders. If they ever pay a check that's supposed to have been stopped, it's automatic dismissal.

"We'll go there after I show you the bank vault and safe-deposit boxes."

We also stopped by the trust and collection departments along the way, and I began to understand why the bank occupied all five floors of the building. Still, I couldn't make out where to find information on loans, and was afraid to ask for fear of being obvious.

The credit department proved the answer, located next to Giddy's office on the second floor. "A loan committee passes on every loan in the bank, no matter the size, unless Tetzel himself gives the go-ahead. You see the reports daily on his desk. Information on loans goes back five years in this department, and there's a credit file on everyone, with an individual financial history. If Mr. Tetzel ever calls for a file on someone—or if you ever need one—you can phone down and order it for him."

I thought of the implications of that, then realized as quickly I could hardly ask for files by the load without becoming suspect. And from the number of filing cabinets in that department, I would have plenty to go through. Giddy was continuing, "Of course, most of the time Mr. Tetzel just calls me and I bring them for him."

"He depends upon you so much, I almost wonder he didn't ask you to become his secretary," I said.

"I'm a whiz with pen and ink, but I can't type my name, and I don't take shorthand either. Now I think we've covered about all the departments except for the storage basement. I'll let you have a peek at my ledgers, but I won't have much time to show you how they're done today. My little 'assistant' is ill and I've got her posting to do along with my own."

She showed me the big bound records, and I could instantly see what she meant about good handwriting. The script—I could denote three different hands—was as beautiful as fancy printing. I noticed a safe in her office like the one in Tetzel's and remarked on this. "Oh, nearly all the departments have safes. We have to keep everything under lock and key—even the department doors. If we have a check or any other customer document overnight, it has to be locked up. That's bank policy."

As I was leaving Giddy in her office, over an hour later, she said, "Oh, and a couple of incidentals that you may or may not learn from experience. We've got some cheeky mullets around here. If they ever try getting fresh with you, just report them. Those guys are even more dispensable than women employees.

"And another thing—watch your personal telephone calls. Minerva, the switchboard operator in the main lobby, will snitch on you. She's an old gossip, and she thinks she's important because she once blew the whistle on an employee who was embezzling, just by some calls he made."

"Thanks for the information . . . I'll be sure to remember."

Walking back up the stairs, I thought if ever there seemed an airtight operation, this was it. Clearly banks were on the watch for dishonest people . . . it only stood to reason. . . .

As for the nosy switchboard operator, Tetzel certainly could not carry on illicit conversations with her around . . . unless she were involved along with him.

4

When I phoned Edwin that night to explain the predicament, he asked, "Does Tetzel keep a master set of keys?"

"Not that I've been told about."

"If so, see if you can slip them out one day and have a duplicate set made. If not, you'll have to take it one department at a time. Try and sneak them out at lunchtime and take them to a locksmith. There's one farther up on Navarro, just past Market. Then stick around one night and do some browsing."

"You make it sound so easy."

"Don't worry. Just be careful. Good luck." He hung up.

Oh, I have to do better, I thought nervously. I should have had the sense to be more nosy when I had the chance. Next morning while Mr. Tetzel was in a meeting, I told Claude I was going to the credit department to observe. "I'll probably spend some time looking over Giddy's shoulder, too, while I'm down that way," I added.

My greatest fear was that Giddy carried her keys in her pocket, and some member of the credit group did likewise. As it turned out, however, I noticed a group of keys in Giddy's drawer while she was busy on the phone. I watched clerks posting into the ledgers all morning, then left around eleven-thirty. When I returned at noon, I was disappointed to find Giddy at work at her desk. "Oh, I've lost my notebook," I said quickly. "I thought I might have left it down here."

She looked around. "I haven't seen it. Check next door in credit."

It was tantalizing to be so near a desk in an empty room, but with Giddy so close by I didn't dare open a drawer to look for keys. On the way out I noticed she was eating lunch. "Staying in today?" I asked.

"Got some catching up to do. Find your book?"

"What? Oh, my book, no. I guess I've put it somewhere in my office. See you later."

I wouldn't have believed such a casual encounter could have set my pulse beating so rapidly, and I thought as I walked back up the stairs, how am I going to hold together through this whole mess?

Overnight I made up a list of questions to get me back down to credit the following morning. My bookkeeping course in business school covered most of the answers, but if anyone seemed surprised at my ignorance I could always use the excuse that I needed some brushing up. In fact the four people comprising the department seemed pleased at my interest, and I got the feeling for the first time that this contact was winning people over. I sensed I'd been looked upon as an interloper from the start. There had been much resentment among the ranks. This was helping to overcome the barriers. I was continually struck by the fact that my work for the BNA, as long as Tetzel came out clean, would actually be to my advantage at the bank. If not, well . . . I'd just have to worry about that when the time came. . . .

Luck was with me that day. Giddy had gone to a meeting and taken her helper along, and they weren't expected back until late in the afternoon. At the first opportunity, I made the excuse of using the telephone at Giddy's empty desk, and at the same time slip her keys into my pocket. On the way to the locksmith I found with relief each key was clearly marked, and the bunch included those of the credit department locks as well. I rushed back before the lunch hour was over, and slipped the original keys back into the drawer.

I picked the night of Friday, December 18, to stay in and do my looking. The Tetzels were headed for a big Christmas ball at the Casino Club that evening, and from talk around the bank I learned there were many parties planned. Probably just about everybody would be in a rush to get out early. With luck, I could wait out anyone staying late to balance.

I was nervous all day, and kept watching the clock. For the previous week I'd made a big project of pulling out files for an end-of-the-year cleanup so that I'd have an excuse to work overtime and get caught up. Mr. Tetzel dictated six letters in the afternoon, which he said could be typed on Monday, then he mentioned, "I'll be going to Europe after the first of the year for several weeks. You needn't trouble with having everything caught up by Christmas. You'll have plenty of time for that while I'm away."

"Oh, but I just can't relax when I have so much in front of me. I think I'll stay late tonight and get some work done, then I can finish up tomorrow morning."

"Just as you wish."

After I closed his door behind me I realized if he was going away that quickly, the sooner I'd have to get into that compartment in his safe, or it might be months before I'd have another chance to borrow the keys from his coat pocket. Then I relaxed a bit. I'd duplicate the key, then plunder the safe while he was in Europe. But what if there were important papers in there that he would take away with him, maybe forever? It was clear, I'd have to get at the contents before he left. I drew in a breath and walked to the typewriter.

Edwin had been wise enough to provide me with a battery-powered light in the package he brought along to our first meeting. Otherwise I probably would have gotten into the darkened room and realized I couldn't see the files. It was very hard for me to carry on this kind of intrigue. I'd always been known for my openness and candor with people, sometimes to the embarrassment of myself and others, nonetheless.

By five-thirty everyone on our floor seemed to have gone.

I left my desk and took a stroll down to the second floor, passing by the credit department and Giddy's office. The cleaning people were in there. All right. Back to my typewriter for half an hour, to give them time to finish. By then I was so nervous I was making ghastly typographical errors on the letters. Mr. Tetzel must never see them in that condition. I pulled out sheaves of paper and started over time and again. When next I looked up it was six-thirty. I rushed down to the floor below, looked both ways, unlocked the door to Giddy's office, and walked in.

It was eerie in that little room. Lights from outside the windows cast long shadows on the walls and silhouetted me as I walked across the floor, bent almost double because it seemed safer. Within a few minutes I was working through the volumes of the general ledger for names attached to large transfers. I covered three months' business quickly through the expert penmanship, then flashed my light upon the wall clock. Quarter till eight. I had nine firm names noted on my pad: Abel, Dixon, Faultless, Flowers, Gregory, Ismell, Mellyn, Stockton, Stuttgart. Truthfully, none of them looked very portentous. About eight, just as I was finishing on the Abel credit file, I heard the cleaning crew coming back down the hall. I almost had heart failure on the spot. I turned off my light and crouched between a window and a filing cabinet as the shuffle of feet and the sound of voices grew louder. Yet they passed without opening the door and continued toward the front stairs, on their way to the lobby floor. I went back to work.

By nine forty-five I was finished. I felt my information amounted to little more than proof for Edwin that I had tried. He could use the full names of the owners, their business addresses, and the amounts of money loaned as he saw fit. When I rose from my position on the floor, I ached from head to toe. I closed the cabinet softly, pocketed the keys, and left cautiously. Downstairs I passed by the night guard, Hector Bolt. He was a kindly old white-haired man, always cheery and personable. "Get caught up, Miss Devera? Just in time for a party, too. Good night."

Party, my foot. All I wanted was a good hot bath, some food, and my bed. There was a frantic moment when I thought I'd left my list lying on the floor, but a nudge of my fingers inside my handbag dispelled that worry, thankfully. Much relieved the business was over, I walked hurriedly home.

In my mail was a letter from Mother. "The whole year of 1914 will go down as one of great progress for us," she wrote.

"However, it only gives us time to take a breath of comfort before 1915 dawns and more work lies ahead." Her thoughts might have been echoes of my own.

She signed her letter "with love." She signed most of her letters to others "yours in v. for w."—vote for women—and each time she wrote me I was compelled to glance at the line over her signature first, to be sure it referred to her feelings for me, rather than the cause uppermost in her mind.

There was also a note, slipped under my door, from Keith Butler. I had seen him several times at the store, but had not really gotten to know him any better because he was busy with exams at school and I was busy in my own more and more complex activities, which I couldn't discuss anyway. He wanted to come by on Saturday evening and take me to a dinner at his brother's house. The note was written at 3:15 P.M.

I walked out on the balcony and looked down at the dark store below. Too late now. About that time there was a knock on the door. I glanced quickly toward my handbag, where the list was hidden, then asked who was there. It was Keith.

I opened the door. "I just got this note—I'm sorry, I had to work late."

"I've been worried silly. I came by at seven, then at eight, then at nine."

"Well, come in. You needn't be an old mother hen. I might have had an engagement tonight."

"I thought of that, but I also kept thinking about your living alone. It seems risky, somehow."

"Why?"

"Young women—nice ones—just don't live alone."

I laughed. "And how do you know I'm a nice young woman?"

"I can tell, that's all. I'll bet you haven't eaten, either."

"I was just about to have a sandwich. Would you care to join me?"

"No, thanks. I can tell by what you buy at the store that you don't eat well."

"You're worse than my mother."

"Look, come along tomorrow night, won't you? It'll be fun—family, mostly, and a few friends."

"I'd love to, but I don't know if I have anything to wear. I haven't had time to—"

"It doesn't matter. I'll call for you at half-past seven. My brother's wife, Christie, can cook out of this world, so be sure to come hungry."

"You can count on that."

He hesitated a moment. "You look awfully tired."

"It's been an . . . eventful . . . day."

"Be sure to lock the door behind me. You never know."

I did as he said, then leaned against it, suppressing a laugh. I had never been so tired, and was hard put to recall the person I'd been a few weeks ago, so full of energy at night I'd scrub everything short of my roommate.

I hope this is the end of it, I thought.

5

Keith's family proved to be a fun-loving lot. Ken and Christie had four children ranging from two to five, boy, girl, boy, girl in order of age. They seemed to be everywhere that evening, crawling around like little mice, in and out of their grand-parents' laps, tugging on Christie's skirt and Ken's trouser legs. When Christie asked about my family, I told her I couldn't help thinking our house must have been something like theirs when I was a kid. "The total disorder drives Ken crazy, but it doesn't bother me," she said amiably. "Ken's mother thinks we ought to have regular help, but a cleaning lady twice a week suits me fine. I like being around my children. When I was growing up we spent most of our time stranded upstairs while my parents had parties downstairs—very strait-laced, you know. Here, cut this apple crisp into squares, will you?" She had blond hair, green eyes that crinkled at the edges when she smiled, and freckles across her nose. She wasn't bothered at all by interruptions from the girls, who wanted first drinks of water, then cookies to eat.

"My brothers were all older—the youngest one four years my senior—and I was never really very close to them. It's nice your children are so near to each other in age."

"Yes. The Lord willing, we won't get blessed with another one at this point. Keith and Ken get along well enough, though their interests are very different. And I worry sometimes that Ken overshadows Keith, being the first son."

It occurred to me she was probably right. When we arrived,

Ken, who looked much like Keith although he was a bit smaller and two years older, had remarked on how well "the" suit (a hand-me-down) looked on Keith. Keith seemed embarrassed. The coat was a little too narrow around the shoulders and the sleeve length just about half an inch short. Mr. Butler had remarked, "It's lucky Ken takes good care of his clothes. There won't be much extra money for Keith's wardrobe till he finishes school."

"Right, Pa," Keith answered, then changed the subject abruptly.

I enjoyed the evening and seemed to fit in comfortably. Keith didn't have an automobile, so we rode to and from the dinner party with his parents. On the way home he seemed pensive and less talkative than usual. When he walked me upstairs I asked if something was wrong.

"Oh, nothing," he told me, and asked what I'd be doing on Sunday.

"I have to meet a—uh, I have a sort of appointment."

"Of course. Well, thanks for coming tonight. See you at the store."

I couldn't believe how easily I'd almost slipped and told him I had to meet Edwin. That was the trouble with living a double life, I was soon to find. Oftentimes what you said was entirely misinterpreted and you couldn't elaborate to clear things up. Keith would just have to assume I had another fellow calling. It didn't matter anyhow. He was only a friend, and that was just as well. Until the situation with Mr. Tetzel was cleared up I'd have to watch about getting too involved with friends of either sex. Even if I did find nothing in his life to incriminate Tetzel, I might one day make the mistake of disclosing the work of the BNA, and I did not want to do that.

I met Edwin near the front of Brackenridge Park on Sunday at two o'clock. I'd taken a trolley close to the church, and arrived early, so I walked around for a while. When we lived in San Antonio before, this place had been among my favorites. My dad took us on Sunday buggy rides along the paths, the big trees on either side forming a moss-laden arbor across them. I could still remember looking up through the trees as we rode along, following the sun till it became hidden by the heavy branches, then waiting for it to appear again in a clearing. Somehow the park seemed an endless labyrinth of trees then, unbothered and hushed. Now, though its boundaries still outlined acres and acres on the north side of the city, it seemed smaller.

Certainly there were more people around, even if it was the wrong time of year for picnics and outings. I couldn't hear the sound of rippling springs as I used to, and was unsure which direction they'd be coming from. I sat down on a bench and waited for Edwin. Soon he appeared—seemingly out of nowhere—and I told him I had the list. He nodded and put a doubled newspaper between us, then motioned for me to place the list on top of it. When I had, he folded the paper once again, and shifted on the bench. I found it amusing. Surely no one could possibly be watching. . . .

"I don't think it's anything important," I said, staring ahead.

"We have to check out everything. Were you able to get into that safe compartment?"

"Not so fast. These things take time. I did find an apartment."

"Good. What's the address?"

After telling him I paused for a moment or two, to give him an opportunity to bring up the money situation, but of course he didn't. Finally I said, "How about a little cash? I'm barely making it, and this is a cheap apartment."

"I can't get anything for you now, but I'm working on it. Get in touch as soon as you've seen the inside of that safe."

"Oh, there was one thing. Mr. Tetzel plans a trip to Europe early in January. I have no idea where he is going, or who he is going to see. It's probably banking business. His former secretary made the arrangements."

"That's very interesting. Ask him if he made an itinerary."

"All right. He's leaving in a week."

"Get right on it, then."

"You know you really make me mad, being so pushy. Remember, I'm not a professional agent, and I'm not getting paid for this."

"Neither am I," he said. "We'll be in touch," he added, then walked off, the newspaper under his arm.

I didn't know whether to be frightened or comforted by his remark. Were they all a bunch of greenhorns? If so, their organization might bumble itself right into oblivion. Espionage was serious work. Spies got killed. Oh heavens, I thought, I wish I could get that list back and call off the deal before I get in too deeply. But Edwin had vanished. He was very apt at doing that.

That night I thought further about the seriousness of what I had done so far. Should that list get into the wrong hands, I could say good-bye to my job. Should Tetzel indeed be involved in anything against the law, supposing my contact were a counterspy actually working for him? I'd never seen any proof Edwin was connected with Michael Stobalt. Neither had I seen Michael Stobalt again. What if Edwin had murdered Stobalt?

Stupid.

Still, not impossible. Didn't I have a right to know before I got into this any further? Tomorrow I was going to have to go another step, actually invading private property. Should I be pressing my luck too far, and get caught with the key to that safe compartment, there was no telling what the ramifications might prove to be. I punched a fist into my pillow and turned over. Why should I be losing sleep over this, I wondered? I got dressed and went downstairs to a phone. Edwin's line rang only once.

"Listen, you're getting me into some risky business. I want some sort of proof you're connected with Stobalt before I go any further."

There was a long pause. "I'm sorry, but I can't get any. Stobalt doesn't live in San Antonio, and anything written down is too risky for us. You'll have to trust us, that's all. We're not well organized yet, and we're scattered pretty thin—"

"What about my list? Can I get it back?"

"I've already turned it in for investigation."

"To the police?" I asked in horror.

"No, to another group within our outfit."

"Did you give them the original?"

"Yes. We don't risk copies except when something has to be returned without being noticed."

I just stood there. I could think of nothing else to say that would sum up my frustration. Finally Edwin said, "Listen, do you think if we were in the business of professional espionage, we'd run the risk of using someone like you, with no experience?"

He did have a point there.

"If you're hard up for money, maybe I can spare ten or fifteen bucks out of my pocket."

"Never mind," I told him, and hung up. I was already realizing that if Edwin were not sincere, he probably would have tried to charm me or otherwise lure me on. His stark candor impressed me. If his organization were really on to something involving Tetzel and I proved an obstacle, I might be the instrument of failure for a good cause. I'd learned enough in history to know of the oppression felt by some of the countries and provinces—especially the small ones—in Europe. It was the very reason so many people came to this country prior to the War Between the States, and after. My father knew lots of immigrants who served with him in the Army, and thought very highly of those he spoke of. He'd probably be proud of me for trying to help the BNA. Yet I still did not believe Tetzel capable of doing what they suspected, especially if his activities involved hurting innocent people over here. This country had offered him the chance of bettering himself . . . he'd made that clear the day I was interviewed for the job of his secretary. Why turn against it?

On Monday morning I set about getting into his secret compartment. It was to prove twice as hard as the task in the credit department, because he carried the key in his inside suitcoat pocket, and very often wore his coat all day, unless the office became stuffy. I was lucky enough to know the whereabouts of the key in the first place, and only just happened to learn this one day as he slipped it there after closing his safe.

Monday and Tuesday passed without luck. They were rainy, chilly days during which even I wore a shawl around my shoulders throughout the day. Finally on Wednesday the weather warmed up, the sun came out, and in the afternoon the heating system proved to be a little stifling. I walked through and remarked on how hot the office was getting.

"They need to adjust the heat," said Mr. Tetzel, and within a few minutes he'd taken off his coat and hung it on the rack behind his office door. I will never forget how spunky I felt that day, as I went around gathering opportunities with the same outward detachment as someone gathering eggs from a hen house. Tetzel had a meeting at three o'clock in a conference room down the hall. He started to reach for his coat, then, as I held my breath, decided against it. He straightened his tie, pulled at the hem of his vest, and walked out. "I'll be back in an hour," he said.

I walked into his office, laid some papers on his desk, checked his outgoing box and left, stopping quickly to reach into the coat pocket and find the key. Once my hand was on it, however, I didn't feel so spunky. I hurried past Claude, telling him I just remembered my watch had to be put into the shop for repairs before closing time, dashed downstairs and up the block toward the locksmith as fast as my legs would carry me and the traffic would permit. When I returned with the duplicate key, Mr. Tetzel was still gone, and even Claude had stepped out. I slipped the original back into its place and sat down at my desk, with a sigh of relief.

That night I made no excuses about working late. I just took my things as though I were bound for home and hid in the ladies' room till everyone was gone. Two days before Christmas, few employees were apt to be staying around late, and besides that I had lucked into a job wrapping packages for the week at Joske's, and had to report to work at seven o'clock every night through Christmas Eve.

I was left with less than an hour to get into the safe, reach a phone and contact Edwin if I found anything, and get to Joske's on Alamo Plaza. At six-fifteen all was quiet. I crept down the hall. Within three or four minutes I was inside Tetzel's office, fidgeting with the combination lock. Once it clicked into place I felt a little better, and rammed the key against the secret compartment lock, then forced it in and opened the door. The compartment was a deep rectangle, and I was pleasantly surprised as I pushed my forearm toward the back that it was almost completely unoccupied.

First I pulled out a small oval-shaped photograph in a fancy silver frame. It was very old, reminding me of some of my father's photographs taken around the time of the War Between the States. I focused the light on the face of a pretty young woman, her mouth turned in a fetching smile, a bonnet on her head. Tetzel's mother? No, his wife more likely. I paused for a moment then, feeling disgusted for this invasion of Mr. Tetzel's private life. It was like going through his under clothing in a chest of drawers.

I replaced the photo then, and pulled out a roll of papers tied with a string. Once I'd flattened them out it was easy enough to tell they were exactly what I'd hoped never to find: a group of invoices from several hardware companies located in a town in the Midwest. Tallied up, they amounted to thousands of dollars in rifles and ammunition. One common denominator among them was the consignment order: R. M. Gutierrez, Inc., Laredo, Texas.

I sat back on my heels. One fact was certain: there was no going back for me now. I rolled up the papers and put them into my bag, closed the safe, and made for the nearest telephone outside the building.

It was six forty-five by the time I reached a phone in a little cafe near Joske's. My heart beating triple time, I was standing on one foot then the other, looking anxiously about, waiting for Edwin to answer his line. When I told him what I had, my voice a few decibels higher than usual, he said, "Don't panic, Camille. I'll meet you at seven o'clock on the Commerce Street bridge. I can have the invoices duplicated and back to you by morning."

"But I have to be at Joske's by seven."

"All right. Give me five minutes. Have you got on an overcoat? . . . Good. Put the papers in your right-hand pocket."

"Hurry!"

True to his word, he was there by five of seven. The air was so chilly off the river I should have been freezing to death, yet I was hot from the inside, even while my teeth clattered and my breath made little clouds on the air. Edwin approached from behind, and I felt his hand slip into the coat pocket and out again. Then he stood there beside me for a few moments, both of us staring at the river below. "You're doing great."

"Oh, this is horrible!"

"Don't take it so personal."

"I can't help it."

"Go to work now, and I'll slip these into an envelope under your apartment door by seven in the morning. Can you beat Tetzel to the office and replace them?"

"I think so." The words came from the back of my mouth as though there were a gag around my neck. "There's no denying it now, is there?"

"Probably not. But we still don't know to what extent Tetzel's working. I'll get back with you as soon as I know something. Till then just try to stay calm and get that itinerary."

"I have it. He'll be in Germany, then up into Scandinavian countries."

"Anything more detailed?"

"No. That was all Claude knew."

"All right. Maybe we can get something from the other end. Get to work. And thanks."

"Sure."

There were crowds of people in the store that night, and I received a few snide glances by the other women on duty wrapping packages when I walked in, plus a definite look of disapproval from my supervisor. I was only five minutes late, but you would have thought it was an hour, and from the way the people were lined up I could understand the irritation I had caused. Without a word I went to wrapping. One woman kept looking at her watch as she handed over box after box, then I heard her remark to a companion as she walked away, "You don't find decent shop girls anymore. Look how long it took to get this done."

I was tempted to shout back she ought to have read the notices in the paper that suggested people shop early, but was saved from the outburst when a man placed a full-sized child's rocking horse on the counter in front of me.

I worked till ten-thirty, and went home exhausted. I was not sure the effort was worth the few extra dollars, but then there was only one night left before Christmas, so I supposed I'd make it. My own apartment was depressing after I'd passed by all the street decorations and colorful shop-window displays. I hadn't even had time to trim a tree, and it didn't look as though I would.

Suddenly I dreaded the thought of Christmas, and this year a long weekend followed because it fell on Friday and we'd be off on Saturday. Mother had to be in Washington in advance of the House vote on a constitutional amendment on national suffrage, so she wouldn't be in town with me for Christmas. My brothers all lived too far away to pay them a visit.

Now all my dreams seemed to be falling apart. I hadn't realized before just how much I had counted on Mr. Tetzel being innocent of any crimes against humanity. The war in Europe had never before seemed to be of any consequence to me, and certainly had not seemed to have anything to do with Mexican troubles. Now it looked as though it were all somehow tied together, and I was right in the middle of the knot.

Too keyed up to sleep, I lay awake half the night. At one-thirty I heard steps in the hall and the sound of Edwin's envelope shooting under my door and across the floor.

6

There are a number of things which I did for the BNA that still keep me awake nights from time to time. If I despised my early and timid peeks into Mr. Tetzel's business, that feeling was nothing compared with the anguish and disgust I suffered later over what I did to the Cabots.

I will never forget the first day Emory Cabot appeared in Tetzel's office, the week following Christmas of 1914. I was busy that morning—with honest banking work—and had just finished typing a stack of letters that had to go to the post office by noon. I was thinking how convenient a time to offer my services as courier for Tetzel as I glanced over the letters for errors, and all at once I became aware of the presence of Cabot at my desk. First his enormous finger ring caught my eye, then I looked up. There he stood, hat on his head, impatiently puffing on a cigar. His gaze on me was startling. I jumped up. "May I help you?"

"I have an appointment with Adolph Tetzel."

"Yessir. Won't you have a chair while I tell him you're here?"

He would not, and paced around the office until I returned to send him in. Although I did not know at the time, Cabot was not accustomed to waiting for anyone, and was rarely still.

He was the most attractive individual I had ever seen up close. Giddy, who was leaving Tetzel's office with an armload of files, met him face-on as he passed through. She obviously agreed with me. After he was inside we both kept staring at the closed door.

Finally she approached my desk and said in a whisper, "Did you see that beard? Now, in my day that was the sign of a real man."

"He isn't bad to look at now."

"Wish I was about twenty years younger . . . who is he?"

"I never saw him before."

"Well I hope he comes around regularly."

"Giddy, your tongue's hanging out, for heaven's sake."

She winked. "I may be old, honey, but I'm not dead," she told me, then walked out. She had a prissy walk that she'd exaggerate at times like these. I was still smiling and shaking my head in her direction when the door opened and out came Tetzel.

"Pull out a commercial account application for Mr. Cabot, Camille, and push through all the confounded paper work, will you?" He handed me a note with all the information I needed.

I didn't have much opportunity to study what I was typing. I noticed his office was located on Commerce, his home on Beauregard at Washington—I knew where that was—and his would be the only signature on the account. He was opening with a thousand dollars. No wonder he was getting special treatment.

It was almost noon when I took the application in for signatures, and I carried the letters in with me. "I could take these right over to the post office on my way to lunch," I offered.

"Why, that's nice of you, Camille."

"As a matter of fact, I've noticed most of your late-afternoon mail doesn't go out until morning. I pass close by the post office on my way home in the evening. I could easily drop it off."

He looked as though he'd agree, then changed his mind. "That's a lot of extra bother . . . I don't think so."

"Oh, but I'd be glad to."

"Maybe so. We'll talk about it later. Mr. Cabot and I are going to have lunch at the International Club. I'll probably be out a couple of hours."

When they were gone I wondered idly about Cabot. His firm name—Cabot Enterprises—didn't indicate his business; rather, it seemed to suggest he was involved in several areas under one company heading. I wondered whether I ought to mention him to Edwin. Probably he was unconnected with Tetzel's undercover activities. The bank eagerly solicited big accounts, and likely Cabot was swinging all his business over here. That was reason enough for special treatment by the president.

They had been gone for a couple of minutes by the time I noticed Tetzel's homburg on the shelf. I rushed out the door with it, through the main lobby, and caught them up just as they were reaching the street. "Why, thank you," said Tetzel. "I don't know why I have such a time remembering this hat."

When I started back through the door, Cabot said, "Allow me," and I brushed in front of him. My heart thumped a little faster all the way back to my desk, and it seemed to me I'd never been in the presence of anyone who generated such power. Boy, I bet you didn't cross him without thinking twice. . . .

When Tetzel returned in the late afternoon, he said, "I'm very pleased with your work, Camille. I went against my better judgment in hiring you, to be truthful, and relied on my instinct. I believe I made the right choice. I'm always glad to see enthusiasm in young people, particularly when they work for the bank."

It was the kind of genuine statement that convinced me he just couldn't be bad, and kept me wondering whether I'd made the right decision in accepting the proposal to spy. That evening I went home in low spirits, yet still with the faint hope that if I dug deeply enough into Mr. Tetzel's affairs, maybe I'd wind up turning a frog into a prince. Yet I was reluctant to go further, always fearing the next step would prove me wrong. Nine chances out of ten he would turn his mail over to me, and because in the late evening I couldn't get postage from the mail department at the bank, it would be so easy to keep a supply on hand and leave it off until I'd steamed open the envelopes and resealed them. In some ways it was so easy to deceive him, and knowing he trusted me, I hated myself for doing it.

Inside my apartment door was a note from Edwin, wanting me to meet him on Main Plaza on the courthouse side at lunchtime the following day. Oh Lord, what now, I wondered? Suddenly the air seemed foul. I walked to the River Avenue balcony and opened the doors. Only seven o'clock, but pitch dark outside. Down below the street was filled with vehicles behind glowing lights. Up the block I caught a glimpse of Keith Butler, his figure outlined by a streetlight, loading boxes into the store truck. Apparently they were catering a party tonight. How nice and uncomplicated his life seemed. His immediate goal was to finish school. His great dream, a rather boyish one it seemed to me then, was to learn to fly an aeroplane.

He had invited me to a winter *dansant* at the St. Anthony's Hotel on the night after Christmas, and wound up spending most of the evening talking about being in the air. His interest was aroused a few years earlier when Lieutenant Honeywell housed his great air balloon the "Centennial" in a hangar at San Pedro Park, and used the park as a departure field on many of his flights. Keith was one of countless youths who hung around Honeywell as he tended to his balloon, badgering the poor guy with questions about what kind of gas he used, what materials he used to build his craft, and details on his famous flight in the Chicago International Race of 1907, when a forty-mile-per-hour gale blew him and his co-pilot through eight fences as well as various other obstacles. Yet in spite of it all, Honeywell had emerged with two cups and established American records for distance and endurance, flying twenty-three hours and over eight hundred and fifty miles.

Keith spoke of Honeywell's experiences as intently as though they were his own, and conceded his most prized memory was when Honeywell took him, along with several other boys, up over the park one windy Sunday afternoon.

"That was it," he said. "I knew then someday I wanted to be like Honeywell, maybe go for the Lahm Long Distance Cup myself."

"Maybe after the war you could pick up a German Zeppelin at a discount, and take people on world tours. I've heard they used to be pretty classy, with dining on board," I told him in jest. He seemed insulted I could take his hopes so lightly and looked across at me seriously.

"That's all changed now," he said. "As soon as I finish school and save up enough money, I'm going to take flying lessons. I want to be an aeroplane pilot."

"Your parents are paying for you to become an engineer," I reminded him.

"I know, but sending me to college was my mother's idea. She felt it only fair if Ken got a college education, I should have one too. Dad just wants a son to take over the store someday, and he gave up on Ken years ago when he swore he'd become a dentist."

"I see . . . what do your folks think about your becoming a flyer?"

"They don't take me seriously. But they will, one day."

I started to remark that I agreed with them, but it seemed ungrateful to hurt his feelings. He'd rescued me from the Christmas doldrums by asking me out that night. What if he was a bit boyish? At least he was an ordinary American, a refreshing departure from the type of people I was becoming involved with. . . .

I watched him finish loading the boxes into the truck and drive off, then went inside and closed the doors behind me. Keith was always after me for failing to eat right, and just the evening before had brought me a box of fresh vegetables from the store. I opened up the icebox and considered making a big salad for supper, but then lost interest and fixed a cheese sandwich instead.

Next day Edwin had some interesting news.

He was so late that I had almost run out of time. I'd been sitting on a bench wondering if the people who built the mighty stone courthouse intended for its main tower to look like a beehive when he finally drew up beside me. It occurred to me for the first of many times that we must have looked like two crows perched upon a fence, the way we looked straight ahead all the time.

That day he was reporting on the invoices, and explained, "Since the British blockade was set up the Germans have been in a tough spot. At the beginning of the war they thought they would outguess the Allies by tying up the American munitions factories with their own orders for weapons, but now with the blockade in effect they can't get the weapons they've ordered overseas where they need them. So they're consigning them to Mexico for sale down there. A lot of them went to Huerta before he got thrown out a few months ago, and exiled.

"Now from other things we've been able to learn, plus the information you found, we're putting together a few pieces and we think Tetzel may be working on a scheme to return Huerta to power."

"Why would they want to do that?"

"If they buy and pay for the head of the government, they'll have all the clout they need if they go after Mexico's help for their own cause. You know, the British depend upon Tampico oil for their fuel supply, and if the Germans can get an embargo on that oil for the duration, they'll have an obvious advantage over the Allies.

"Also, it would be to the benefit of the Germans to keep Mexico tied up in fights with the United States, to keep America busy. If they throw Huerta into the sizzling brew down there, fireworks are going to go off, especially since the U.S. is breaking its back trying to mediate a peace so they can recognize one of the governments, then wash their hands of the whole mess.

"From the consignment of these invoices, it's possible we have a tie-in, but nothing is definite."

"If not, there's nothing wrong with Tetzel selling weapons down there."

"That's right, but if so, then that involves him in fomenting a revolution on U.S. soil and that's breaking a law."

"Oh, those neutrality laws are on and off like a bee on a blossom."

"Even so, we've got to watch and see what develops. We don't want to do anything hasty. This may be more extensive than we know. No use throwing a small fine on Tetzel now, when we could let him operate for a while, then get him by the neck."

"I resent that. You have no proof against him yet."

"That's right. What we have to have is more written evidence. Did you ask about the mail situation?"

"Yes, but he hasn't given me an answer yet. He may not let me do it."

"Don't press him too hard; it might alert him. But don't miss a chance to take it on if you can. Oh yes, and one other thing. This list of accounts you got looks all right except for Stuttgart Printing. See if you can find out anything more about the owner."

"Why?"

"Printing currency for use in Mexico. It's a long shot, but he is German, and revolutionary currency has been printed up here in the past."

"I don't know what I can do about it. I don't have access to information on a day-to-day basis unless he borrows more money. I'd have to be checking his credit file all the time to see if anything showed up there, and that is unlikely anyhow. Oh, I'm getting to hate all of this."

"I know, but you got to stick with it. Just pay attention to calls between Stuttgart and Tetzel, visits from him, one thing and another. Have you seen anything unusual lately? Any new people on the staff, or unusual breaks in Tetzel's routine?"

"No. He did go to lunch at the International Club the other day with a new customer named Cabot."

"Hm . . . that club was under some fire during the Madero revolution in 1910, but I don't think anything is going on there now. I can check it out. Who's this Cabot?"

I told him what little I knew.

"All right, but watch for visits. We may have to wire Tetzel's office eventually, but I want to wait until we have more before we risk that. You might be checking around for possibilities of setting up equipment."

"What sort of wire are you talking about?"

"To get recordings of his voice . . . you know, like they use for a Victrola."

"Oh! I didn't know you could do that kind of thing."

"It's a little tricky. We have one man on our team who's an electrical expert, and I learned what little I know from him. We put a wax cylinder recorder in one room, then wire to another room—in this case, Tetzel's office—and install a receiver. The recorder has a headset attached, so you can listen in while you're recording. I have a diagram you can see."

"The idea seems pretty dangerous. The whole floor—plus the one above and below—are occupied by bank offices."

"How about a storage room, or closet?"

"I'll look around. How big is the recorder?"

"About a foot and a half long, and maybe eight or ten inches deep."

"All right."

"Remember, the Germans have a habit of committing important words to paper. If you could just get at the mail—"

"I'll try."

"And every now and then check again in the safe. He might keep memoranda in there. Also, make yourself useful. Offer to do odd jobs, deliver things, anything that will get you close to Tetzel or any of these other people. Shadow them whenever you can."

"What do you expect me to do, hide behind the bushes?"

"It wouldn't hurt," he said, and laughed. "I know it's dirty work, but remember, the end justifies the means."

"Maybe I'm just not right for this. You might be better off hiring somebody professional. I feel awfully inadequate."

"We don't have enough money to hire professionals. Besides, they often prove to be low types who buy and sell information to both sides, so there's a built-in risk right there.

"Also, your position makes it possible for you to see many things we could never have access to. We might work for months and never get anyone on Tetzel's staff, much less right inside his own office."

"That's true," I admitted and thought how relieved I'd be if all of this would end.

Yet, like a small twig working its way downstream, the complications went further. The day before Tetzel left for his overseas trip Cabot came by again, and this time as he left I overheard Tetzel say, "All right. I'll transfer five now. Let me know as you need more."

Later in the afternoon, alone in the office, I called down to credit and said, "Mr. Tetzel wants to verify an amount transferred into the Cabot Enterprises account as a loan. Was it five thousand?"

"One moment."

An eternity passed, with my eyes on the door, looking for Tetzel to appear. Finally came the answer. "That's right. Did you need that loan number?"

"No thanks. That's all."

When Mr. Tetzel returned from a meeting, we worked together until around seven o'clock because his trip was to begin the following day. His wife phoned then to remind him they had dinner guests arriving in half an hour, and he handed me a bundle of mail and said, "You needn't bother with this tonight, but would you see that it goes first thing in the morning?"

"Of course, sir, have a safe journey."

A cursory glance over the bundle seemed to prove it was innocuous, but I had an uneasy feeling future batches of mail might prove otherwise. Still I took it home like a good spy and steamed open the envelopes I couldn't readily identify. One was addressed to an R. M. Francke in New York. A brief memo, it stated, "I understand you will be out of the city during my stop in New York within the next few days, so I'll try and reach you upon my return back to the States a few weeks hence. I have a matter of urgency to discuss, so we need to talk before V.R. comes over. This may change the picture somewhat. Please wire M.K. at the German Foreign Office per usual."

I called Edwin, who picked it up for copying and commented, "Aha, this is going to be our tie-in, you can bet on it." Then he noticed my lack of enthusiasm and said, "I'll get in touch with you after I've done some checking. I think your attitude will change."

7

Late in January, Mother came down for a brief visit. Just when I was feeling low over the recent—and still undigested—development with Tetzel, and equally disturbed by the fact he was to be away for the rest of the month so that my whole life seemed suspended, I could have used some of her good-sense talk. Yet she was more depressed than I had ever seen her. She'd returned from Washington where Vote for Women had suffered overwhelming defeats. The national suffrage constitutional amendment had been defeated in the House, denying its chance of going before the states for ratification. As an added disappointment, the President stood firm against suffrage on a national scale, although he was in favor of it himself.

"Sometimes I wish Taft were still in office," she said bitterly. "His attitudes toward women trying to get ahead are a lot more advanced."

"But Wilson isn't against you," I told her.

"Nor will he get behind us. Would he wield his power our way, we could be years ahead. One national amendment would save all this traveling hither, thither, and yon. Each state is like another field to be plowed, and there are still fourteen left without even so much as limited suffrage for women. You're living in one, don't forget."

I'd been giving a lot of thought over the past few weeks to human rights and the work of little provinces like Bohemia trying to keep from being gobbled up by the German empire, so I remarked, "I don't know, Mother. Maybe there's something good in Wilson's stubbornness about leaving this to the states."

"That's a fine thing to say. Look what happened a few years ago when he stood up for California's anti-alien act. The Japanese have never gotten over the fact they lost their right to own property they'd worked, out there. That confounded, obdurate governor ought to have his head examined for doing them that way. It's silly to risk the friendship of another country over that, especially in this day and age, when countries are falling into line on one side or another," she said, then stopped and knitted her brow. "That isn't what I meant to get off on. Are you at liberty to discuss your BNA work with me?"

"I suppose so. You got me into it."

I told her briefly of the clues uncovered, and included my secret visits into the files and Mr. Tetzel's safe. After I finished she took a sip of hot tea and said, thoughtfully, "Hm . . . I really wouldn't think they would get you too involved if it gets rough. Probably bring someone down from higher up in their organization. To be honest, I didn't think it would go as far as it has."

"Is that why you were so eager for me to stick my neck out in the beginning?"

"No. I truly believe in their cause, but not at the risk of— of—"

"My life?"

"Of course not, silly, your job."

"I'm afraid it might be getting a little stickier than that."

"Well you can always get out if it is something you don't feel you can handle."

I shook my head at her. "You never cease to amaze me. One minute you'd see me hanging by my toenails for the V. for W. or some other worthy cause. The next minute you tell me not to risk getting my feet wet in the rain."

"I know . . ." she said slowly. "It's the mother in me, I guess, love. I'd never forgive myself if you got hurt or anything, but at the same time I expect you to be a wildcatter like me."

"Well you sure have a way of bringing that about."

She smiled and put a hand around my chin. "You're made of strong stuff, Camille. . . . I guess I blame myself for pushing you out from under my wing so early. But I trust your judgment to get out of this thing if you feel it's too dangerous. You're dealing with a high-principled group of people. They wouldn't hold it against you if you didn't come through for them."

"I suppose you're right."

"Well now, what are you doing in your spare time? Have you met any nice young men?"

"I don't have much spare time. I've been seeing the son of a grocer down the street, but he's just a pal. Nice guy, but it's nothing serious."

"Good. You're young yet. You are to be admired for holding down a good job and seeing that the cupboard is filled and the rent's paid . . . it is, isn't it?"

I laughed. "Oh Mom, you're so cagey. You'd make the better spy. How about a salad? And as to the rent, well I'm making it, but just barely."

"You ought to be used to that. All the time you kids were growing up, we managed by the grace of God and army benefits, such as they were."

When Mother's train left there was a light snow falling, and, whether because of the downcast weather or because I treasured her visits so dearly, I felt very lonely as I waved good-bye to her figure on the other side of the train window and wiped away a tear, warm against my cold cheek.

When Tetzel returned at the end of the month, he was preoccupied more than usual and a bit edgy. I still had not heard from Edwin on the note Tetzel sent to R. M. Francke in New York, and kept trying to read something into Tetzel's actions that would tell me whether he'd gotten wind of what was going on behind his back. In fact I wondered what would happen if something went wrong. Would Edwin simply disappear, and leave the BNA's dirty laundry on my doorstep? Surely not. . . .

First thing, Tetzel asked for the arrangement of a meeting with Emory Cabot. I rang his office but got no answer. "It's almost noon . . . maybe he's out to lunch," I suggested.

"He has a man working for him—what's his name?—Nathan Hope, that's it."

"Apparently he's out too."

"Confound it. Try and reach Mrs. Cabot at their home, find out where he is and tell her I need to see him as soon as I can."

"Yessir."

I found Electra Cabot to be a soft-spoken and seemingly refined woman over the telephone. She asked me to tell Tetzel that her husband was out of the country on business, and she was not sure just when he would return. I asked her to hold the line while I checked for a message, but Mr. Tetzel wouldn't leave one. I began wondering what sort of woman a man like Cabot would be married to—timid and fragile, yielding to a strong spouse? Or tough underneath, like Cabot definitely was on the surface? A few days later, quite by accident, I began finding out.

I saw her standing at the counter at Butler's, talking to Keith's father. "I used to live in Colorado, and now that I'm here I never miss the opportunity to buy fresh vegetables and fruits in season. When I saw your ad about strawberries I hurried over."

"Well, they're a mite expensive now, but pretty good for the first of the season. There's a quart," he said, eying the scales. "Can I put these on your account?"

"I don't have one."

"Then, allow me to open one for you. What was that name?"

"Cabot. Mrs. Emory Cabot."

I had been listening because there was something slightly familiar about her voice, and now I knew why. I edged in a bit closer as she continued to chat with Mr. Butler. He was telling her he'd always wanted to go to Colorado, but in spite of his many questions about the conditions there, the only information she related was that the climate was too cold, and she liked it better here. As she phrased her brief answers, her voice became lower and lower so that I could barely hear her at all. Finally he told her of a man he'd known several years back who went to Denver and opened a small grocery store, whose business had now grown to a chain of six or seven stores in the Denver area. He told her the name and asked if she'd ever shopped in one of them.

For some reason, the question seemed to startle her, and she faltered, "I . . . didn't ever . . . that is, actually I lived in a little town not far from Denver." Then, as though in a hurry she wished him good day and gathered her parcels. I kept my eyes on her as she walked out the door. She was well dressed and very striking. Looked as if Cabot had good taste in women. . . .

On the way home I kept thinking of the curious fact she'd spoken as though she came to this city alone . . . so maybe she had not been married to Cabot very long. And she was obviously nervous when asked about Colorado.

For the first time then I realized I'd failed to be on my toes since Mr. Tetzel returned, too busy worrying over his own discovery of me to catch a possible tie-in. Why had Cabot been the first person he wanted to see? I redoubled my steps and went to the nearest telephone to call Edwin. I was fairly bursting with curiosity over the mysterious note to R. M. Francke anyway. Maybe Edwin would have some information for me.

There was no answer. I checked the time. Six-thirty. He ought to have been there. I went to my apartment, determined to check with him again in an hour or so, but found a note from him inside my door. "Meet me at lunch tomorrow, twelve-thirty in front of Roach and Barnes Kodaks on West Commerce."

After that, I didn't sleep all night.

Next day Edwin told me the link was definite. "Tetzel has been responsible for a major part of the weapons being shipped south of the border, and will play a definite role in the planning for Huerta's return. This month the Germans are to send a man by the name of von Rintelen over to mastermind the plot. He'll be meeting with Huerta in New York, and instructing Tetzel as to weapons."

"So V.R. in Tetzel's letter stood for von Rintelen. . . . I wonder if he got to talk to Francke in New York upon his return, about the 'change in the picture.' "

"Our people weren't able to find out about it, if he did."

"Well, with this link, all you have to do is catch the two men on the spot, right? Then—" I began nervously, but Edwin interrupted.

"We think Tetzel is involved still further, and we don't want to pick him up yet."

"What more could he be doing?"

"You mentioned his trip to Europe . . . while there, he arranged for the transfer of copper through Norway into Germany. It is the only way to get raw materials past the British blockade. Denmark and Holland are co-operating with the Allies, but Norway maintains an attitude they'll ship to whomever, wherever they choose; see, they also produce a sizable amount of copper themselves, so they want to leave all the doors open."

"I still don't see any wrong in that. The British blockade is starving them to death. Neither do I blame the Germans for declaring a war zone all the way around the British Isles, if you want to know the truth." I hadn't intended to be so blunt, but I was getting edgy myself.

"Good points, but the important item here is that the further we dig, the further down we find Tetzel, and we want to see how far the cable goes before it runs out. Now, what did you learn since we last met?"

"Only one thing that looks significant. The first man Tetzel asked to see when he got back was Emory Cabot, and Cabot was out of the country—I don't know where—on business. I also ran across his wife in the grocery store, and overheard her indicate she and Cabot haven't been married very long."

"How old a man would you say Cabot is?"

"Oh, mid-thirties, probably. I wish I'd looked over his papers more carefully when he first came into the bank."

"Why didn't you?"

"I was busy," I said, not about to admit I was busy looking at Cabot. "Besides, I attached no particular importance to him at the time."

"All right. Anything else?"

"Yes. Mrs. Cabot lived near Denver, Colorado, before."

"Hm . . . that's copper-mining territory."

"Oh . . . I didn't think of that," I told him, then described her reticence in talking with Mr. Butler.

"She might bear some checking out. Can you shadow her? Find out what her name was before. We'll need a line on her before we can get any further."

"Oh, and Mr. Tetzel mentioned Cabot had a man working for him named Hope."

"See if you can find an excuse to go by Cabot's office one day —deliver papers or something. You still on the mails?"

"As much as I can be. But Tetzel hasn't asked me lately, and he hasn't been back very long." I was beginning to perspire. "Look, couldn't you just slap a fine on Tetzel for his part in the Huerta thing and let him go? I'm sure he'd never—"

"Don't be naïve. One thing you've got to learn is that you can't afford to get off the train until you've reached the end of the line, and don't let kindness fool you. I can probably get some information on Cabot with what I have, but you've got to work on his wife and his man.

"What I really need is a wire in Tetzel's office now. Did you find a place big enough for a machine?"

"There's a storeroom nearby, with one wall backing up to his office. No one ever seems to go in there. It's full of old office furniture, mostly."

"Perfect. Does it lock?"

"Everything in that bank has a lock on it."

"Have a key made for me, and meet me here with it tomorrow. I'll take care of the rest."

"All right, except—"

"What's bothering you now?"

"The same thing that has bothered me all along. I just don't see why Tetzel would be involved in a dirty thing like you suspect. People do things for reasons, and he has nothing to gain in all this. He already has money, so it can't be that. He has position in society, belongs to all the right clubs, knows influential people. Why risk it all?"

"That's something we may never know."

I sighed. "It's very hard for me to . . . you know . . . cast the first stone at him."

"If we're wrong, he doesn't have to know what we suspected, but we're looking for something bigger than what we've uncovered so far. The Germans have fifty million dollars invested in sabotage over here, and it's beginning to look like Tetzel is in charge of distributing a large share of it."

"Well if it turns out all he's really doing wrong is helping Huerta to get back, what will you do?"

"Maybe nothing, and remember, all we can do is gather evidence and put it into the right hands. By the way, I haven't been able to get anything on Stuttgart. How about you?"

"Nothing," I said, then looked at his profile. "What do you do in your spare time?"

"I don't have much." He laughed. "See 'ya tomorrow."

He walked away and eventually disappeared among the people crowding the sidewalks. I turned around to face a camera display in the shop window, and was reminded I hadn't taken one picture of the bank staff. I hadn't even been able to throw all my energies into the crusade because I just couldn't convince myself Tetzel was as bad as the BNA believed him to be. For Edwin, dealing with me must have been like swimming against a strong current.

I made up my mind then I was either going to have to give it my all or get out. So far my only concern had been with one man. Now a whole new group of faces and names had been thrown into the can to be shaken up and sorted out. I just couldn't give up my faith in Mr. Tetzel's goodness, and never really feared anything worse from him than being fired, should he discover me in an act of sleuthing.

But Emory Cabot was an unknown quantity, as were his wife and his man Hope. How far would any of them go to save their necks, or to avenge anyone connected with undermining them?

Suddenly Stobalt's opening plea—that plots involving Tetzel might well be endangering the lives of innocent American citizens—echoed in my mind. I shoved my hands into my pockets and went back to work. I decided I would go on.

8

Setting up a recording machine in Mr. Tetzel's office proved a nearly impossible task. Difficulty enough arose from the fact the bread-box-size machine had to be concealed in one place, then connected by wire to a sizable receiver in another, several yards away and down a hall. Edwin installed the machine out of sight at the back of the storeroom with relative ease. However, the only place inside Tetzel's office for the receiver was behind the credenza next to the safe at the rear of his desk. Edwin had to hook it as near to the top as possible while still hiding it from view, and up-end the head in the hope of catching at least part of the conversations carried on there.

"It might work, but these things don't have much scope, and a lot will depend upon how loud people are talking," he said doubtfully. "Does Tetzel have a loud voice?"

"No, rather low."

"Hm . . . and his back will probably be to the receiver. Well, we'll have a go at it, anyway."

Neither of us realized we had a deceivingly simple problem facing us which would take a long time figuring out. I soon thought the whole scheme pretty fruitless, as Tetzel didn't make a habit of talking any but banking business on the phone, and in the weeks between his return from Europe and Cabot's return from what proved to be Mexico no conversations of significance were recorded on the machine. Neither did he place any mail in my hands for delivery to the post office, although I offered to serve as courier several times. I was beginning to think he might suspect me, and was afraid of pressing the point very far.

Between February and mid-April of 1915 was a long period, during which Edwin was called away several times to the East Coast, where German involvement was proving out in connection with the sudden and mysterious burning of ships in United States harbors, and the incitement of strikes among harbor workers. At the time I was given little detail, and assumed Edwin's trips had no direct relation with what I was doing.

During the lull, I took the opportunity of getting to know Keith better. I spent one afternoon with him in March, following a snowfall which left a white blanket one and a half inches thick all over the city. I'd been in real blizzards when we lived up north, so this little snow seemed a mere inconvenience to me. Keith had not seen much snow, however, and his excitement was infectious. He managed to get an old buggy with a poor hag of a horse connected to it from somewhere, and met me at the front door of the bank at lunchtime, red-nosed and red-cheeked underneath his blazing blue eyes.

Mr. Tetzel happened to walk out at the same time. Noticing I was being picked up in a buggy, he smiled broadly and said, "Children should have a good time. Take the whole afternoon off, Camille."

Keith gave the horse a gleeful "giddyap," and we thrust forward down the icy street toward Alamo Plaza. "Oh, he's so darned nice," I said under my breath.

Keith looked surprised. "You don't sound too grateful."

"Oh, I am, I am," I told him.

Through ingratiating snorts by the swayback horse conveying us, we made our way to the plaza, where Keith insisted on starting a snowball fight. Suddenly he disappeared. I looked around and called his name several times. Nothing. Then, from behind a snow-laden bush off to the right came a whistle, followed by a whizzing white ball. I turned just in time to see Keith's arm shoot out, before catching the ball square in the face. "Come out of there, I'll fix you," I cried, and started gathering ammunition.

Before I knew it he whammed one into my backside and darted across to another bush, giggling like a baseball player headed for third base. On his way I whacked him a good one, then threw another, missing him, and, now unarmed, took cover behind a frozen shrub. We sparred like youngsters long enough that I really began to laugh and enjoy myself, and to realize how serious I'd become of late. I'd almost lost my sense of fun completely.

After an hour of battle, we were thoroughly winded, with arms trembling from the motions and backsides aching from numerous slips to the cold ground. We helped each other off the field, arm in arm, and boarded the buggy for a ride through Brackenridge Park right down the old path referred to as lovers' lane. The route proved to be just as I remembered—overhung with tall skeletal trees and silent as a frozen brook.

We were at ease with each other, like school buddies. As we rode along I told him about outings with my family during the years we were all together, and he told me of summer picnics under the shade of the big trees in the park. He never made overfamiliar moves toward me. If he had, I'd have been more astonished than insulted or embarrassed, and probably would have burst out laughing. He'd been busy with exams after Christmas and we had not really spent very much time together, so we just enjoyed the laughter and the silences in between.

Around five o'clock, darkness gathering suddenly, he said, "You know what would be swell? Some Mexican food. I'm chilled to the bone."

So off we went to his favorite Mexican-food cafe down on the river. The smell of hot spices met us at the door, increasing my appetite three times over. We sat at a table close by a crackling log fire, overlooking the strange sight of mist above the water.

"Almost spooky, like a moor in Scotland, isn't it? Wonder what causes that?" I said.

"When the warmer water of the river is touched by the cold drizzle coming down, it throws off a steam."

"Like a veil. You could almost get lost in it, couldn't you."

"I guess so. I never thought of it that way," he said.

Just then the Mexican waiter appeared and Keith ordered food enough for a banquet without batting an eye. Soon there were hot platters before us with chili, tamales, enchiladas, frijoles, refried beans and rice threatening to overrun the edges. All of it was permeated with the smell of onions and cheese, and accompanied by crispy tortillas. Keith bragged as the waiter left. His family knew the owner, and he could testify to the quality of ingredients in the dishes. In one sitting I ate more than I'd eaten in the previous week, and I'm not sure who dug through the delicacies with more vigor, but Keith and I were a good match and afterward sat back groaning happily.

"That was the best Mexican food, not to mention the best meal I've eaten, since I moved out from Mother's place," I said.

"I'm going to take you out more often. You can't survive on—"

"I know, I know. Save the lecture, please. Keith, I can't remember when I've had so much fun."

"Gosh, me too," he said. Then he paused and shifted in his chair. "Of course, you're awfully busy with other guys, I guess."

"Who, me?"

"Well . . . you don't seem to stay at home very much."

"Oh, have you come by to check on me?"

"A time or two."

"I work late sometimes, and take odd jobs to make ends meet. It costs a lot to live alone."

He studied me for a moment, then said, "I've never known anyone like you before. Most girls sit around wondering who's going to marry and support them. I admire you a lot."

I told him thanks, and he quickly looked away. "Listen, I've got to return this buggy and get back to the store before closing time," he said. "I'll take you home now, if it's all right."

"Sure. You may have to carry me to the buggy, though. My feet might give out under my weight."

He saw me up to my apartment, our spongy shoes depositing wet tracks all the way up the stairs to the fourth floor, and when I unlocked the door I said, "I was really sincere about today. Thanks again."

He propped an arm up high on the door facing, and looked down at me. "You meant it, too, about not seeing a lot of other fellows?"

"Since I came to San Antonio I haven't had time to make many friends—boys or girls."

He dug his hands deep into his pockets and smiled. "Well, good night. See you soon."

I walked out onto the River Avenue balcony and looked down toward the store. The streetlights were like moons encircled with haze. The snow had already begun to melt and a couple of automobiles poked along the street carefully. I watched Keith's buggy go the length of the block then turn to the left, headed I supposed for the place where he'd picked up the contraption in the first place. Where, I wondered? He'd never said. About the time the horse started cautiously around the corner, an open car full of joy riders, laughing and singing, came barreling down the avenue. The driver blew the horn rudely and, taking the corner much too quickly, almost slid the auto right into Keith and his old buggy, then roared away to the other side of the street and off again. The old horse could have formerly served as an army draft horse for the little upset he showed, and in a moment Keith set him back in forward motion and disappeared around the block.

I stayed out on the balcony for a while, still wrapped in my overcoat, savoring the day. It was to be the last of its kind for a long time to come.

Huerta arrived in New York around April 13, just ten days behind von Rintelen, and soon the newspapers were bursting with stories of the ousted Mexican dictator's return, assuring the public that he was being watched by United States authorities. President Wilson was openly seething over this development, and quickly locked new restrictions on the vague neutrality laws. Huerta had only to make one false move and the authorities would have him in a noose.

I must say it was a time when I enjoyed being one who was "in the know," as I read statements in the papers issued by Huerta himself, declaring that only a Mexican would save Mexico, and (so innocently!) that he did not know who it would be. He also defended himself in the death of the revolutionary martyr Madero, announcing to the press he had no part in it, but that he did know who was guilty and that it was a "professional secret."

Many people who kept up with the news in Mexico had wondered about the parties to blame in the assassination of Madero in 1913. My only reason for keeping up with events down there was that one of my classes in high school was devoted almost entirely to current events and thus had followed the revolution of 1910, studying its basis, the reforms planned by Francisco Madero, and his aborted attempts at carrying them through. By the time Huerta had betrayed him I was far away from San Antonio and could find little in the local newspapers where we lived.

I asked Edwin if his guilt had ever been proven.

"Only by strong circumstantial evidence," he said, "but personally I have no doubt Huerta did it."

"I don't think the Mexicans do either. Even Pancho Villa and Carranza seem to concur on that. I can see how returning Huerta to power will be like pouring salt on an open sore."

"Just what the Germans want."

"Do you think von Rintelen will come here to meet with Tetzel?"

"More likely Tetzel will go there and sit in on the negotiations between Huerta and von Rintelen. However, there may be a rift because Tetzel's request for delay was shelved. We're bound to pick up something on the machine or find something in the mail. Be extra curious and try and get something on it. Tetzel's a dangling end in an otherwise tight operation. As soon as we get enough evidence, we can scuttle plans for Huerta, but the question remains about Tetzel and you're the only one who can get a clue."

"I'll do my best."

On the day following the news release of Huerta's arrival in New York I went into the bank early, eager to get a head start on the day. Soon Mr. Tetzel came in and dictated a batch of bank letters to me, and I went to work on them. He was quiet, but not out of sorts. I was a little nervous at first, and almost jumped out of my shoes when he brought his empty inkwell to me. "Oh, I'm sorry, sir, I know you don't like—"

"It's all right," he assured me pleasantly, and went back to his desk.

After a while my nerves settled down and the day began to shape up into normal routine. I told myself it was silly to keep expecting something to happen. But then suddenly the door burst open and in came Emory Cabot, fuming mad.

"Where's Tetzel?" he demanded.

Apparently Tetzel overheard him. He was instantly outside his door, inviting Cabot in with an appeasing tone. When the door was shut, I leaped up and made for the storeroom. I knew something of great consequence was going to be said, and I was determined to have a recording of it. Once I set the wax cylinder revolving, I put the headset on. I couldn't hear anything. I figured it wasn't attached properly, and took it off. Then I put my ear to the wall behind the machine. Though the storeroom backed up to one end of Tetzel's office, I didn't expect to hear anything through the thick walls. Yet, to my surprise, I was able to hear most of the words. Doubtless the fact both men were in a state of excitement and talking louder as a result made a difference.

It was obvious Cabot was upset by Huerta's return. I heard Tetzel say, "I did everything I could to get them to hold on longer, but they can only afford to burn the candle from both ends for just so long. Keeping border trouble stirred up by financing Villa, and keeping any number of other fires ablaze while they await the moment of takeover by a party they can be sure to trust—"

"You mean, someone bought and paid for with German money."

"Ah well, however you wish to express it—in any event,

they're impatient in the Foreign Office. Our friend Barrista could perhaps be a bit more decisive."

"I don't give a damn how impatient those son-of-a-bitches are, I want Huerta out, do you hear?"

"They are discussing terms just now, in New York."

"I gathered that from the San Antonio *Express*," Cabot said acidly.

"Believe me, my friend, no one has double-crossed you. The plans for returning Huerta had been discussed for months before you ever approached me about financing Barrista. Once the wheels are in motion, it is difficult to slow them down. However, I have some inside information that von Rintelen is quarreling with Boy-Ed and von Papen. It is just possible the whole Huerta plan will suffer failure as a result."

"Well you can tell your friends if they want any more copper from Cabot Consolidated, they'd better deal straight."

"I have told them already. Try and keep your boots on, and let this situation resolve itself. I believe it will. Now, where does Barrista stand?"

There was a pause, then the sound of pacing footsteps. Cabot said, "I've just spent a couple of months on a saddle instructing the family and close friends of the Plan de Pacifica Reforma. But Barrista's tired of the bloodshed. He wants to go in peacefully if he can."

"Of course. Have you need of more money?"

"Not yet."

"Just let me know. I'll be in touch with my friends in New York about our visit. It is to everyone's advantage if someone agreeable to all factions can take over. A Mexico at peace will serve us better in the end."

After that I heard the door slam shut. I listened hard, thinking I might hear Tetzel make a phone call to New York. Yet I heard nothing, and I supposed either the sound was inaudible to me or he was communicating with New York by the mails and the telegraph alone in deference to a meddlesome switchboard operator. It was also possible he was leading Cabot on. . . .

I looked down at the cylinder, still rolling. There was so

much contained in the conversation I decided to take it off and get it to Edwin immediately. My hands were so moist and shaky I was afraid I'd drop it on the floor and have nothing to turn over to the BNA but a collection of shattered pieces. When I had it safely off, I relaxed somewhat.

Little did I know the cylinder would prove a total blank.

9

"I just can't understand it," I told Edwin.

"I'll try and get in there over the weekend to see if the machine's fouled up somehow. You're sure you've told me everything you overheard?"

"Yes, oh fudge!"

"Don't worry, these setbacks are part of the game. Just keep up the good work. Now you've got to focus your attention on the Cabots."

"All right. Tetzel mentioned a 'takeover' by someone they could trust—does that mean another revolution?"

"Most likely. The trouble is, there are so many over there all the time it's hard to know which of them to take seriously. We'll check out Barrista as far as we can, but that's going to be difficult."

"Do you think they're only using him?"

"I don't know. It's possible . . . once he serves their purpose in stirring up trouble, they might ditch him."

"That means Tetzel could be lying to Cabot."

"It's possible. Just keep your eyes open. This guy Cabot keeps lookin' more vital."

"All right. When he said copper I nearly fell through the floor. The way he talked, Germany must be depending upon him for a good percentage of their supply. He certainly seems to think he wields some influence, anyhow."

"Well, that's somethin'. Either he has his hands on quite a few producing properties or he's paying a premium to Pancho

Villa to keep some good ones open in the north. Maybe German money is footing that bill, too." He paused, then continued, "It's hard getting great quantities of anything out of there right now, with all those wars going on, so unless . . ."

"What?"

"Nothing for now. Just keep your eyes open."

"Who are those others with the queer names—Boy-Ed and von Papen?"

"Boy-Ed is German naval attaché; von Papen is the military attaché in charge of sabotaging munitions factories in this country. They probably resent von Rintelen's intrusion on their territory."

"This is becoming awfully complicated."

"You're not wolfing. Without your help we'd be a lot longer finding out as much as we know. By the way, how's your money situation?"

"Terrible."

"I've put in a request for a little dough for you, but no answer yet."

"It's all right. I'm making it."

In fact I had looked at a pair of Lady Betty pumps in the window at Joske's, and, with holes worn nearly through the soles of my work shoes, I was tempted to break through the window and steal them out of sheer desperation. But there was also a shoe-repair shop nearby with one-day service, so I took my shoes and had them fixed. I could never tell Edwin of my true feelings about the financial straits I was in. Each time we got together there was so much of importance to be discussed, my meager needs seemed to dissipate by comparison, especially when I was working for a group that had little funding. And from the looks of Edwin's dowdy attire, he wasn't very well fixed either.

When Edwin wasn't in sight it was a different story. Sometimes I got so angry I came near calling him up and quitting. I could go back to the Y for a while, live with a roommate, and with my salary at the bank I could manage new clothes now and then if I budgeted carefully. As it was I could scarcely afford a matinee, and when Keith invited me to go with him to see Billie Burke in *Jerry* at the Grand, I couldn't accept because I had to meet Edwin that evening.

At the end of the month Cabot came back twice again to see Mr. Tetzel, and, although Edwin's surreptitious visit to the storeroom to check on the equipment proved it to be working perfectly, again we got nothing on the cylinders. Both times I was denied the chance to hear what was going on during the visits, because I was working on urgent letters when Cabot arrived. I could slip out only long enough to turn on the machine without arousing suspicion as to my whereabouts. Once I opened a file drawer near Tetzel's door, and listened hard. But I heard nothing, and couldn't chance putting my ear to the wall. In fact, the farther away from that side of the office I stayed, the better. I got back to my work, in hopes the clacking of the typewriter would encourage Tetzel and Cabot to raise their voices.

When Edwin and I discussed the continually blank cylinders, I was afraid he'd think me some sort of counterspy, withholding information. Yet he didn't seem to doubt my word, instead cautioning me to try and see what went on in that office during the Cabot visits. "See if the cabinet gets covered up somehow. That could muffle the sound and keep the recorder from picking it up."

Mr. Tetzel left for a trip through his "old homestead country," as he referred to it, during Fiesta Week. In a jovial mood the day before he left, he said, "What I'm really trying to do is avoid all the crowds that pour into the city during Fiesta. I haven't enjoyed the Battle of Flowers parade since the year one of Sophie's ladies' clubs had a float and I got hoodwinked into driving. You should have seen the flowers on that wagon— thousands of them—they wired them to the wheel spokes and even to the poor horses' harness and blinders. On top of that I sneezed and sniffled for a week because I was allergic to pollen and didn't know it. I told Sophie, 'Never again.' . . ."

We both laughed over the story, and he told me he had a good picture of the float at home and would bring it someday for me to see. I was so taken off guard by the conversation I forgot myself and came dangerously close to asking him about the photo in his safe. Thank goodness he spoke before I did and began another funny reminiscence.

At the end of the day—we worked late because he had letters that must go out before he left town—he asked me into his office on a more serious note. Everyone else was gone; my heart quickened as he called my name. I was beginning to live more and more in fear of being suspected. So many conversations with Edwin. Had someone working for Tetzel and the Germans been listening in? So many trips to the storeroom. Had he gone in himself, to check on my activities in there? So many involuntary jerks of my shoulders if he should say something while I was occupied, startling me. Had he begun putting two and two together, just by watching me?

I walked in and sat down, pencil in hand.

"This doesn't concern any more work for today, Camille," he said, looking through the lap drawer in his desk. "It's another little matter."

"Yessir." I gulped and gripped the pencil tighter.

"I've been very pleased with your work here, and as of the first of May I'm increasing your salary again by ten dollars a month."

I let out an audible "gosh," then added more calmly, "You're very generous, Mr. Tetzel. I don't know what to say."

"Unlike many bankers, I believe in paying my good staff well. On the other hand, my employees who don't show so much initiative make considerably less, so I guess it evens the score. Banking business is improving all the time, you know. Since the Federal Reserve System went into effect it's much easier for banks to grow and prosper. We can hold less in reserve nowadays, without fear of people running scared and pulling their funds out.

"I believe those who take on more than their share of the extra work resulting should be repaid in kind."

"It's so much, though . . . I really wish I could take on still more work for you in return. I know my job well enough. I could take over other things for you, or maybe help someone out in another department where the load is heavier. I could help more with your personal correspondence. You always seem reluctant to ask me, but believe me, I wouldn't consider it an imposition at all."

"I'll have to do some thinking on that. For now . . . perhaps I ought to let you carry my late mail for me. Sometimes I get so exasperated with the mails nowadays. In fact I have a lot of envelopes ready to go out tonight, and I'd like to stay around for another couple of hours. Could you take them by on your way?"

I was up on my feet. "Anytime, sir," I said, and reached out for the stack of paper and envelopes on his desk. I noticed they were turned facedown.

"Not quite yet. I'll bring them out shortly," he said.

As I walked out of his office I felt lower than ever. Not only had I accepted more money from him, but I'd used my job to my advantage again, to hurt him. I almost wished he'd be unreasonable or impetuous instead of nice. Then I wouldn't feel so bad about betraying him, regardless of what he did on the outside of the bank. Soon he brought out the stack. The letters were now folded and inserted, the envelopes sealed.

I left around six-thirty and hurried home to have a look. What I found gave me the feeling of sinking little by little into quicksand. Again, to R. M. Francke in New York: "I shall endeavor to purchase several small newspapers in the Fredericksburg-Comfort area, where we have much sympathy for our cause. I believe I can get them for less than twenty-five thousand dollars. I will report upon return. I have made several inconspicuous overtures to the *Frie Presse* here, but have been met with cool reception."

Still another memo to the same Mr. Francke: "I entreat you to consider the possibilities I hold in my power down here re Mexican situation. We all know already that V.H. has a history of betrayal. I remind you again, if we can get someone who believes in loyalty to his friends such as B., we are more likely to be able to deal with him should it become necessary.

We can persuade him to support our cause in recompense for our services."

Still another brief memo: "Perhaps M.K. has vision beyond mine, but I believe at this point third party he mentions is hardly plausible even in vague and remote future, due to lack of trustworthiness and industry. He is not serious, surely?"

Even if the recording machine proved of limited service to us, the letters surely helped. I called Edwin and had them picked up. They presented many cryptic messages, I was certain, but because he was extremely careful in his wording they surely could never be used as supportive evidence, only clues to an ever-unwinding spool of yarn.

Edwin and I discussed at length the memo on "B."— Barrista. The BNA had done some checking, and believed the name to refer to a well-known family in Mexico. They were stumped by the fact that no first name or initial had surfaced at this point, however. There were five Barrista brothers, almost any one of whom might have political leanings. The most prominent among them was Fernando Barrista, the renowned historiographer and journalist, yet perhaps even more likely to have aspirations to power because of his fiery temperament and vast influence on the Mexican Pacific coast was Carlos Barrista.

"Those two are the best bets, even though the name Barrista is common enough down there that we might not even have the right family line."

"Are you going to have them watched?"

"No. Unfortunately, we have no agents down there."

The final memo on the "third party" baffled Edwin completely. Who was untrustworthy and lacking in industry? Certainly many Germans looked with contempt upon people who were not industrious, yet the memo had not mentioned if it was a German in Germany, or a citizen over here, or somewhere else. It said enough only to cause the BNA to continue digging into Tetzel's activities.

During Fiesta Week, when he was out of town, I became very ill with a mild case of influenza. (The doctor called it "mild." I had several other names for it.) Torrential rains beginning on the weekend may have brought it on, as I got caught in a downpour with no umbrella or any other protective gear, but it was just as well because the streets were still so full of determined merry-makers I preferred staying in anyway.

I probably wouldn't have gotten a doctor except that Keith came by with a box of groceries on Monday night and I was too sick to go to the door. I was aching all over and running a high fever, and had lost count of the days. I had no idea it was Monday. I didn't even think to report for work, and I suppose no one there considered investigating my absence because Mr. Tetzel was out of town. Keith was frantic.

"I'll be back with a doctor. Stay right where you are," he said through the door.

I could not have moved if I'd wanted to. He also went for his mother, who demanded the landlord admit her and looked after me until the doctor showed up, and, as I was told later though I had no idea of time passing, she stayed all night and into the next afternoon. The fever broke then and I was able to sit up and move around some, so she went back to the store and returned later with dinner for me. In between I watered my thirsty ivy plant, which seemed to like my apartment better than Cecelia's shelf in our room at the Y, and had accordingly sprouted runners in all directions. One was climbing steadily up the River Avenue wall. It seemed to me I lay in bed for hours just staring at it.

I recall also that, during the delirium of fever, someone asked, "Where's her family? Is she here all alone? Can't we reach her mother?"

When I was feeling better and able to think straight, that little interlude of conversation made me feel sorry for myself and brought a lump to my throat.

Tetzel was due to be gone for the whole week, not returning until May 3, so I stayed home and tried to take care of myself. The Butler family literally treated me as one of their own, Christie coming over two or three times during the day and

Mrs. Butler coming whenever she had an opportunity to leave the store. Keith often came too, but stayed politely outside the door.

When the end of the week came he asked if I was up to a drive out to the San Jose Mission for a picnic. The weather was deliciously cool and breezy, bicycle-riding weather, but Keith insisted on borrowing his father's car and driving us out because of my weakened condition.

"You've lost weight, just look at you," he said on the way.

"I'll gain it back again."

"Camille, I don't know what you do at that bank, but you certainly are overworked. The doctor said you were exhausted. I think you ought to consider finding another position if that man overworks you so pitilessly."

"He's pretty nice, really," I said, looking at the pleasant countryside as we trundled along.

"Well just don't let him get the best of your good nature, that's all. Some employers really use their employees unfairly, especially where women are concerned. They know how hard it is for a young woman to make her way, and they seize on the opportunity to take advantage."

Sometimes it works precisely the other way around, I thought.

Although the more we learned, the more was yet uncovered, we finally did resolve one baffling situation about the Cabot and Tetzel meetings. Cabot came by one afternoon shortly after Tetzel returned, and this time I made a point of knocking on the door to ask a question once they were in session. One glance at the credenza told me all I needed to know.

Cabot had a habit of tossing his wide-brimmed hat in the same spot every time he visited, right in front of the receiver planted and concealed so carefully by Edwin.

10

I had been back at my desk but a few days when headlines of the *Lusitania* explosion streaked like the tongues of angry dragons across the newspaper, and suddenly everyone became very concerned about the war in Europe.

People in the office were discussing it the Monday following the disaster, and beginning to talk for the first time of choosing sides. The Germans vowed that the British merchant ship was carrying munitions, so they had every right to bomb it. Also, and this was not to be denied no matter which side was taken by an individual, the passengers were warned before they boarded ship and sailed for the war zone. Eventually the whole incident would be diverted from the attention of the public by a mass of bureaucratic red tape, memos, and papers back and forth between the United States and Germany. Yet it held a sharp and lasting significance for me, though I knew no more about the tragedy than anyone else at the time.

A couple of weeks later I was visited by Michael Stobalt. It appeared that the most inexperienced spy on behalf of the BNA cause was suddenly placed in a position of crucial importance. He began in his clipped and precise phrases, "Miss Devera, the developments over the past few months are such that we feel it unfair to involve you any further unless you have a complete understanding of what dangers you might be facing and are willing to face them. I cannot make your decision for you, but a moral obligation forces me to outline the situation for you and warn you. If you wish to cease helping, it will be completely understood, and the facts you've uncovered for us to date already far exceed anything expected."

I stared at him, wondering if he realized just how little I had really done.

"Through information you passed to us, we've been able to link certain shipments of copper from Cabot Consolidated Copper to destinations here in the States. We have certain proof that a large quantity has never left the country for points overseas."

"But I thought Germany was in dire need of copper and other raw materials to fight the war—where's it been going?"

"You know of certain instances in the past of munitions ships in the New York harbor exploding, and you will remember I explained to you in the beginning we knew that German sabotage was responsible for the planning of this sort of activity.

"Now we've been able to link copper going from Mexico to points where it is used in the making of several types of explosives, including old-fashioned clockwork—time—bombs, and just lately an incendiary bomb which is small yet lethal, and cigar-shaped, called a pencil bomb. These small bombs are equipped with time devices and are easily slipped into hidden places aboard ships headed for Allied countries, hours, or even days before detonation.

"We know that Adolph Tetzel has been responsible for the supply of much of the copper used in the making of such explosives."

I felt like someone had punched me in the stomach. I whistled under my breath.

"We have reason to believe that, contrary to information given to the public, it is almost a certainty that two of the time bombs—somewhat unreliable but more frequently used until recently—were placed on board the *Lusitania* before she sailed from New York harbor.

"But the papers said—"

"I know, and still we have no proof—perhaps we never will.

However, the fact remains that we have a definite link between
Tetzel and explosives, which we have suspected for some time,
not to mention his services in spreading German propaganda in
the States and aiding in the plot to return Victoriano Huerta
to power in Mexico."

"But you know he was against Huerta, in favor of the man
named Barrista."

"Yes—part of the puzzle as yet unsolved."

"Couldn't he be picked up, then? That would be sure to
scuttle the deal with Barrista."

"Not necessarily."

"But isn't it wrong to go on letting the bombs be used?"

"We have managed to take measures to control them, at
least for now."

"So, what's left?"

"We do not know how directly Mr. Cabot is involved, nor
how much he himself knows. And there is also a possibility his
wife may have ties in Colorado which prove significant. To
blow the whistle now would be to lose any opportunity for getting entirely to the bottom of activities being carried on among
the German Foreign Office, Mexico, and the United States. In
short, Cabot holds the key. Should we pick up Tetzel, he may
well turn to other sources within the German secret agencies,
may continue to carry on activities detrimental to Mexico and
to the United States, and to the advantage of those in Germany who wish to use him and others like him."

"Can't you pick up Cabot, too?"

"No, because there is no proof he was aware of the ultimate
destination of his copper. Now, there is also the matter of the
unnamed 'third party' in Tetzel's correspondence."

"So what happens next?"

"We intend to let the line out just a bit further on the plot
to return Huerta to power, because we believe in-fighting
among the German agents here in the States will eventually
uncover more for us. Authorities can pick up Huerta any time
before he actually crosses the border into Mexico, and manage
to hold him."

"What do you want from me?"

"If you decide to stay with us, you must redouble your efforts to find out more about this man Cabot, his wife, and his employee or employees. And if you can, discover a possible channel for written proof of Tetzel's activities from this end. So far he has been able to retain a link of some kind which protects him from holding much material which would be invaluable testimony to his espionage activities."

I thought of the proverbially empty safe compartment and said, "So, nothing has really changed."

"Nothing except that now we know the extent of Tetzel's activities is a great deal more far-reaching than we at first supposed. He may be a great deal more dangerous than we believed, may have lines open with persons much higher up in the German Foreign Office than we at first projected. He may be capable of deeds to which we would not want to subject you, Miss Devera."

"You mean, like murder or something?" I asked, jokingly.

"Exactly," he said. "It would be only too easy to rid himself of a young single woman, living alone in this large a city, should he become aware of your activities. You must know this risk is a very real one."

Suddenly I began to believe his earnestness might be well founded. As I carefully laid a trap for Tetzel, leading him along as though on a leash, while bothered by feelings of guilt about what I was doing, I may instead have been laying my own trap.

"Well, what do you say? Or, would you like to think it over?"

"Who will be able to do what I'm doing? You can't pick Tetzel's secretary for him . . . it occurs to me now that it might have been my naïveté that convinced him to hire me."

"Precisely."

"Then if I go, you lose your grip on San Antonio—or at least your mainstay."

"Yes."

"I don't suppose there's really a choice. I've gone this far. I guess I'll stick by."

His mouth relaxed into a smile, but his eyes expressed concern. "Do be careful, and stay in frequent touch with Edwin. Be cautious about creating dangerous situations for yourself, and go to him for advice whenever you are in the least doubtful. Good luck, Miss Devera."

"Thanks. I've a feeling I'm going to need it."

11

The following months were the roughest yet. Most of my time was spent in ferreting out the Cabots and Nathan Hope, and if anything of lasting value was gained, I suppose it was being forced to take a good, hard look at myself.

I discovered two strong parts of my nature that are absolutely contradictory, and caused me no end of grief all along. One is my initial trust and belief in the goodness of people, which I inherited from my father. This must be the worst property for anyone involved in espionage work, and has to be overcome constantly in order to succeed.

The other trait—being naturally inquisitive—proved quite an advantage. I believe this part of my make-up was largely subdued in the early months of shadowing Tetzel, because I was too inexperienced to let my instincts come forth, and too preoccupied with the mechanics of my work for the BNA to rely on my own initiative. After my meeting with Michael Stobalt, however, I began to get my bearings. Once I began my new task, I soon found myself staying awake nights preparing conversational hooks to get what information I needed. As time went on, my natural curiosity became compelling, and often I felt disgusted with myself for the way I used it.

While the Cabots were tough cases to unravel, I immediately recognized in Nathan someone unsteady, easily toppled, suffering from something acute which he tried desperately to hide. I have never met a more perplexing man.

Three weeks passed before I found an opportunity to meet

him. Then one day Tetzel asked me to send for a mullet to deliver a sealed envelope to Cabot's office. Luckily, the noon hour was approaching. "I can take it by. I have to go down that way anyhow, to pick up some shoes at the cobbler," I told him.

I whisked by my apartment and steamed open the envelope. The contents were three sheets of paper giving a rundown of Cabot's loan picture over the past three months, including interest accrued on several different notes. Unfortunately, time did not permit a trip to Sam's Print Shop, so I had to write down the most important figures I read. I was astounded to total up a balance due the bank in the amount of nearly four hundred thousand dollars. The paper showed a beginning balance of only around fifty thousand, and the rest had been transferred during the three-month period. The loan picture was drawn up by Tetzel's own hand, so apparently he had ordered Cabot's file from credit himself. This wasn't unusual. Often if I were busy on a project, he phoned downstairs for what he needed instead of bothering me.

I'd already used up thirty minutes, most of it awaiting the iron to heat up, so I hurried over to Commerce and walked into the Cabot office. I found Nathan Hope seated before a monstrous desk piled high with papers, staring at me through a thick pair of eyeglasses. I told him why I was there.

"Mr. Cabot is gone for the day, miss."

"Well then, maybe I ought to take this to his home. I believe it's important."

"Suit yourself."

I hadn't expected this, figuring instead he'd offer to take the envelope himself. I stood on one foot then the other, trying to think of a reason for sticking around. Finally he asked me if I had further business.

"No . . . I've just always wanted to see what an important businessman's office looks like. You must be Nathan Hope. Mr. Tetzel says you are Mr. Cabot's right-hand man."

"I work for him. It's that simple. Good day."

"Well, you needn't be so abrupt."

"I have work to do, as you can see. I don't mean to be unkind, but I have to get back to it. We—the Cabots live at

Beauregard and Washington in the brick house on the river side. If you like, I could take the envelope home with me this evening."

"You live with them?"

"Yes."

"Well, then you must be awfully important."

He crossed his arms and leaned back. "That's none of your business. Just leave the envelope, and—"

"I know, and go. All right then, I guess it's all right to be conceited when you work for a man like Mr. Cabot."

I was amazed at being met so coldly, and decided I needed to retreat and consider a new tactic. Just as I neared the door, however, I thought of another angle. "Say, don't you ever break for lunch?"

"Hardly ever."

"Well, you ought to. Your eyes are red. You could work better if you would give them a little rest."

"Thanks for the advice. Good-bye, miss."

"My name is Camille Devera. I'll come back tomorrow at twelve o'clock with sandwiches. We can sit out by the river somewhere."

He turned around and picked up his pencil. It was probably a rebuff, but I took advantage of the fact he had not thrown me out headfirst. On the way back to the bank I began analyzing him. So he lived with his boss. That seemed a little funny, as he was obviously up into his twenties and more apt to have quarters of his own, not to mention a wife and family. And from all I could gather, he was a little touchy about that situation.

I decided keeping him on the defensive might be the best course. I would show up at noon the next day with sandwiches —this would be a real step beyond the call of duty, as I would have to get up fifteen minutes early to prepare a lunch, when ordinarily I didn't bother with that meal—and try to develop some kind of friendship with him.

When I presented myself with a basket under my arm the next day, he looked surprised and started to send me away.

"Oh, but if you don't come it will hurt my feelings awfully," I said with all the innocence I could feign.

He considered a few moments, then said, "Well, I *have* been here since six-thirty," and pulled his coat off the hook. Walking toward the river I could sense he was ill at ease. A small man, he took quick, uneven steps. I had trouble falling into rhythm with him and was reminded of my first time on the dance floor at fifteen, trying to make the best of a waltz with a pimply-faced boy whose hands were warm and clammy. One thing you couldn't miss about Nathan, however, was his unusually tidy appearance from head to toe—every hair combed into place, fingernails so well manicured I was soon wishing for a pair of deep pockets in which to conceal mine. Even his shoes were as immaculate as my father's regulation army boots used to be.

I found it easy to convince him I'd fallen prey to his charms, though he was painfully short on them. Yet I had to give my all to unraveling him because he was the closest person to the Cabots and probably the only one with any knowledge of their lives. I was soon convinced he was privy to all important matters concerning Cabot, but was to change my belief back and forth as I tried to pinpoint his loyalties.

As we got acquainted over those first few weeks, I could tell he thought the whole world revolved around Electra Cabot. He told me all about what a cultured, knowledgeable lady she was, that she attended the symphony and art exhibits with a distinguished old English gentleman named Woodstone. He said she was a widow before she married Cabot.

Between our conversations I was feeding all this information back to Edwin, yet for a very long time it led to nothing. I could get Nathan to say much less about Cabot himself, and at the time could not understand why. He seemed to have almost an unhealthy attachment to the man, like an oath in blood. Perhaps, in a way, you could say that was the case.

Obviously, the man was lacking romantic attachments, so I batted my not-so-long eyelashes at him and tried to appear all goggle-eyed whenever we were together. Yet he didn't seem to take to that bait. He wanted to tell me more of how wonderful Electra was, that he built her a summerhouse and they sat together when Cabot was away and talked for hours, and she depended upon him for comfort and condolence in her loneliness. Actually he could say an awful lot without relating much, and after a while I began resenting the time wasted on him. It seemed there was not an hour of the day left when I was free to do what I wanted to do. Apparently Keith was tired of waiting around for me because lately he'd kept his distance. Likely he had found another girl, I supposed, one of those uppity finishing-school types that college men like. And here I was, literally giving away my lunch break to the BNA, sitting across from a young man I could scarcely talk with, and normally wouldn't bother.

Still I kept at Nathan persistently, though he was too close-mouthed to help until the end. Then of course he was telling a great deal that I was unable to make any sense of until it was too late. . . .

Oh, how I drove the poor man. I used to think up ways of finding out what made him react, not to mention keeping a mental list of subjects at hand that I could use should there be an empty silence between us. There often was. About the only time he talked at length on one subject was when he began reminiscing about his boyhood home in Mill Springs. Very often this would lead him into comparing his own widowed mother with Electra. I could see he held the two women on almost equal pedestals.

Regardless of what other topic I mentioned, he remained noncommittal, his expression changeless. Though I tried in every possible way I could think of, I never could satisfy myself as to whether he knew exactly where Cabot's copper was bound, and, indeed, how much he knew about Cabot's business altogether. He remained an enigma, at least for a long time.

Obtaining information—important, vital facts—from Electra Cabot proved less difficult. She was more open, especially in the beginning. Yet before I met her face to face I came across her in another place, following the day I watched her buying strawberries at Butler's.

One day at lunchtime I was sitting on a bench across from the post office awaiting a rendezvous with Edwin. I had picked up some more invoices from the safe compartment during Tetzel's brief absence from town, and had to return the originals that afternoon because he was due back in the office on the following day.

Electra came from my left, becomingly dressed in a pale pink suit with matching scarf frothing gently from the neck to the top button of her cape-collared suit coat. On her head was one of those huge Gainsborough hats, with deep pink flowers around the crown. Except for a small handbag and a closed parasol, she carried nothing in her gloved hands. For her looks and bearing, she might have been a queen about to be handed into a royal carriage.

I watched her go by purely out of admiration, my head full of fantasies, before I started to wonder what she might be doing at the post office. As she disappeared inside I decided she must be picking up a package too large for delivery at her home. Yet when she returned a few moments later, she was holding a small envelope. Still that could have led to no end of simple explanations. But when she reached the bottom of the stairs she suddenly stopped and looked quickly both ways, folded the envelope, and tucked it into her handbag.

Before she was out of sight, Edwin had approached from behind, and when I pointed her out to him he said, "Good-looking lady." After I explained what happened he said, "There's no way we can get into a post office and snoop around. Just keep your eyes open and see what develops."

Nothing came of it at first, though I did see her repeat the little trip from time to time both before and after we met. Several months passed before I was actually introduced to Electra, and in the meantime the Mexican General Huerta's so-called friends from the German underground seemed abruptly to lose interest in his welfare. His plans to cross the border, join his compatriot Orozco, and stage his return to power by the forces awaiting him, courtesy of German money and ammunitions, were supposedly laid with great care. Yet he was quite handily intercepted in El Paso by United States agents and died before he felt the soil of his own country beneath his feet again.

The failure of the plot was blamed by each German agent on the other. Von Rintelen blamed Boy-Ed and von Papen, whom, he vowed, scuttled the plan from the beginning because they resented his coming over here and meddling in their business. Edwin had called that one correctly, and so had Tetzel.

Regardless of who was at fault, the BNA agents were shadowing Huerta from the time he first reached New York, and after the matter was concluded a few months later, there was a very interesting conversation between Tetzel and Cabot, which I listened to from the storeroom while the recording machine rolled merrily and futilely along:

"You see, my friend, I told you Huerta would be taken care of," Tetzel said. (I could almost see his self-satisfied smile through the wall.) "Von Rintelen will be sent home like a bad boy, one the less thorn in my side. Now, how goes it from the other side of the border?"

"Propaganda is being circulated; everything is going forward as planned."

"Good. Now, with Huerta out of the way I can easily begin stockpiling munitions in Detroit for Barrista."

"But we still have to keep Villa on our side for a while. He's keeping my mines open. I'm going to need some more money to keep him happy. And he needs arms."

"All right. We can see to that. The stronger we keep Villa's forces, the longer it will take the Pan-American countries and the United States to mediate peace; and the busier they are kept working out Mexican problems, the less likely they are to interfere with our plans in Europe. All goes well. Why do you look so glum?"

"I just don't want a rock slide to begin on my mountain before I'm well out of the way."

12

One Saturday afternoon at the beginning of summer, I stopped by Butler's to pick up some groceries. I didn't really need anything, but I did want to see Keith.

Because I could never tell him why I was so often unavailable, he'd finally become convinced I had another suitor. The last time I saw him he invited me out for oyster rolls at the Manhattan. I almost accepted, then remembered a meeting scheduled with Edwin, and stumbled over a silly excuse. There was resignation in his reply: "Well, see you sometime."

I'd watched him walk away, seething. But I had stupidly expected him to ask me out again, and when he didn't I tried to convince myself it was just as well if he was spending his time with someone else. After all, he was only a friend. And yet . . .

I pulled a pickle from the barrel and drew up to the counter across from him. "How've you been?"

"Busy," he said, pretending to study a list of specials. "You know how it is, end of the school year, exams and so forth."

"Sure . . . but it's all over now, isn't it? I'm free tonight if—"

"Oh? That's too bad. I've already made plans."

I was sure my face was turning as green as the pickle in my hand, so I left a coin on the counter and said meekly, "All right, 'bye."

I was nearly to the door when he called, "How about tomorrow?"

"Sure." I smiled back, and right then I made up my mind I

was going to put Keith in front of the BNA more often. Edwin would just have to suit his schedule to mine for a change.

Keith arrived the next afternoon in his father's automobile. We weren't together five minutes before I was laughing and enjoying myself, and wondering why I hadn't realized that seeing him made it easier for me to face the daily burdens of BNA work.

That Sunday we attended a municipal band concert. It was such a hot day that the hint of breeze in the air brought people out of their homes in search of relief, and the crowd was so large at San Pedro Park that we had to leave the auto nearly a quarter of a mile from the bandstand. Keith's mother had packed a lunch—my inability to put meals together was a fact largely recognized—and after we ate we sat close to each other on the ground and listened to a cornet solo of "Love's Old Sweet Song" and a good rendition by the whole band of the "Blue Danube Waltz," one of my favorites, played upon request by someone in the audience. As the sun went down and the crowds began to disperse, Keith and I sat above the creek. He threw pebbles into the water while the descending sun cast dim light on the ripples. The breeze was soft and gentle, soothing as it fondled my hair. Keith looked almost handsome as his strong profile became more and more a well-defined silhouette against the darkening sky.

"I wish I could see more of you," he said at last.

I brushed the hair from my cheeks and looked toward the water. "I know . . . but you have other girl friends, don't you?"

"No one special."

"Neither have I."

"Then, why—"

"It isn't the way you think, Keith," I interrupted. "I just can't—settle down yet."

"Maybe you're right," he said with a shrug, and threw one last pebble into the glassy pool. Then he rose and helped me to my feet, and held on to my elbow for a prolonged moment. He looked as if he might kiss me, then changed his mind and led me toward the car. We rode all the way back to my apartment in silence, and when we reached the door I said, coyly, "I had such a good time today . . . wonder if there's another concert next Sunday?"

He looked half amused and said, "We could plan on taking a drive there just to find out."

I closed the door and leaned against it. How nice it was to know someone who really cared, even if he seemed to have a lot of growing up to do. I wished at that moment I could confide in him, tell him everything that I was involved in. I was so alone in this whole mess. Talking to Edwin was not to be confused with confiding. Apart from our work in the BNA, we had nothing in common as far as I knew. We were like two machines designed for exchanging information with nothing built into our parts for expressions of sympathy or comfort. I always had the feeling when this thing was over he'd tip his hat and disappear in a cloud of smoke.

Mother was of no help either. My last letter from her had arrived in July, and consisted of a lecture on the value of observing "sacrifice week" for the suffragettes. "I know you have few luxuries, dear, but cut expenses wherever you can. Women are giving up everything from trips to the hairdresser, clothes and new shoes and stockings, to using the streetcar and eating dessert. Savings will help to pay the pledged quota of the state association."

I'd thumbed my nose at the paragraph when I read it, but the letter did have its effect—every time I started to reach for a box of sweets, I wound up pulling back. At the end of the week I had twenty-five cents to contribute. Mother also mentioned she'd be in New Jersey in October, where V. for W. was to go before the polls. This was especially important because New Jersey was the President's home state and he was expected to vote in our favor. It was hoped his personal feelings would sway other voters.

I wrote to tell her of my savings, and wish her luck in New Jersey, then thought, if I didn't know so much about Emory Cabot I'd be wishing myself into Electra's shoes . . . being married to a man who could afford any luxury—no sacrifices necessary.

As it happened my feelings about the Cabots were altered before the summer was over. I still cannot explain the way I began to feel or why, yet I was faced with one more example of the bitter part of the work I was doing, which often led me to wonder what kind of man or woman could choose to make a career of espionage work. Watching, analyzing, and smoking out the Cabots was for me worse than being a youngster again, standing by helplessly as my older brothers captured a beautiful butterfly and stuck a pin through its body, stilling its majestic wings forever . . . a death mask mounted on a wall, put there for the purpose of a science project for school.

One afternoon Mr. Tetzel mentioned he and his wife planned a big celebration in their home for their wedding anniversary. I offered to address the invitations by hand, so that I could have a look at the list. After glancing over it I was convinced I had to be at that party, somehow. Not only would the Cabots be invited, but also the Stuttgarts—who had thus far remained an elusive pair.

"My penmanship isn't much compared to Giddeon Sparks', but I'll take care to be extra neat," I told him.

He looked puzzled for a moment, then said, "Of course," and laughed.

"I could help with table settings, or arrange flowers, too," I said.

"No, we'll have plenty of help with that."

"I could serve at table."

"That's already been taken care of. It's kind of you, Camille, however—"

"I know! I could be in charge of hats and handbags. That's always a real problem, and it would free your domestics to do other things. How about it? I can always use the extra money. I need a few things for my apartment, and I want a blouse I saw at—"

"All right, all right," he said, throwing up his hands and smiling. "You just can't keep down an industrious young person."

"That's me, industrious," I repeated, thinking of the memo

he'd sent to R. M. Francke the previous spring informing him of his view that the third party suggested by M.K. lacked "industry."

I gave much consideration beforehand to what I must achieve during that party, so that I would be ready to seize every opportunity. I bought a secondhand maid's uniform, gray with a white organdy apron and matching cap, so I could move about the house a little less obtrusively if I got the chance. I knew this might prove the ideal time to use the vest-pocket camera—I still had no pictures of any of the people under surveillance. But I didn't feel confident with it, and was afraid I'd lean over and lose it from my apron, or that some other revealing incident would give me away, so I decided not to use it.

By the night of the party I was practically in a fit of nerves. It had rained all day—an intermittent downpour that was a result of a storm closing in on the upper Gulf Coast. I'd planned to ride the River Avenue streetcar part of the way and walk the balance of the trip out to Laurel Heights, but the rain forced me to order a taxi to pick me up at half-past six. As luck would have it, the Tetzel home was outside the limits of the fixed routes for the five-cent jitneys.

I paced back and forth by the front windows as the minutes ticked by . . . six thirty-five . . . six-forty . . . six forty-five. Finally I caught sight of the taxi headlights glowing through the splashing water and, grabbing my umbrella, rushed to the door. As I opened it, there stood Keith in his slicker, one hand poised to knock; the other holding a box.

"Oh, say, I brought you some fresh peaches—hey, where are you . . . ?"

I whirled past him, calling behind me, "Leave them inside and lock the door, please," then fled down the stairs. On the second-floor landing I turned and shouted, "Thank you," but just then a clap of thunder shook the building and obliterated the sound of my voice. I made for the taxi without looking back again.

When I took on the job of looking after hats and other

accessories, I had not counted on the extra array of rain slickers, umbrellas, and rubber boots. At least six couples had already arrived and Mr. Tetzel was looking anxiously out the window for my arrival, while a maid, neglecting other assigned duties, sullenly carried soaked galoshes and other gear into the front parlor where a huge tarpaulin had been laid to protect the floor from the wet garments. Undoubtedly the Tetzels were a great deal better prepared for the occasion of rain than I was.

The party had been under way a good two hours before I got through grouping hats, gloves, and other apparel, and had a chance to walk into the magnificent ballroom. I'd been told it was the envy of many San Antonio families, and there was no wondering why. I could almost imagine the day Tetzel walked into the lobby of the Menger and told his building contractor, "I want you to duplicate this for my house."

I stood against a wall among the other hired helpers for a little while, before my eyes fixed on Electra and Emory Cabot coming out to dance. Little footlights had been placed here and there around the rectangular floor, and although there were many others dancing, the Cabots stood out like royalty among the peasants. My heart was pumping hard. Though I'd always admired them separately, I had never dreamed they'd make such a striking couple. Cabot wore a black evening suit and Electra wore a flowing rose-colored gown with a sheer mantle hung loosely around her throat, setting off her golden hair. Their arms extended for a Strauss waltz and he held her not quite, but almost dangerously, close, and looked right into her eyes. The lights from above played on their faces as they twirled around to the three-quarter waltz time, and when the lights caught them just right I saw his eyebrow raised, his mouth moving as though he whispered words meant only for her. Her radiant face was demure, her lips almost, but not quite, smiling. I was so wrapped up in watching them as they moved, I nearly swayed into a waiter carrying a tray of drinks. That reminded me I was supposed to be spying, not romanticizing.

Later, Lyla Stuttgart approached and asked, "Have you any cigarettes, love? These parties are a frightful bore, aren't they."

Before I could answer, her husband, Arnold, came from behind and said, "Come, dear, you must dance with Adolph while I waltz Sophie around the floor. It's the courteous thing to do."

She grimaced and went off with him.

By the time the evening was at an end, I had seen enough to know the Cabots and Stuttgarts were acquainted, particularly the two women, and I could not wait to tell Edwin this first piece of information about Arnold Stuttgart. Could he have been the "third party"?

Although I managed to wind up the evening as clumsily as I began, by losing Cabot's hat temporarily, I felt it was well spent. Mr. Tetzel reimbursed my one-way taxi fare, and offered to drive me home, but then a nice couple who would be passing down River Avenue on their route home insisted upon dropping me off.

All the way, the storm raged outside the auto window. I could not get the Cabots out of my mind. How handsome they were, commanding the dance floor, seeing nothing except each other . . . the very air around them seemed to sparkle. . . .

Later as I lay in bed, each time I shut my eyes I saw the Cabots. Round and round their images swirled, one-two-three, one-two-three, dancing, dancing, in and out of my mind and through my dreams like china figurines, they waltzed the hours away, the music resounding with as much liveliness as if it had never ceased. . . .

In the morning the spell was finally shattered, and I lay awake, sickened by the thought that these same two people could conceivably be separated by the horror of prison walls only months from now. Their beautiful clothing would be replaced by institutional rags. Authorities might cut her hair, shave his beard. The only space left to their command would be a small area in a dingy prison yard. They'd be kept from each other for years, maybe even forever. . . .

It was too awful to imagine. Oh Lord, forgive me, I thought, I know they're probably both rotten from head to toe, but I wish somehow they could be spared the price of guilt.

13

When I told Edwin about the party, he was pleased and said, "Make it your business to run into Cabot's wife when you can."

"I'm hardly in a position to—"

"Watch the house, follow her, ask questions of Nathan Hope. Also, keep your eyes on the mails and get into that safe whenever you can. And hire out to parties—that's a great idea —anytime you can."

Edwin had a way of making difficult feats sound easy. For the next couple of months, however, it seemed I was at another stalemate. Although I did get a chance to have a look in the secret safe compartment, and found a group of invoices which proved Tetzel was still in charge of getting arms across the border, there was a new consignment address in Laredo that stumped me until Edwin was able to check it out: Maxwell Coffin. A new name in the hat, I thought, puzzled, one more strange ingredient in the hobo stew. I contacted Edwin as usual, and thought no more about it.

Once or twice I got my hands on outgoing mail for Tetzel, but he seemed to be curtailing his communications with the German Foreign Office of late—perhaps because of the botched-up affair with Huerta—and in any case, his messages were so cryptic that I felt the only sure way to learn who he so often referred to as the "third party" was to get my hands on the mail coming to him. This I was never able to do. Nothing except bank business ever came to the main mail desk. Though

I searched his desk, his cabinets, his briefcase, and everything else I could think of, I found nothing. It was possible he kept mail in his home somewhere, but on the night of the party I had been able to steal into his study for a quick look, and found his desk locked. I checked the key chain he carried, but found no key small enough for a desk lock. The only way to get in, then, was to have a key made for the desk by bringing in a locksmith, and this little bit of dirty work would almost have to be performed when the Tetzels were out of town and the house closed. They never seemed to travel together, and they kept a staff of at least six regular servants apt to pop up anywhere at any time. The desk-key dilemma was one example of the endless frustrations hampering our progress.

I kept up with my mid-day meetings with Nathan, in hopes of gathering some useful information, yet as the weather cooled off our lunches on the riverbank would have to cease and getting moments alone with him would be more difficult.

As the evenings grew dark earlier, I began working a little later, then leaving the office and making straight for the little neighborhood headed by the house with the square tower and transversed by King William Street. There were lots of bushes, shrubs, and trees to use as camouflage while I watched for any comings and goings from the Cabot house, and the triangular park was a good vantage point for watching the Stuttgart house.

One night I reached the edge of the Cabot yard just at dusk, and noticed Electra tugging a basketload of pecans toward her back door. I rushed ahead and offered her a hand.

"I meant to bring these in earlier, but they were so heavy I decided to leave them for Nathan to carry. Now he's called to say he'll have to work late. How lucky you happened by—what brings you down here?"

"Why . . . I have some friends a couple of blocks from here."

"Are you in a rush to get there?"

"No, ma'am."

"Then come in and have some refreshment with me. I'm lonely these days. Emory's in Mexico, you know."

Inside I was full of questions as to her husband's business.

She told me about his mining properties in Mexico, and said he
was seeing to a supply shipment of some kind, and checking on
production. "I really know very little about how his business is
run, because I never go down there."

"It's hardly a place for visiting these days."

"How I wish all the fighting would stop. It scares me to
death when Emory travels down there. He never knows what
he'll find."

"I can imagine. But he probably has friends who look after
him, doesn't he?"

"Oh yes. In fact, he has ranching property next to that of
Fernando Barrista—have you heard of him?—he's very distinguished. We've had him as our guest here a couple of times."

I tried not to show my excitement. "Uh—yes, it seems to me
I've run across that name before."

She opened her mouth as though to add a further remark,
but changed her mind and took a sip of coffee. "More currant
cake?"

"No, thank you."

"Camille, since I don't really know you well, I hope you
wouldn't feel . . . insulted . . . if I advised you about something. I admire you a lot for taking on extra jobs and working
so hard to make your way. However, I couldn't help noticing
something at the party not long ago. I don't want to mention
names . . . but I think you ought to look out for people—men
—who might try to take advantage of your position. Sometimes
young women who are single and bright, and attractive, are
. . . well, noticed a little more, shall we say." She paused and
shook her head. "I know I'm being vague, but just be on guard
when extra attentions are paid you by people you might be indebted to."

I couldn't imagine what she was talking about, but it was
clear she wasn't about to divulge any names, so I pretended to
be in the know, and nodded agreeably.

All the way home and into the rest of the evening I puzzled
over what she told me, trying to think of every incident at the

party which might have led her to caution me. I was only "indebted" to one person—Mr. Tetzel—but surely she wouldn't have read anything into his actions toward me. He'd never come close to trying anything fresh.

Maybe she was the jealous type, and meant to warn me against getting involved with her husband. If I had a husband that good-looking, I might be inclined to be suspicious now and then.

I was still mulling it over when I met with Edwin several nights later, but saved it till we'd discussed other business first.

He said he'd get to work right away on Barrista, and added, "I wonder when they intend to pull the rug out from under Pancho Villa?"

"Looks like the United States is going to do that for them. They're about to recognize Carranza."

"Yes, but that won't stop an old bandido like Villa."

"What can you do about the Barrista revolution?"

"All depends upon what is being done on this side of the border. I'll have to find out what I can. Unless they're exporting guns directly to him, or drawing up battle plans, there isn't much we can do. I'll say one thing for Cabot and Tetzel. They run a tight ship. We've had a lot of tough cases to open, but I never saw one like this, at least not in my territory.

"Oh, by the way, the invoices you found were consigned to a coffin company."

"You're kidding. I thought Maxwell Coffin was a proper name. What in the world for?"

"A good way to smuggle arms across the border."

"Inside coffins?"

"That's right."

"Well then, as soon as you fill in the U.S. agents, they'll confiscate the guns and blow Tetzel's whole operation wide open."

"That's why nothing will be done yet. We're going to let out some more rope."

"I wonder what'll happen when Carranza is recognized."

"On an official basis, Washington will be able to wash its hands of the trouble down there. It'll be cut and dried from this side of the border as far as selling him arms. It ought to solve a lot of problems about embargoes."

"Then, what about Barrista? Do you suppose the Germans will drop the idea of financing him?"

"Not if it means they can keep trouble stirred up by continuing."

"I don't understand why the United States can't pluck out everybody concerned. All you have to do is pick up a newspaper to read of German plots being uncovered all the time."

"Because they have no proof of anything, yet. What we know and what we can document are as far apart as one end of Texas from the other."

I told him then about my guarded advice from Electra. He paused, considering, then said, "I wish we could get something on her background. She may be in deeper than we think. That post-office routine is especially interesting. Next time you see her, ask about her maiden name and her former married name if you can. We haven't been able to turn up anything so far on either of the Cabots before they got to San Antonio.

"In the meantime, beware of men who pay you too much attention."

I looked across at his profile. He was smiling.

Next morning a mullet delivered a tin box with my name on it, full of shelled pecans from Electra Cabot. "Oh, fudge!" I said, dismayed again at the fact the people I was after made me feel awful by being so nice.

Giddy, who was standing by, said, "Excellent idea. I have a marvelous recipe passed down from my mother."

"What?"

"For fudge, of course, with lots of pecans. Delicious!"

Bewildering, how weeks would pass when nothing would turn up, then suddenly, just as light gleams at the end of a tunnel at last, so would come another smattering of puzzle pieces into our laps.

In December the German agents Boy-Ed and von Papen were recalled to their homeland, leaving only von Bernstorff, the German ambassador, in the States. From what Edwin told me they'd gotten pretty sloppy in their plotting in this country, probably because they were so tied up in internal conflicts, and they became an embarrassment to the German high command. I attached no particular significance to this until late in the month, when Cabot returned and met with Tetzel.

I stationed myself in the storeroom to listen in. Cabot apparently wasn't feeling very well. He kept pacing back and forth, complaining of his aching head and limbs. "I was afraid Barrista might buckle under once the United States recognized Carranza, but I think I've got him talked into holding on."

"Good."

"He still wants to go in peacefully, by a vote, if possible."

"That's all right . . . if it can be done."

"Just in case it doesn't work out that way, I'm going to lay out some plans for taking up arms. And I'll need to collect hospital supplies, as well as weapons."

"You know we are stockpiling arms. You can purchase hospital supplies under one of your company names. Here's the address of a firm in Corpus that can be trusted to remain discreet. How much money will you need—five, ten?"

"Make it ten. Oh yes, and there's another matter, too. That damned push for national prohibition. I'm going to have to pour more money toward the antis, although I think it's going down a dry hole."

"I think you're playing a losing game for time, Cabot. Why don't you just sell out now, and take the loss? I can lend you more if you need it, when the properties you're looking at down there become available."

"We've sure as hell got to get rid of Carranza. He's never going to honor those land titles from Villa, and he controls most of the north now. My production's almost at a standstill."

"That's all right for now."

There was a pause then and Cabot finally added, "Your patience is to be admired. I wish I had some of it."

"Recent developments have lessened my worries somewhat. There's no need to rush. If we do, plans go awry. Take time and care, everything will work out perfectly."

"I gotta get home. My head's killing me."

"Take care of yourself. You might have picked up something down there, eh? Perhaps you behaved badly?"

A silence followed, then Cabot replied, "Hell, I wouldn't touch any of those broads down there. I've just got a fever or something."

Again, I thought with satisfaction of his devotion to Electra. Just after he left, Mr. Tetzel locked his door for an hour. When he came out he laid some sealed envelopes on my desk. It was still plenty early for the mail pickup, but I intercepted the envelopes anyway, as I often did, a least until I had a chance to look over their contents. One of them was addressed to the New York contact. I slipped it into my drawer.

When I steamed it open that night I found a brief note inside: "All plans go forward in Mexico. Now that I have more control over business at hand, I am certain we can realize our aims. I trust B. and V. will have a more successful journey home than V.R."

Lots of things came together then. There was no doubt to whom B. and V. referred, and V.R.—von Rintelen, had been picked up recently, carrying a fake passport in Switzerland. He'd been taken by the British to a prison of war. Apparently Tetzel had long hoped for a situation like this, putting him more in control. Add those facts to his vagueness with Cabot and it seemed a fair chance even Cabot did not know the full extent of the puppet strings manipulated by him.

There were new questions surfacing all the time. Had Tetzel been responsible for scuttling Boy-Ed and von Papen? Was he continuing to finance Pancho Villa—now labeled an outlaw as he battled Carrancista forces—only until Barrista was ready to step in? Or did he intend to double-cross Barrista in the end, keeping his little embryonic revolution on tap until such time as Villa forces whipped Carranza and more trouble was needed to keep the United States busy?

Did Villa know of Barrista and co-operate in the whole plot? In the end, would they join in dual control? I had read that Pancho Villa wanted a civil government. Was the idea that

Barrista would head the nation while Villa led the armed forces?

Was the whole thing a complicated game for just one purpose: keeping the United States out of the war by continually stirring up trouble? If so, who knew the full truth, and what was in it for Tetzel?

That is what I wondered most of all. What could he possibly gain that would be worth the risk of losing everything he had so carefully and wisely built here? If the Germans won the war, it would be the generals and the monarchy who took the spoils, not the lowly espionage leaders whose dirty activities were best swept under the rug.

The more I thought about it the more I wondered who was deceiving whom, and the more I feared we were all being pulled under by a current stronger than we could fight.

14

I had not seen Keith since the night of the Tetzel party, when I rushed by, leaving him with his gift of fresh peaches in my doorway. I had never thanked him properly or apologized for my rudeness, although I'd consumed the sweet and succulent fruit with all the abandon of a drinking man who opens his first bottle of whiskey after a long ride on the wagon.

Every time I went into the store he was either busy checking stock or carving a piece of meat for a customer, or out on a delivery. When the holiday season rolled around and the pace slowed down at the bank, everyone infected by the spirit of peace and thanksgiving in one way or another, I thought of Keith a lot. His family would all be together on the important days, while I'd be alone unless Mother surprised me with a visit. She had been campaigning hard in New Jersey, where, in spite of the endorsement by the President, the women's vote lost. Next week she would be back in Washington for a big protest meeting of some kind, which she didn't take time to detail in her letter. It seemed doubtful she would come all the way down to San Antonio in between.

I'd taken an early job of writing up orders for signature handkerchiefs at Washer Bros., and would begin late in December at Joske's, this year as a clerk instead of a wrapper. I supposed I'd just get lost in extra jobs and let the season slide by as painlessly as possible, and considered asking Giddy what her plans were for Christmas day, in case she might be alone, too.

Yet Keith came by one evening unexpectedly and said, "Mother asked me to invite you for Christmas dinner at Christie and Ken's. I told her I figured you'd have other plans, but I'd see." He addressed me from the stair landing, having walked back there after knocking on the door.

"Oh no. I'd love to come," I said, so eagerly that Keith's eyes widened. He moved closer to my door. "I haven't seen your family for such a long time . . . it sounds like great fun."

"Won't you be seeing that other guy?"

"What other guy?"

"The one you have lunch with all the time, down by the river."

"Oh, him . . . uh, he works for an important bank customer and I have to be nice to him, that's all. It isn't what you think."

"Seems I've heard that one before."

"Well, just what are you doing spying on me?"

"I'm not. I happened to see you there a couple of times, on my way somewhere. Say, have you seen *Birth of a Nation* yet? Everybody's talking about it."

"No, and I'd love to go if you want to. Just name the date."

"How about tomorrow night?"

I was supposed to see Edwin, which caused me to hesitate momentarily, then I made up my mind and said, "What time will you come by for me?"

Next morning I called Edwin and told him I had other plans. "I have a friend who's beginning to suspect something is going on because I have to say no to him nearly every time he invites me out. Don't you think I'd better say yes?"

"Probably so. But lets make it lunch the following day."

"All right. The weather's gotten too cool to try and spirit Nathan out very often."

"Did you get a former name on that Cabot woman?"

"Yes. It's Dexter. That's all I could find out."

"Who gave it to you?"

"Nathan."

"That might not be for real."

"Well it was the best I could do," I said, irritated. "Look, you want me to be nosing around all the time without looking suspicious. There are only certain natural ways to get into conversations that personal. I have to use them."

"Right. See 'ya. Tomorrow, in front of Duerler's Candy."

When we met, Edwin had some new developments to discuss. He'd put a check on the name Dexter in Denver, which might take months to track down, especially in the absence of any first name, and he had also found out that Fernando Barrista's daughter, Aegina, was right here in the city attending school. "Nine to one, she's also busy working on the revolution. She's enrolled in Sacred Heart Liberal Arts College up north of town, taking advanced courses in languages and education."

"Oh, swell. What do I do now, quit my job and enroll in college?"

"No. We have a person on the staff here in the school office. His code name is Hubert. He's going to check on her. I've already had him working on Stuttgart Printing, and he has found some invoices from a small city in France on Stuttgart's desk. We're investigating them."

"How many people do you have working in San Antonio?"

"Just the three of us, plus Sam the printer. Well, if that's all—"

"Incidentally, my rent's going up in January—five dollars more a month. I got a notice this morning."

"I'll see what I can do. Maybe you could find another place."

"From what I hear others say, it's still cheaper than most apartments in the area."

"You better stay there, then. If you get short, holler."

"My Christmas job pays more this year because I'll be clerking. Maybe I can find something else after that."

"No, you won't have time to do any shadowing if you have too many jobs."

The President was making his tour around the country, speaking on national defense, increasing the army strength and spending millions on new equipment and ammunition. When I mentioned the subject to Nathan it proved to be another touchy spot with him. "I think it's time and money foolishly spent," he said.

"But what if we're drawn into the war in Europe? Between the British interfering so much with our shipping, and the Germans bombing first and asking questions later, it looks to me as though we ought to be prepared."

"We've stayed out this long. Who'd be left to mediate if we had to go in?"

If the Germans have their way, probably Mexico, I thought.

"That's a good point," I said. "Who do you think will win?"

"Who cares?"

His face was growing redder, but I couldn't figure exactly why he was so bothered, unless both he and Cabot were involved in Tetzel's intrigue with the German Foreign Office, which would instantly label them as traitors if we went to war. So far the facts I'd learned didn't add up to that. There was a prolonged silence. Finally I said, "What does Mr. Cabot think? I always believe good businessmen have wise opin—"

"What does he know?" Nathan snapped back, and glared at me.

"I suppose so . . . well, I hope we don't get into the war. I'd sure miss you if you had to go off soldiering."

That did it. He was on his feet at once. "You silly little brat! What do you know about important matters of the world, always putting in your two cents' worth where it doesn't concern you?"

"Gosh, I didn't mean to make you angry."

"I'm not angry, why should I be? I've got to get back to work. You waste more time than a gossippy old woman," he stated, then stalked off. If I could just get at the bottom of what's nagging him, it would be worth all the trouble I've gone to, just satisfying my curiosity at last, I thought.

It was the sort of conversation that characterized the whole end of the year—a time of loose ends that continued to wind like spaghetti around a fork. At Christmas dinner in 1915, Keith's father offered a lengthy blessing before the sumptuous feast in front of us, thanking the Lord for keeping us out of the war and praying for His guiding hand on our government's shoulder. After dinner Keith and Ken occupied the floor with talk of aeronautics, especially what they knew of the Royal Flying Corps' deeds in Europe, and Keith's every phrase made it more obvious that he was bursting at the seams to get over there in the midst of it. I noticed his father smoking his pipe, watching Keith with a father's special kind of seasoned expression, and wondered whether there would be another Christmas when we'd all sit around, stuffed fuller than the Christmas turkey, and talk academically of the war that already involved us much more dangerously than any of the Butlers were aware.

15

Though I couldn't see it then, even from my informed position, the minutes were ticking off faster and faster toward the inevitable explosion of forces. Since the reluctant but nonetheless official recognition of the Carranza government in Mexico, the United States had been gradually shifting focus to the war in Europe as it affected our shipping, reacting with indignation both to British and German violations of the neutrality laws, veering dangerously close to the precipice of war yet managing to stay behind a point of safety.

Though I probably will never know for certain, any more than others, whether the speculation by Edwin and other BNA people that the Germans were responsible for the turning of the tide in January of 1916, it certainly seems plausible they backed Pancho Villa when he massacred the mining engineers near Chihuahua City. It did eventually bring on our intervention down there, keeping us busier than ever just when we had supposed ourselves done with Mexican troubles. And of course Villa was getting money and weapons from somewhere for his gradually diminishing troop force. However, there was no proof that Adolph Tetzel was dealing with it.

Through all the months that I had worked for him, though I had found invoices in his safe and copied vaguely worded memos, never had I picked up a check voucher or check, bill of lading, or any other incriminating document that actually carried his signature, and after the Chihuahua City incident the evidence I was able to glean became even more disturbingly scarce by comparison.

He may have become more careful than ever. One particle of proof that he had anything to do with the increasingly futile and expensive chase of Pancho Villa deep into the mountains and out again, up and across the border of Mexico, and there would have been no further hesitation by the U. S. Government to pick him up, thereby breaking what was probably one of the best-kept espionage rings ever dreamed up by the Germans.

I believe up to that time the BNA and its ever-growing network of agents in the States had been largely responsible for holding U.S. authorities from beginning their own investigation. Yet suddenly there was nothing in his desk anymore, not even invoices, to link him with Pancho Villa and his gang of raiders. I wondered from time to time whether all of it had been my imagination in the first place. If he made any contact with the German Foreign Office during those early months of 1916, he certainly did so without my knowledge. In short, he effectively absolved himself of any danger of immediate capture. Even his involvement with Cabot and Barrista could not be proved. All he had done, according to documented evidence, was to lend money to Cabot.

Soon after the tragic incident in Mexico, Cabot came by to talk with Tetzel, and from my side of the storeroom wall, it seemed the conversation on Tetzel's side of the desk was unusually guarded.

Cabot was reporting he feared Ralph Jones, his mining engineer, had been among the men executed near Chihuahua City. He was obviously much relieved the man was safe. Yet, the next thing we knew, Jones had been killed and Cabot was off to El Paso to claim his body. The day he left, Tetzel made many telephone calls behind closed doors, and though I strained hard to hear him through the wall—the headset again was useless—I couldn't make out anything except that he was trying hard to locate a mining engineer to replace Jones. He spoke in vague terms about someone who would be suitable to take over, and whether he could handle such things as "additional duties," and so forth, never detailing the specific things he wanted. I gathered Jones had known little or nothing of the ultimate destination of copper from the Cabot mines.

That evening he left a little early, and said he had to stop off at Cabot's home to leave some information for him. I offered to stop by for him and he seemed to consider it for a moment, then said, "It's only a note, but I can take care of it." I paused momentarily and looked through the door. In a short time, he'd circled back again, catching me cold. "Your thoughts are many miles from here," he remarked pleasantly, then took his homburg from the rack and walked out again. I made sure he could hear the loud tapping of the typewriter keys before he was out of earshot down the hall. I chastised myself for slipping. Usually I thought of the homburg and went chasing down the hall with it. What must he be thinking . . . ?

Several days later, when Cabot got back into town, he met with Tetzel again and talked of his sad duty of relaying Jones' body to his home state of Michigan. Cabot seemed very depressed about the matter, and when Tetzel asked if Electra had given him the name he'd passed to her, Cabot said, "Yes, I've contacted the man. I guess he'll do. Hell, at this point I don't really give a damn anymore. Everything seems to be coming apart in my hands."

Tetzel counseled patience, and managed to talk him into borrowing another ten thousand dollars from the bank. "It's very hard now on the mines down there. When this is all over, paying back will be small change."

"Well go ahead and transfer it, but I'm still working on a buyer for my properties here. If I could just hold back that goddamn prohibition campaign for long enough—ah, well. . . ."

"One cannot control everything, sadly."

"Yep."

"You heard Huerta has died in prison."

"Bladder cancer, so I heard."

"According to reports."

There was a long pause, then Cabot said, "Were the reports of his illness true, or—"

"My friend, one can believe only half of what the papers say, so who knows? In any case, he is better out of the way for good, eh?"

"You can bet your ass on that."

16

Through the early months of 1916, it seemed the obstacles were endless. Though I checked the secret compartment in Tetzel's safe time and time again, I found nothing except his gilt-framed picture. And, from all evidence, he continued to be out of touch with his contact in New York, R. M. Francke.

Cabot came by a time or two—his eyes bloodshot, his voice a bit slurred—and spent most of his visit with Tetzel denouncing the proposed 50 per cent increase in income tax on people worth a million dollars or more. I had not realized his wealth amounted to so much, and made a mental note to tell Edwin. He had not yet found where most of Cabot's financial strength in San Antonio lay. He owned no bottling companies or whole-sale liquor houses, or if he did, they were not in his name.

Through all of Cabot's raving, Tetzel remained calm and amiable. His demeanor of inward contentment when so much was at hand no doubt puzzled Cabot as much as it did me.

Even Edwin did a lot of head shaking during our meetings. Finally one night he said, "Since we can't find out anything from listening to Tetzel right now, maybe we could find out something from listening to Cabot talk behind Tetzel's back— to Electra, or his man Hope. We've got to find out what goes on in that house of theirs." He'd already ascertained the design of Cabot's cramped office would make wiring it impossible, and anyhow, he seldom seemed to be in it. Dangerous visits during the wee morning hours on three occasions had not turned up anything on paper we didn't already know. The last time Edwin tried to steal in—around two in the morning—

he almost came face to face with Nathan, still at work. "Have you noticed anything unusual about their house lately—any changes?" he asked.

I thought for a moment. "At night—when I'm able to get by —the car is often gone from the garage, but the lights are on upstairs. And once or twice I've seen Electra looking out the window—I suppose from their bedroom. I've never been in any of the rooms except the kitchen."

"Wonder if they have a basement, where I could conceal a machine."

"Probably. Many of those houses have an underground floor."

"Find a reason to go by there and have a look."

"I'll try. I owe Electra a favor. She sent me a tin of fresh pecans last fall. Maybe I could take her a quart of strawberries from Keith's store. They ought to be coming out soon, and she likes them."

"Good. Flatter her about her house. Ask her to let you look around."

"Couldn't you get into trouble for wiring a private home?"

"I won't tell if you won't."

He started to walk away, then said, "Oh yes, we had that Stuttgart lead checked out."

"Oh? That was quick."

"Yes. It turns out Stuttgart's wife has expensive taste in clothes. She'd ordered several little creations—worth about two grand—from a fashion house outside of Paris—perfectly legitimate."

I laughed, and Edwin added, "At times like these, it helps to have something to laugh about . . . but if I had a wife like Stuttgart, I'd wring her neck."

Typically, he'd departed before I had a chance to ask a further question, and I stood there wondering whether he had a wife, or any other family.

The following Saturday I walked down to Beauregard Street, a bucket of strawberries in hand. Actually I followed Electra home from a visit to the British gentleman's house. I held back until she had time to get inside and settled, then I knocked on the door.

I was surprised to see her face very drawn, her eyes worried. She seemed greatly changed from the last time I had visited with her. But she managed a smile and invited me in for tea.

Soon she told me she was concerned about her friend. "Woody's quite old, and his only close relative has joined the British Army. He's worried about him, and I'm afraid the strain might affect his health."

"He's lucky to have a friend like you to look in on him."

"I'm not much help; it's frustrating—not being able to do anything to stop this madness. Emory accuses me of taking the whole war too personally, but then he doesn't know Woody. He's a kind old fellow." Then she brightened and said, "Well, it does me good to see your face. You always make me feel good and lively."

"Thank you, ma'am," I said, though the remark surprised me.

"I do so admire you for making your way in the world. I don't know how many times I've told Emory. It is so hard on a woman, yet you strike out and manage a greater degree of self-reliance than any woman I know."

"It's odd you should say that. I must admit I've wished myself in your shoes a few times."

"Mine? Oh, my dear, you don't know what you're saying. Not that I haven't had a good life here in San Antonio, but whereas I'm totally dependent on . . . circumstances, you've learned to take care of yourself. You're three strides ahead of most women. I just don't know why Nathan doesn't . . ." her voice trailed off.

"What?"

"Don't tell Emory I said so, but I think you two make the nicest pair. Yet Nathan won't take any girl seriously. It's a shame, I think. He just isn't interested."

"I've noticed that. And lately something seems to be really bothering him."

"It's the Army. He's scared to death of being called to duty. I don't know why. Emory taunts him about it—I think he considers Nathan's attitude unmanly. But I think Nathan deserves more compassion than that. Men seldom give much understanding to each other in friendship, do they?"

I was so thrown by her talkativeness, her change in demeanor, that I all but forgot my errand and was forced to bring up the subject of her house as though it suddenly popped into my head. "I've always admired your home. I'd love to see how you have it decorated. If you could see my little apartment, you would understand my fascination about all the houses down here. Yours is one of the nicest."

"Why, thank you. I'll show you around."

I made light chatter as we went, in order not to be terribly obvious: "Do you know Mrs. Steves down on King William? Her house has the natatorium, and its own artesian well to water her pecan grove. It's one of my favorite houses."

"I don't know her well, though I met her once, at a coffee klatch, I believe. My only close acquaintance since we moved here besides Woody is Lyla Stuttgart. Do you know her?"

"Not personally, but her husband is a bank customer. I met her briefly that night at the Tetzel party. She's very attractive."

"Yes, though I don't think she realizes how lucky she is. Travel and education—finer things of all kinds—have been handed to her freely. Yet she seems bored most of the time, and doesn't like to be with her children very much. She could stand reminding what blessings they are. Why, I'd give anything if—" she began, then abruptly stopped.

Eager to bridge the awkward pause, and even more anxious to learn the answer to the question she had brought to my mind, I said, "From what Nathan told me, you and Mr. Cabot haven't been married very long . . . maybe in time—"

She cut me off so quickly I was sure she was offended by my nosy remark. "That isn't what I meant. I was about to say I wish I'd had Lyla's material advantages. I've learned everything I know on my own, just about. And I can thank Woody for my acquaintance with art and music, such as it is."

This surprised me. I assumed she'd been wealthy and involved in cultural activities for years, probably a former socialite in Denver. I'd have to tell Edwin. Suddenly she said,

"Emory and I were very poor growing up. He's worked so hard, and put up with so much pressure and strain, to amount to something. I admire him."

"I didn't realize you two were children together."

"Yes. Emory was the champion of my youth, you see, and I never quite forgot him. It's too bad he had to miss your visit tonight. He's out on . . . business."

From the picture I'd gotten lately—his symptoms of heavy drinking, his conversations with Tetzel—I could see she was defending him as much to herself as to me, and I was sorry for her.

Before leaving I had established there was a basement with a fair-sized storage closet, where Edwin could hook up his equipment and run his wire upstairs from the outside. It wasn't easy. I had to lure her down there to show me all the fresh fruits and vegetables she'd put up in jars, and couldn't get away without gifts of pickled okra, pear preserves, and spiced peaches from her shelves. Because of this spontaneous generosity on her part, and the fact she was so open about her feelings with me, I left her home hating myself for intruding. Edwin should feel the evening was well spent, I thought bitterly, walking home. Now he could hook up his machine, and duck into the basement window to listen, whenever he dared.

The question remained of how and when he could go to work on it. Surprisingly, the opportunity proved ready-made.

In April, Electra phoned me at the bank to see if I'd work at an anniversary celebration. Though I jumped at the chance, I never dreamed this would be Edwin's opening. Yet when I mentioned the party to him he said, "Good. I can be out there right after dark."

"The place will be crawling with guests."

"All the better. I'll be on the side of the house where you've drawn the diagram, and everyone else will be entering the front door. Perfect. Noises I happen to make won't be noticed. Couldn't beat it."

I failed to count on the gay idea of Japanese lanterns being strung between the house and summerhouse to entice the guests out there. By the time I learned of the lights it was too late to reach Edwin, and anyway, though the job would be a bit more risky than we'd expected, I felt he'd probably choose to go on with it. We were getting pretty desperate for information, and becoming a little more inclined to take bigger chances. The basement storage closet was on the same side as the summerhouse, but far to the rear of the main house. So I figured Edwin could size up the situation when he arrived, and if he felt it was too risky he could leave. We scheduled a meeting at nine o'clock under the window where he'd be working, one well concealed with luxuriant shrubs.

Since Cabot didn't keep a home study as we had hoped, and it was hardly possible to wire the kitchen in order to catch round-table conversations, we had decided on a small sitting room that looked more often used than the formal front rooms. On the night Electra had shown me the house I'd noticed a tray of cigar butts beside one chair in that room, so I gathered they spent some time there together in the evenings, perhaps. There were newspapers around and a crocheted shawl hanging on one chair. In fact Electra apologized for the appearance of the room and told me she just couldn't keep it tidy.

I stole away from the busy party at the appointed hour, and met with Edwin's indignant remark: "Whose brilliant idea were the lanterns?"

"I don't know."

"Did you see where they're hooked up inside?"

"Yes. I can turn them out for a while, I think, without arousing suspicion. Bad connection, faulty switch. Don't worry. Just say when. I've already unlocked the basement window and checked the sitting room."

"Has everybody gotten here?"

"I don't know, but I think so. It's been going on almost two hours."

"All right, I ought to be able to have this thing connected before people start leaving. I've got the machine hidden behind the shrubs. I'll have to put it downstairs first, then wire up along the edge of the window facing outside, then in again. I've got a new receiver that's supposed to be better than the one we have in Tetzel's office. We'll give it a try, anyway."

"How long before you'll be at the window? That's the dangerous part."

"Give me half an hour. Then lights out. When they go, I'll begin."

"Right. Oh Lord, I hope this works."

"Don't worry. I've done this so much I could do it blindfolded."

"Yes, but I haven't."

Nathan was making himself most useful all evening, and I kept watching to see where he'd show up next. The only thing we had going in our favor was that, so far, none of the guests seemed to be interested in taking a stroll out to the summerhouse. Who would, anyway? They were all married couples. Electra told me it was Lyla who insisted on the lanterns, and once she had taken a glance at them, on her way into the party, she gave them no more notice. "That's typical of her," said Electra. The punch bowl on a table inside the summerhouse remained untouched all evening long.

At nine-thirty I managed to disconnect the lights; yet, afraid it would be obvious if I just pulled out the plug, I pulled it out so that it still hung on just barely. Anyone might have stepped on the wire and pulled it part of the way from the socket. Yet the connection was in the anteroom between the dining room and kitchen, and there were no windows, so, after several moments of hesitation, I darted outside to see if the lights had indeed gone out. When I got far enough around to assure they had, Edwin was just coming out the window of the basement with his wire. I started back toward the house when all at once I heard Nathan calling. I could have gone right through the ground, headfirst.

Nathan had been responsible for wiring the lights, so it was a good guess he'd go feeling around, trying to find out what was wrong with them. I couldn't warn Edwin to get back in, because of the noise of the party drowning my voice unless I shouted. Edwin couldn't see Nathan because of the bushes concealing him and his ladder. Thinking fast, I rushed toward the summerhouse and yelled, "Over here, Nathan." I hoped Edwin would hear my voice, but as luck would have it, he didn't.

Nathan came charging toward the summerhouse, each step more indignant than the last as he mumbled his irritation over the failure of the lanterns. Finally when he mounted the little steps he demanded, "What are you doing out here? Mrs. Cabot has been looking all over for you."

"I came to check on the punch bowl. Look, the ice has melted and it's about to run over. Do you think we ought to take it back inside?"

"Hang the punch bowl. You'd better get inside on the double, young—"

"Nathan, why don't we stay out here for a little while? Don't you think it's romantic—the lights out, the moon above?" I coaxed him, drawing nearer.

"What? See here, if you put out these lights intentionally—"

"Don't be silly"—I giggled—"but I've never been one to miss a perfect opportunity. I might even let you kiss me," I said, oozing charm. I pretended not to notice his intractability, and kept drawing him on, whispering to him, stroking the white fabric of the shirt underneath his coat. All the while I watched over Nathan's shoulder as Edwin emerged from the bushes like a determined weed sprouting from the earth, and started with the wire up the window facing, quickly driving tacks toward the opening above. But Nathan was too stubborn, or shocked—I'll never know which—to do what any ordinary red-blooded young man would have done in the same situation. I pleaded for him to return my kisses, one eye fixed on Edwin, then suddenly Nathan just yanked himself loose from my embrace and began to lecture me on what would happen if I didn't get myself back to the party. He was about to walk off, right toward Edwin. I turned from him, unsnapped the apron, unhooked the uniform blouse, and pulled down my undermuslin, then turned toward him just in time to catch his arm. "Please, why don't you like me?" I pleaded. He looked down at my bared breasts, then his glance shot up again to my face. He opened his mouth. "I can't believe—" he began, then gulped. Poor Nathan, poor me. Dear God, it was horrible!

However, it worked. He was soon taking off his coat and looking (thank goodness) to his right, away from Edwin's direction, out of politeness. "Here, keep this over you while you get decent," he commanded. "I won't look. Hurry up. The very idea. You ought to be horsewhipped. Hurry up."

There was no time to think about it through the evening. While Electra and I washed dishes after the party, she brought up the subject of his sudden disappearance just now when we could have used his help. To divert her, I sliced the tip of one finger with a small knife, and made much over the injury to keep her otherwise occupied.

Much later, home in bed, I lay wide-eyed, unable to believe the things I had done. Were all the previous months of intrigue and daring to blame for my quick and drastic decisions? I kept piecing it together, rationalizing, telling myself I saved the day, that any good spy would have acted the same. But the truth was still there: I had never bared my breasts in front of anyone. Past the age of nine, my brothers were locked out of the bathroom when I was in, and likewise I was never allowed to see them unclothed. How could I ever face Nathan again, not to mention continuing my efforts at getting information from him? Oh heavens, what must he think of me? What did I think of myself? Was I ruined, tarnished forever? What if he told someone? Lucky, he wasn't the social type. One day I'd have to tell the man who proposed marriage to me, out of fairness, if I intended to spend the rest of my life with him. Yet how could I? Oh dear, what would Mother say?

By morning the situation was better in perspective.

So I'd acted hastily. Nathan probably hadn't even gotten a good look. The moonlight was fairly bright, but not that bright. Anyway, why did anyone else ever have to know? I'd just have to gather courage . . . sometime in the next couple of weeks . . . and swear Nathan to secrecy. Let him think me a foolish young girl—he did anyway—play on his honor as a gentleman, yes, that was it. I raised my cut finger and succumbed to the temptation of congratulating myself. Now, that took real courage. Electra would never guess her line of talk was hitting too close to home.

In spite of the way I bolstered myself over the next few days, the first time I was forced into another meeting with Nathan all my defenses were down and anticipating it was a plain case of out-and-out torture. If not for the fact Mr. Tetzel sent me to Cabot's office to pick up a string of pearls with a broken catch that Sophie had lost during the party, I would have put off seeing Nathan again forever, if possible.

By the time I spanned the few blocks between the bank and Cabot's office, my hands were as cold as ice. I hoped Nathan would react to my appearance with his usual detachment, and maybe even have the decency not to look around from his desk. In fact I found him surprisingly kind. Though I could not have judged at the time, in the light of everything that happened afterward, I believe this was my closest look at the man Nathan might have become if his life had not taken a sharp detour long before I met him. He was like a flower that had unfolded too near sundown, and thus never fully bloomed, all too quickly secreting the finery that was lodged deep down and close to the stem, as shadows gathered.

He handed over the pearls and said, "Let's take a walk."

"I—I don't want to take up your time."

"I can spare a few minutes."

So off we went, a few blocks down Commerce, and wound up sitting on a bench. We both faced ahead. I don't think he felt any easier about looking into my eyes than I felt about looking into his. Normally spasmodic in movement as well as speech, he was calm and almost nurturing that day. He spoke first. "Listen, Camille, I'm probably the last person in the world to be handing out advice, but you just can't go around chasing after men. Heaven only knows why you chose to like me, but regardless, one day you might fall for a fellow who'd take advantage of you. I wouldn't tell anyone what you did the other night, but some men—"

"Thanks, Nathan . . . I really have dreaded facing you after that. I don't know what could have gotten into me," I told him honestly. "Maybe you can understand, though. I've done everything to get you to notice me. Have you ever liked someone who didn't like you back?"

"Of course. I've liked lots of girls—I was quite serious with one—yet some of them didn't return the feeling." There was just a touch of defensiveness in his voice. "There's nothing wrong with you that a little growing up wouldn't straighten out. But you are wasting your time on me."

"I don't see why."

"Because I'm not going anywhere that would interest you," he said, then turned to face me for the first time. "You need to find a man who can offer you a decent future."

"I don't see why that couldn't be you," I told him, thinking maybe I could press him just a little further. . . .

"I can't tell you that." He looked away again. "I wish I could, but I can't. I have to get back to work."

"All right. But we could still be friends, couldn't we?"

He stood up. "I suppose . . . I don't have much time," he said, and walked away. I assumed he meant he was awfully busy. Watching him as he disappeared down the street, I wondered what might have happened between us if we'd met under different circumstances. It was the first and only time I ever came halfway close to being truly attracted to him.

I was spared further shadowing of the Cabots for a while. I'd just hang back and check on the appearance of the Cabot automobile in the garage. When it was there I would call Edwin, who'd come out and turn on the confounded machine.

The information we gathered through it turned out to be of little more help than anything else, and only proved to further illuminate Cabot's growing impetuosity and moodiness. We also learned he apparently confided little in Electra. He seemed, in fact, to keep everyone in the dark as far as possible. One point of interest we did learn from Edwin's hours of wearing the headset was that he spent much time riding Nathan's back when he was at home. I hadn't realized the full extent of this from Electra's remarks on the night I toured her house.

Again it led me to wonder just why Nathan was so loyal to Cabot. One day I asked him how he'd like to apply for a position at the bank, just to see what his reaction would be.

"There's a job in bookkeeping opening up, and a chance for eventual elevation to auditor of the bank," I told him.

"No, thanks."

"But it would be such a good opportunity. Mr. Tetzel's bank is one of the fastest growing in San Antonio. One day you might even be an officer."

"No, I think not. Thanks anyway."

"Boy, it must be peachy working for Mr. Cabot, if you won't even consider leaving him—regardless of the offer."

"That's right. I've got a good deal—a great job."

"What would it take to get you to leave him?"

"Why do you ask?" he said guardedly.

"Just curious."

"Well it would take a lot more than anything you could dream up. So just forget it, all right?"

Even that brief exchange didn't seem of any importance, except in terms of my growing curiosity about the whole group of people who lived at Beauregard and Washington. Otherwise, we still were gathering almost nothing in the way of information about Tetzel. His conversations with Cabot centered mostly around the difficult situation faced by all mine owners in Mexico at the time, wondering what Carranza would finally decide on as his policy for governing foreign investors, wondering what would become of the increasingly hot situation with Pancho Villa. He'd been terrorizing the countryside in all directions since the night he raided Columbus, New Mexico, bringing on the punitive expedition under General Pershing across the border. Villa was no man's friend now, with the exception of the Yaqui Indian and his ever-decreasing band of raiders. If it was Germany's intention to finance trouble below the border that would suck us into a hole, and keep us too occupied to bother them in their own war, you couldn't prove it by Tetzel. And the queer fact was that we were convinced he participated very actively in what was going on.

The slow pace gave me a chance to accept invitations from Keith, yet all he talked about was the work of the aeronauts in Mexico. Half our time together was spent around Fort Sam, watching the testing and dismantling of the planes that were destined for use on scouting missions down there. He would have given the clothes off his back to be among the eighty men of the first squadron sent below the border, although he predicted before they left that the planes weren't going to be strong enough in lift capacity to be useful in the mountainous terrain, and nodded in wisdom when returning aeroscouts reported they almost lost their necks. He was more approving of the planes sent later, but still itching to be down there himself.

"Can you imagine, Camille, they're the ones who found Villa being carried around on a litter. I tell you, one aeroscout can do the work of a hundred foot soldiers."

"Yes; now if they could just guess whether he's alive or dead, we'd really have something."

"I didn't say they were wizards. Boy, for two cents I'd quit school and join the reserves. As much as I've studied about flying, I know I'd be a natural up there."

"No doubt about it," I told him, in all seriousness.

Then he paused and became thoughtful. "I know you think I'm silly sometimes, Camille, but it's important for a guy to think about how he's going to make his mark in the world. I get so tired of just being the second Butler son who helps out at the grocery store. I want to be where the action is, and I want to see it from the air. That's where the real power is."

"Doesn't seem to be much we can do from the ground," I admitted.

17

At last, in early summer of 1916, results of our efforts began to come through. Edwin set up a meeting one Sunday afternoon at the Navarro Street bridge.

"Cabot's money is tied up in saloons down in the red-light district," he said. "We know now he has been trying to sell out at a good price."

"But failing."

"That isn't all. He's dealing now with some real pros, an eastern syndicate. Those guys would as soon kill you as look at you—we've got an agent who knew something about them before the war—and it's a cinch Cabot is desperate. Tell you another thing. Those guys deal strictly in cash."

"Hm . . . that would mean he could bypass paying income tax on the sale, wouldn't it?"

"Right."

I thought that over for a few moments, then asked, "Is all this money he's trying to make going toward Barrista's rise to power?"

"We think a lot of it is. Financing Barrista, plus buying all the good properties he can get his hands on down there, must add up to a small fortune."

"And if Barrista fails, his properties won't be worth any more than his saloons . . . maybe less."

"I have some news about Tetzel, too. Now we know why he has suddenly become very idle. Since the border has become such a hot spot, with Pershing down there, the Germans have been getting arms into Mexico another way. They're pulling into coastal ports, aboard free-lance oil tankers."

"Still going to Pancho Villa?"

"Yes. But from what we can learn, von Eckhardt, the German ambassador in Mexico City, is handling it. For the moment Tetzel is sitting tight. For a while we thought he was at work on sabotage of Russian arms, but—"

"Russian arms?"

"German money is helping finance the revolution in Russia. We've found out lately that munitions made in this country consigned to the Tsarist field forces are being switched out at the factory for scrap iron. Now and then a box of ammo is mislabeled, with the wrong caliber, so that when it arrives in the field, it doesn't fit the guns."

"Oh, that's really dirty . . . but Tetzel isn't involved in that, is he?"

"No. We think that Tetzel is working directly with the German Foreign Office on something highly secret. It doesn't appear anyone else is in on it, and that explains why the memos to Francke in New York have stopped. He's probably wiring information back and forth, probably coded."

"But I thought the British cut the cables at the beginning of the war."

"They did, but not through Holland. He could wire messages from here through the Dutch cable, and if they were carefully coded they'd go right past and into Germany.

"Our electrical wizard could be brought down to tap a telephone wire into Tetzel's office, but just now he's busy on other projects."

"Sometimes I feel as though we're the orphans of the BNA."

"Between the Bohemian National Alliance and the Slovak League, we have around three hundred and twenty thousand people. Do you know how that compares to the German espionage system? They have around three million sympathizers."

"Golly . . . I guess we're spread pretty thin."

"You get the picture."

"Well . . . how about one person—a spy in the telegraph office here?"

"We've already tried that. It's tighter than a cork on a bottle of vintage wine."

"Anything turned up on Aegina Barrista?"

"Not yet. Have you got anything more on Electra Cabot?"

"No. I really don't think she's into anything, do you?"

"It's possible, because we haven't been able to trace anything on her in Colorado. For all we know she could have come out of any crack. I think the Dexter name was a fake. Why don't you try to get with her again, find out a maiden name if you can?"

"All right," I said petulantly. I wished we could leave her and Cabot and Nathan Hope alone. Whatever their personal motives, it was my guess they were being used by Tetzel. Shortly after, however, I was in for a number of surprises.

One day in July while I was out on a banking errand, I glanced toward the post office to see Electra hurrying out the door, gripping a letter which she soon began tearing to shreds as she descended the stairs, obviously in a huff. I stared at her in wonder as she reached the bottom stair, looked both ways, and drove a fistful of paper fragments down into her handbag. Next she turned in the direction of her home and it was then I got a good view of her face. I had never seen her look so distressed. Even her normal gait had changed from one of grace to a quick, animal stalk. I stood there for a while, wishing there were some way I could have a look at the letter she picked up. I felt it would tell us an awful lot.

When I reported the incident to Edwin, he could make nothing of it, but encouraged me to keep watching her. Later in the month I managed to chat with her when by coincidence we met at the train station. She may have been a little nervous, but otherwise seemed her normal self. She'd come with a group to meet the influx of soldiers being moved to Fort Sam and Camp Wilson and offer them refreshment. I was there awaiting Mother's arrival for a short visit. During a temporary lull I sidled over and began with lines designed to lead her into a trap. We spoke of Lyla Stuttgart, who sat in a corner looking ill. "Funny name, Stuttgart, some German city, isn't it? Wonder what her name was before."

"I don't know," said Electra.

"Mother and I get into conversations sometimes about the fact a woman gives up her name when she marries, often to something far less pleasant. Seems unfair, don't you think? I sort of like my name now . . . I hope I marry a man with an equally distinguished name."

She laughed, and shook her head. Oh, how easy it was to play the game of silly young maiden girl to my advantage. "Well, you can laugh," I said. "Look what you wound up with. Cabot. That's a strong, powerful name."

"Well it certainly beats Weems," she said, then closed her mouth abruptly. Now almost an expert at diverting conversations, I was speaking of something across the station even as I noted her sudden silence. I wanted her to believe I hadn't really been paying attention to her last remark, and I am fairly certain she did. Since we had never disproven she was once married to a man named Dexter, I assumed Weems was her maiden name. However, I realized as she walked away the name might be spelled any number of ways. . . .

I stood around for a while, keeping an eye out for Mother and now and then glancing toward Electra's group, still busy serving the soldiers. How simple life used to be, I thought. It seemed as though now we all existed in layers. Before I got mixed up with the BNA, I was always candid and forthright, living on the first layer and assuming everyone I knew lived the same, at least to a reasonable degree.

If not for that day Michael Stobalt knocked on Mother's door, I would have an important job as the secretary to a bank owner named Adolph Tetzel, not knowing he was anything other than what he appeared to be on the outside—a hardworking, prosperous businessman, inclined to be generous toward me in return for my capabilities, my sincere eagerness to serve him, and my loyalty.

I would probably be acquainted with both Electra and Emory Cabot somewhat by now, believing them to be nothing more than an extraordinary couple with money, good looks, a place in society—all things normally to be admired if not envied. I might even have chanced to be courted once or twice by their quiet and modest employee Nathan Hope.

I would know nothing of the layer just beneath the surface of the lives of all these people that was built of betrayal, secrecy, hidden motives. . . . And I'd be awaiting my mother today, believing that the life I'd made for myself in this city would go on until I decided to change it, for some normal, everyday reason. Watching Electra smile and hand out cups of beverage like any young matron anxious to aid a good cause, I could almost imagine that if I wished hard enough and shut my eyes, there might be but one layer after all, and everything underneath that would be the product of a bad dream from which I would soon awaken.

When Mother got off her train, I found the sight of her cheery face unusually refreshing. She'd been in Missouri for a meeting, and was curtailing all other activity until September, when she had to be in Atlantic City. In between, she'd manage a visit with each of us kids. We went directly to my apartment, and sat down to talk.

Right away she observed me carefully and concluded, "You look a little tired, and definitely thinner."

"You're looking a little tired yourself."

"But not any thinner. I go to too many luncheons," she said with a laugh, then paused before continuing. "Something's bothering you very much, isn't it? I can always tell. You're less bubbly."

"It's only that . . . well . . . I went into this thing believing people were either all bad or all good. I'm beginning to see it isn't quite so simple."

"That's a good lesson to learn, my dear, though sometimes a hard one."

"We keep digging away. Some of the people we're working on are not going to prove to be involved in anything wrong—at least too wrong, anyway, I don't think—and somehow it makes me feel bad. Dirty, underhanded. Yet I have to admit that when I'm sniffing someone out, my curiosity is pitiless. Sometimes I despise myself. . . ."

"I wonder if I didn't do you a terrible injustice by introducing you to that group," she said.

"I've been giving some thought to that myself. Remember, I was going to prove Tetzel was a knight in shining armor."

"Instead you keep finding more tarnish."

"Yes. But you know, I still find I can't dislike him, or even fear him. I've never admitted that to my contact here, but it's the truth. Funny, isn't it."

She smoothed the hair back from my forehead and said, "You're growing up, honey," then she took me in her arms and we held each other for a long time. I wonder if she could ever imagine what those moments between us meant to me, how much support I felt in her embrace. Certainly it was a gesture that helped to bolster me through the next few crucial months.

One afternoon in mid-August I returned from an errand to hear Cabot's voice in Tetzel's office. I rushed to the storeroom, turned on the machine just in case, and put my ear to the wall. Cabot was incensed. Barrista had backed out altogether.

"He's got no more sense than that fool Madero," he told Tetzel, who listened silently. "He thinks Carranza will be reasonable enough that in time he can get a cabinet seat, then when his turn comes around, he can run for President. He wants to drop the Plan de Pacifica Reforma altogether."

"Perhaps you push too hard; give him time."

"He's had too much time. He has been listening to his brothers—especially Carlos—who never wanted into this thing anyway. I've been marooned up here with no control over what was going on.

"It looks like we're finished. I'll have to pay you back the notes as best I can."

"Slow down a bit. If you aren't one of the most impetuous men I have ever known. Don't we both know how hungry Carranza is for power? He did not hang on this long with any idea of letting go easily. Let me see what I can do about bringing about the truth a little early. Leave it to me, eh?"

"You know you can't get to that stubborn son-of-a-bitch."

"Ah, but the press is a powerful tool . . . we are as anxious to get him out of office as you are. Let me work on it. Barrista will see."

"And what if he doesn't?"

"Don't borrow trouble. I will extend your notes if need be. But Germany is more than ever in need of big imports of copper. We have other sources, as you know, both here and below the border. But try and eke out as much as you can and let me worry about the rest."

"If we could get Barrista back on the track, I could be prepared to take up arms within a few weeks."

"Just don't go off half cocked."

"How do you convince the people on your end to have the same amount of patience as you?"

"It isn't easy. Von Eckhardt in Mexico is in favor of negotiating an alliance with Carranza. Even he cannot see that would be futile."

It was the word, "alliance," that sent chills up my spine. When I got back into my office Tetzel was waiting for me. "Get Giddeon Sparks to bring down Mr. Cabot's file, and leave it on my desk. I'll be back shortly," he said, pulling on his coat.

I felt sure Tetzel was about to send a wire that would incriminate a whole group of agents involved in this affair, so I started to phone Edwin to send him to the telegraph office. Then I remembered it was too early for him to be at home. I called Giddy and ordered the file, then waited for her to appear with it, afraid to follow Tetzel myself for fear of being seen.

At least I did get a look at the Cabot accounts. In rough figures he had been lent seven hundred thousand dollars in the past year. I had no idea that much money had been transferred. No wonder the man was nearly mad with worry.

That night I reached Edwin by phone. After I blurted out everything, winding up with the part about the negotiation between Mexico and Germany, he said, "Holy Moses."

We knew then that the German Foreign Office was still a house divided. While von Eckhardt favored an alliance with Carranza, someone apparently was pushing to continue the old routine of stirring up border troubles, courtesy of Pancho Villa. We did not know who Tetzel was working with, or whether the "third party" felt by him to lack "industry" had been brought in. However, it occurred to me then the third party might refer to Cabot himself because it now seemed clear he was not aware of the full extent of his copper consignments—that much of it had been kept here in the States for the making of explosives, rather than exported to Germany. Yet Cabot would never have been thought of as someone not industrious, though he might well be considered untrustworthy.

Then all at once the truth appeared obvious: "third party" referred to someone below the border—maybe von Eckhardt, whom Tetzel apparently disliked or at least whose wisdom he doubted; maybe someone else, charged with sabotaging Carranza through the Mexican press; maybe even Carlos Barrista, being aided by someone to stage a separate revolt. . . .

Since the possibilities seemed endless, I'd let it go at that and gotten busy with some banking work, when I ran across the name of Arnold Stuttgart, Stuttgart Printing. One thing we had learned about him was his employment of Mexicans. He had a Mexican typesetter who was renowned for his speed and skill. Currency for revolutionary governments . . . papers for smearing the reputation of Carranza . . . printed over here and circulated below the border. Carranza could not then control what was being said of him before at least a good percentage of Mexicans who could read got their hands on the material. Perfect!

I'd have to allow some time for the ball to roll—perhaps a week or more—then I'd pay a visit to Stuttgart's office one night. The word "industry" continued to bother me for a while. Then I remembered something overheard one day when Tetzel was trying to reach Stuttgart over the phone about some problems with his account. It was during the hottest part of the summer and Stuttgart was out of town at his house in the hills. Disgruntled—I assumed at the time more from the heat than anything else—Tetzel had wiped his brow and remarked, "Every time I need him he's off on holiday in the country."

Then he'd mumbled some German word I didn't understand, and closed his office door.

When I told Edwin of my plan, he didn't seem convinced I was barking up the right tree, but offered to do the snooping for me. As it turned out, he was right. "All I found was a copy of *Fatherland* in a desk drawer."

"What's that?"

"German propaganda sheet. But it doesn't mean anything. It might be headed for the trash in the morning."

He was interested in recent events concerning Electra and asked whether I'd seen her since the day we met at the train station.

"No. Is someone checking out the name Weems?"

"Yes, but no news yet. Well, keep your eyes and ears open. I'll check on Stuttgart again. We may have acted too hastily . . . or not quickly enough. It's hard to tell. And as soon as I have the chance I'm going to get inside Cabot's office. Maybe right now with tax time nowhere near, Hope won't be working late so much."

18

One day shortly after, Cabot paid a visit to our office. Tetzel had someone with him at the time, so he was obliged to wait outside in my office for a few minutes. I have never seen such a remarkable change in anyone, and was itching to get into the storeroom and listen in on what brought about the congenial mood he'd acquired. He sat in a chair, rather than pacing, and even had the courtesy to inquire whether his cigar smoke bothered me—if so, he'd put it out. "My wife says the smell gets into all the furniture cushions and in the draperies. Every time I leave town she airs out the house for a week," he remarked, smiling.

"It doesn't bother me," I assured him.

He leaned back then and told me he'd wrecked his Cole Six, and had ordered a new Overland. He detailed its luxurious features from end to end. I tried to appear all wide-eyed and impressed, as he would have expected; yet I wondered how a man so deeply in debt could get excited about having to spend still more money for a new car.

When he got inside with Tetzel, the reason for his ebullient frame of mind became clear: plans for the revolution were on again. Tetzel kept repeating, "Didn't I tell you in a little time our efforts would pay? Now, when does Barrista begin?"

Cabot explained it would be early spring before all preparations could be made, and that Barrista would first make the gesture of opposing Carranza as a political candidate. "Of course, he'll never get his name on the ballot. Carranza has the race tied up fine and dandy. The appearance of the single name on the ballot will be the signal for the call to arms. We can figure on at least between one hundred and twenty-five and one hundred and fifty thousand troops.

"Barrista believes he can persuade Zapata, Villa, and Diaz to join him. But I'm wondering whether Villa will tell him who's been footing his bills. Can you see to it that doesn't happen? It might just ruin—"

"Don't worry. He'll never admit to that in front of Barrista. Anyway, even if he should, he won't be mentioning my name. He has no way of knowing I am connected with the Germans who are supplying his arms. And, his aim is to win for his country. You can be sure he takes our money and laughs at us behind our backs. I'm wondering, though, if you couldn't be ready a little sooner? Time is at a premium now, with von Eckhardt pressing—"

"Hell, you can't prepare a revolution over night. People have to be contacted; currency has to be printed—more than we planned initially because we'll have more troops to pay. Munitions have to be transferred down there and stockpiled in the central points."

"Have you drawn up battle plans?"

"Yes. I'm going down in January, carrying them with me. I'm a little worried about his brother Carlos. I'm going to hold off telling him the strategy until closer to the end. I don't want him to have time to think about how to scuttle it."

"Ah, there is always a weak point somewhere, eh?"

"Otherwise, everything is set."

"The grand finale, as they say."

"Yes, just before the new beginning, I hope."

"Perhaps a new era on both sides of the ocean."

"Things are getting rougher in Europe, aren't they?"

"Crucial better describes it. War is expensive both in human lives and materials. Yet it seems we are powerless to end what has begun. Italy and Greece have now fallen in line with the Allies. More and more sympathy in this country goes toward them. Right here, more than fifty per cent of the war materials being used by the Allies is manufactured, yet the United States claims no favoritism.

"There is talk of a separate peace . . . in time, Russia may be sympathetic . . . in the meantime our people are starving for the failure to get raw materials. I think surely some kind of terms of peace must be negotiated soon."

There followed a brief pause, then Cabot said, "Just how far are you into this?"

"Frustratingly distant . . . how much can I offer? A few tons of copper because of my association with you and with neutrals in Scandinavia."

"And an ace up your sleeve—Barrista. He could do much for you that would wind up this mess—embargo British fuel in Tampico, pump out more raw materials."

"It is fair exchange, and once the war is over, debts will have been paid."

"I just hope Barrista sees it that way."

"What choice will he have?"

"You know when he finds out German money put him into office, it is I who will be blamed."

"You will be around to reassure him, help him put things into perspective, as they say."

Following that conversation I told Edwin it was the closest the two men had ever come to discussing enough so that I could tell how much each of them knew. "I think Cabot has figured out a lot more than Tetzel has told him, but he doesn't care now so long as he profits in the end. It's a vicious circle— Cabot uses Tetzel, Tetzel uses Cabot, and they both use Barrista. I got the feeling there were certain things Cabot didn't want to have said. Tacit agreements, if you get what I mean. I still don't believe Cabot knows his copper—or at least part of it—went into explosives in this country. I think his feeling is that he doesn't care one way or another what happens in Europe as long as his investments in Mexico are looked after. But I don't think he knows of his complicity in sabotage over here."

"Why?"

"Because Tetzel always stays clear of discussing it."

"That isn't going to help Cabot very much, when the truth comes out. . . . Anything else new?"

"Not exactly . . . just a feeling. But I guess you're not interested in my instincts."

"Of course I am!"

"It isn't so much what I heard in that conversation, but a difference in Mr. Tetzel lately. He's spending more time inside his office, with the door closed. Seems preoccupied, tense."

"Any other changes in his habits?"

"No."

"I'm going to give the Stuttgart Printing Company one more check tonight," Edwin said. "I suggest you keep your eyes on the mails again—Tetzel may be keeping in touch more often now with his friends overseas. Check his safe again, too."

"All right. I can't help wondering what's going to happen next."

"A lot depends on the outcome of the election here. With a mandate and four years ahead of him, Wilson may become more decisive than he has been so far."

"I don't follow you."

"He may be looked to for mediation, since he'll be more in a position to speak for the country than he has been for the past few months."

"And that could mean an end to it?"

"I hope so."

"Then what would happen to Tetzel?"

"There's enough evidence now for the U.S. authorities to pick him up for violating neutrality laws, and maybe enough for a case of conspiracy if we could find his signature on checks."

"So his days are numbered," I said, still puzzling over the reasons for his involvement.

"As well as those of others mixed up in the same type of activity."

Edwin's final remark made me aware for the first time of the real scope of espionage and counterespionage operations we were involved in. Tetzel was busy working toward his own ends, totally ignorant of how closely he was being watched, how extensively he was being investigated. How many others, like him, were over here conducting conspiracies or channeling funds down into Mexico and into other countries such as Ireland and Wales, for causing unrest and dissension in order to keep people busy? How many Cabots, profiteering off the misfortune of others; how many Barristas, knowingly or not, using them as stepladders toward their own goals?

I recall feeling very small then, walking back from my meeting with Edwin down a sidewalk slickened by rain and reflecting off the streetlights above. Lucky I didn't decide to settle in Washington or New York, where really important things took place.

What could happen in a faraway city like San Antonio, where all of us were simply very small cogs in an enormous wheel, gathering momentum?

I returned from work one evening in late September to find Edwin had slipped a message under my door. He'd been by at three in the afternoon, and requested that I call him at the usual number after six. When I reached him, he had some news for me about Electra Cabot.

"I was on my way from a meeting with Hubert up on the north side today, and who should I see coming out of an antique store but her? She was carrying a box under one arm, so I figured she was out shopping—"

"But of course you followed her, just to be sure," I said through a smile.

"The lady was having a vase appraised. I got near enough on her last stop to overhear her dickering with the dealer over the price. Finally she accepted twelve hundred. She asked for cash and got it.

"I followed her taxi from there all the way to the post office, where she got out with an envelope and headed up the stairs."

"So she's sending money to someone."

"And probably without Cabot's knowledge," he added.

"But you don't know that for sure, just because of today. He is in pretty bad straits financially. Maybe they've decided to sell off some of their things," I suggested.

"While he's busy ordering a new Overland? Come on!"

Edwin was always eager to believe the worst about Electra, I thought with dismay. Yet, within a short time I was to find myself more suspicious of her than I'd been before.

While Tetzel was working with his door ajar one morning, the telephone rang. Long in the habit of listening hard, I took my hands from the noisy typewriter keys and stared at the book with my steno notes, as though trying to jolt my memory on a word I couldn't decipher. I heard Tetzel say, "Yes, yes . . . she's having the pearls restrung. It was kind of you—" and I realized he was talking with Electra. Presently he closed his door and at once I had to decide whether to dash to the storeroom or to the filing cabinet just outside his office. Afraid the call might be brief, I had my hand on a drawer handle within seconds. For several moments he was silent, then he said, "All right, I'll see you tomorrow around twelve. No, I'm not expecting Cabot today . . . don't worry, I won't mention it if he comes by."

I could hardly wait until six o'clock that evening to phone Edwin. There were obvious built-in problems with my eavesdropping on the meeting they scheduled, and while Edwin recognized Electra, I wasn't sure he'd know Tetzel. It would have been so much easier if I'd overheard the name of the place for their rendezvous.

Excitedly, I blurted out all the garbled thoughts in my mind, and Edwin answered, "Which door does Tetzel usually go out at lunchtime?"

"The main lobby, as far as I know, but how will you—"

"Since you haven't gotten around to using your camera, I've done some shadowing of my own. I know Tetzel when I see him."

I ignored the rebuff. "If by some chance she comes up here, I'll be standing by in the storeroom. But since they're trying to keep this from Cabot, she probably won't be meeting Tetzel anywhere in this area."

"If he goes out the back door, though, we're whipped."

"No, he parks his car nearer the front of the bank. Good luck. I'll call you again at six, tomorrow evening."

I lay awake most of the night, fretting over the fact I could not be the one to listen in on that meeting. Whereas I would be looking for inflections in Electra's voice, phraseology, anything which might indicate justification for dealing behind Cabot's back, Edwin would be listening only for the meat of the conversation. He looked upon both Cabots with the same degree of detachment that I should have exercised, and oftentimes I felt we almost competed as to who would prove right in the end, especially when it came to Electra.

All the following day my stomach churned. I watched Tetzel calmly take his homburg and walk out at noontime, return two and a half hours later, somewhat preoccupied, and work the balance of the day with his office door closed. When I phoned Edwin at six, my fingers trembled on the receiver. Just as I expected, he was terse in his report, yet he wasn't entirely to blame. "I'll say one thing for that Cabot woman, she sure knows how to conduct a private meeting. She led Tetzel to a table for two way over in the corner, and even though I sat nearby, I could hardly hear. She spoke almost in a whisper, and her back was to me.

"The only real advantage I had was seeing Tetzel's face, and it did turn pale a few times."

"I guess you didn't find out much, huh?"

"Enough, I think. She was asking for money, and apparently a good deal of it. He was not buying what she was telling him, that was clear. I heard him tell her something was 'risky business.' But that didn't stop her. They talked for a while after that, then left. I think he put her off."

I stood there shaking my head for such a long time that Edwin finally asked, "You still there?"

"Yes . . . I just can't figure it. I would have never thought she'd betray—"

"Camille, you've got to face the facts. You don't really know this woman, and just look how little we've been able to find out about her. She did say something in the beginning about Cabot having looked her up, and I've got a hunch he may have had her traced. I'm going to try and get into his office and look around."

Several days later I overheard a telephone conversation in Tetzel's office. His habit of vagueness was present in every transaction he made, and in the case of telephone calls even more so, probably because of the danger of alerting Minerva, the switchboard operator. Only when I heard him mention the word "Colorado" did I realize the conversation was important, though I was not able to figure out who was on the other end of the line, and whether the call was long distance or local. He might have been checking on a prospective bank customer from the way he talked.

"You found nothing? Yes . . . well, that only proves she isn't with us." (A pause.) "No, but I needn't be in any hurry about that. These days, one is less and less certain who is to be trusted, eh?"

19

I had been in and out of Tetzel's secret safe compartment so many times, largely to no avail, that I'd begun doing so more or less perfunctorily, while keeping a sharp ear for possible surprise intruders. Usually I moved the small gilt-framed portrait out from the front, reaching way to the back in the dark, and felt all around; then, finding nothing, replaced the portrait and closed the box. This time, however, my hand quickened upon the discovery of a sheaf of papers. They were sales agreements for four small newspapers in the Central Texas area that Tetzel had visited several times, though not lately. Also with the papers were check vouchers amounting to just above thirty thousand dollars. Apparently it had taken long months of negotiation before the deals were finalized, and a few extra thousand dollars also. It confounded me then as it had many times before that Tetzel seemed to draw from an inextinguishable source of funds and, with few exceptions such as this one, distributed them through some still undiscovered channel.

The papers in my hand now were just the sort of evidence Edwin would be elated to hear about, I knew, but for me it faded in comparison to what happened the afternoon of the following day. Cabot was sporting around in a taxi these days, awaiting arrival of his new Overland, and just as I rounded the corner after a shopping errand on Commerce I saw him board a waiting cab and head down the block, then turn up a small side street north. I made a quick decision and hopped another waiting cab to follow him. When I got in and on his trail, I checked my handbag and told the driver he'd have to stop when I'd used up four bits, because that was all the money I had. Cabot was headed for Aegina Barrista's school, it became evident, and when he reached it he dismissed his taxi. A block behind, I stopped my driver, who looked back puzzledly and said, "But that's only twenty cents, miss."

"It's all right." I left the cab, ducked out of sight, and watched. In a few minutes a tall young woman with dark hair parted down the center and pulled into a knot at the nape of her neck came from the school and crossed the street to a small drugstore and ice-cream parlor. Cabot was a few steps behind her. Once he was in I walked to the store window. They were being seated in a little booth near the back. The booth this side of them was occupied, so I had to wait a few minutes until it cleared. Aegina would see me walking through, but she didn't know me and Cabot's back would be facing me. If I got caught I could just say I was in the neighborhood and had a passion for ice cream. I didn't have time to consider whether my excuse would work. I wiped the perspiration from above my lips and walked in. I would browse close by, to be sure no one new took the booth I needed before I could reach it. From where I stood I could see Aegina face on. She was every bit as beautiful as I'd heard—her features a combination of Greek and Mexican. Her eyes were like dark topaz stones, encircled with thick lashes. Her skin seemed flawless over her high cheekbones. Her lips were wide and full. Immediately I thought, she might be Cabot's sister, as much as they favor.

Ten prolonged minutes passed before I slid into the booth behind Cabot to listen. I had thought to buy a newspaper outside the door, to hide my face should they look my way upon leaving. I ordered a double fudge sundae and listened.

". . . and you can have it by the time I come back in February?" he said.

"Don't worry. Artemio works quickly."

"I've noticed that."

"You are always teasing, Cabot," she replied, laughing. "Besides, my father approves of Artemio. He is good to me, and works hard for the cause. We'll marry, probably, as soon as the revolution is over. Father will have the big fiesta."

"That will make my wife very happy."

"She still suspects there is something between us?"

"Yep, though considering how much money I spent tracking her down and getting her here, she ought to realize how much I think of her. I never figured I'd pay five thousand bucks to get a wife."

I pressed my ear to the booth.

"You were thinking of her, even while we were together, weren't you?"

"Sometimes, but you did a commendable job of holding my attention."

She laughed again. "But you always really loved that woman, didn't you? With me it was for fun—a little *interludio* before you found her?"

"No . . . I never thought I'd see her again until I started looking. But she's always been my woman, and always will be. She's gone through a lot of agony since I brought her down here. I'm going to make up for it once this is over."

"What you are doing for my father is worth the waiting she must do. He would not have come this far without you, and would go no further. I'm grateful. He will be, too, even more than he is now, once he has gained the presidency and sees his dreams turning into realities. If my mother were still alive, he wouldn't have needed your fire, or mine. When she died he lost some of his ambition. He worries more about me because he has no one else. He worries too much about everything to work effectively in his own behalf. He will be good for Mexico, but he won't be able to envision the future as clearly as you until he has the worst behind him.

"He knows all this. He says you bring him luck."

"I hope he's right. Let's get out of here. I'll check with you again before I leave the country."

"Artemio will carry another batch when he goes down next month. The circulars are being read in all parts of the country, now, Father writes. He complains of his hands being tied. Even right there in Mexico, there is so little he can do.

"We probably won't have to move the press again, do you think?"

"I hope not. Hell, with the government buying up property and renting all the warehouses in town, we might have to. That was a close call last time." The wooden booth groaned as his big frame rose from it.

"Good-bye, Cabot. *Buena suerte.*"

I covered my face as he walked past, and soon after, she went by and out the door behind him. My untouched sundae had become a marbly puddle.

When I reached Edwin that evening I told him it was a cinch Aegina was in charge of currency. What else, aside from circulars, I didn't know. Edwin wanted to know where their operations were.

"They didn't say. Apparently they've been operating out of the basement in a warehouse or something, and recently moved, maybe more than once. There's no telling where they are now."

"We'll start checking. What else?"

"You were right about Cabot tracing Electra to Colorado," I told him and explained what I'd overheard.

"I knew it," Edwin said excitedly.

"And one thing more . . . it seems that Cabot was once linked with Aegina Barrista . . . romantically, I mean . . . and Electra has been pretty jealous over it."

"Hm . . . that's interesting. Maybe it was jealousy that led her to Tetzel."

I had to admit that had crossed my mind, but I'd already dismissed it.

"By the way, we're short on recording machines so I'm going to have to find a way to pull that one out of the Cabot house, then get it up to Maryland. It hasn't been all that much help to us anyway."

"Oh Lord, how will you—" I began, thinking of the trouble we had getting the thing installed.

"Don't worry. I'll figure a way, probably do it sometime next week. Hey, have you seen the papers today?"

"No."

"German subs sunk two British steamers fifty miles outside of Boston harbor."

"My goodness! Have we declared war?"

"No. The subs stayed within the bounds of international waters. We won't even make any claims for indemnity unless we prove they violated international warfare laws."

"They just got the *Lusitania* incident settled, and now this. Seems to me they're getting too close for comfort."

At moments like these I found the whole situation confusing. It seemed the Germans on one hand were trying to keep us out of the war, and with the other suck us in, daring us further and further until we had to fight. Yet before the end of the year Edwin's prediction came true: Wilson, re-elected by a narrow margin over Charles Evans Hughes, offered his services as mediator between the Centrals and the Allies, and it looked as though at last the world was on the road to peace. Though the terms made on either side were a little preposterous at best and the Germans—betting high now—were obdurate, they were at least talking so surely that had to be a step in the right direction.

Yet, still our government talked up national defense, preparedness, and planned civil aeronautical schools, more Navy ships and guns, an increased Army, and a possible conscription. Keith had set his mind on joining the military reserve and going straight to aviation school as soon as he finished college in the spring. He read everything he could get his hands on about preliminary and advanced qualification tests so that he could be among the first men picked for aero squadrons.

The contrast between his attitude toward military service and that of Nathan was the difference between springtime and bleak winter. I didn't see a lot of Nathan but it was clear from the talks we had he was unsettled by the thought of conscription. "Men like me, with no wife and family, would be first to go," he said more than once.

"Isn't it easier for you to go than it would be for a man with people to support?"

"Cabot wouldn't have to go."

"Maybe not . . . maybe so. But if he stayed out, there would probably still be a good job awaiting you when you got out, as much as he depends—"

"Get out?" he repeated, and glared at me as though I'd lost my mind. Then he narrowed his eyes and his voice became very soft. "It wouldn't end there for me. I'd never get free."

"Of course you would. Look here, it seems downright unpatriotic for you not to want to serve your country for a couple of years. Look at all the men around here in khaki—the town's crawling with men eager to serve if there's a place for them—"

"Then let them go. I've got more important things to do."

"Like what?"

"I've got to look out for Electra, for one. She needs me more and more, and I'll be hanged if I let—"

"What?"

"Never mind. None of your business. All you do is pry. I can't stand the way you pick at me all the time. Go away."

Nathan spoke in riddles—what did he mean, look after Electra while Cabot was away fighting a revolution? Probably so, but it was likely I would never know for sure, I thought in exasperation. It seemed nothing ever got accomplished for all the "picking"—as Nathan accurately described my work.

Actually, could any of us have seen ahead, we would have been grateful for the knowledge that the travail would soon come to an end. The wheels, set in motion so long ago, were turning at such a high speed, they hardly seemed to be moving at all. . . .

In mid-December a new man was promoted to head the German Foreign Office. His name was Arthur Zimmermann. Around the same time the BNA learned there was much infighting in the German Reichstag over the next measure to be taken to stop the war, particularly over the use of a new submarine with a far more powerful cruising range than those used up to that point. Edwin told me the fighting was over whether to unleash the new submarines in an all-out campaign against merchant vessels of any country.

"Won't that force us into the war?"

"It might . . . that's why their congress is fighting. The military leaders are favoring it. The civil government is against it, as far as we can tell."

"Which side is that new fellow heading the Foreign Office on—you know, Zimmermann?"

"We don't know."

"I wish we could find out how well Tetzel knows Zimmermann."

He laughed. "You're not the only one."

By the end of the year we had our first break in months—an opening in the telegraph office was promptly filled by a Czech, sent by the BNA as soon as the position became vacant. Allan —his code name—was to prove the master key for all hitherto locked doors.

20

The death of Geoffrey Woodstone seemed a hard blow to Electra. She visited my office one day unexpectedly, entreating me to take the old Englishman's terrier Scoop, because, as she explained, her husband would not let her keep the dog indefinitely.

It was very hard for me to refuse, yet pets were not allowed in my apartment. I just couldn't tell her "no" flat out because she was obviously desperate. I hedged a little and told her I was thinking of moving in a few months, and wouldn't mind having the dog if I could find a place that permitted him. In fact, as I mentioned the idea it sounded pretty good. My only companion for the time being was the healthy ivy plant that favored my River Avenue balcony.

She seemed somewhat consoled by the suggestion, and told me she wouldn't bother me further about it, that I should let her know when I could take the animal. As usual, I was struck by her elegance. She both dressed and conducted herself like a lady whenever I was around her, and could always retain her dignity and composure. She spoke at length of her friendship with the English gentleman, and said only since his death had she fully realized what a great friend he was.

I told her the only experience I'd had with death was that of my father, and there were many things about him I never appreciated until a long time after he passed away.

She faced me directly then, her eyes intent, and said, "Yes, in time, many things have a way of coming to light."

I thought she'd say more, but she looked away quickly then. and rose from her chair. "I have to go now, or I'll be late for a sitting with Miss Onderdonk. She's doing a miniature of me as a surprise for Emory."

Long after she left I was still sitting idly, wondering about her. She could at once seem so open and frank, while remaining very private. She could pour out her heart over something which mattered to her, yet leave you without a clue as to why she felt so strongly. With many questions now open about Electra's activities, both before she came to San Antonio and after she arrived, she might well have been two people. The Electra I had come to know, and who seemed fond of me—judging by her generosity toward me, and her eagerness to confide in me, even to look out for me in certain matters—might have appeared one day out of nowhere . . . someone with all the usual human qualities, yet at the same time not quite real, though altogether sincere. . . .

It was but a few short weeks later that I was forced into reconciling Edwin's harsh, realistic view of her with my own. He asked that we meet one Friday near the front of the arsenal to exchange information. Since the hiring of one of our group at the telegraph office, he was now turning the tables and telling me about Tetzel's doings.

"He's sending wires to von Eckhardt's office in Mexico, as well as to the Foreign Office. Before, all we knew was that he was connected with Germany on the wire. His telegrams carry his special code of vagueness—the best in the world. If we could have seen his letters, or even his wires, from the beginning, we might be able to tell more.

"As it looks, though, he's running a one-man show on this Barrista thing, so far as Germany is concerned. He is apparently reporting everything that Cabot says directly to M.K. in the German Foreign Office. There is a Mortimer Krantz who works as an underling there, and he seems to be Tetzel's contact. R. M. Francke has disappeared. Tetzel wired von Eckhardt's office a duplicate that Barrista would be in touch with Diaz, Villa, and Zapata, and that they should follow up in the usual way."

"What does that mean?"

"We think Tetzel is playing both sides of the fence. The German agents are apparently being instructed to assure each of the three leaders that Barrista is on the German hook, in case it comes to 'them against us.' That ought to suit them fine. The Pershing expedition effectively turned just about all the Mexicans against us anyway."

"That's a far cry from what he told Cabot."

"I know. Now, we already have confidence that the Germans are hot to get Carranza bought and paid for, and that Tetzel has been against this move from the beginning. So there is an underlying plea for patience in all of his wires. He's trying to tell them they're wasting their time by trying to bargain with Carranza, and that he can deliver Barrista all wrapped up and tied with a ribbon by spring."

"That may seem a long time to them. . . . What about Zimmermann?"

"Tetzel wired that he was personally gratified about the promotion, and confident they could work together. His 'personal gratification' probably stems from the fact Zimmermann came up from the ranks. There's a little clique in German political and social circles that separates the 'vons' from the common man."

"Anything more about the third party?"

"No."

"It still seems that it would take strong reasons for Tetzel to be so entangled. If the United States helps to bring about a peace settlement, and the war comes to a close, surely Germany isn't going to take friendship with Mexico seriously. And since they're so fired up about keeping us out of it, I don't see why Tetzel goes to the trouble," I said, but Edwin disagreed.

"If we get into the war it would tie up arms shipment to the Allies because we'd have to be stockpiling for our own use once we got men over there. That would take at least a year, probably, and in the meantime Germany could have the war won and be enjoying the spoils of victory," he pointed out.

"I see. So, Tetzel wants to play it safe in any event, and Carranza can't be counted on."

"Right. Like I told you before, regardless of the stand our government takes, Mexico alone could be a pretty strong ally because it controls British fuel, and there's a wealth of mineral resources that would be at the disposal of the Centrals," he said.

"But apparently those dealing with Tetzel are getting too edgy to go along with his waiting game," I said.

"That's what we think. I guess when you're the one out in the lake, trying to keep your head above water, you'll settle for a floating log instead of awaiting a rescue ship."

"Has Tetzel mentioned anything about Electra Cabot in any of his messages?"

"Not by name, but he has warned both von Eckhardt's office and the German Foreign Office that any interference at this point could be damaging to them all."

"That could cover a whole list of subjects."

"Yes. It's apparent that as the time for Barrista's rise comes nearer, Tetzel gets more nervous. Remember that phone conversation you overheard that seemed to indicate he was having someone check Electra out? He could be wondering if her object in dealing with him is to get information to pass on to his adversaries right in his own back yard."

"Gosh, I never thought of that. I guess you're better at putting two and two together than I am."

"I'm no genius, just persistent. I'm going into Cabot's office tonight."

"Oh! I won't sleep a wink until I talk to you."

"I ought to be back home by nine-thirty or so, unless I run into trouble."

That evening I sat around my apartment and waited. I was reminded of a conclusion I'd made earlier: spy work was in many ways not quite what I would have expected. One of the greatest surprises was the amount of time spent waiting for something to occur. This did not suit my nature, particularly. I wasn't sure whether it was worse to be hiding inside a dark building, searching through files, or sitting on a couch awaiting news. Either way, it was far from glamorous.

I was to leave my apartment at ten o'clock and go to a phone to call Edwin. Full of my old nervous energy, I cleaned floors and dusted and rearranged cabinets from the time I got home from work until eight-thirty. Then I heard a knock on the door. Startled, I nearly dropped a glass tumbler. I wasn't expecting any callers.

It was Christie, Ken, and Keith, and the three of them had obviously begun a party before deciding to include me. They toted in two dozen bottles of Lone Star beer. Ken opened four of them while I glanced nervously at the clock. Christie looked at me sideways and said with a wink, "Don't tell the Butlers I enjoy a beer once in a while."

Keith was excited about the new aviation center planned for Fort Sam, and even Ken seemed to have been infected with his enthusiasm. They talked of the Army's attempts at picking up privately owned property between the parade field and the fort. One of Ken's dentist friends owned a big chunk of it, and as Ken said, "He's holding out as long as possible for a high price."

"If he holds out too long, they'll just condemn it anyway. He ought to be reasonable and sell out while he can get the true value," said Keith.

"Well, you know how Harry is. . . ."

I kept glancing at the clock. Nine-thirty. We were on the third round. No one seemed to notice I wasn't talking much, and I sneaked off and poured my beer down the drain. Seemed a shame to waste it in the face of the certainty of prohibition, but all the same I seldom drank beer and I didn't want to get caught by the party mood and be late calling Edwin. I had to get this bunch out of my hair in time.

Finally at ten minutes before ten I said, "You know I've really had a rough week. Why don't we call it a night? Maybe Sunday we can get together again. I'll fix supper here."

"Translated, that means Keith will furnish food and Christie will cook it," Keith piped up, and everybody laughed. Thankfully they didn't seem to get their feelings hurt when I bustled them out the door. As soon as they were all the way down the stairs I walked a block up Houston to a cafe with a telephone. It would have been nice to have a phone in my apartment at times like these, but I couldn't afford one and also it was better to use a different phone all the time as a safety precaution. If the BNA knew how to tap a wire, then surely the other side was capable as well.

By ten o'clock I was awaiting the sound of Edwin's voice through the receiver. Yet there was no answer. My first thought was that he'd been snared by Nathan Hope. Tax time or not, Nathan kept odd working hours.

I drank a cup of coffee and tried again at ten-thirty. Nothing. Growing nervous now, I ordered another cup of coffee. The place closed at eleven o'clock, and I didn't know where I could find access to another phone this time of night. At fifteen minutes before eleven, I gave it one more try, and this time Edwin answered. I drew a sigh of relief at the sound of his voice.

"There's a lot to tell. Maybe we ought to try and talk tomorrow night," he said. His voice was husky. I attributed it to his being fatigued, but I wasn't about to let him off so easy.

"Tell me now. I just won't make it through—"

"All right. I spent most of my time trying to pick the lock in Cabot's desk, but I finally found a folder way in the back of one drawer with a contract drawn between Cabot and a private agency, a couple of invoices, and some letters that pretty well sum up his wife."

"Well?"

"Electra Cabot was a prostitute."

My mouth fell open. I couldn't speak.

"The agency began their search in a Texas town. They had the name Leslie Weems. They lost her—she apparently dropped out of sight for a while from what I could tell—then they picked her up again under the name Electra, kept a line on her up into several eastern cities and finally across to Colorado. The letters indicated she was pretty classy—as night ladies go—and the little town near Denver may have been her last stop because she'd been there five years, longer than at any other place.

"It's a pretty unfortunate story. In her early twenties she had one of those . . . uh . . . abortions—evidently a real butcher job that nearly killed her." He paused, then asked, "You all right, Camille?"

"Sure," I said weakly. I felt dizzy, and was thankful for the chair underneath me.

"Anyhow, when they finally located her, Cabot instructed them to buy out what was left of her contract with the house madam where she was working, and meet her expenses to bring her to San Antonio. Buying her out cost twenty-five hundred, and the agency fee was another twenty-five hundred."

"So that's where the five thousand went that he mentioned to Aegina."

"Listen, somehow I'm inclined to believe you're right about Electra's motives, now that I see what Cabot did for her. But we've still got to find out what she's doing with Tetzel. With a past like hers, she could have any number of reasons for becoming involved in espionage, whether or not she's doing it willingly.

"Remember, she's paying somebody behind Cabot's back and there is that gap in her history that even Cabot may not know how to fill in."

"I understand . . . any suggestions?"

"Not tonight. I'm too tired to think straight. I'll meet you tomorrow at twelve, near the rear entrance of the Gunter Hotel. Maybe by then I'll have an idea."

For all I slept that night, I may as well have obliged Edwin by holding off any discussion of Electra until the next day. I stood out on my River Avenue balcony for a long while, watching the headlights of the few automobiles still cruising down the otherwise deserted street, thinking of her. At least a couple of riddles were now solved: the night she hinted to me that someone—a man—might be taking advantage of me, that I ought to be careful of attentions paid me; and the night she reacted too abruptly to my inference she might one day be a mother. . . .

How did she get into that sort of business? For her looks and polish, she could have been anything she chose . . . or could she? What options did she have as a young woman? It seemed to me then that all my mother fought for in her crusade for the rights of women made sense for the first time. I remembered once, before I moved away, Mother participated in some hearings in Chicago about the limitations upon women who had to make their own way, and I went along to watch and listen. This was at a point when she was trying her hardest to get me to join the crusade for women's rights.

A group of prostitutes testified in the courtroom that day, each one of them filing in, dignified, their faces hidden behind dark veils and their names withheld. I had been fascinated by their mysterious qualities, their soft, refined voices. Electra. Oh, it seemed so wrong . . . yet so right.

*

Next day Edwin laid out his plan. "I've composed a little note, offering her a job, which I will slip under her door."

"That's dirty," I told him.

"But quick, and hopefully effective. Don't worry, I'll take care of it."

"Let me see it," I asked him and, after reading it over, remarked, "It's very vague—'business opportunity.' That could mean anything."

"Exactly. She won't come down there unless she thinks it's her admission slip into the game. Remember Tetzel warned her about getting into 'risky business.' On the other hand, if she isn't up to anything she'll assume someone who knew her in her former life has seen her here, and is trying to blackmail her. 'Business' would have only one meaning for her, and Durango crosses Flores near the district. She'll recognize that and pitch it into the garbage, having no reason to fear it because Cabot already knows what she was."

"But what if he sees it?"

"She won't let that happen if she's up to something of interest to us. Just to be on the safe side, I want to get it to her while he's out of town."

"Why can't we just ask the postal clerk to put it in her box?"

"Because we have no way of knowing when she might decide to stop by and pick up her mail."

I started to hand it back to him, then thought again. "Let me do it," I said. "I want to think about it . . . maybe there's another way of—"

"Believe me, I've considered all the alternatives, and this is the best. You can do the job if you wish, but remember that time is not on our side. And let me know, so I can be waiting for Electra when the time comes."

As we parted I felt a little better. Now that I was in control of the note I could put it off for as long as possible—Cabot would be gone at least through January, probably longer—and maybe, just maybe, something would happen to save me from having to slip it under Electra's door at all.

During this period Tetzel was away from the office a lot—for days on end—and when he was there, his manner was again quiet, and more and more withdrawn. I could now almost use Cabot and Tetzel as barometers for events to come, just by watching their behavior. Tetzel was letting bank business go undone. Mail piled up on his desk after he gave it a cursory glance once or twice a week. I took care of the items that I could handle without his help, but when I broached him about our need to write a certain letter, he'd wave a hand and say, "Another day. I have some business to tend to this afternoon."

When I reported this to Edwin, he thought for a moment, then suggested, "Keep your eyes on the Cabot house, and deliver that note soon."

"I'll do some watching," I told him, but avoided mentioning the note. On a Wednesday night in January I walked down, without any expectations. Yet before I came within two blocks of where King William begins, I saw Cabot's car turn west on Durango. Walking down Presa, I got a good view of the automobile from the side. There was no mistaking it. I grabbed the first taxi I could find, and instructed the driver simply, "Go over to Durango as quick as you can." The driver gave me a questioning glance, then sped on. Luckily this time I had more money in my bag. I'd just gotten paid, and had not yet handed the bulk of the money over to my landlord. Watching from the window, I kept thinking, Cabot's supposed to be gone . . . what's he doing here?

We were nearly to the South Loop before his car came back into view and I leaned forward eagerly. "Slow down," I said frantically. I didn't want to overtake him. The driver gave me a suspicious glance, so I added, "The place I'm looking for is along here somewhere, I think."

"You sure, miss? There isn't much out here except the asylum, and I think there's one of them tent meetings going on out here."

We were too far out to be headed for the red-light district by now, and I thought, it would be just my luck Cabot's headed out of town. Finally we approached a big canvas tent off to the left, lit up like an amusement park on Saturday night. I saw Cabot's car turn off and enter the field close by in a line of other automobiles. After that I couldn't see it anymore, but it was clear we'd reached his destination.

"Stop here."

The driver turned around, eyes wide. "I can't leave you here. You sure this is where you want to go?"

"How much do I owe you?"

"Let's see . . . fifty cents. You want me to wait?"

"No, I don't know how long I'll be."

"I'll come back. It's a slow night downtown."

I considered for a moment. "All right. It's seven-thirty. Come back right here at nine. I don't know how long these things last, do you?"

"Honey, why don't you go to one of them big churches downtown? These things aren't for people like—"

"Be back at nine," I said, and hopped out.

21

I had never been in a gathering of so many people.

Throngs converged on the big tent, and I could hear the sound of gospel tunes being pumped out of an organ within. I was soon lost in the crowd, and I realized Cabot was just as likely to find me as I was to spot him. It seemed the people appeared from all directions. I saw many on crutches and in wheel chairs, being helped along by others. Old men, toothless and unshaven; younger men with searching, frightened eyes like escaped convicts, or even inmates from the asylum—perhaps some were; blind figures who depended upon companions to substitute for their eyesight; women, young and old, some dressed in rags, some dressed to the hilt and wearing thick rouge, their hair wiry from dye applications. I thought of Electra. Surely she could never have been a part of such a class of people. Then I thought, suppose she's here too? I pulled my collar up around my ears and looked both ways.

It was very hard to avoid becoming mesmerized by the milieu of faces and bodies clustering so near that at times the stench was unbearable. Just outside the tent opening a big banner had been driven into the ground with stakes. "Brother Billy Sanblack—Revival—January 7 through 13." The words billowed out in the stiff winter wind. I must be crazy, I decided. I'll never find Cabot in all this.

Inside the tent seemed even larger than from outside. Wooden benches lined the sawdust floors. Kerosene lanterns hung from above. Up the big center aisle a platform with a lectern awaited. The music had stopped, replaced now by the sound of a bass drum being pounded by a big woman in a dark coat and bonnet. I took a seat near the back and looked around again for Cabot. No sign of him. The bench soon filled, and the woman on my right shifted closer as still more people edged in. The man on my left smelled so strongly of whiskey I nearly fell faint.

At eight o'clock the booming on the drum ceased, and the audience hushed. A woman wearing a mound of white flowers on one shoulder approached the lectern and introduced Brother Billy. When he came across the floor the people jumped up and cheered, whistled and wailed. I had never seen anything like it. The woman on my right, her face a study in deep ridges and age spots, pulled on my elbow. "Stand up, honey. It's Brother Billy." He was a monumental figure in a dark suit, with a shock of silver hair. We were still standing as he raised his arms, Bible in hand, and began a round of robust hymns. He threw out his chest and reared his head back. His voice was deep and compelling. He carried his audience like a forceful wave in the surf. He walked around and smiled into faces, like a coach inciting his team to victory against impossible odds. They swayed and nodded, croaking at the top of their lungs. The sound rose and fell in mighty discordance. I looked at the lady next to me. Her eyes were raised to the ceiling; the veins in her neck stood out and quivered. Perspiration rolled down her face. If he has them this stirred up by Wednesday, think what a state they'll be in by Saturday, I decided.

As the hymns came to an end, and the big collection baskets appeared, it seemed as though my own mission was not to be completed. I glanced at my watch. Eight-thirty. The sermon was about to begin. Then, I suspected, there would follow a coming forward of poor lost souls hoping to be saved. If I waited out the whole process, my taxi driver would leave and I'd have no way to get home. Then I looked to my right, and there, several rows ahead, sat Nathan. I craned my neck to get a better look, and was immediately nudged back by my neighbor on the right. She wanted to get a full view of Brother Billy as he preached.

I knew then I couldn't leave, even if I missed my taxi and had to walk home. I was able to see there was no one familiar to me beside Nathan. My neighbor's hat kept obstructing my view of him, so finally I asked her if we could switch places. This she was glad to do. When she moved over, I noticed she was missing her right arm. Now, oblivious of the words belted out with so much conviction by Brother Billy, I watched Nathan closely. Throughout the sermon he sat with eyes closed, head inclined upward slightly, rocking back and forth with his palms between his knees. He looked very odd, and as I continued to scrutinize him I began to feel nauseated. It was the closeness of the people around me, the stench in the air of unwashed bodies, I thought dizzily. Yet I knew I would have been far less affected by these things if not for the fact I was seeing someone I knew in what appeared to be an almost catatonic state. Before that time I had never actually pitied Nathan. Now all the troubles he suffered inside were being paraded before me even as they were concealed. For the first time I removed myself from the situation which had forced my attention on him originally, and wondered what else might be bothering him. In trying so hard to ferret out the information required by the BNA, I had become totally blind to any other facet of Nathan's life that caused him to be as he was. Though I was not aware then, I know now that in all the melting pot of people present during that revival, there was not a soul more lost than he. . . .

I left just before the last of the individuals who'd gone forward to confess their sins returned to their seats. Nathan had not moved from his chair to join them. Outside the cold air was so invigorating I took several deep breaths before I looked for my taxi. After ten o'clock. I didn't think the driver would be around, yet he was. I couldn't imagine anyone worrying more over a person he didn't know, but as he explained on the way back to town, he had a daughter my age and he was by habit cautious. He also had at one time driven a streetcar in San Antonio. "I've seen my share of mischief," he told me. "Young ladies belong at home after dark."

He let me out at a cafe, where I ducked inside to phone

Edwin and report. He didn't seem to believe it meant anything, as indeed it did not, in terms of espionage. By that time he was able to recognize Nathan, however, and offered to attend the revival if I thought he should.

"I suppose not. I heard someone talking about a group baptismal service down at San Pedro Creek on Saturday, though. I'm kind of curious as to whether he'll go. I'll just continue to shadow the Cabot house all week, and go down there early Saturday morning to see if he leaves in the car. One of the peculiar things about this is that he has always been so reluctant to use Cabot's car."

"Sounds like he's becoming a little on the sly side, doesn't it."

"Yes—that's unusual for him."

"Well, be careful."

I replaced the phone receiver. Lately Edwin was always cautioning me.

Very early on Saturday morning, I was stationed not far from the Cabot house, awaiting the appearance of Nathan in the Overland. My gloved hands thrust deep into my coat pockets, my breath coming out in icy puffs, I was wishing for an invitation into any warm parlor and chastising myself for being such an eager spy. Eventually, Nathan did round the corner in the Overland, and I thought, so what does that prove? Almost everybody gets baptized at some point in their lives.

There was no longer any question our country was tooling up for war. Draft age had been set between eighteen and forty-five years. The Army was buying more property to expand Fort Sam, and opening a school for chauffeurs and mechanics to maintain the legion of new Army motor trucks arriving. Keith could hardly study for midterm exams, his mind was so involved in the prospect of military duty, and Nathan would not even look up at me from his desk.

Edwin was picking up a huge zero from Allan at the telegraph office, and his only question for me was regarding delivery of the note to Electra. I was about ready to start biting my nails, wishing something would happen, yet afraid it would, and grasping for something to tell Edwin to divert his interest from Electra.

Toward the end of the month an interesting development came about. Tetzel brought a group of four men into his office, none of whom I had ever seen, and when the door was closed I hurried to the machine and turned it on. It was obvious they had been discussing the possibility of the sale of the bank, apparently for some time. Why this should have so astonished me, I can't tell. Regardless of the way things turned out, Tetzel would probably wind up divesting himself of San Antonio interests and going—where?—to Mexico? Back to Germany?

Edwin was called out of town for a couple of weeks, so it was not until his return that I was able to tell him about the news. What he had to tell me, however, was far more important and a great deal more startling.

22

The German Foreign Office had made two choices: first of all, they intended to begin unrestricted submarine warfare on February 1. Yet officially they still hoped to keep the United States neutral. In the event that was impossible, they intended to seek out the Mexican President for an alliance under the terms that Germany would give general financial support, and the promise that Mexico would reconquer lost territory in Mexico, Arizona, and Texas.

Further, the President of Mexico was to be encouraged to communicate with Japan regarding a triple alliance among the countries.

"Reconquer part of the United States—are they serious?" I squealed.

"They're not playing tiddlywinks."

"And Japan—where does it come in?"

"Your 'third party.' We assumed they referred to a person."

"How did you get this information?"

"A cable from Zimmermann, transmitted in code to the German ambassador at Washington, for forwarding to von Eckhardt in Mexico, was discovered and deciphered by the British. There is only one reason for you and me to be in on this little surprise. We have to find out if Tetzel plays a part in it.

"I've checked the telegraph office. There have been no wires sent by him, or received lately. What do you find?"

"Nothing. Except, he's trying to sell the bank."

"Keep a close watch. It looks as though Tetzel is possibly being kicked . . . out."

"Why do you think Tetzel was so against Japan?"

"Exactly the reasons he named. They're as fickle as a southern belle, although they've been disgruntled with the United States since the trouble out in California, and that leads some of the Germans to think they might be willing to side with them."

"But not Tetzel."

"Right; anyhow, they're not industrialized enough to be of much help as an ally."

" 'Industry,' " I repeated. "We always thought it referred to a personal trait."

"Just goes to show you the power of words."

"Do you think they shoved him out because of that quibble?"

"More than likely it was just so much political backbiting. In my opinion Tetzel is smarter than the rest of 'em."

"They're also going against his wishes in dealing with Carranza."

"They're selling arms to Carranza now, and dispatching German and Austrian reservists below the border."

"Does that mean he's co-operating?"

"No. It just means they're confident he will."

"Golly."

"Oh yes, I've got something for you from someone high up in the organization." He felt around in his pockets, then brought out a small envelope from one and stuffed it in my hand. When he was gone I opened it up to find fifteen dollars.

We had both been mistaken that Tetzel's corner of the triangle had been chopped off, however, as we soon found out. Though no copy of the wire for von Eckhardt followed from the German Foreign Office to Tetzel, there came a brief wire dispatching Tetzel to Mexico City for a meeting with von Eckhardt. On the morning of January 25, the day which marked the beginning of Pershing's troop withdrawal from Mexico, he walked in brusquely and said, "I have to leave town on business today . . . I should be back by late next week."

"Anything you'll need to take along?" I asked.

"No. I believe I have everything I need. If I should receive a call from a James Parker, tell him I'll return it next week."

I'd overheard the name Parker during the meeting so recently conducted about the sale of the bank. Mr. Tetzel looked tired and drawn that morning. I offered to bring him a cup of coffee, and he gave me a sort of wistful smile—or so it seemed to me—and said, "You take such good care of me, Camille." I knew it was not right to feel sorry for him, yet I did.

He returned right on schedule the following week, and Allan in the telegraph office reported that on the day of Tetzel's return, he promptly sent a wire to Mortimer Krantz in the Foreign Office. "I believe I have persuaded V.E. to hold off a bit longer on that which concerns us. However, there is of course nothing that can be done about the other. The edict has been signed." Tetzel's spirits were undeniably brighter.

"So he's still in the game," I told Edwin. "You know, when I think of the times I've wondered why you didn't just round up the evidence and pick him up, I feel ridiculous."

"Yes . . . the plot is gettin' thicker than molasses."

"And the German Government has no idea the secret's already out."

"The decoded message from Zimmermann is sitting on President Wilson's desk, like a death warrant."

"While they continue talking 'officially' about peace terms."

On the thirty-first of January, Wilson was handed Germany's official announcement of their intention to conduct unrestricted submarine warfare, briefly stating that since their efforts at peace had been declined by the Allies, they would establish a U-Boat blockade along a line twenty miles from the coasts of Allied countries across which no one would pass, in order to bring an end to the war by the use of a "starvation blockade" of England.

Their only concession to us was the permission of one ship per week to pass unharmed between Falmouth, England, and the United States, plus the guaranteed safety of our ships already en route from neutral to Allied countries.

Wilson immediately broke off diplomatic relations with Germany, sent the German ambassador his passport to go home, and ordered our ambassador, Gerard, to return from Germany to this country. Still, the public did not know about Zimmermann's telegram, and many people wondered why the President took such drastic steps over what surely was an understandable measure on the part of Germany. People in the office chatted incessantly about the prospects of going to war, their views toward President Wilson's action divided almost equally. I stayed out of the conversations altogether, pretending to be terribly busy.

News releases began appearing in the papers from Zimmermann himself, expressing surprise at our reaction to the "starvation blockade," not knowing that the telegram over his signature, proving his country's betrayal of us, had been unmasked a couple of weeks earlier.

Tetzel went about his work much as usual, except that he did begin sifting through old mail and directing memos to be sent now and then. He held another meeting with the men interested in buying the bank, and from this meeting I got clear indications he was holding out for a higher price, stock options less attractive than cold cash. I believe he was trying to appear to be a hard bargainer. Should he rush through too quickly, he might arouse suspicion at such unorthodox terms. He wanted to work them into a corner where they would be obliged to come to his terms, before time ran out and he was forced to disclose his impatience at ridding himself of the bank so he could flee the country with his pockets full. I am sure this was why he began negotiations so many months in advance.

On the evening of Monday, February 5, Edwin contacted me. Another telegram for Tetzel had been picked up: "Come at once," from someone at the German Embassy in Mexico City called "Toto." Neither of us knew the reason for the sudden summons, and doubtless Tetzel was puzzled by it, too. He phoned the office Tuesday morning to tell me he had to leave town again, with obvious irritation in his voice, and he said he would be back by the first of next week.

When he returned there began a series of events that were as quick and irreversible as the spark on the fuse of a powder keg.

23

Tetzel came in early the following Monday. In fact he was already at his desk, hat and coat off, sleeves rolled up, before I arrived. I slipped in unobtrusively to fill his inkwell and glance over his desk as I laid down the bank reports. All I could gather was that he was composing something long and detailed. He mumbled a terse "good morning," indicating he didn't want to be bothered, so I took off my coat and went to work.

Around eleven o'clock he left the office. I looked over his desk after he'd gone, but found nothing unusual. I was afraid to take time to go through the safe. By afternoon he was back, phoning Parker to set up another meeting in his office for three o'clock, and looking with renewed interest at untended items on his desk. He called me in to dictate a few memos, and when we were finished he said, "By the way, Mrs. Tetzel has some friends coming in from another city this Friday, so she wants to plan a dinner dance for Saturday night. Do you think you could come over and help us?"

"Of course. That's—let's see, the seventeenth?"

"I believe so"—glancing at his calendar—"yes."

At three o'clock I was stationed at the machine, listening with growing bewilderment as he called off the sale of the bank, disregarding all arguments of the buyers.

I went home at six wondering, what gives now? There was a note under my door from Edwin, asking that we meet at a little cafe on Commerce at seven. The answer to my question was soon forthcoming.

Tetzel had sent a rather lengthy wire to Mortimer Krantz in the Foreign Office earlier that day, which stated that since they had dealt him out, and decided to act now toward making an alliance, he would be willing to call off their association and to keep their secrets in return for their keeping his.

"Sounds like blackmail," I said.

"I believe the Foreign Office dealt directly with von Eckhardt in urging him to begin alliance talks now, rather than awaiting either the entry of the United States into the war or the takeover by Barrista. It's likely the seat is growing hot over in Germany about now.

"However, they dealt behind Tetzel's back, obviously, and whoever the code name 'Toto' refers to in the embassy in Mexico is undoubtedly on the lookout for Tetzel. Since his agent in New York—R. M. Francke—suddenly disappeared, I have a feeling they are one and the same. The wire we picked up today, from Tetzel to Krantz, said that it was 'unfortunate V.E. was unable to spare me an appointment.'"

"From what happened today I can tell you what is in the works," I said. "Tetzel is figuring on moving right out of this thing as though he was never part of it. There's no evidence of any consequence against him, as far as he knows. He can just go back to normal now as if none of this ever took place. He has called off the sale of the bank and planned a big party for next Saturday night."

"Oh? Hm . . ."

"Did the note to Krantz say anything about calling off the revolution?"

"It said as far as he was concerned everything below the border would go as planned, that it was out of his hands at this point, anyway."

"So he intends to leave Cabot and Barrista dangling in midair?"

"Not necessarily. The money's already been spent and the plans are made. If Carranza decides to play ball with Germany, then Barrista and Cabot are subject to being betrayed, but then Tetzel did speak of keeping secrets. Anyway, how can the Germans lose? If they go after Carranza now and he balks, they still have Barrista to fall back on, right?"

"Then why is Tetzel burning his bridges?"

"Could be pride. He has been frozen out. It isn't likely he'll be able to go back to Germany in glory now, unless the present department heads begin to roll," Edwin answered.

"And if they do, he'll have leverage by having disassociated himself from Zimmermann, von Eckhardt, et cetera," I said.

"So he's proven habitual at playing both ends against the middle. If Zimmermann's plan works, Tetzel is safe over here, as far as he knows and as long as he keeps his mouth shut. If it doesn't, he'll have some clout.

"We just stand by for now. We can't afford to disclose anything yet because it will expose what we know of Zimmermann's telegram about the alliance. That could send any number of rats back into the woodwork before we have sufficient proof. Which reminds me of Electra Cabot."

"Oh, that . . ."

He looked at his watch. "It's a little late for you to go down there tonight. How about tomorrow night?"

"I'm supposed to go out with a fellow."

"Well, suit yourself, but don't wait too much longer."

As it happened I neglected the note for the following week because Mr. Tetzel decided to clear his desk of all the old business, and I worked late every night and most of Saturday. I had just enough time to slip down on Washington and shove it under the door before getting home and dressed for the Tetzel party. I did not know Cabot was back in town, and for that reason assumed I would not find myself face to face with either of the couple that night.

Totally unprepared for what was about to happen, I arrived at the Tetzels on time and got to work checking wraps. The party was smaller than the one I'd worked before, so there was far less confusion. When the dinner was under way, I looked into the large rectangular dining room, just to feast my eyes on all the bounty—one thing to the Tetzels' credit was their fine taste in entertaining—and noticed two empty chairs up near one end of the table. I thought nothing of this at first, looking instead at the wife of the man I'd been shadowing for nearly a year and a half. Sophie just wasn't anything special to look at, regardless of the fact she did seem to attempt to dress stylishly at social affairs. She was chunky and plain, and seemed almost devoid of spirit. Over the telephone she seemed aloof and distant, unsure of herself. In person she was much the same, hardly an asset to a man like Tetzel, whose business was bound to overlap into social affairs frequently. Well, each to his own taste, I thought. I went back to the foyer to wile away the time before the guests invited only for the dance would arrive. I straightened coat sleeves and smoothed out gloves for a while, then found a comfortable place to sit.

Suddenly the door swung wide open and there stood the Cabots. Frozen in my chair, I tried to mouth an audible "good evening," then rose slowly. One look at Electra's face told me she'd read her message. She was as stark white as her evening frock was black. Cabot, very much in command, guided her in as though she were a fragile doll. He wished me good evening, put out his cigar, and helped Electra off with her wrap. The cut of her gown was shorter both from the hem up and the shoulders down than anything I had ever seen her wear. The aigrettes in her headband and her silk stockings and shoes finished off the trend-setter appearance. She had never looked more stunning, even while obviously very much distressed.

She looked at me and made a valiant attempt at smiling, though she didn't speak, and Cabot, unusually protective and attentive, ushered her into the dining room, where they were met with greetings all around the table.

I lowered myself into my chair again, for fear my knees would buckle. It seemed plain this woman was no secret agent any more than I'd believed her to be. I'd never felt dirtier, lower, or cheaper in my life as I sat through the eternity of a six-course dinner in the next room. Mrs. Tetzel's personal maid, whom I'd met at their party before, took one look at me and brought a glass of water. "Are you ill?" she asked.

"No, just sick to death," I answered. She knitted her brow and stared at me. As I sat there, gripping the glass of water, I kept thinking over and over how I wished all of this would end. I hated it, hated it. Worse, I hated myself. . . .

Later when the dancing was under way I stood with the

other help at the door and watched the couples moving around on the floor. Perhaps it was only my imagination, but it seemed there was more drinking, more loud talking and laughter, less restraint than normal. Without a doubt Mr. Tetzel was acting with more gay abandon than I would have ever expected. It struck me maybe this sort of party was just what he needed to lessen the strain he'd been enduring over the past couple of years. In fact, maybe it was what they all needed in the face of what was about to happen. Anyone with a modicum of common sense could see the handwriting on the wall. We would soon be a country at war, suffering at least a taste of the deprivations already demanded in great measure of the countries in Europe. Surely our government, knowing the secrets in its possession, would keep anything too dreadful from happening over here, such as an attack by Japan and Mexico from the south? It was almost too incredible to imagine, yet someone in a high place had conceived it as a possibility. . . .

The music continued to flow with the whiskey and wine that evening, and toward the end Mr. Tetzel suddenly appeared at my side and invited me out on the floor for a waltz. "Oh, but I can't!" I protested, aware of my starched uniform and cap as well as my trembling knees.

"Oh, but you can," he insisted, "my goodness your hands are cold," and whirled me about on the floor, through three waltzes. Mrs. Tetzel stood off to the side all the while, following the music with her shoulders and head.

When finally he relinquished my arm, the other helpers were clapping from the corner. I stood back with them, winded, and watched as a tango began. The tango was my favorite of all dances, and while I couldn't execute it—I'd never learned how —that did not keep me from being entranced by watching others perform it.

It seemed very soon that couples began to disappear from the floor, and eventually there was but one still dancing: the Cabots. I kept looking into Electra's face—was I dazzled by the pain I expected to see there, compelled to watch with some sort of morbid curiosity? I don't know even now, but I couldn't stop watching, watching, as they made the uneven, sensuous moves across the floor. At first her expression was as timid and uncertain as when they walked in, but Cabot was talking to her all the time. I could see his lips moving. He held her so near and in such a daring embrace that there were whispers around me labeling the Cabots "shameful" and "risqué." Yet to me it was a beautiful exposition, a dance of love in the strictest sense. A man who wouldn't any more let the world take his woman down than he'd let it get the best of him. How she must have adored him that night. How many of her grievances against him of late must have been wiped from the slate. If I had ever had any doubts up to that point, they were then dispelled. Those two loved each other in a way that was enviable to see, that made me hope someday I might have those feelings myself and have them returned.

All at once Electra lifted her eyes. Gradually her color returned. I think Cabot said something to her to bring this about because it occurred with suddenness, as though in reply to a command. Before it was over she was smiling and animated, moving smoothly and gracefully. When the music stopped the audience which had congregated off to the side shouted and whistled their admiration. Before leaving, the Cabots hesitated on the floor and looked about momentarily. The night was conquered. I stood transfixed, tears rolling down my cheeks, thinking of what a hideous thing I had done to her and, accordingly, to him.

I lay awake through the night.

Memories of the party fluttered through my mind like autumn leaves blown by the wind across a cold countryside. What were the Cabots saying to each other, I wondered? What would they do, now that it was clear their best-kept secret was no longer confined? How could I have done what I did; why didn't I insist on following my instincts, regardless of Edwin's feelings? He was the one who'd be standing near Durango and Flores streets at the appointed time, awaiting her arrival. Well, I could tell him right now he'd be wasting his energy. Emory Cabot himself might show up. He might beat the living daylights out of Edwin, should he know what was behind the deed. For that matter he might beat the dickens out of me. We both deserved it. Oh, how awful, how despicable. I punched at the pillow and turned over and over again. I was dangerously tempted to do a little plotting myself. I could go to the Cabots, explain the whole picture, and urge them to leave the country immediately. For a short while I let my imagination take hold, thinking how I'd get them secretly on a train for Laredo some dark night, and wave to their grateful faces as the engine roared and the smoke shot up from the powerful wheels, eager to speed them on to safety. . . .

Then all at once it occurred to me there was no reason I couldn't warn them. I raised up, excitedly. While releasing the Cabots would amount to a betrayal of the BNA, how much could it really matter in the end? They were primarily after Tetzel, not Cabot, who from all evidence had no certain knowledge of the gruesome extent of his involvement in German espionage.

I was practically to the point of jumping from the bed and throwing on my clothes, when I thought about the unresolved matter of Electra. If she'd really involved herself with Tetzel in an incriminating way, losing her might mean far more to the BNA than losing her husband, might undermine their efforts severely.

Yet all my instincts still shouted of her innocence. From the time I watched the Cabots glide across the dance floor like figures in a magical midnight dream, I had been caught up in my fantasy again, wanting them to be just what they appeared. . . .

Finally I decided to wait until Wednesday. After she failed to appear at the meeting place, there would be no gamble left, even for the BNA. Then perhaps I might tip them off. No one would ever have to know.

Morning light was peeping through the windows as I finally began to doze off, yet another specter got in the way—the face of Sophie Tetzel as I whirled around the dance floor with her husband. Then something else hit me. The picture in the safe. I had only once looked at it closely, but it seemed to me the woman didn't look like Sophie would have looked as a younger woman. I determined to have another, careful look at the picture, then fell asleep and awoke at one o'clock in the afternoon.

On Monday evening I pulled out an accumulated pile of work from my bottom desk drawer and announced I intended to stay late and finish it. "Suit yourself," said Mr. Tetzel. "You are the most conscientious worker in this entire bank, a model for others. Well, good night. Take care getting home."

I did indeed work away till after seven, the cleaning people dusting and sweeping around me, then disappearing down the hall. Then I went into Tetzel's office quietly and got into the locked compartment of his safe. I wanted a good long look at the picture, and this had been my main reason for staying late instead of coming back when the lights were out. There was no one around to see. First I checked for papers in the compartment. Nothing. Then I looked at the picture and knew at once the features did not belong to Sophie Tetzel. The nose was different, the eyes more deep-set and dark. The hairline was different. Every telling feature confirmed my suspicion. Yet it proved nothing. Could have been his sister for that matter. I slipped the picture back and closed the compartment.

Just as I reached for the outer safe door I realized someone was behind me. My heart took a wild leap. But then I realized with relief it was Giddy. "Oh, hi! I didn't know you were still here," I said, closing the door slowly as though it were quite an ordinary errand that caused me to open it.

"I had to work late, too, and noticed the lights on when I came up to the ladies' room. Now, old fogies like me just work because we haven't got anything more interesting to do, but you . . ."

"Yes?"

"Well, my dear, if I didn't know better I'd suspect you were bucking for a raise."

I sat back on my heels and laughed nervously. "Oh, fudge! I guess the truth's out."

24

During the week following the party I watched Tetzel more closely than ever. Daily I opened the newspaper expecting to see publication of the full text of Zimmermann's intercepted telegram, yet it did not come. Edwin speculated, "If the President turns it loose now, he might be accused of trying to influence the Congress toward going to war out of sheer indignation. He'll try and get his Armed Ship Bill through first, out of a last-ditch attempt at keeping neutral, while protecting our merchant ships. But he has a lot of enemies in the Congress, particularly the Senate. They could tie up his bill there interminably."

"Doesn't this session of Congress end early in March?"

"Yes, but they could call an extra session or something if they wanted to be really stubborn. Once they adjourn, Wilson has the whole ball game for nine months, and I doubt they'll want to part company with him at this crucial point, leaving all the decisions in his office."

"Who wouldn't want the Armed Ship Bill to go through—isn't it logical to anyone that we need to protect our merchant ships?"

"The pacifists will call it a move toward war, and they're powerful in Congress."

"Wilson's hands are sort of tied, then, aren't they? I mean, he's going to be made out a villain either way."

"Probably so."

"And if he can't get his bill through, he could use the telegram as a little leverage, couldn't he?"

He laughed. "Camille, they might need you in the Capitol one day."

In the middle of the week, Cabot paid Tetzel a visit. True to his inevitable habit which had foiled us all along, he walked in and threw his hat squarely above the receiver of the recording machine. If not for its unwieldy size, we might have been able to move the piece of equipment to another place. I hurried to the storeroom, ready once again to get what I could by listening at the wall. Cabot was apparently making firm his plans for the next month. Mostly, Tetzel just listened without comnent.

"I've collected some boxes intended for electrical bulbs going inside the mines. We're going to put the currency in them to ship it down," he said, then added, "Beats coffins."

Tetzel laughed.

"It'll be on the train by March fifth. Everything else will be arranged by the time I leave here on the first. I'll go by Barrista's, then on to visit Carlos, to lay out his battle plans. By then he'll have only a couple of weeks to get organized, and I'll stick around to help him. He thinks I've held back because of some crucial decisions in strategy that I hadn't been able to make. Barrista assured him of that.

"On March tenth, the general election will take place. If Barrista's name appears on the ballot, the whole plan will be off. If not, the call to arms will follow in exactly one week— March seventeenth.

"Is everything set from your end?"

"Oh yes, count on it," said Tetzel. He neglected to mention that events over the past couple of months had left a great deal more to chance than Cabot expected.

"I'll be in touch the morning I leave, in the event anything new develops. Oh yes, and let me leave this with you—just in case."

"But I don't think I'll need—"

"Just the same, you'll be handling things for Electra anyway if anything happens to me."

"All right. And Cabot, best of luck."

"We're going to need it. If this works, you'll be a big German hero."

"Ah, maybe so, maybe not. It's a long way to the fatherland. . . . But you will be a very wealthy and powerful man."

"That's what it is all about, isn't it?"

"For some . . ."

When I reported the meeting to Edwin I couldn't resist remarking on the irony of Tetzel's confident state. "Even if we never get our hands on the vouchers and other material we kept looking for in that safe, there is enough evidence stacked up against him to put him away for years. As soon as Barrista raises a gun, we'll have even more."

"Any way you look at it, that makes you a pretty valuable agent."

"Don't get any ideas about me continuing this kind of work. I wouldn't live to see thirty."

"By the way, I went down to Durango today at three o'clock. Mrs. Cabot didn't show up, but her husband did."

"I knew it!" I exclaimed, then quickly asked, "What happened?"

"Nothing. I kept out of sight."

"Well, I guess that closes the case against—" I began, thinking once again of alerting the Cabots.

But Edwin interrupted, "Just the same, keep an eye on her. She might be prompted to contact Tetzel again."

"Oh . . . I didn't think of that," I said deflatedly.

It would be a long time until the Mexican elections in March, still longer if the plans went through on the seventeenth. I noticed an ad for Joske's, hiring extra clerks during their February clearance sale, and decided to apply. The lady in personnel liked me, since I'd clerked at Christmastime and proved pretty good at selling. She was more than glad to place me in the undermuslin department, expected to be one of their busiest areas during the sale. It was only for the final week in February, but it would at least get me through a few more days with my mind diverted as much as possible from other matters.

I thought maybe I could talk my way into an extra job somewhere in the store beginning in March, too, if nothing complicated my evenings.

I began on Saturday the twenty-fourth, and one of my first customers was Electra Cabot. "I've let my stock of undergarments get very low lately, and I need some new petticoats too, shorter than my old ones. Styles are getting further up the calf by the day, it seems." She bought several boxes of merchandise, and just as I was totaling up the sale, thinking the sum was going to throw her into shock, she said, "I'm considering a little trip next Wednesday, and I have to get ready for it."

"Oh. Going far?" I asked eagerly.

"Not very. I haven't really made up my mind about it yet."

"Will you be gone long?"

She laughed. "I can't say about that, either. Emory's going to be away for a while, and he thought it might help me pass the time. I could use a change of scenery."

"So could I."

"By the way, have you found a new apartment yet?"

"No, haven't had time . . . but I will in the next few weeks."

"Think you might still take Scoop?"

"If I can find a place that will permit him. That's eighteen dollars and thirty cents altogether. Shall I put it on your account?"

"Please. And I'll carry these two boxes, but I'd like the others delivered. Be sure to have them there by Tuesday afternoon, because I'll be leaving at mid-day Wednesday."

"Who's going to look after Scoop while you're away?"

"Nathan. Thank goodness, he doesn't object to him like Emory does."

After she walked off I got to wondering what Nathan's plans were after Cabot returned to Mexico, perhaps for good? Electra would no doubt expect to go where her husband went . . . that is, unless she was dealing behind his back . . . and from the looks of all the packages she carried out of the store, including what she bought from me, she was preparing to take along what necessities were probably lacking down in that country.

Surely she wouldn't cross the border until after the shooting was over, should there be any. Cabot wouldn't want to risk her life needlessly, and since he had no more idea his plans had been laid open than did Tetzel, he would have considered her perfectly safe here in the States.

If not for the fact Nathan had changed so much over the past few months, and had gone off on some kind of religious tangent, I would have been certain he would go along to Mexico too, perhaps waiting until Electra went down. Yet there was now something peculiarly disturbing about him. . . . I had the feeling he was laying plans for himself that didn't include anyone else.

On Wednesday morning Keith called to invite me for lunch at his favorite little Mexican cafe on the river. This was unusual for him—normally he attended early classes then worked through the lunch hour—but, as I soon learned, there was a special reason behind his impromptu invitation. This was the day before his birthday, and he had just picked up his first tailor-made suit at Fomby-Jones, a combination birthday and early graduation present. He could hardly wait to show it off—a tapered light-brown tweed with belted back and leather buttons. The outfit also included a new white shirt and brown tie, brown Stacy-Adams shoes, and a handsome cap with a leather bill. Only when I saw how proud he was of his ensemble could I fully appreciate how demeaning his hand-me-down clothing had been for him. All through lunch he kept raising his arms as if to reaffirm the sleeve length was just right. "Tomorrow night, Ken and Christie are going to cook dinner for me—can you come? Mom and Dad and I can pick you up after work."

I hesitated a moment. My job at Joske's was over tonight, and I'd planned to ask about extending it for a couple of weeks when I went on duty at six o'clock in the evening. To complicate matters, tomorrow was March the first, the day Cabot would leave for Mexico. It didn't seem a propitious day for making plans. However, as I watched his face, never lacking in boyish anticipation and particularly so as he awaited my reply, I realized I couldn't tell him no. Joske's would have to wait a day in between, that was all, and as for Cabot, there probably wasn't much I could do one way or another as he left for Mexico. As Edwin had explained, the United States officials could pick him up on the strength of his copper shipments inside this country a few months previous, and avoid the risk of losing him for good once he was down in Mexico. However, to do so would be to expose the findings on Tetzel before rounding up the remainder of evidence against him and the names and locations of the people he was working with, whom we still had not been able to identify.

"Sure," I told Keith, unaware that we had let out the lines just a bit too far. Someone we would never have suspected was about to snap them.

25

Since Tetzel had a meeting elsewhere and didn't plan to return to the office until around four o'clock, I took the luxury of a two-hour lunch with Keith, never having enjoyed his company more, nor appreciated the fact that he was so detached from my other life—refreshing as a cool breeze after a rain.

Around three o'clock I meandered slowly back to the bank, and, crossing Alamo Plaza, noticed Electra Cabot disappearing into the post office. It did not occur to me just then that she should not have been there. I thought of this after I returned to work and typed the date at the top of a letterhead. She was to leave at mid-day on her trip, I remembered, then figured she might have changed her mind about going, or decided to delay till the following day, when Cabot went to Mexico. It did seem a little odd for her to have preceded him by a day, missing the chance for some more time with him, now that I thought about it.

People change plans all the time, I told myself. Yet, now that Electra was suspect, I just couldn't get her departure from schedule off my mind. By the time I walked into Joske's at six o'clock, I'd decided to go down to the house at Beauregard and Washington after work, just to see what was going on.

I arrived at ten o'clock. Picking the nearest house to theirs with its automobile missing from the garage and the lights out —my usual custom—I crouched down among some bushes nearby and watched. The only lights in the Cabot house across the street were those burning in Nathan's window. I couldn't be sure from my vantage point, but I thought the garage was empty.

I sat looking at the same unchanged scene until eleven o'clock, and, thinking how foolish I was for worrying in the first place, rose to leave. It was then the big Overland rolled down the street and turned into the drive. I waited long enough to see two dark figures start across the grounds from the garage toward the house.

Though they were too encased in shadows for me to be sure, I had no real doubt it was Cabot and Electra. She had on a big Gainsborough hat. I didn't see any other lights go on in the house, though I assumed they turned on lights at the back. I was about to leave when the people who occupied the house beside the shrubbery where I was hiding came down the street. I dropped to my knees just in time to avoid being caught by their headlights. I'd have to wait, then, till they'd gotten out of the car and gone inside. They had several children along, and there was much complaining and shifting around before they all got out of the car and inside. I wasn't sure whether there were more still out there, or if the father would come out and unload the car should it be necessary, so I waited a bit longer. Crossing would have put me in full view of anyone going back to the garage.

Meantime I kept my eyes on the Cabot house.

The lights continued to burn in Nathan's quarters. Midnight. My curiosity about him was at a peak anyhow, and I decided to steal across the street and peer in the window, just to see what in the world he could be doing up so late. Maybe I could see something that would give me a clue as to his odd behavior of late.

Oh, this is really dreadful, I thought as I crossed the street, pulse pumping. Edwin would murder me for taking this kind of an idiotic chance. But then my curiosity had truly gotten the best of me. I was spying for myself, not for the BNA. Edging up to the window, I saw Nathan seated very still in his chair. Profile to the window, his eyes were closed, his shirt collar unhooked, sleeves rolled up. At first I thought he was asleep. Then slowly his hand came over the side of the chair. He picked up a handgun and turned it over and over in his grip before laying it aside again and leaning back in the chair. All at once the things he had been saying and doing over the past few weeks made sense. He was going to take his life. I had to stop him.

The only usable explanation for banging on his door was my old starved-for-love routine. It would just have to do. The Cabots, by now asleep upstairs, would probably not even hear a gun fire between the thick walls. If not for me, there would be no one to save him from himself.

He opened the door slightly and looked out. His face was haggard. "You! What do you want?" he demanded.

"It's cold out here. May I come in?"

"Come back some other time."

I thrust an arm inside the door. "Couldn't we just talk for a few minutes? You haven't talked to me much lately."

He left to close the other door, leading to the foyer—it was slightly ajar—then returned. "I guess it's all right. But only for a few minutes."

I walked in and sat down near him. The only light came from a dim desk lamp. His quarters seemed close and overpowering. He was halfway through a bottle of whiskey. He poured himself another glass, looking ahead at the wall above the desk, as though I weren't there. I glanced down at his lap and saw a black Bible there. It looked ominous somehow, in that position. I felt the blood rise in my temples. Finally I cleared my throat and said, "You're putting away an awful lot of that whiskey . . . how will you be able to work tomorrow?"

He looked across at the ledgers covering the desk and said, "I finished tonight. Everything Cabot has done is down there in those pages, all balanced and reconciled. . . ." Then he added with almost a smile, "Just like me."

I ran my tongue over my lips. I would have given a lot to have those ledgers in my possession. "Swell. Why don't you take some time off?" I said brightly. "Do you good."

He smiled to himself. "Oh, I am . . . I won't ever have to touch one of those filthy things again."

I sat back. The liquor was apparently loosening his well-guarded tongue. There was no end to what I might find out from him tonight, if I asked the right questions. "So, you're quitting Cabot at last. I've always suspected you didn't really like keeping books."

He raised the Bible in front of him and said, "I've found all the answers right in here . . . funny, all those years I was afraid, and the answers were right under my nose."

He sounded like a fresh convert, as, in a way, he was. "This book has given me courage to do what must be done . . . I don't have to be afraid anymore. The Lord loves me. He forgives me of all the bad things I've done, and He uses me to reach His own ends." He put the Bible down again. I didn't see how this had much to do with what interested me. I wanted to get back to Cabot.

"You worked for Cabot a long time, and passed up the chance to go elsewhere. I could have gotten you a job at the bank, remember—"

He considered me for a few moments, and gradually his peaceful expression changed. His eyes narrowed, his lips hardened. In the shadows he had an almost demonic look. His voice was low. "You stupid little bitch . . . coming around me when I never wanted you, pestering me because of the way I live. Do you think a man would live like I do if he was free? Don't you recognize the devil incarnate when you run into him?"

"Who—you mean Cabot?"

"Of course, you little fool. The Bible says the devil will bring evil to our lives, but that with the power of Christ we can overcome him. And now I know that it's true."

"But Cabot's not—"

"Oh, you think you know so much, but you don't," he said. His eyes were little flames. "Electra knows. She wouldn't tell you, but she knows, and now I've freed her. She's safe and far away. He'll never be able to hurt her again."

I started to tell him she was very much here in this house, but before I could he was talking again. "I'll bet you didn't know he beat her once. And if you could hear the horrible things he has said to her . . . oh, when I think of the times

I've heard him lash out at her with his poisonous tongue, powerless to stop him. More than once I've felt the force so strongly I've crawled into a corner and covered my ears."

I swallowed hard. "Well, if that's so, why didn't you interfere?"

"Because I couldn't. Much as I wanted to, I couldn't because he might have killed me, then no one would have been around to help her when the opportunity came. And if I was lucky to be quicker than he was, and kill him, nothing would be gained because I would still be subject to his will. Can't you see the devil emerging even as I tell you how he works?"

I sat still and quiet.

"The Lord promises those of us who suffer travail upon the earth shall find peace and happiness in heaven. . . . I don't have anything to fear anymore," he said, and put his head back again. "You're not convinced, poor little lamb Camille. . . . It follows, though, because the devil has enormous powers of deception. I'll tell you something, will you believe me? Even after Electra left on the train today, he brought another of those harlots home with him tonight, brought her to this house Electra worked so hard to keep for him. She was trash, just like him. I heard them go up the stairs, talking and laughing. They're lying up there together now," he said, glancing above, then across at me. His eyes were very bright for a moment. He looked down again and continued, "No one has ever known how much I could hear in this house, and Cabot himself caused the mistake that made it possible. He hurried me when I was working on it before we moved in, and I left a hollow wall without intending to. It was his fault, driving me to finish when I was so tired I could hardly stand up. He foiled himself, and because of that I was led to the Lord at last."

"I don't understand."

"If not for the desperation, knowing time was running out and I didn't know what to do, I would never have gone to a prayer meeting. I was nearly mad after he struck her, but I lacked the courage and the wisdom to defy the devil. But now I've done it. He can never hurt either of us again."

I wanted very much to get him to the core, and it seemed

that each time I came nearer he whirled off on his religious reel again, talking nonsense, thinking he was led by the Lord when he was spurred on by the liquor. His voice was becoming more and more slurred. If I could only get to the bottom of what he was talking about. . . .

Finally I said, "You were with Cabot for years before Electra came along. I still don't understand why you stayed, hating him as you did."

He paused and blinked at me. I had the feeling he was not really aware of my presence any longer. He looked back toward the wall. "Cabot saw me kill them."

26

I realized then Nathan was someone we all had miscalculated. At once I wished to be as far away from him as I could run, yet was seized with curiosity. I didn't dare ask a question. I could only hope he would continue to go steadily from that point on, and he did.

He became retrospective, and gazed up at the ceiling, as though it was with some relief he finally told what he had kept secret for years. "Sam Arnesty was big as a bull and strong. He had a ring of black hair around his head and dark, distrustful eyes. He took a shine to my mother as soon as he hit town and went to work as foreman of the mill. I didn't mind him. Mother said he made good money and if she married him she wouldn't have to sew for people anymore. And it wasn't bad at first. He'd take me with him on the buggy sometimes; when something broke that couldn't be fixed at the mill, he'd put it on the buggy and take it to Lufkin to the foundry there. And all along the way he'd talk about the mill and there wasn't anything I'd rather listen to.

"But then a few months after the wedding Mother got sick and Sam brought Doc Barnes to the house to look at her. He was the mill doctor. He said he didn't know, he'd have to run some tests and send them off. So when she felt a little better she went down to his office and he did the tests. When the results came back he said he wanted to send her to a big clinic in Baltimore where they'd do some more tests.

"Sam didn't like it much, said it was probably all her imagination when it came right down to it, but he sent her anyway. When she got back she told him she was real sick and would have to go to a big hospital for treatments. I don't know what she had. I was just a kid. No one would tell me anything. I think she had cancer, but she wouldn't talk to me about it.

"Sam got mad. He came home drunk one night and accused her of knowing she was sick before she married him, and using him to pay her doctor bills. At least he didn't hit her—even Sam Arnesty wasn't as brutal as Cabot—but he said awful things to her and made her cry. Then he left and didn't come home for a week.

"When he did, he apologized and said he just didn't have the money to send her to a fancy hospital, and was too ashamed to admit it at first. I heard her tell him that if he'd just promise to look after me after she was gone, and see that I grew up all right, that was all she'd ask. He agreed to that. We hardly ever saw him. He was always on call at the mill, and I think he stayed there even when he didn't have to.

"After she died—she was hardly cold in her grave—he brought Clove Sutcom in and told me he intended to marry her. Said she would be my stepmother. She was fat, with a little pig face and four chins. He'd known her up in another mill town where he worked before. I don't know how long he'd been carrying on with her before my mother died, but that was the first thing I thought of. My mother had very high morals, and Clove Sutcom wasn't anything more than a common night woman." He paused, then as if in a trance continued:

"One day right after they married I got sick at school with a fever, and the teacher sent me home. When I walked in they were sitting at the table, talking about buying into the mill. Sam said he had several thousand dollars saved up. When I heard him bragging about that money I flew into him. I would have torn his guts out, but he flung me off so hard I hit the kitchen wall. He started toward me, but Clove pulled him back. She said they ought to put me to bed, and that she had a better idea than for Sam to beat me up.

"I don't know what went on for the next few days. I was delirious with fever, and all I remember is Clove giving me calomel. It seemed the room around me was swimming all the time. Then one night about the time I was beginning to be better, and thinking about how I was going to get back at Sam for lying to my mother about not having the money to save her life, the two of them came in together. Last thing I knew I had a wet towel slapped in my face. When I woke up I was on a train slumped down between them. Each of them had an arm around me. Sam said if I made a move toward the aisle, he'd make me wish I hadn't. Clove said I was a bad boy and would be better off in a school she knew about out in West Texas, and that was where I was headed.

"I was trapped in that place until I was seventeen, then I escaped. There was only one place I wanted to go, and that was Mill Springs. I got me a gun to kill Clove and Sam, and after that I was going to set that stinking mill afire, and every building connected to it.

"It took me three weeks to get there, and I sneaked down the little hill in back of the house one evening and waited till they sat down to supper in the kitchen. I shot her first, then watched him lunge toward her, then look toward the window where the shot came from. I let him see my face, then I shot him, and he fell over on her."

"And Cabot saw this?"

He nodded. "I can still hear his voice. 'Drop the gun,' he said. I looked around. He was sitting on a horse up on top of the hill, aiming his rifle at me. He guided the horse slowly down the hill, then came on over, leaned real close, and stared into my eyes. Then he straightened up and started telling me what to do. He made me go back in there and take all her jewelry and empty Sam's pockets, then bring everything back to him. When I got back he looked over each piece carefully and put it all in his saddlebags. Then he made me clean up all the blood from the table and chairs and the walls—oh, he was a monster if ever there was one—and bury Clove and Sam under the house. All the while he sat on his horse and watched me, and stood lookout to be sure no one saw.

"After that he sent me back to put their clothing in suitcases, so people would think they'd gone on a trip, and bury those things in another spot under the house. When I got through my nails were bleeding and my arms and legs were numb from bending under that house. I did not know what had come upon me. I didn't know there was anyone in the world that evil.

"We camped out in the woods that night. He asked me why I'd killed them, and I told him. He said no one would ever know about it, and made me sign a confession he'd written down on a piece of paper. He said the paper would be kept with all his legal papers that wouldn't be opened till his death, so if I ever killed him it would be found and the law would get me, that the evidence would be right there, buried just where it said on the paper.

"I asked him how he happened to come by there, and he smiled in that diabolical way of his and said, 'Just lucky, I guess.' "

He paused for a few moments then. I didn't want to think that what he was saying of Cabot was true, but it had an undeniable ring of plausibility about it. Always quick to grasp an opportunity, Cabot had taken himself a slave. . . .

Soon Nathan continued, "He told me he could use me to keep his books, that he'd teach me how he wanted them done. So we came to San Antonio and he moved me with him into his apartment close by the district, and every night he went down in there and gambled and drank, and half the time brought one of those whores home with him to stay all night.

"He was lousy as one of those rats running free down in that hole where we stayed, but he didn't bother me as long as I kept up with who owed him what and made sure no one ever cheated him. Later on, when the government taxes started to get in his way, he made me cheat for him. I used to tell myself, if they catch him at least I'll have the chance to see him behind bars, and it will be worth something when he tells on me, just knowing he got at least part of what was coming to him."

He leaned back in his chair again and closed his eyes. I thought he'd pass out then and I sat silently, watching to see what he'd do next. One eye was on the ledgers. If I could just get them. . . .

In a moment, though, he began to talk again. "But then Electra came, and everything changed. I was shocked he'd take up with someone as fine as her, and more surprised she'd take up with him. I know she wouldn't have except she had known him when he was younger, and probably not so mean. I figured she must have thought he was still that way, until after they married.

"At first when he brought her here, you'd have thought he really had changed into someone decent. He stayed real nice for a while. But then he began to abuse her, and I could see how frightened she was. She hated him just like I did, but she didn't know how to get away from him. Oh, the times I've seen her face when he's around. . . . She'd have run away before but she was always afraid he'd come after her."

"Did she tell you that?"

"Certainly not. She's too much of a lady to tell anyone about her husband. She just put up with him. Before he had the wreck it was worse. I was nearly insane, wondering what to do. I knew he'd try to cheat on that cash deal he made down in the district, but the draft was hanging over my head, and I knew I'd probably be taken before he was found out, then what would become of Electra? There would be no one to watch her, and once they started digging into my past for my records, they'd likely discover what I had done.

"But then, thankfully, the Lord interceded, and started directing me. I watched her, and waited for Him to give me a sign. She didn't seem frightened for a while, but then last week, when Cabot came back to town, I knew it was happening again."

"How?"

"When they went to that big party over at the Tetzels'. I didn't hear them argue and I don't know what it was about, but she was scared to death when they got into that car, and he stuck close by all the time, afraid she'd try to get away, see, so I knew I had to help her. And one afternoon the very next week

I came home to find her cowering in the parlor, with the shades drawn. You see, the closer the time came, the more she was caught in the grips of fear. So just to be safe, I got her ticket for the train today. Just in case . . . She's down in Corpus Christi, knowing I helped her, and she won't ever have to go back to him."

He looked across at me and smiled. "The Lord has used me as His instrument. I learned all about how He works through us to help others. He'll forgive all the bad I've done because I confessed my sins and accepted Him as my savior, and I let Him use me to help someone who couldn't help herself."

All at once everything about Nathan began to make sense. I didn't know how much of his rambling about Cabot was true, but I did see how twisted his conception of Cabot's relationship with Electra had been. If not for the fact he mentioned the Tetzel party, I would not have understood, but that gave me the necessary clue. I sat there wondering what to do. His eyes were closed again now, and he had his Bible on his lap. It seemed evident he intended turning those ledgers over to the authorities while Cabot was away in Mexico. Apparently he'd fixed them to reflect some cheating over a long period—I could only guess, not having seen them. He truly felt Electra only awaited a chance to get away from the wicked husband she was married to. I could imagine every time he saw the shadow of fear or distress cross her face, he was certain Cabot had put it there. He knew nothing of her past, and of the obsession she must have had about keeping it quiet. He knew nothing of the dangerous activities she might be carrying on at present.

It occurred to me then that he may have felt if he turned on Cabot while he was in Mexico, he just might be able to get away before Cabot returned. He would have time to leave the country, and run far enough that he might never be found. Badly as I wanted the ledgers, I didn't want to risk taking them until I spoke with Edwin because of the predicament it might put me in.

Finally his head fell on his chest. I couldn't go upstairs and waken the Cabots without taking a chance of revealing myself

. . . yet I almost did. I thought of playing on them the same trick I'd used on Nathan, even if it did seem a bit absurd. It would be easier and safer just to take the gun with me, I finally decided. When Nathan awoke tomorrow morning he would no doubt have regained some of his senses. At least I could save him through the night and by morning think of something better. I reached across gingerly and picked up the weapon. I'd never held a handgun before. It felt big and awesomely powerful in my hand. I left the house with it and went to my apartment, looking at several places along the way for access to a telephone. Yet everywhere I looked was locked up tight. It was one-thirty in the morning. When I got home I found a note under my door that proved the futility of calling Edwin. He had gone to Washington early in the morning of the twenty-eighth, and would call me sometime during the day on March first, when he arrived, to let me know his number. He added, "Apparently Carranza not playing ball—looks like Germany might be depending upon Barrista after all. If so, Tetzel might be 'in' again. Check our agent Allan at Western Union for messages."

Exhausted, I fell into bed consoling myself I'd kept anything horrible from happening. Had I been less tired I might have been able to reason out other eventualities, but there was one thing I would never have thought of because I had never been exposed to drinking very much and didn't know its effects.

Nathan would sleep, but not all night.

27

After going to bed I tried again to sort out Nathan's bemusing words, but the more I went over them in my mind the more confused I became. Finally, the obvious occurred to me as I went back again to the beginning and considered the way he fondled that gun. He handled it in a gentle, almost loving fashion. He was contemplating suicide, but not until Cabot was on the train to Mexico. Then he could turn over the ledgers to the authorities, his final act. "All balanced and reconciled . . . just like me," he had said. Once I had figured that out, I knew I had done what was right. I could explain away the fact I had taken the gun. It would have been very awkward explaining my theft of the ledgers. I had effectively bought some time . . . time to check with Edwin about the next step. . . .

I slept until after eight the next morning and, still exhausted to the point of fogginess, I decided not to jump into my clothes and rush to the office. I was already late. A few more minutes wouldn't matter. I went to the River Avenue balcony for some fresh air, hoping to clear my mind. Yawning, I stepped out into the sunshine and bracing chill. It was second nature to look down toward the Butler store by now, often to see Keith loading the truck for deliveries of the day.

Instead I saw him dash suddenly out the door. His blue eyes were ablaze as he glanced down the street below me. He jumped in the truck, and shot off in a wave of exhaust fumes. His father followed him outside, holding a newspaper under his arm. My first thought was, Zimmermann's telegram had finally been released to the press. Yet even if I was correct about that, it didn't explain Keith's behavior. I went back inside, quickly dressed for work, and took a detour by the store.

Mr. Butler was leaning against the doorway, reading the newspaper headlines, mumbling, ". . . those dirty Germans" under his breath. He showed it to me and I read, at last, the full text of what the BNA had learned of weeks earlier, the message intended for the eyes of von Eckhardt:

> We intend to begin unrestricted submarine warfare on the first of February. We shall endeavor in spite of this to keep the United States neutral. In the event of this not succeeding, we make Mexico a proposal of alliance on the following basis: make war together, make peace together, generous financial support, and an understanding on our part that Mexico is to reconquer the lost territory in Texas, New Mexico, and Arizona. The settlement in detail is left to you.
>
> You will inform the President (of Mexico) of the above most secretly as soon as the outbreak of war with the United States is certain and add the suggestion that he should, on his own initiative, invite Japan to immediate adherence and at the same time mediate between Japan and ourselves.
>
> Please call the President's attention to the fact that the unrestricted employment of our submarines now offers the prospect of compelling England to make peace within a few months. Acknowledge receipt.
>
> Zimmermann.

Somehow it appeared even more sinister than I had imagined. "Make war together; make peace together." It gave me the shivers. I handed it back to him. "Where's Keith?" I asked.

"Gone down to the river. They found a body caught in the brush down near Guenther Mill—no, that's Pioneer—I always say it wrong."

I brought a hand to my mouth. Mr. Butler thought he had shocked my feminine sensibilities by his bluntness, and offered me a chair close to the door.

"No," I said, gulping, then took off toward East Guenther Street, at the foot of King William. With every step I tried convincing myself it wasn't Nathan. Someone else could have lost his footing and slid down the viney slope, someone who couldn't swim. Could even be a woman—Mr. Butler hadn't said. Oh, but if it was Nathan, the fault was mine. I'd taken the gun. Oh, what a magnanimous gesture to save someone bound for suicide. Around Alamo Plaza, then on down South Alamo, it seemed a longer distance than ever to the quiet little bend in the river around the mill. Across Nueva and up Garden, then finally left onto King William past the house with the square tower, then the triangular park, I wasn't conscious then of my legs tiring, or of my raised skirt hem, which must have shocked people of the neighborhood who watched as I sprinted by. I wasn't even conscious of the fact that this impetuous reaction might tell more than I wanted known about my activities of late. It didn't matter. All I wanted to know was whether I'd helped to seal the fate of a poor, mixed-up young man who thought he was friendless and had only one route of escape from torture I didn't understand and couldn't quite piece together. Along the way I was reminded of Tetzel's remark when I first met him. "It is very deep there," he had said of the river, near the mill. "We used to say the river had no bottom. . . ."

Down four long blocks of King William Street, I finally reached East Guenther, and shortly after came to a halt. I saw many automobiles, including police cars, and Keith's delivery truck near the corner. Then I thought of the Cabots—I should have gone down Washington instead, to pass their house and see if they were up and about. Yet Washington ran out and the river curved and left it, making King William the most direct route.

There was much talking, and someone near me asked, "Did they ever get his hand open?" Finally, I was able to see between the spectators. The body was on a litter, covered end to end with a white cloth. The medical attendants were about to carry it off. I pushed my way through the crowd, still with only one aim—finding out if it was Nathan. I guess I would have lifted the cover myself, but suddenly Keith was in front, blocking my way. "Camille, what are you doing here?"

"Let go. I've got to see who it is."

"Are you out of your mind? You don't want to see a dead body. Come on, get into the truck. I'll take you away from here. I can't understand your morbid—"

"Does anyone know who it is?"

"Yes. One of the neighbors identified him. His name is Emory Cabot. He lived up on—Camille, you're going to faint. Sit down on the ground."

28

I crouched on the ground with my head down. I was vaguely aware of Keith telling someone, "She'll be all right, I think. Could someone go for a cool rag?" I was holding on to his forearms, strong as logs in a swift stream. My head was spinning.

I recovered before I let him know, and kept my head down to think. I had somehow to get back to the Cabot house to find out what happened. I had to get rid of Keith. I had to go to the bank. I had to contact Edwin. First I had to get rid of Keith. He wasn't about to leave me alone down here. I'd have to let him take me home. That was it. In his truck it wouldn't take much time. But the police would be at the Cabots' by now, probably, oh Lord, I would just have to tell Keith something.

"Keith, I'm all right, really," I said, and rose. "Listen, I can't go back with you now. I'll explain later, all right? Just go on. Call the bank and say I'm ill this morning and will go in later. If Mr. Tetzel is there—oh—if he's there—just tell them I'll be in later."

After many protests, I finally won, and sent him away, his expression doubtful and concerned. Poor Keith. Then I walked up to the corner of Washington and Beauregard. Cabot's pearl-gray Overland was still in the garage. The police were then knocking on the front door. I hurried toward them. "I know the Cabots," I said, "Mrs. Cabot left on a trip yesterday, and I believe their lodger Mr. Hope is—away, too."

One of the officers said, "We'll have to have a permit to go in there anyway even in a case of foul play like this one. Let's go on. Do you know where Mrs. Cabot can be reached?"

"She's in Corpus Christi in a hotel, I believe. You might check down at Mr. Cabot's office if anyone's there. They might know where she's staying. Otherwise you could just check the bigger resort hotels for her name."

"Hey, a little police work, eh?" some officer said, smiling at me. Then they laughed and went off. I expected people to stay around the house through the day, and had no idea how I'd ever get in there. Yet within a few minutes they dispersed. Now the grapevine would take root and travel before others, curiosity roused, came by. No doubt the Stuttgarts would be around soon, yet she had the new baby so maybe they wouldn't after all. . . .

I walked around to the back of the house and waited till everyone had gone. Then I doubled back to the window where Edwin had once tacked recording machine wire. I didn't see any faces staring at me from the windows of other houses as I crept in. Apparently no one saw.

I heard Scoop's whimpering from the kitchen as soon as my feet touched the floor. He'd been left there all night, no doubt. Yet I couldn't deal with him yet. When I was standing in Electra's sitting room it occurred to me that it was odd how normal everything could seem. Her house plants were thriving as usual, her shawl thrown over the chair, the smell of Cabot's cigar lingering, magazines lying on the table by the door, a copy of the *Mexican Mining Journal* on top. I had moved too quickly to reason things out; otherwise I probably would have knocked on Nathan's door first, thinking him still in a heavy alcohol-induced sleep.

Yet I passed his rooms by and went carefully to the stairs. It seemed absurd to be so quiet, yet I hardly dared breathe for fear of making noise. On my way up I saw muddy footprints that preceded me like those of a host leading a guest to a chosen room. I checked two upstairs chambers before I finally found the right door, and pushed it timidly open. The first thing that caught my eye was the sight of blood spattered all over the wall behind the bed. "Foul play," the officers had termed it. My God. I was biting my hand to fend off dizziness.

I approached a little nearer. The bed was disheveled, and empty.

I looked around at the otherwise orderly room, left as though its occupants had a penchant for neatness. No clothing scattered about, or stockings on the floor, or shoes. Had Cabot brought a prostitute home with him, surely they wouldn't have taken care to put away their things before they got into bed. Yet if Electra had been with Cabot, where was she now?

I stole quietly again down the stairs, poor Scoop whimpering away hoarsely—he must have been at it for hours—and scratching at the kitchen door. I could not make sense out of anything at all. I knocked dumbly at Nathan's door for a long time before I fully realized he either wasn't in there or in too deep a sleep to be roused, or . . .

I saw only enough to tell me what I had to know. As the door opened his stockinged feet came into view, hanging freely around three feet above the floor. The chair I'd sat in the night before lay on its side close by. I shut the door without gazing farther up, and leaned against it to get my breath. Then I realized I had to look again, to see if Electra was in there. I gripped the knob and pulled it slowly open again. I still avoided looking up too far, afraid of the sight of Nathan's whole body, but went all around the periphery of the room twice. Nathan's bathroom door was open and I could see enough of its interior to know Electra wasn't there. Just before I pushed the hall door shut again I noticed tracks across the floor. I traced them to the corner, where Nathan's normally immaculate shoes stood together, caked with mud.

Some source of strength that comes when needed took me over then, and got me through the balance of the day. I went to the kitchen and picked up Scoop, who was shivering and nearly delirious. I found some food and gave it to him, and filled a water bowl, which he emptied three times. I wanted to take him back with me to my apartment, but I was already beginning to reason more clearly. Proving my presence in the house would implicate me. I opened a kitchen window about a quarter of the way and let him out the back. If the police were curious, they could satisfy themselves he'd jumped out.

On the way back to the bank it finally occurred to me that I held the gun which probably had killed Emory Cabot and, perhaps, Electra as well. Things that Nathan said the previous night could lead to only one conclusion: he'd killed them. Then he'd killed himself. I had been crouching in the bushes even as he climbed the stairs to commit the murders. Then, in between, I'd knocked on his door, expecting to save the day. . . .

By the time I arrived at the bank, Tetzel had learned of Cabot's death and left the office. There was a message I'd had a call from someone who left no name, but that the call would be replaced in the afternoon. That would be Edwin. Meantime I had to pretend to do my work as though I knew nothing except that a good bank customer had been found in the river, his body riddled with bullet holes. Everyone was talking about it, speculating, gossiping.

During one of my frequent trips to the percolator, I overheard a young man say he'd been to lunch with a buddy from the *Express*, and learned of the contents of Cabot's closed hand. "It was one of those Onderdonk miniatures . . . they had to break the guy's hand to get it out. Doesn't that beat all?"

I felt suddenly nauseated. I barely made it to an alcove in the ladies' room before vomiting. My body quaked so hard I had to sit back on my heels for several minutes, clasping my abdomen. I had the sensation that everything inside me was coming loose, and I started to weep, harder and harder until someone came in and noticed my crouched body beneath the alcove door. "Are you all right? Did you faint?" she asked. The unfamiliar voice served its purpose. I sniffed and got up, thinking, I've got to hold on. . . .

I numbly walked back to my desk and rearranged papers over and over again, trying to pass the longest day I had ever experienced. The only honest-to-goodness work I did was to give Tetzel's inkwell a good scrubbing in the lavatory and refill it with fresh ink. Emory would hardly have been holding on to Electra's portrait if he were in the company of someone else. . . .

Finally Edwin phoned from Washington. I took his number, told him to wait right where he was, left the bank, and went to a telephone a block away. I told him in detail what had passed the night before, and where we were at the moment. Finally, voice quivering, I added, "What do I do now?"

"Poor kid," he said. "When you get home, hide the gun but don't get rid of it. Remember during that last meeting when Cabot gave Tetzel something to keep? It may have been the paper, or a box, or even a key. Check around."

"Paper? Box? What are you talking about?"

"The signed confession by Hope. You might need it. You've done a lot of running around this morning, and may well have implicated yourself—I'm not complaining, but you've left a lot of holes. Look in Tetzel's safe for a key or an extra box or something."

"Yes, all right. When will you be back?"

"I can't get away for a few days and Hubert's up here too. Things are popping right now over Zimmermann's telegram. I've got to sit in on a meeting tomorrow and I'll be tied up all the next day. Boy, what a time for a thing like this to happen."

"No fooling," I said, biting my lip.

"Tetzel's going to think there's some kind of plot to mess him up because of Cabot's death."

"Oh Edwin, I can't even think straight. Why?"

"Because Cabot was carrying around the rest of those battle plans in his head, and Barrista is waiting for him in Mexico."

"Oh, yes."

"Be careful. I'd have Allan stick with you but he has to keep the telegraph covered. Oh, and one thing more—you can use my car if you need to. I wanted to tell you that before I left but I couldn't reach you."

"But I don't know what I'd need with a car. I don't know how to drive."

"Oh, swell . . . the first thing you look for when you're in a tight spot is a way to get the hell—I mean, get out of town. You've never been behind a wheel?"

"I drove my brother's car once but I don't remember anything—"

"It'll come back to you if you get behind the wheel again. You might not even need the car, but just in case, it's parked at my duplex on West Pecan, number 602. Got it? Tools are under the back-seat cushion. It's full of gasoline."

"All right. Oh, Edwin, I wish you were here."

"Me too, Camille, but the whole world's cratering up here."

Down here, too, I thought.

Tetzel didn't come back for the whole afternoon. I stayed after everyone had gone so that I could look for whatever it was that Emory Cabot had left with Tetzel. I thought once it might have been a copy of the battle plans for the revolution, but then that wouldn't have done Tetzel much good at the time. When the floor was empty I went into his office and opened the big safe. There was no box, and no papers that I hadn't seen before. I pulled out the key to the secret compartment and shoved it in. At first I found nothing except the picture. Then my hand touched a small key near the back. I recognized it as one that fits a safe-deposit box. I put it into my pocket, and was about to close the secret compartment again when I heard a noise behind me.

"Were you looking for something, Camille?"

My hard-stretched luck had finally played out. It was Tetzel.

29

He locked the door behind him and said, "No need to hurry, my dear. I was just returning to pick up something myself. Give me both keys, please."

I handed them over. I moved away from his desk and he took off his homburg and sat down. "I'll need the safe-deposit key, you see, as executor of the Cabot estate."

"When I get through, you won't be executing anything—" I began, then realized the folly of my own words. What Michael Stobalt said about women who are single disappearing, never to be heard of again, came back to me then.

"Who do you work for? You might as well tell me, because it won't make any difference." He paused before continuing, "To think I was so busy worrying about Electra Cabot while all the time . . .

"When she came to me and asked to borrow money to pay off some obligations Cabot knew nothing about, I was suspicious at once. Then she said forty thousand dollars! Quite an obligation, I'm sure you can see.

"Then she offered her collateral—do you know what it was? —no more than her word. She was coming into some money soon, she said, three to four months hence at the outside, she assured me. Did she have a document to prove it? She had nothing. She feigned to reason that if I trusted her husband's word, I surely could trust hers.

"What really took me aback though was her statement that

she knew everything. How much did she know—how much was 'everything'?

"I told her we had policies at the bank regarding loans, that I simply could not grant one without authority of the loan committee and this was highly irregular. Well as you know, Camille," he said, his chest rising, "I answer to no one in this bank. I could have handed the money to her then.

"But I didn't dare risk it. Her story was just preposterous enough to worry me. Should she channel funds from this bank into the wrong hands, that would be the end for me.

"The more I questioned her, the more wary I became, and after our meeting I began a little investigation on her, but it led to nothing. I still don't know for certain about her motives, and now she's gone . . . or is she? Do you know?"

I shook my head, eyes wide.

"Was she mixed up with you, eh?"

I shook my head again.

He narrowed his eyes. "I was so certain Electra was up to something that I wouldn't listen to Giddy when she tried to convince me about you."

"Giddy?"

"You are surprised? How odd a person so thorough could have overlooked her value to me."

I thought then of all the files she carried back and forth for him, her long tenure on the bank staff, and the impediments standing in her way of promotion. Giddy, then, served as the channel for vouchers and other materials we were never able to uncover. And there was the night she'd caught me in the safe, and apparently had seen more than I realized. It made sense. Tetzel wouldn't have hired a secretary who would have been the least bit suspect, but a person working in Giddeon's position wouldn't be looked at with wary eyes. Giddy . . . on the phone with Tetzel that day I heard him discussing Electra. . . .

"I was at fault. I let one innocent modicum of sentimentality ruin everything for me." He reached into the safe for the picture. "You reminded me just a little of Johanna, faintly of her spirit and vitality. Why else would I have been interested in hiring someone as young and inexperienced as you? Didn't you ever stop to wonder how you were so fortunate as to begin in the top clerical position in the bank?"

"What . . . happened to . . . Johanna?" I asked, stalling for time. There had to be some way to get out of that office.

"She was to be my wife. Her family and mine came over here together—she and I were intended for each other long before we left the fatherland. We had not been here long when our farms were raided by Indians. They massacred both my parents and hers, her brothers, my sisters, and Johanna. Last, before me, they took Johanna.

"Six renegades raped and tortured her to death before my very eyes. . . . I managed to get away from them and fled into the woods. They burned everything to the ground before they left. That is what we came all those miles over the ocean to find. We left all the social prejudice of Germany behind, so sure that over here we would get our chance for hard work and success . . . all we wanted was a chance. And that is what we got for our trouble. . . ."

He was lost in his story by that time, reliving his past as though it were happening all over again. "Sophie came much later along with a boatload of girls sent for domestic work. I married her. She has been a good wife, all these years, but she is not my Johanna.

"For a long time I have waited the chance to go back to Germany, not as someone oppressed and confined to a miserable class treated by the nobility like so much dirt and filth, but as one who holds his head high in the world. I was very close . . . had things worked as I had them planned, everything would have been so perfect. Had they only been more patient I could have had Fernando Barrista moving at the snap of my fingers.

"That idiotic group of people running the Foreign Office would have stepped down. I would have used them as a platform under my feet. Had Zimmermann himself not sided with them I could have saved us both; but he was stupid. Lately I thought his time would be over, but not necessarily mine. With or without him I would have gone back with dignity, obtained my position of authority, risen up as the whole monarchy crumbled. It is, you know. The time for crowning kings is over."

He paused and narrowed his eyes at me, then asked, "Which of my enemies hired you to undermine me? You have been listening. You led them to Cabot so they could kill him, didn't you? Barrista will not rise without him. There is little hope for my situation now."

I was shaking my head.

"No? Well then, who have you been dealing with, tell me? It hardly matters to you now because you won't be testifying. Tell me, Camille, you owe me that at least."

With one swift motion I grabbed the inkwell from his desk and threw the ink into his face. I unlocked the door just as one of his hands caught at my sleeve, ripping it from the shoulder. I ran down the stairs, faster and faster, until I was outside the bank in the cold night. I needed time to hide the gun sitting on the kitchen ledge in my apartment. If the police got an idea I'd had anything to do with the murder of Cabot and caught on to my lies about Electra and Nathan, they could have the landlord open my apartment and search it. Still, to run there would be the obvious trap. Tetzel would go there first. I could not run for the police. I could not run home. I ran for Keith.

I made my way to the store, seeing no one behind me, frightened at every corner that Tetzel would jump out and grab me. Yet he didn't seem to be following. I got within two blocks of the store, though, when his car drew up alongside me and the door opened. An arm thrust out at me. His face, tinted by the ink, looked like that of the resurrected corpse of a man who had burned to death. I gasped and threw off his arm, and kept running. When I got in view of the store he turned the corner and waited.

Keith was cleaning up the meat counter, preparing to close the store. His parents were in the back office talking over accounts.

"Camille, you look like a ragamuffin. I've been worried all day. What's happened?"

He was wearing his good suit under the apron, and when I

saw it I remembered the birthday party. "Keith, you have to come with me and hurry. Where's the truck? Can you take me to West Pecan Street?"

I suppose one good look at me was enough to answer all doubts. He threw his apron aside, picked up his coat, and called to his parents, "I'll be back."

In the truck I asked him where Pecan Street was. "One block over and up Jefferson a block. What's there?"

"A car."

"Listen, Camille, I don't know what you're mixed up in, but —what are you looking for?"

"We're being followed. We have to detour to throw him off. I can't answer any questions or involve you in this. Just get me to that car."

He put his foot on the accelerator and began darting in and out of alleys so deftly you would have thought he was accustomed to covering his trail. "I haven't been delivering groceries all this time without learning a few shortcuts here and there," he said, and in spite of everything I had to let go for a moment and smile in relief. Around and around we darted, backed up, cut to the left then to the right, until I could see no sign of Tetzel's car. By that time I had no idea where we were and how far away Pecan was, but we still had to get there.

"Where are we—how far from the street? Oh, this confounded town. You can get lost going around the block."

"You just have to understand how it's laid out," he said calmly. "We're on Santa Rosa, not too far from the—uh—red-light district."

"Oh!" I laughed.

Within a few more minutes we were on Pecan, looking for 602. When I saw it I yelped and started to jump out of the truck. Keith's arm was on mine. "Where do you think you're going?"

"This fellow I know has promised to lend me his car. I'll be all right."

"You're crazy. Wherever you need to go, I'll take you."

"Oh, Keith, you can't."

"Yes I can."

"All right. But let's switch to that car. Tetzel may recognize this truck by now, but he won't know the car. Park in an alley or something."

"Tetzel—your boss? What's going on? Did he try to—"

"Oh Keith, you don't know anything. Come on."

When we got into Edwin's old Ford, the thing almost wouldn't start at all, and when it did, it sputtered and jerked, almost leaped forward, then died. I was nearly frantic. "Can't you drive? I can do better than that myself," I said, then quickly added, "I'm sorry. What's the matter?"

"This automobile hasn't been taken care of," he said. "It needs—"

"I don't care what it needs. Will it get us to Mill Springs?"

His eyes widened. "Mill Springs? Camille, that's in East Texas. Are you serious?"

"We have to go there—it's the only chance I've got to prove I didn't kill Cabot, and I can't go to the police about anything else until I can prove that." Since he looked totally perplexed, I added, "I'll explain later."

"Mill Springs," he repeated, already thinking ahead. "I think it's this side of Lufkin—must be around two hundred and fifty miles northeast. It'll take us all night, maybe longer in this heap. How much money do you have? We'll need gas before we get there."

"I don't even have my handbag."

He dug into his pocket. "I've got a couple of bucks. All right."

We never saw Tetzel again—I don't know how long he drove around San Antonio trying to track us down—we drove all night and into the morning, over roads that weren't fit for cows, part of the time across fields because we got lost. We had a total of eight flat tires along the way. Thankfully Edwin did at least have provisions for such emergencies. The car chugged and generally grumbled all the way there, and when we arrived at the edge of the little town, we had been on the road sixteen hours. Smoke was coming out of the radiator like dust in the wake of wild horses.

I'd had to tell Keith about the BNA and about the strange trio of the Cabots and Nathan Hope, and exactly what we would be looking for when we arrived in Mill Springs, not to mention the sparse amount of information that I had to go on. At the mention of Electra's name, Keith at once said, "Dad connected her with the man they found in the river as soon as I told him about it this morning. I never met her but I saw her a few times in the store. Boy, she was one fine-looking woman."

There was something that had nagged at me since the evening I last spoke with Nathan, and I remarked on it to Keith, having shoved it to the back of my mind earlier because of all the other events going on at the same time.

"I just don't believe in coincidences . . . maybe because I've been spying too long. But it strikes me a little odd that Cabot just happened to be on that hill overlooking the house when Nathan killed those people."

"Why? It's plausible."

"I know . . . but somehow I just can't quite believe it."

"From everything you've told me Cabot was a smart, crafty opportunist. He wouldn't have missed the chance to get someone like Nathan in bondage."

"That's true . . . bondage is a good word. A century ago he would have made an excellent lord of the manor. No threats of prohibition or taxes or other tiresome little laws to get in his way. I suppose you're probably right about the coincidence."

"I'll tell you what bothers me more. . . . What happened to Mrs. Cabot?"

30

Mill Springs was a town that had withered and died in the shadow of nearby Lufkin, which had grown and flourished by comparison and absorbed most of Mill Springs' industry and residents along with it. That was the gist of the dissertation—far more lengthy than necessary—given us by the old man who ran the gas station on the main, and perhaps only, real street through the town. He didn't recognize either of the two names I connected with the town—Hope or Arnesty—having lived there only for the past five years. He and Keith discussed the various problems of Edwin's automobile, now shuddering in place as though it were exhausted and short of breath. All four tires were flat and had to be pumped up.

I walked past the dirt-encrusted gas-pump dome, down the street to a cafe, never pausing to consider how I must have looked without hat or handbag, Keith's suit coat wrapped around my shoulders to keep me from freezing.

The waitress in the cafe, pouring coffee for an old man seated at the counter, did not miss an inch of my appearance, head to toe, however. The smell of bacon and eggs turned my stomach over with hunger, but there was no need in admitting this when I had no money to buy breakfast or even a cup of coffee.

I asked if she'd ever heard either of the names. She thought for a moment as she popped her chewing gum and forked the bacon over. Then she said, "I'd nearly forgot. Arnesty was the name of that feller who owned part of the mills for a time. That the one you're talking about?"

"Yes," I answered eagerly. "Did he live in a house with a little hill behind it?"

She laughed. "Honey, there's lots of little hills around here. But if I remember right, he and his wife disappeared about thirteen years ago. Just took off. I don't know what they'd been doing, but there was an investigation by the marshal from Nacogdoches.

"He never found nothin' though, and finally they dropped the case. Course I was just a youngster then, and I don't remember much about it except what my folks said."

"Do you know if the house is still there?"

"No, but it probably is. Ain't no reason why it shouldn't be."

Then the man at the end of the counter, thus far occupied with his bacon and eggs and coffee, rose from the stool, flipped a coin onto the counter, and wiped his mouth. "That's the place up there on the ten-mile road." He pulled out a handkerchief and blew his nose. Then he added, "Gotta big old dead tree in front, with ivy growing all through it."

"Yes, yes," I told him excitedly. Nathan had mentioned that tree. "Does anyone live there now?"

"I don't think so. Nobody's lived there all these years. Kinda gave people the creeps, after what happened."

"Could you direct me to the ten-mile road?" I asked.

He walked to the window and pointed with his finger. "Go on up here to the end of this road about half a mile. There's a fork. Follow the left tong. Go about three, four miles down that road and it begins to curve off to the left. When you get to the cemetery, turn to your right and go about another mile and a half. You'll see the ten-mile road there. There ain't no sign or anything, but there's a rock pile, or was last time I was up that way. Used to be a chicken ranch on further up where I bought my eggs. Turn to your right on the ten-mile road and go on till you come to the house. It's the only one around."

I wondered how he was able to sit quietly while the waitress unloaded her thimbleful of information, when he could have led me right to it. "Wait a minute. That's too much to remember. May I borrow a pencil and some paper?"

While the waitress was fiddling about for a piece of paper, I found out the reason for the old man's reticence. "You related to Sam Arnesty?" he asked.

"No."

"Well he was a mean rascal. I worked under him as foreman up in the planing mill till he disappeared. If you want my opinion, the marshal dropped the case because everybody in town despised him."

He lifted his arm again toward the bright morning sky. "This used to be a darned good town. As long as the mill was operating, everybody done just fine. Wasn't a night passed you didn't see that smoky blue haze rising above the main plant. Only twice in my life the mill closed down for a while because of bad drought, and the haze disappeared. Those were bad times. Yessir.

"But when Sam Arnesty came along he started to bleed the mill of money—that didn't come out till later, of course—some Oregon outfit come down here and bought it out and moved the equipment away. The buildings were left there to rot, till finally they caught fire and burned down. Probably some old hobo spent the night there and built a fire, they was always doin' that, and burned the place to the ground.

"It all started with Sam, though. When he disappeared, no one wanted too much investigating done, and they let the marshal know it."

"I see . . . well I wasn't related to him," I reassured him. The waitress was handing me a tablet. By the time I had the directions down, Keith was pulling up out front. "Oh, we'll have to have a shovel," I told him.

"Yes, but if we buy one we'll have the whole town watching us, and besides that, we're nearly broke."

"Maybe there's one around the place that we could use, or maybe we could steal one along the way."

"Steal?"

"All right, borrow."

Keith rolled his eyes. About halfway there we came across a farmhouse and barn that looked unoccupied. "Stay here, I'll check the barn," I said. "Honk the horn if you see anyone."

I was out of the car and halfway across the front yard before he could react. When I came back, shovel in hand, he was laughing in amazement. "Did you learn to work that quickly before or after you joined the BNA?"

"I haven't joined the BNA. I was impressed into service. Oh Lord, I just thought of Mother. I wonder if she's tried to reach me since the telegram was released to the papers. And your parents. They must be sick with worry."

"I called them from the gas station and reversed the charges. They thought we'd eloped."

"Oh, that's funny," I said, and we both dissolved into laughter.

Then Keith said, "I told them we had."

My mouth fell open.

"Well, what else could I tell them? You swore me to secrecy."

We drove up in front of the dead tree around eleven-thirty. Just as Nathan had told me long ago, the tenacious ivy crept up its trunk and pushed out along its branches. Seeing it gave me a spooky feeling . . . something living taking sustenance off something dead. I felt the hair rise on my neck. In fact the whole place was a little eerie, though surely it would not have been except for the things I knew about it. The house itself was merely a shell of a structure that was probably fairly decent at one time. The wood had rotted and turned silvery brown from a long period of neglect. The features of the house that gave it lingering respectability were the finials on the pitched roof and the gingerbread trim around the front porch, now broken in places. I thought of Nathan's mother, in there sewing dresses for the ladies of the town. . . .

We left the car and walked up. From our first step on the porch stairs, the boards creaked beneath our feet. The front door squealed on its hinges. Inside there was no furniture left

—who had taken it, I wondered?—the place had long since become a roosting place for wild birds and, from the smell of it, a place of shelter now and then for barnyard animals who'd wandered by. There was one large gaping hole in the roof where the sun shone down in the center of the kitchen like a heavenly ray of light. Keith suggested lightning might once have struck the roof. I thought of the two people, seated at the table one pleasant evening when, from the distance, came a shot. . . .

I turned around and looked at the wall across from the window. It was hard to tell whether there was stain from blood there, or simply shadows caused by the glancing sun.

Only after we had walked through and wound up in back, facing the small hill, did I realize what a tremendous job we had in front of us. It was one thing to dig up a grave underneath a house, and quite another to locate it after thirteen years. The house seemed all at once three or four times bigger. Keith looked underneath. "The ground's pretty uneven. I don't see how Nathan got a grave dug without breaking his back, but I'll tell you one thing. We won't have to worry about going down too deep.

"Now, let's see. He would have had to go under the house at a place where Cabot could keep his eye on him and if we can assume Cabot stayed on the hill, then Nathan would have to have gone under from this side, so the graves are probably in this vicinity. . . ."

I started to ask if he didn't think he ought to go on and become an engineer and forget flying, the way he busied himself calculating. He felt around the ground a bit and finally stood up, rubbed his hands together, and announced, "They must not have had any rain around here in sixty years. The earth is packed down like cement."

"We'll take turns," I said. "I can go first. I got you into this mess."

He was rolling up his sleeves. "I'll give it a try. If I wear out, you can dig for a while."

I did some snooping and found a rusty spade in the barn, then followed him under the house. There was around four feet of headroom. "Consarne it, we don't have any light. See if your friend left a lantern or anything in the car."

We were in luck. As I carried the lantern back I thought to myself, Edwin may not have taken care of the car, but he apparently did remain prepared for quick trips, just as he indicated over the phone.

Back on my knees again, I realized for the first time I was sore from all the running since the morning before. . . . It seemed such a long time ago that I'd headed down King William, certain I was going to discover the dead body of Nathan Hope. We dug around to no avail until about two o'clock, then came up for air. We were both so tired we could hardly stand up. "Look, why don't we give up and rest a little," said Keith. "My back's so tired I can hardly bend over anymore, and I know you must be exhausted. We don't need to hurry. No one's going to be looking for us, I don't imagine." I thought of the young Nathan, exhausted from digging, frightened and perplexed by the figure on the horse, watching. . . .

We walked to the car and sat inside with the top pulled over. The wind was picking up and it was getting colder all the time. Keith sat back. "Here, you can lean against me," he said, and held out his arm. I never thought we'd fall asleep, let alone sleep for such a long time, but when we awoke the sky was purplish pink with puffs of gray splashed against it.

Arms and legs aching and weary to the bone, nonetheless we both got back to work under the house, by the light of Edwin's lantern. Finally I struck something hard, like metal, and called excitedly to Keith. I'd hit one of the hinges of a suitcase. We dug it out and busted the rusty latches. It was full of limp, musty clothes. "Well, this is great, but it won't get the job done," I told Keith. So back we went.

It must have been close to nine o'clock when finally Keith reached something else.

I rushed over behind him to watch. His face, lit by the lantern, grew more and more intense as he threw away the shovel and started moving clay-like soil with his hands. Then slowly and carefully—I would have never considered the danger of damaging or even destroying our find, as he did—he moved the

426

dirt around with his fingers until at last he disclosed a skull, and leaned back momentarily, staring at it. Finally, with an effort at joviality, he said, "Ken would have a ball with that set of teeth."

I was beside him then, ferreting out the one that must lie next to it, but I was on the left side and he discovered it, minutes later, on the right. "This is it, Camille," he said excitedly. I peered over his shoulder as he smoothed away the dirt, and saw perspiration roll down the side of his face and drop off. The whole back of his brand-new white dress shirt was sopping wet and dirty. I reached out to touch him, but drew back my hand. Then I took a hanky from my pocket and wiped his face.

"Hold up the lantern," he said, and as I did he slowly and carefully dug away the rest of the soil until the full skeletons were disclosed. By then my heart was thumping madly. Keith sat back for a moment to catch his breath, and I said, "If not for you, this moment might never have come. . . . I could be down at the bottom of the San Antonio River right now. . . ."

"Let's get out of here," he said, and we crawled out and stood up. His whole suit was rumpled, and there was a big tear in one of the trouser legs. For the first time in my life I could think of no adequate way of expressing what I felt. I flung my arms around his neck.

He kissed me then, not a peck on the cheek like one buddy gives another, but long and hard, like a man kisses a woman he cares about.

"I guess we missed your birthday party," I said breathlessly.

31

Adolph Tetzel was picked up by United States agents on March 2, as he boarded a train for Laredo. A lengthy wire he had sent to Mexico City, announcing his scheduled arrival and his plan to replace Cabot in the Barrista revolution, along with a special section regarding his provision of munitions, was used as evidence to hold him until the balance of proof against him was uncovered in the apartment of Giddeon Sparks. After hearing of this, I wondered whether he would really have harmed me. Then I shook my head and wondered if he'd remembered to take his homburg.

In her statement to authorities, Giddy claimed to have discovered Tetzel in his espionage work "far earlier than anyone else," through a slip-up in one of his transactions at the bank. She then presented herself as willing to help him in exchange for the official position she so longed for—auditor of the bank. She became his distribution system for all the German funds we could never tie down by spreading the money over some twenty-five to thirty different fake business checking accounts, creating different signatures for each with her versatile talent for penmanship. She laundered the money through the books with ease, breaking down the substantial amounts into sums that escaped my early probes through the ledgers and files.

Tetzel assured her the position at the end of the war (apparently failing to mention that he intended ultimately to sell the bank and leave the country). At the close of her statement she remarked, "Just like a man, isn't it? I tried to warn him about Camille, but he wouldn't listen. If I'd worn trousers, it would have been different."

Aegina Barrista and her boy friend Artemio were discovered as they loaded currency into electric-light-bulb boxes in the basement of an old warehouse less than two blocks from the arsenal. Her father, Fernando Barrista, was picked up by Mexican authorities but quickly released on the guarantee that he would take exile in one of the Latin American countries where he was so renowned, and take his daughter with him. All of his properties as well as the Cabot Consolidated Copper properties were confiscated by the Mexican Government for redistribution among the poor, with mineral rights reserved for the government. There was speculation by the press that if Carranza had not been so anxious at the time to make a name for himself as a peacemaker eager to spare any further bloodshed, and also reassure the United States that he had no knowledge of Zimmermann's plan, and wanted only friendly terms with his neighbor to the north, he might have dealt more harshly with Barrista. Of the Barrista family, Carlos alone was allowed to retain the properties which he owned for lack of evidence that he planned to participate in the revolution against Carranza.

When finally the safe-deposit box belonging to Emory Cabot was opened by authorities, a small box containing a man's gold watch and chain, a woman's pendant, and other jewelry was discovered inside. There was also some correspondence between Cabot and a private agency that had been engaged to locate his mother, Clove Cabot, beginning in early 1903. The final letter from the agency, dated in 1904, pinpointed her in Mill Springs, Texas, where she had married a man named Sam Arnesty. The letter further stated this was her fifth marriage, and there were no offspring discovered from this or any of her marriages following the first one, to Emory Cabot's father.

So Nathan, in the act of murdering Sam Arnesty and his wife, Clove, had unwittingly taken the life of Cabot's mother. And judging from my conversation with Nathan on the night he died, he never learned it was more than coincidence that brought Cabot to Mill Springs around the same time that he returned there, in 1904.

There was no note of confession by Nathan Hope among the papers in the safe-deposit box, which leads to speculation as to what happened to the note which he claimed held him in slavery to Cabot. Knowing of all the other circumstances, it seems likely the note did at one time exist. The only question is, for how long? Did Cabot keep it only long enough for Nathan to be assured it was in his possession, or did he keep it until the day he turned over his key to Adolph Tetzel, or destroy it at some point in between? It was not found among any of his things, nor among Nathan's possessions. The truth went down with Cabot to his grave among the cold depths, but I chose to believe he destroyed the note before he gave the key of the box to Tetzel, and perhaps I've always been just a bit soft for Emory Cabot, but I believe, too, that he intended to tell Nathan he'd destroyed it before he left for Mexico on March 1.

Would Nathan have believed him? Perhaps Cabot would have considered it a nice and final twist of irony that Nathan should never be sure, a sort of lasting punishment for his murder of Cabot's mother. This brings on a further question that will never be answered: when Cabot located his mother, what did he plan to do? Would he have murdered her himself? Surely not. One doesn't murder his own mother regardless of how badly she abused him. Yet, knowing Emory Cabot you simply could never be sure. . . .

Many times I have wondered about the night Nathan killed Cabot. I believe he must have taken the gun up the stairs, believing Cabot to be with a whore, and opened fire on both of them without even switching on the lights. He was deathly afraid of Cabot, and would not have dared given him a chance to react in time to win that final game. The ledgers that I had been so certain were of great importance showed nothing that Cabot might not have written down in his own behalf.

After I had left he must have wakened, certainly before daylight, and gone back to check again on the work he had done up there. Was it his discovery of Electra with Cabot that drove him to prepare his own destruction, or was she there at all?

The muddy footprints on the stairs would indicate Nathan took one body down, then returned for the other. Or did he return for something else?

Electra's reservation at the Nueces Hotel in Corpus Christi was recorded, but she had not shown up to honor it. Days later, I was nearby when three charges of dynamite shocked the peaceful waters of the San Antonio River, down by the mill, as authorities attempted to draw her remains to the surface. With each rumble, my body stiffened a little tighter. Keith closed a hand around mine to steady me. The explosions availed nothing. Someone standing near us recalled the whirlpool close to the arsenal side.

When permission was obtained to open up the postal box still held in the name of Electra Cabot, we found three letters addressed to her and postmarked New Orleans, mailed between March and April of 1917. There was enough information in these letters to prove she was being threatened. We expected this, although we were puzzled by the fact that the letters reflected she owed around ten thousand dollars, not forty, the amount she tried to borrow.

What really surprised us, however, was that the sender proved to be the older brother of Emory. Upon tracing him to his boarding-room address in New Orleans, we were told by the landlady he had been thrown in jail a week or so before. She didn't know why. "Since last fall, he has roomed there more than he has here," she said.

I was present during the questioning which followed, and it struck me his features resembled Nathan's description of Clove Cabot: "fat, with a little pig face," he had said.

Mark Cabot told us that twenty years before, Electra had taken up with him after Emory went away. "I always thought she was a homely little twerp, and I used to pick on Emory about walking home with her from school." He paused here and added, "I used to get the biggest kick out of makin' Emory mad—it was so easy to get him stirred up. Lordee, how he hated me . . . 'specially after Daddy died and I made him bring all his money to me. . . .

"But anyways, after he left town, in the next year or so,

Leslie turned plum pretty and I took to her myself. She was a sly one all right. I tried to get her to run away with me, but she said I'd have to prove I could buy her all the things she wanted first.

"So I went out on the road, three or four towns away, and robbed a store. I took the money back and showed it to her one night. She was a'settin' on that horse behind me quick as lightning."

From there, he explained, the two of them pulled a few robberies together, and finally held up a train with a shipment of cash on its way to an Army post out in West Texas. The take was forty thousand dollars. The law was on their trail quickly, but they managed to hide the money before they were apprehended, and made a pact that whoever got back to it first would take only half. Then they separated.

"Leslie got off as an 'accomplice,' while I got a twenty-year stretch," Mark said with a sneer. "She was out in two years, and I got off on good behavior in about fifteen. When I got back to the hiding place, sure 'nough the money was all gone.

"Took me a while to find her, but I had some friends along the way that helped me out. From what I heard, she must have waited quite a spell before she went back for the forty grand, and while she was goin' through it, she took care to spread it all over instead of spending it in one place. I don't know whether she become a whore before she went after the money or later, but she didn't start calling herself Electra until after.

"I guess you know the rest," he said, and as we parted he added, "So you can't find her? She'll turn up again one day, you can bet on it." Then he slapped his knee and started to laugh, and it seemed to me the laugh grew louder and louder as it resounded down the hall which led away from his cell, toward the exit and the afternoon sunshine.

In the huge inventory of clothing owned by the Cabots, it wasn't possible to account for every single item, and isolate the frock she may have been wearing had she escaped and fled. Lyla Stuttgart was asked by authorities to help, but declined and was excused on the grounds of her still delicate condition. Again impressed into a service I wanted no part of, I walked back into the house at Beauregard and Washington.

It was a cool, rainy morning yet the bedroom was stuffy. I opened a window to let the breeze off the river rush in and circulate through the room, then stood there for a few seconds, thinking how long ago it seemed since I came to San Antonio, hoping for a room of my own with a river view. Down below, the new leaves on the trees along the water path swayed to and fro, and birds made loops among them, calling. . . .

The big bed of the Cabots' had been stripped of its fine linen. Just as I gazed upon the stark sight of it, I thought I heard a noise from somewhere, and listened . . . nothing. I drew in a breath and started to work. I went carefully through Electra's things, trying to remember each of the stunning ensembles which I had so admired. Every one I could remember having seen was there, in her room. Stacked inside the wardrobe were boxes of garments she'd recently bought, including those she purchased from me at Joske's. In a drawer of the bureau, the black-aigrette headband was carefully folded and boxed. I could not look at it again without recalling the details of the party to which she wore it, the tango music that thrilled her steps to those of Cabot; and for a moment I thought it was just as well they died together, that last study in motion a fitting nocturne for two people whose lives were a swirl of shadows. . . .

I was more than ready to leave after replacing the headband and closing the drawer. I circled the room with my eyes, only then noticing a small chest just outside the bathroom. Probably nothing to worry about . . . still, I'd been told to be thorough.

The drawers were full of lacy undermuslins and filmy sleeping gowns. As I opened each one I was gripped by the same distaste I'd always felt when plundering Mr. Tetzel's safe. Yet I checked each one, four in all, and in the last caught a glimpse of the corner of something blue near the rear. It proved to be a booklet detailing the boundaries of the red-light district in San Antonio, and including the names, addresses, and telephone numbers of both houses of pleasure and ladies residing there.

I sat back on my heels and turned over its pages, wondering why Electra would have wanted something like this. I checked in the drawer again, and this time drew out a small business card for a man named Richard Boscomb, of New Orleans. That no doubt tied it to Mark Cabot and his threats about money. Just how, I would let the officials investigate.

Anyone who takes his life leaves many open questions as to the motives involved and the final working through toward the end result. So it was with Nathan. By the time President Wilson declared us in a state of war in April, I had made up my mind not to worry about mysteries I couldn't solve . . . at least for a while.

The last meeting I had with Edwin, he was in uniform, passing through Fort Sam Houston on his way to some station on the East Coast. We chatted briefly about Cabot and Tetzel.

"You know that guy Cabot made only one bad mistake— borrowing money from Tetzel."

"Oh?"

"The United States uses the neutrality laws to its convenience. If Cabot hadn't been using German money to put Barrista in, Washington would have worn a blindfold about his participation in the revolution. Barrista's well liked up there, and he said something during the first Pan-American Peace Conference up in Ontario that made a few of the mediators suspect he might be planning something. We learned of that just lately."

"Do you think Barrista might have succeeded?"

"It looks like he would have had a healthy chance, at least, with a little luck. One reason Carranza was particularly inclined to go easy on him was that he eagerly agreed to make a sworn statement to United States authorities about his lack of knowledge that the Germans were paying his way, and also his complete reform plan as well as his revolutionary battle strategies. He claims to have had wide support, and whether or not he could have counted on Zapata, Villa, or any other rebel chief, he sure had more going for him than any other Mexican revolutionary. And he had Cabot. From all we've been able to learn, Cabot was pretty shrewd."

"And what about Tetzel? From his final wire before he left, it looks as though he certainly had no intentions of ditching Barrista in the end."

"It seems you're right, though by that time he was a desperate man, grasping for straws. However, had the others in the German Foreign Office listened to him all along, they may well have gotten just what they wanted in Mexico. I'll defend his intelligence right down the line."

"And he was nice—misguided, but nice."

Edwin chuckled. "You'll never give up, will you, Camille?

"Hey, someone from way up in the organization is going to come down to pay you his respects, but I'm here to tell 'ya, you did a first-class job for us. You scared the daylights out of me from time to time, but you came through when it counted. Thanks."

"Good luck, Edwin."

Like all the others in the BNA and the Slovak League, Edwin was true to his word about being first an American. How his homeland fared as a result of all the prewar efforts on its behalf in America is yet to be known.

I have moved into the house on King William Street once owned by Geoffrey Woodstone, along with four other girls who work with me at the Red Cross. Scoop, who returned to this house as soon as I let him go on the morning after the Cabot murder, is our mascot and sleeps at the foot of my bed. Once just a few months after we got into the war and shortly after we rented this house from the Woodstone estate, following the young couple named Brandon, who left the city when Gregory Brandon went into the service, an attorney called to inquire after Electra. He had traced her first to Washington and Beauregard, and had been sent to this house by a new lady in the neighborhood who thought I might know of her whereabouts. "It's most distressing," he said. "There was a will found among Mr. Woodstone's things after his death which postdated his earlier one. In the event of his grandson's death, he had made Mrs. Cabot sole benefactor of his estate. I find her home has been turned into a boardinghouse. I don't know what we shall do now that the woman has disappeared."

I explained that there had been extensive efforts to locate her, since February 28, the last day she was seen alive, but that no trace had been found.

"If only the estate could have been settled earlier," he said, shaking his head. "But you know it took some time to complete the inventory and make sure it was adequately insured while awaiting Mr. Woodstone's daughter to come over here and take charge of it. His books were the last property to be appraised, and most of them were in a large breakfront. It was in removing the books that we found the new will. After that it took quite some time to investigate its validity."

He took in a breath. "Well then . . ." he added helplessly, tipped his hat, and walked back to his taxicab.

After he left my mind kept returning to his use of the word "time," though I didn't know why. Finally its significance dawned on me, and I realized what Electra was trying to tell me on the day she visited me about taking Scoop. She spoke of failing to understand the full extent of Mr. Woodstone's friendship to her until after his death, and said, "In time, many things have a way of coming to light."

So she had somehow learned of her friend's new will, and that was her bargaining point with Tetzel, which had sounded unbelievable even to me. She had been perfectly sincere. She was also doubtless smart enough not to lift a finger toward revealing it herself because she would have been labeled an opportunist right off, and with her background, would never have been able to withstand the contest bound to follow.

I was about to walk back into the house when another thought occurred to me. We had never learned why she attempted to borrow forty thousand dollars from Tetzel, when she could have asked for ten and probably would have been more likely to have her request honored.

She must have intended to repay the forty thousand she and Mark had stolen together so long ago. It was her only defense against unending blackmail from him, and she must have been convinced from his letters that Mark was not going to wait whatever time it might take for Mr. Woodstone's new will, benefiting her, to be revealed.

When Tetzel continued to put her off, she must have become desperate. And then along came the little note concocted by Edwin and slipped under her door by me. . . .

That night, neither for the first time nor the last, I dreamed of the Cabots dancing, and woke up in a sea of perspiration, wondering what would have happened had I obeyed my instincts and warned them before it was too late.

There has been little change in the neighborhood, with the exception of the sight of more and more uniforms in the streets and the sound of cannon going off at the arsenal, which brings great annoyance to some of the older residents. I don't believe anyone pays much attention to the fact that King William Street—originally named for the Prussian ruler Wilhelm—has been changed to Pershing Avenue. People still refer to it as King William, regardless of its new official status. It does cause a great deal of confusion over the delivery of packages, however.

Keith stayed in school until graduation in May, then took the direction we all expected—into aviation. Mr. Butler, both his sons now in uniform and with no likelihood of having anyone to take over his business upon his death, has arranged for the sale of his store to a large chain of grocers here. I think he has felt it less painful to take care of this now than to await Keith's return and be told it is his heart's desire to go on flying aeroplanes forever instead of taking over the family business. Keith took his preliminary training close by in Austin, then went overseas to train with the Royal Flying Corps. He was quartered at Queen's College, Oxford, for a while, and from his letters it didn't seem such a bad place to spend the war. Now he's flying an aeroplane called a "Pup," which seems an odd name for a plane. However, I don't suppose it's any worse than a "Jenny." I miss him.

Just before he left, they opened the new Japanese Sunken Gardens in Brackenridge Park, and we went there one Sunday afternoon, along with several hundred other curious people, to walk among the beautiful flowering plants and cross the bridges built in the shape of a dragon which lead up to the pagoda tearoom. It seemed to me that the sunken gardens embodied the spirit of San Antonio—a man disturbed by the unsightly quarry hole left when a cement company moved out thought it would be nice to plant exotic trees and flowers there instead, and went over to Japan to pick them out. I suppose that's the reason I've always liked it here. With all the desecration inflicted overseas by the war, and all the beautiful things which have stood for centuries being destroyed, it is nice to live in a place where people go out and do things just for the sake of beauty, instead of progress or money or anything else. I told Keith this while we were on the bridge in the gardens. He said he'd like to have a look at that dragon walk from the air. I told him he had a single mind. As we stood on the bridge, someone took our photograph together. I have it on my desk at the Red Cross.

It is very strange about Electra Cabot.

On two occasions I thought I saw her. Once was at the train station on the day Arnold Stuttgart departed for duty. I was there with the Red Cross, handing out cookies and punch to the soldiers. I saw Lyla say good-bye, holding the infant in her arms, its long lacy dress spilling down past Lyla's knees. The other Stuttgart children took their father's kisses in turn, and Lyla stood there waving a handkerchief with her free hand, looking so very grieved at the parting. I always wondered if she was sincere. . . .

Just then I saw a woman walking away, in one of those big Gainsborough hats Electra wore so beautifully. Her pace was smooth, her carriage erect and regal. I ran up behind to see if it was her, but then she'd disappeared among the crowd before I caught her up.

Another time I saw the profile of an elegantly dressed woman as she crossed Santa Rosa. She was pretty close into town at the time, but headed down toward the red-light district. I followed her three or four blocks, more sure with each step that I was almost within reach of Electra. But then I was stopped by a convoy of troop trucks passing by, and when I could see again, she was gone.

By far the most peculiar incident occurred this morning, though, when I got the mail. A letter from Mother, who's now in Washington pushing hard for the Susan B. Anthony amendment, came at the same time as a letter from Keith in France. I read Mother's letter first and saved Keith's until I could stop my work and read it several times, which is my custom.

He said he saw someone who resembled Electra, dressed in a volunteer's uniform at a military hospital. Somehow these lines really put a lump in my throat. She always felt so bad about the war, and what it did to Mr. Woodstone . . . maybe she also felt guilty for her husband's part in helping the other side, and joined a Red Cross chapter somewhere under another name, trying somehow to make it up for all that happened. . . . Maybe I'm just becoming too much of a romantic again. . . .

Keith wound up his letter, "I miss you," and signed it, "Love, Keith." I folded it tenderly and pushed it back into its envelope. Then I put the letter into my pocket and went on about my work, praying as I do time and again that, through all this, his life will be spared, and he will get back to me.